RUINS OF CAMELOT

THE ABDUCTION CYCLES

JOHN ELIJAH CRESSMAN

MAVERICK-GAGE PUBLISHING

ISBN: 978-1-954524-09-5 (Paperback)
ISBN: 978-1-954524-10-1 (Hardcover)
ISBN: 978-1-954524-08-8 (Amazon Kindle)
ISBN: 978-1-954524-11-8 (Audiobook)

Any references to historical events, real people, or real places are used fictitiously. Names, characters, and places are products of the author's twisted imagination.

Front cover image by Christina Myrvold

Editing By Celestial Rince.

Printed by Maverick-Gage Publishing in conjunction with IngramSpark, in the United States of America.

First printing edition 2021.
Maverick-Gage Publishing
Allentown, PA

info@maverick-gage.com
www.maverick-gage.com

John Elijah Cressman
www.johnecressman.com

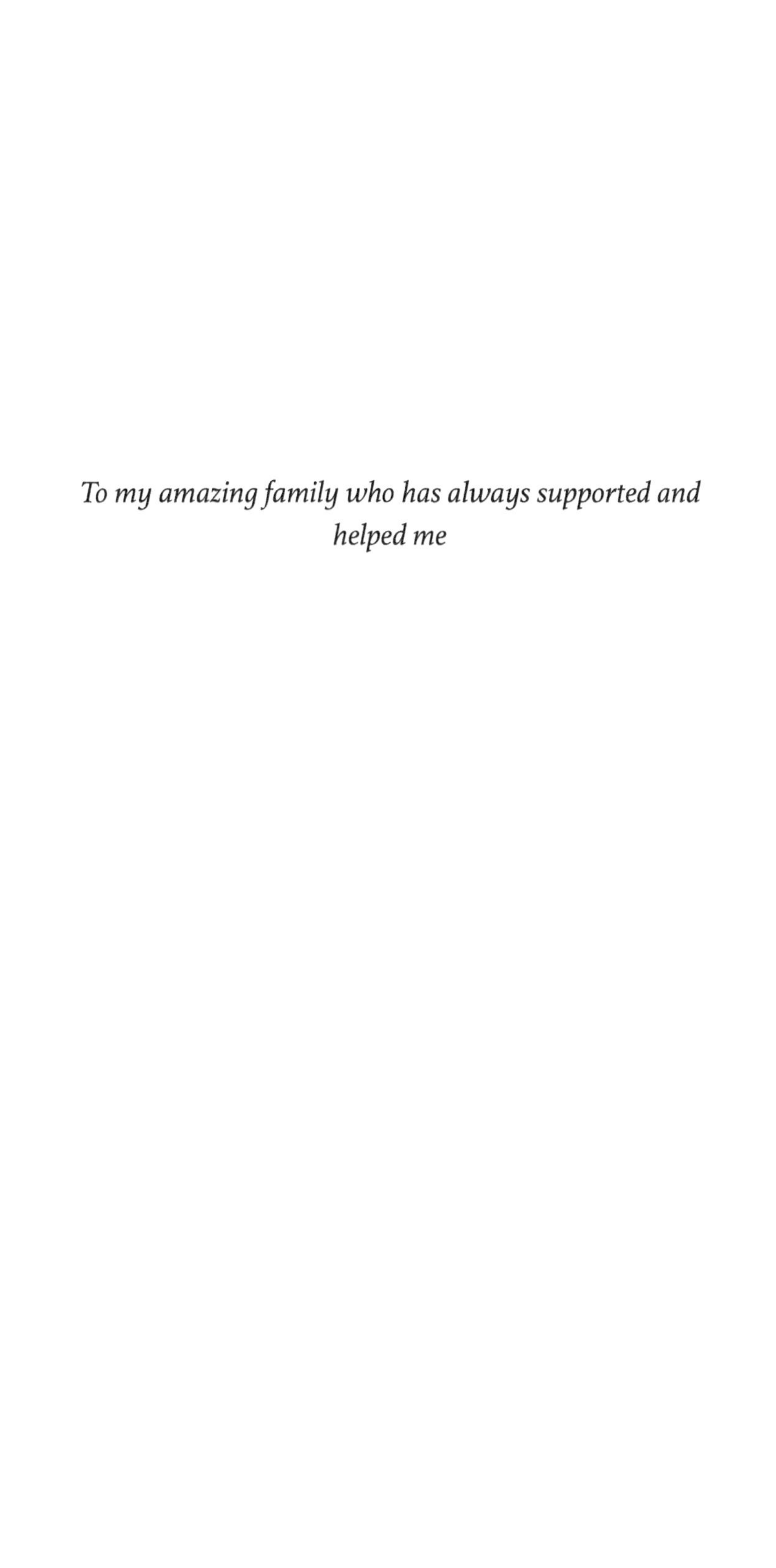

To my amazing family who has always supported and helped me

PROLOGUE

Ethan lay in bed with a dim ball of light hovering near him. It was a magical orb of light he had learned to conjure as one of his first bits of magic when he'd arrived on this world. It took almost none of his *Mana* to create, nor did it require any concentration to maintain.

He chuckled silently. Magic. Magic was real on this world, and Ethan was a wizard. The very thing he'd role-played in MMORPGs and tabletop RPGs back home on Earth. It still boggled his mind when he took the time to really think about it.

Nearly four months ago, as best he could estimate, Ethan had been abducted from his home and dropped on this world. A world that had real monsters and real magic.

Almost as strange as the monsters and magic was the fact that he now had a HUD, a heads-up display. It gave him information on his statistics, like *Mana*, *Health* and *Stamina*. It was almost like he was in a video game.

At first, he had actually believed he was in some sort of sophisticated alien virtual reality simulation or game. But the level of detail in the world seemed far beyond any sort of simulation. Tiredness. Fatigue. Muscle aches. Even bodily functions. It was all too real.

Simulation or not, Ethan had quickly met up with other abductees who had joined together with him for self-preservation. They were all from unique worlds but they were straight out of Earth mythology.

First, there was Ainslee, the ebony-skinned dwarf. Stocky and muscular, she was from a harsh underground world of caverns and lava oceans. The dwarf had an uncanny knowledge of stoneworking and was a talented blacksmith. Sometimes crude and abrasive, she had nevertheless proven herself a loyal companion.

Like him, Ainslee had a HUD and had chosen the knight class. While not an experienced combatant, the strong and sturdy dwarf could hold her own in a fight. This effectively made her the group's tank.

Next was Yuliana. Yuliana was a green-haired, copper-skinned elf. Slender and graceful, the elf had an amazing sense of hearing and was hundreds of years old. Despite her age, because her species was long lived, she appeared to be a 20-something-year-old.

On her homeworld, Yuliana had tended a grove and had gravitated to the druid class in her HUD. Her healing abilities had kept the group alive in a number of sticky situations. Not only that, but her animal companion, a mountain lion she had named Luna, added some additional DPS to their group.

Next was Par'karr, the three-feet-tall lizard man called

a kobold. Unlike Ethan's other companions, the kobold was a native to this world. After another kobold tribe had destroyed his village, Par'karr had joined Ethan's group.

Perhaps because he was a native to the world, Par'karr had no HUD. But he did have a class. The kobold was a summoner and was able to summon large, demonic rabbits who were surprisingly good fighters. Combined with his knowledge of the world, Par'karr had proven a valuable asset to their group.

Finally, there was Nia. Ethan turned his head and looked at the sleeping woman next to him. Nia was a foxgirl. While she looked mostly human, she had fox ears and a large, bushy fox tail. Like canines of his world, she had an uncanny sense of smell and was able to track like an Earth dog.

The foxgirl was also an incredibly talented and experienced warrior who seemed to be proficient in nearly every weapon she picked up. From what he'd learned from Nia in their conversations, her world had been a world of warring clans and violence was a way of life for them.

When they'd first met, Nia had chosen the acrobat class. She claimed she'd been a dancer back on her world, but he had later found out that she was the daughter of an alpha. Ethan didn't fully understand the ramifications of that, but it seemed she was basically like a princess. A dancing princess?

Oh, and Nia was also his wife. Or, at least, that's what she claimed since they had first had sex in the wasteland on their way to the Library of Daemonium. Afterwards, she had claimed that - by her people's standards - they were now married, and he was her new alpha. Among other things, this allowed her to actually truly fight enemies, rather than being bound by some "no kill" order from her previous alpha.

Ethan didn't know how the marriage laws worked on this world, but he wasn't about to argue with the foxgirl. She was incredibly cute, had a killer body and was easily the most attractive woman he'd ever been with. Plus, she could probably kill him about two dozen ways without breaking a nail.

As if she knew he was thinking about her, Nia shifted in her sleep, draping a slim, muscular arm around him. Ethan looked down at the foxgirl with a little envy. At least she was able to sleep. Not him. His mind was racing with a thousand thoughts.

When they'd first arrived on this new world, he and the group had stumbled into a conspiracy by the previous mayor to loot a tomb that had been discovered and sealed up in the old silver mine near Hawkshead.

The mayor had died to the traps of the tomb, but not before his plan backfired and almost got the village itself destroyed by one of the kobold tribes he'd armed and ordered to keep the trade caravans out of the village.

The kobolds had done so but then had other ideas. They had used the weapons to destroy the other kobold clans, shifting the balance of power in their favor. Then they'd decided they wanted the entire area - including Hawkshead.

Ethan and his companions had organized the defense of the town and after a hard-fought battle, had sent the kobolds packing. For a reward, Ethan was made the mayor of the town - with all the duties and responsibilities that came with the job.

One of the first things he'd had to do was to travel to the nearest city and restart the trade caravans. This proved more difficult than he had expected, and he'd ended up on a side quest to the Library of Daemonium to retrieve some valuable tomes.

He'd found them but then been ambushed by a warlock from the Order of the Scroll and a priestess of Hel, who wanted to enslave and then sacrifice Ethan and his companions to her dark goddess.

They'd overcome the warlock and her minions and, in the end,, Ethan had decided the secrets contained in the tomes - namely how to contact a powerful demon lord - were too dangerous to just hand over. He'd destroyed them and effectively missed his chance to join the Order of the Scroll and gain access to their vast library of knowledge.

When he'd returned to Hawkshead, he'd learned that something was causing all of the game to flee the area and, of course, he and the group needed to figure out what was going on and fix it.

The new quest had led them back into the mine and into the tomb where the former mayor had met his end. In the process of investigating the tomb, Ethan learned it was actually the resting place of King Arthur.

Ethan still wasn't completely sure how an Earth legend like King Arthur had ended up on this world. It didn't make sense unless the aliens that abducted him had also abducted King Arthur and his knights over a thousand years ago.

But Ethan knew it had to be the real King Arthur because atop his tomb, they'd found the Holy Grail - the actual Holy Grail. The magical cup had healed Ethan from the brink of death and healed terrible scars Ainslee had received from one of their battles.

The Holy Grail was also the source of the missing game animals in the area. Ethan didn't fully understand how or why, but the cup had been enchanted to give off a high-pitched noise whenever it was removed from Arthur's tomb. While inaudible to humans, it drove animals crazy and had forced them south.

They'd found that a cave-in had knocked the grail from its resting place and also opened up the tomb to a colony of giant spiders. After defeating the spider queen, they replaced the cup on Arthur's sarcophagus and the noise had stopped.

But the discovery of the tomb of King Arthur had made Ethan even more curious about Merlin's journal. He'd been reading it every spare moment he had since they had returned. As the town's wizard and mayor, spare moments were hard to come by. The village was still recovering from the kobold attack and there was always work to be done.

Evenings were really the only time he had to read the journal. He'd been calling it Merlin's journal, but it was most likely only a single volume what appeared to be a set of Merlin's journals. Possibly, the last volume. It detailed what Merlin had done after Arthur's death.

And while some of it was written in a strange form of runes that Ethan had also encountered in the tomb, most of it was in English - or, at least, what his HUD translated into English.

He wanted to read more but a sleepy voice next to him snapped him away from the book.

"No more light," she moaned. "You sleep too."

Ethan smiled down at the foxgirl and then looked back to the journal. He'd just gotten to a part in the journal where Merlin had taken the sword, Excalibur, and decided to return it to the stone in Camelot. The legendary wizard feared what the sword might do in the wrong hands.

"Ethan," the foxgirl whined. "Make the light go away."

Nodding, Ethan set the journal down and with a thought, made the light disappear. He wrapped his arm around Nia, and she snuggled closer against him.

So many things were racing through his mind, Ethan didn't think he'd be able to sleep. But it seemed like only moments after he closed his own eyes, he too was fast asleep.

1

It was a new day and work around Hawkshead continued. Despite the villagers' earlier apprehension toward Ethan and his magic, they seemed much more tolerant - even appreciative - for his magic now.

Whether it was the fact that he'd brought back the animals or that he was simply too useful to ignore, the villagers and farmers were literally lining up outside his house to ask him to help them.

This new development was both good and bad. It was good because he was glad the villagers were actually talking to him and asking for help. It was bad because he was now busy all day and no longer had much free time to work on his side projects.

Ethan had hoped to make a few more portal pouches but there just hadn't been time. He'd also had a few more interesting projects he wanted to experiment with but now he was simply too busy.

He had also wanted to spend more time with Michalus now that the old wizard had recovered from his injuries. The older elf had hundreds of years of experience with magic that Ethan wanted to learn from. The problem, once again, was lack of time.

Like Ethan, Michalus was in demand too. Once the villagers had learned how much easier things were when a wizard was around, the ones that couldn't get Ethan to help had eventually asked the elven wizard. Michalus had been happy to help them. Ethan guessed it was good to be needed.

"That's a bit too high, mister mayor wizard, sir," Ayden said, snapping Ethan's thoughts back to the present.

Ayden was one of the farmers from the outskirts of Hawkshead. The kobolds had burned down his farm and he had asked Ethan and a few of the other men from the village to help do what was effectively a barn raising - but with a house.

They lacked the manpower to do a real barn raising. There simply weren't enough able-bodied men in the village to help out properly. So, the villagers had turned to Ethan. And now he was screwing it up.

Ethan looked at the beam he was holding aloft with Air. It was about a foot higher than where it should have been. Ethan lowered the beam and gave the farmer a sheepish look. "Sorry about that. And call me Ethan!"

Ayden insisted on calling him mister wizard mayor and even added sir on the end of it. Ethan didn't really care for titles much. Back on Earth, he'd been a Senior Computer Support Engineer, which was a fancy way of saying he fixed computers. He didn't like stupid titles there and he didn't like them here.

Lowering the beam into place, Ayden and the three men helping him immediately set to tying the beam to the existing crossbeams. Ethan watched them do it, fascinated by the men's speed and efficiency. Then again, if you weren't self-sufficient on this world - you didn't live long.

The men finished up tying the beam and Ayden gave him the signal. They'd done this a few times before, so Ethan knew what was expected. He slowly released the tendrils of <u>Air</u> supporting the beam to make sure that the corner of the roof didn't collapse.

"Okay," Ethan called to the men as he released the last of the <u>Air</u> keeping the beam in place. "I'm not holding it anymore."

The men looked around the roof and pressed down on the beam in different places before erupting in a cheer.

"That's it, mister wizard mayor, sir!" Ayden grinned. "It looks like it's holding! Thank you kindly! We just got done in two days what would have taken us a week."

Ethan smiled. "Glad to help."

He meant it too. In general, Ethan had always enjoyed helping people. It was one of the reasons he'd gotten into computer repair. To help people. Little had he known back then that it would be a thankless job back on Earth.

At least here, these people were genuinely thankful for the help. Plus, Ethan felt good that he was one of the only people who could give that help. It wasn't like he was a dime-a-dozen computer tech. He was one of only a handful of wizards left.

That thought sobered him. He remembered why there

were so few wizards left - because something was killing them and sucking out their brains.

"Would you like to stay for supper?" the farmer asked, bringing Ethan's attention back to Ayden. "Cara's going to be startin' it soon."

"Thank you," Ethan replied with genuine appreciation, "but I need to get back to town."

"Suit yourself, mister wizard mayor, sir," Ayden said. "But you'll have to come back some time for supper."

"I will, Ayden," Ethan promised. He meant it too. The farmer and his wife, Cara, were appreciative for his help. The couple had insisted on feeding him and the other men the last few days, even though Ethan knew food had to still be somewhat scarce.

Waving to the men and grabbing his shirt from a log, Ethan began walking back to town. It was a good half hour walk back to Hawkshead and the suns were already beginning to set. As usual, he'd get back in time to eat with his companions and then it would be off to bed, with Nia.

The thought of going to bed with Nia brought a smile to his lips. That part, at least, he looked forward to each night. Maybe he'd even have time to read some more in Merlin's journal.

Ethan thought back to the previous night. He'd been reading in the journal and learned about the aftermath of the death of King Arthur and most of the knights at the hands of the Doemenagg.

He hadn't understood what the Doemenagg were until he remembered the carvings in King Arthur's tomb. The final one had been Arthur being fatally wounded by giant praying-mantis-looking creatures. They had to be the Doemenagg.

After Arthur's death and the defeat of the Doemenagg's queen, Merlin and the remaining knights had taken Excalibur, Arthur's body and the bodies of the fallen knights and returned to Camelot. There, Merlin had to break the news to Guinevere.

A shocking revelation to him had been that Guinevere had actually been Merlin's daughter. Ethan couldn't remember if that had been the case in the Earth stories he remembered, but he didn't think so.

Ethan had just read about Merlin and the knights arriving when Nia had made him turn the light out and get some sleep. He'd put the light out, but he'd been up for some time, thinking about Camelot and Excalibur.

He would love to have seen the city of Camelot, or whatever remained of it now. It would be like seeing a legend or piece of ancient history. Unfortunately, the location of Camelot was never mentioned. So, it remained a mystery.

Ethan started to pull his shirt over his head but stopped as he caught sight of his chest and his abs. He grinned. He could actually see his chest muscles and the beginning of abdominal muscles. Months of walking, no junk food and daily exercise had flattened his little beer belly and toned his body. He was probably in the best shape of his life.

Looking at the flawless skin on his chest, Ethan remembered a number of the scars that he'd gotten from various fights since arriving on this world. The worst had been the troll claws. Yuliana had healed the wound, but the claw marks had never gone away.

Or rather, they hadn't gone away until he'd drank from the Holy Grail. It hadn't just healed his wounds; it had actually healed all of his scars. He didn't fully understand how a wizard could have created a magical item that healed. All he knew was, it worked. And it was powerful magic. So powerful, it had been able to revive Michalus from near death.

Thinking about the elven wizard, Ethan finished pulling on his shirt and quickened his pace. If he were lucky, he'd be able to talk to the old elf tonight at the inn. He wanted to ask Michalus if he knew anything about the Doemenagg.

For the moment, Ethan assumed that the Doemenagg had been some other alien race, brought to the planet by the aliens who had abducted him and the others. But for all he knew, they had been some sort of indigenous species.

Michalus was the oldest person he knew. Over eight hundred years old, according to the old wizard. If anyone would know what the mantis creatures were and where they'd come from, he might.

Ethan also wanted to ask the wizard about Camelot. It had been over a thousand years since Arthur had lived, according to Earth legends. That was a long time for humans. How many human generations had come and gone? But Michalus was over eight hundred years old. Maybe he knew something about Arthur. He had actually known someone named Merlin. Perhaps it had been THE

Merlin. Perhaps Michalus even knew of Camelot's location.

If so, Ethan knew he'd have to go check it out, even if it was just ruins now. He wasn't sure why he felt the need to visit it so strongly, but he did.

It had grown darker and Ethan looked up to see that the first sun had already set. Soon the other would set and it would be dark.

Ethan brought up his HUD and checked his *Stamina*.

Stamina: 21

He was under a third of his *Stamina* but it should be enough to allow him to go a bit faster. Picking up his pace, Ethan jogged towards Hawkshead.

2

———

"You mentioned you knew Merlin, right?" Ethan asked Michalus as he bit into a leg of roasted pheasant.

The meat was tender. It had been salted and seasoned and was the best thing he had tasted in a long while. Ethan turned to Elspeth, who sat at the other end of the long tavern table. "This is really good!"

"Glad you like it," the innkeeper's wife called back to him. She nodded at Nia. "Was your missus who caught the birds."

Ethan looked over at Nia and gave her a smile. She returned it and then went back to eating her own pheasant.

"I knew A Merlin," Michalus replied, waiting patiently for the banter to finish. "I told you before, I don't think it could have been the Merlin your legends speak of. He would have been hundreds of years old and he was a human."

"But he could have been," Ethan said. He wanted to add "if Merlin had drunk from the Fountain of Youth" but stopped short.

They'd all agreed not to share the fact that there was a magical pool of water in the tomb that stopped people from aging. At least for now. Ethan had pointed out that once word got out, people would come from all over for a chance at immortality.

It could even start wars. After all, who wouldn't want immortality. He had laid out a bleak picture of what the greed of people would do, not only to the people of Hawkshead but to the entire area. No, for now, it must remain a secret.

Ethan wondered if that was why the pool had been hidden in Arthur's tomb, or why the tomb had been built around the fountain. Or was there some other reason why Arthur's tomb was built around the fountain of youth?

"I don't see how," Michalus responded, bringing Ethan's thoughts back to the conversation.

"What about Camelot?" Ethan asked. "Any idea where it might have been?"

The old wizard chuckled and then took a sip of his mead. "I'm afraid not, dear boy. But there might be some information in the library in Castlehaven, maybe even Moonpoint."

Ethan sighed. He'd had the chance to join the Order of the Scroll and have access to their library. He'd been given a quest to retrieve lost Tomes from the library in Patheos. He'd done so, but upon learning they were basically a guidebook to contacting a demon lord, Ethan had - wisely in his opinion - destroyed them.

Unfortunately, that act had effectively robbed him of the opportunity of joining the guild, since he had no new knowledge to offer the Order.

"I'd offer to take you..." the old wizard began but then trailed off.

Ethan knew why. The laws had changed recently in Castlehaven. They now allowed slavery and even human sacrifice of slaves. And unfortunately, they were targeting elves and foxlings.

Moonpoint was different, since it was mostly elves and foxlings at this point. There was no slavery there. But Michalus, who had recently returned from the city, reported that because of the actions of the humans and dwarves in Castlehaven, they weren't really welcome in Moonpoint.

"I still can't believe it," Fearghas said. "We've been isolated here for some time, but I can't believe they reinstated slavery. And my kin went along with it."

"Doesn't seem like our folk," Ainslee agreed, wiping her mouth with the back of her sleeve. She took a long drink of mead and then slammed the mug down. "It's not right."

There were murmurs of agreement from around the table and the conversation seemed to stall while people continued eating.

Ethan took a few more bites himself before turning to the old wizard. "Have you ever heard of Doemenagg?"

The wizard stopped chewing mid-bite and lowered his piece of pheasant to his plate. He finished chewing before turning to Ethan, a serious look etched on his face. "How do you know of the Doemenagg?"

That was when he noticed that both Fearghas, Elspeth and their son Sawney had stopped eating as well. Ethan suddenly felt he had asked something wildly inappropriate.

"Sorry if I said something offensive. I learned about them from Merlin's journal," Ethan answered quickly. "They're what killed Arthur."

There were shared nods from the innkeeper, his wife and Michalus but their faces remained grim. He saw Elspeth look at Sawney with concern.

Michalus saw it too and gave the dwarf a slight nod. "It's something we can discuss later."

"Aw," Sawney whined. "I want to hear about the Doemenagg!"

"That's enough of that, young dwarf," his mother told him in a stern tone. "You finish up your dinner and let the big folk talk."

"But..." the boy started and then Fearghas turned a glare on his son too. The boy, probably realizing the futility, lowered his head and took another bite of his pheasant.

"Ahem." Fearghas cleared his throat and looked meaningfully around the table. The message was clear, no more talk of Doemenagg. His expression turned into a smile and he looked at Ethan. "Ethan, the other villagers wanted me to convey their thanks for letting us keep the magical bag. It's been immeasurably helpful during the hunts."

Realizing the innkeeper was trying to change the conversation to something lighter, Ethan nodded. "That's what I made it for. To help the village."

He'd made the magical haversack to help the village

when the animals had fled the area. There had been no food nearby and those that could hunt were forced to venture days away to find game. Much of the meat would spoil before they could get it back so Ethan had created a larger portal pouch that transported the meat to a stone chest in the river.

"We have to be the only village in these parts with a magic bag," Fearghas chuckled.

"Certainly, the only village with one so large," Michalus added. "I have to admit. When I saw it, I was a bit jealous."

"Jealous?" Ethan asked. "Why? You're the one who gave me the idea with your portal pouch."

"True. But the portal your haversack creates is much larger." The old wizard looked down at the magical pouch at his waist then looked back up. "I have to confess, it's impressive."

Ethan chuckled until he realized the elf was serious. He became serious. "If I managed to do it, it's all because of your tutoring."

Michalus smiled wryly. "I wish I could say that's true, but I barely taught you anything. No, Ethan, you have a real talent for the magical arts. Your progress is uncanny."

Unsure how to respond to the old wizard's praise and feeling a bit awkward, Ethan shrugged. "I've kind of been doing things because I had to do them. If I hadn't made the haversack, some of the villagers might have starved."

Fearghas and Elspeth exchanged grim looks. The innkeeper nodded. "You don't know how true that is. I think most of them had given up hope until you gave us that."

Not knowing what else to say, Ethan simply nodded to the dwarf. Fearghas looked him in the eye and nodded back. It was the acknowledgement of two men who knew that additional words weren't necessary and would probably just be more awkward.

"Got any more mead?" Ainslee asked suddenly. Whether she was saying it to break the tension or was completely unaware that there had been tension, Ethan didn't know. But it worked all the same.

"Mead, you say?" Fearghas gave Ainslee a wicked smile. "I could give you some mead, if that's what you really want. But then my new batch of dwarven spirits would go to waste."

"Dwarven spirits?" Ainslee gasped, eyes widening. "You have dwarven spirits?"

"Just tapped the keg earlier to make sure they were presentable." The innkeeper grinned.

Ainslee licked her lips and looked around the room. "Well?! What are you waiting for? Get those spirits!"

Grinning, Fearghas pushed his chair and left the room.

While he was gone, Yuliana looked anxiously around the room. "Is that not the substance we used to create the firebombs?"

"Oh yeah." Ainslee grinned.

"And we are going to... drink it?" Yuliana asked hesitantly.

"Oh yeah." Ainslee nodded more enthusiastically to the elf.

The green-haired elf looked around the room. "And this is wise?"

"Loki's balls, no," Ainslee chuckled. "Wise? No one drinks dwarven spirits because it's wise. They drink it because it's good!"

"Good?" Yuliana raised an eyebrow, but her expression remained skeptical. "The substance we used to create fire bombs."

"Oh yeah." Ainslee nodded, a lustful look creeping into her eyes. "I haven't had spirits since...."

"Since you passed out at the inn?" Nia said dryly. "And Ethan had to use magic to lift you."

"Oh," the dwarf chuckled. "You mean the time Ethan lost his breeches and did the teleportin' thing?"

Ethan tried to feign indifference but, remembering the scene, felt his face flush. He purposefully stared down at his plate and took a bite of his meat while the women shared a chuckle.

Michalus clapped him on the back good-naturedly. "And he managed to teleport without killing himself. Quite an accomplishment."

Ethan was saved from any sort of response by the appearance of Fearghas. The innkeeper carried a small keg, similar to the ones Ethan had seen before when they'd used some of the spirits to create firebombs to defend the village.

"Come to Mama!" Ainslee bellowed, gulping down her remaining mead and holding her cup out to the innkeeper.

The old wizard leaned into Ethan, his voice low. "She's an impatient one, especially when it comes to alcohol."

"You have no idea," Ethan replied, watching the excited dwarf. "You have no idea."

3

————

Dwarven spirits reminded Ethan of a well-aged whiskey as it burned its way down his throat. It was smoother than some whiskeys he'd tried and had a pleasant smoky finish. He wasn't a huge drinker, but he managed not to embarrass himself as the spirits felt like it was dissolving the tissue of his throat.

Yuliana was not so lucky. She took a large swig of the spirits before anyone could warn her to go easy on it, and then immediately spit it out all over the people gathered around her.

"Hey!" Ainslee scolded the elf. "Don't waste good spirits!"

Red-faced and gasping, Yuliana thrust the remainder of her drink at the dwarf. "Why... would you... drink that?"

Ainslee snatched up the elf's mug and poured her share of the spirits into her own cup. She grinned at Yuliana. "Are you kidding? This is good stuff! Best drink I've had since I got here!"

Fearghas sipped his, seeming to take the time to enjoy it. He grinned at Ainslee's words. "And this is only aged for a year. Wait until I manage to make some 10 or 20-year spirits."

Ethan finished up his spirits and then motioned Michalus towards the door. The old wizard set his own mug on the table and followed Ethan outside. The two of them walked down to the river and sat down on the corners of the bridge.

Glancing around to make sure they were alone, Ethan faced the old elf. "So, tell me about Doemenagg."

Michalus sighed. "It's not something people generally like to talk about or hear."

"That bad?" Ethan wondered aloud.

"That bad." The wizard nodded. He settled down on the side of the stone bridge, trying to get comfortable.

"The Doemenagg," he started, "were a race of insect-like creatures that very nearly took over the world over a thousand years ago. They were finally stopped, no one knows exactly how or by whom, and the scourge just disappeared one day. But not before they had... consumed... much of the world's resources and inhabitants.

"They're myths to most people now," the elf continued. "Stories to tell children when they're bad. 'Don't be bad or the Doemenagg will get you' and such."

Michalus gave him a hard look. "But make no mistake. They very nearly killed every other lifeform on this world. They came into an area, consumed everything and everyone and then left it barren. The area around Patheos is still barren because of them."

Ethan swallowed, remembering the utter desolation around the library. "They sound like locusts."

"Locusts?" Michalus cocked his head.

"They're insects," Ethan explained. "A few inches long. Their swarms number in the millions sometimes and they come into an area and decimate crops. If you don't know what they are, maybe they don't exist on your world."

"I do not know of them. They sound like the Doemenagg," he told Ethan. "But the Doemenagg were as large as a man."

Ethan remembered back to the carvings. The mantis creatures had been depicted as the size of the knights. If the paintings were right, Arthur and his knights really had fought them.

Of course, based on the carving in Arthur's tomb, he'd had no idea the creatures had been terrible. "According to the carving I saw, it was King Arthur who killed a really big one. Maybe the queen or something."

The elf smirked. "When you've been around as long as I have, you realize that kings and princes like to make people believe they did great deeds. Some of them have actually done great things but most rewrite the legends to include them."

"You think the carving isn't real?" Ethan asked. He hadn't actually considered that it might be made up but it did make sense. There were certainly examples on Earth of famous leaders who took credit for things other people did.

"They might be true." Michalus shrugged. "But then again, they might not."

So far, Ethan hadn't told Michalus about the fountain

of youth or the holy grail. He thought he could trust the old wizard, but in all honesty, he barely knew the elf. He certainly seemed like a decent fellow, but something like the Holy Grail or the Fountain of Youth could make people crazy.

"The tomb was very well constructed and magically reinforced. It even had some sort of anti-magic enchantment that prevented me from directly interacting with the stonework," Ethan told him.

Michalus raised an eyebrow. "Anti-magic?"

"Magic couldn't touch the walls, ceilings or floors," he explained. "As soon as it did, it just... fizzled."

"I've never heard of anything like that. Though I think I remember talking with someone about the concept. But I've never seen a working example of it," Michalus admitted. "I'd love to study it."

Ethan wasn't sure how to respond to that. He didn't think the old wizard would figure out all of the puzzles and get to the final resting place of Arthur, but who knew what knowledge Michalus had after eight hundred years of life.

"You'd have to be very careful," Ethan retorted. "There were a ton of traps. And spiders too. Though hopefully they're gone."

"Yes." The old wizard smiled. "Ainslee was telling me all about the spiders."

"I bet she has." Ethan smirked. The dwarf had arachnophobia and hadn't been the most useful person around the spiders. But she'd managed to overcome her fear and help them out at the end.

"Thirty feet tall, a hundred eyes," the wizard chuckled.

"Or so she says. They get bigger and have more eyes with every telling."

"I bet." Ethan grinned.

"Can you tell me any more about the Doemenagg?" Ethan asked, trying to stir the conversation back to the creatures.

"Most of what I know is from the books I've read," the old wizard admitted. "With some rumors thrown in. How much of it is true, I have no idea. But I do know that whomever or whatever killed them must have done a thorough job because they never came back."

"That's good?" Ethan asked. "Right?"

"It is," Michalus agreed. "But have you ever tried to kill insects? I don't know anyone who has ever succeeded in killing all of the insects that plague them. They scurry away and hide beneath things, procreate and then come back twice as bad."

"You think the Doemenagg did that? Scurried away and procreated?" Ethan asked with a sinking feeling.

The old wizard shrugged. "If they had, you would think they would have been back in the last thousand years or so."

"**Then** you do think they were all killed?" Ethan asked.

"I guess you'll find out eventually," Michalus sighed grimly. "You do have an inquisitive mind."

"Find out what?" Ethan asked, a sinking feeling forming in the pit of his stomach.

"There was a prophecy... several actually... that said the Doemenagg would return," the elf said.

"When?" Ethan swallowed.

"Like most prophecies, it's a bit vague on exactly

when," the elf mused. "Something about the waters of immortality revealed, the lost city found and a bunch of other equally vague stuff."

Ethan swallowed again. The waters of immortality sounded much like the fountain of youth. "Does someone defeat them, in the prophecy?"

Michalus wrinkled his forehead. "If I recall, it said something about the instrument of their fall being the instrument of their destruction - whatever that means. Have I mentioned I don't believe in prophecies?"

"Why tell me?" Ethan frowned.

"Because," the wizard chuckled. "Many others do. Some people even believe that the murder of the wizards is part of it... the ones of power will be devoured, or some such nonsense."

"Ones of power devoured?" Ethan repeated. "That does sound like wizards."

"Or princes, or rich merchants or even dragons for that matter," the wizard countered. "That's the thing about prophecies: they're so vague that you can read almost anything into them."

Ethan was silent for a moment as he thought about the pieces of the prophecy. The waters of immortality certainly sounded like the fountain of youth. Lost city found? Could that be Patheos? And the part about, instrument of their fall. Arthur had killed the queen with Excalibur. Did that mean Excalibur would be needed to finally end them?

"Do you know where the complete prophecy is?" Ethan asked.

Michalus sighed. "I knew I shouldn't have said anything. But yes, I'm sure there's a copy in..."

"... the library of the Order of the Scroll," Ethan finished with a grimace. It seemed like most of the knowledge he wanted to learn about was in the Order's library.

"How right you are," the elf chuckled.

"Ethan!" came a familiar voice. It was Nia's voice and the word had been slurred. Was Nia... drunk? He turned to see the foxgirl staggering down the road towards them. How much of the dwarven spirits had she drank?

"Come on, my alpha," the foxgirl bellowed. "It's time for us to mate!"

He gave the old wizard an embarrassed look, but the elf just chuckled and gave him a wink. "When a beautiful woman tells you it's time to have a bit of fun, it's impolite to turn them away."

Ethan cocked his head at the old wizard and the wizard gave him a smirk. "I wasn't always eight hundred years old, you know."

Nia staggered over to him and collapsed onto his lap. She pushed her face into his, kissing him roughly. Pulling away, she gave him a huge grin. "I feel really good."

Ethan shook his head. She wouldn't feel good tomorrow when she had a killer hangover.

"Come on, Ethan," she slurred. "I am Tal'Cha! I want to have you now!"

The drunk foxgirl began fumbling with her clothing, obviously trying to get them off.

"I believe I heard someone calling me," Michalus said, excusing himself. He gave Ethan a grin and another wink. "You two have a good night."

Not wanting to have sex on the bridge, Ethan scooped up Nia in his arms. She gave a little giggle and nibbled him hard on his neck. "Carry me to our bed, my alpha!"

Shaking his head in amusement, Ethan carried his wife back to their home. It promised to be an interesting evening.

4

———

The evening turned out to be significantly less interesting than Ethan had initially thought. No sooner had he carried Nia into the house and laid her in the bed than she promptly passed out. He gently shook her several times, but she was unresponsive.

"Just great," Ethan growled, his excitement quickly waning.

Stripping off his clothes, Ethan hopped into bed next to his inert wife, he sighed and levitated Merlin's journal. He would have preferred a few hours of passionate love-making with Nia, but he'd have to settle with reading the journal. Thumbing through the pages, he found where he had left off and continued reading.

The pages told of Merlin and his journey south to Camelot. The legendary wizard related his sad duty of telling his daughter, Guinevere, about the death of Arthur and of her weeping over the body. Merlin had thought of Arthur as a son and the wizard was heartbroken too but had to be strong for his daughter, as well as their teenage son, Mordred, who was now the new king.

Merlin recorded his misgivings about Mordred, his grandson, though he did give the boy his father's sword, Excalibur. The wizard loved his grandson but recognized that the boy had grown up spoiled and lacked the courage of his father and the compassion of his mother.

Mordred, as the new king, commissioned a grand tomb for his father, one worthy of a king and begged Merlin to build it. The wizard had taken the commission and worked on the design for nearly a year, all while using magic to preserve Arthur's body.

During that year, Merlin had seen that Mordred had become increasingly insolent, shunning the advice of both Merlin and Guinevere. The boy-king had also begun dabbling in the ways of the channeler. Merlin began to realize that the boy could not be trusted with the secret that he had shared with Arthur, Guinevere and the other knights - the secret of the Fountain of Youth.

Ethan stopped reading and re-read the passage. Did that mean Merlin, Arthur, Guinevere and the knights of the round table had all been immortal like he and the others were? Could that mean some of them could still be alive somewhere? He quickly delved back into the book.

Merlin changed his plans and decided to build the tomb in the mountain home of the magical pool, effectively locking it away from Mordred. Taking his leave of the royal court, Merlin left Camelot and traveled east to the coast and then north for three months by horseback before cutting west to the mountainous home of the Fountain.

There, he spent nearly a year building the tomb, reinforcing it with magic, puzzles and traps to not only protect the tomb, but also protect the Fountain of Youth. When he was finally done, he left a marker and teleported back to his chamber in the castle.

That's when he found out the terrible news. His beloved daughter was gone. Guinevere had fled the kingdom and her son, who was no longer recognizable as her son.

Mordred had fully embraced his channeler powers and his continued use of the power had changed his body and made his mental state even more unstable. The new king now ruled the kingdom with an iron fist, warring with the nobles who had stood against his tyranny and who were still weak from their war with the Doemenagg.

And Mordred was winning. And he was winning because he not only had Excalibur and his channeler powers, he also had the Holy Grail. With the magical cup, all but death could be healed.

After questioning the servants, Merlin learned how Mordred had become increasingly antagonistic and controlling. Fearing for her life, Guinevere had fled the castle. One of the servants even admitted helping the queen escape through the city, dressed as a commoner.

In a rage, Merlin sealed off the Great Library, the largest collection of books in the world, to prevent Mordred from learning any more about the dark powers. He then went to confront his grandson on the battlefield near one of his nobles.

When Mordred attacked Merlin on sight, the wizard knew his grandson had indeed become the monster his daughter feared. Merlin easily overcame the boy-king and his black knights but could not bring himself to kill the boy. Despite his demonic appearance, he was still the son of Guinevere. His grandson.

Instead, Merlin stripped the boy of both Excalibur and the Holy Grail. He embedded Excalibur into the stone just inside the castle at Camelot, proclaiming that only the true king could withdraw the sword and placing some sort of enchantment on it to back up his words.

Then he teleported back to the tomb and left the Grail on the tomb of Arthur. He placed an enchantment on the Grail. Mordred's transformation had left him vulnerable to high-pitched sound. Merlin's enchantment would generate a high-pitched sound that would make it impossible for his grandson to be within miles of the Grail without excruciating pain. After that, the wizard sealed the tomb up and left to look for his daughter.

Ethan stopped and wiped his sweaty palms on the bed sheet. He swore loudly and then grimaced. He quickly glanced over at Nia, but the foxgirl was sleeping soundly.

He tried to process everything he'd just read. If the journal was true, then it really was the real Merlin who had written it. The real Merlin who had known and helped King Arthur. And, the real Merlin who had created the tomb and set all of those puzzles and traps.

Now Ethan knew why. The wizard had done it to keep the Grail and the Fountain of Youth from his own grandson. A grandson who had become a tyrannical channeler. Someone who had become so twisted that his own mother had run from him. Ethan snorted. Talk about family drama.

Now Ethan understood why the tomb had been built around the Fountain of Youth. And why the Holy Grail gave off the noise when removed from the sarcophagus. The high-pitched noise was not meant for animals. It was meant for Mordred. To prevent the channeler from gaining, or keeping, the power of the Grail.

All of that was very interesting to Ethan but the most interesting part was Merlin's description of his journey from Camelot to the resting place of the Fountain of Youth. If Ethan understood it correctly, it was a three-month journey south from the tomb.

Ethan read that part several more times. Two weeks to the coast, nine weeks north and then a few days west to the Fountain. Almost three months. He grew excited.

If Ethan could find out the average number of miles a person traveled on horseback and had access to a map, he might just be able to figure out the general area where Camelot was. And Camelot had a library. A vast library. At least, it had been vast over a thousand years ago.

Still, it might contain information on the abductions or even the rest of Merlin's journals. Surely, they would document how he'd come to be on this world. That might give Ethan some insight on how he might get home.

Feeling an overwhelming urge to find the library, Ethan wanted to jump out of bed and rush over to talk with Michalus. The old elf may have some maps or know where they could find one. He might even know something about the area the journal was referring to!

He stopped himself and, with difficulty, reined in his enthusiasm. It was now late, and the old wizard was probably sleeping. As excited as he was, he wasn't about to go waking the elf this late just to satisfy his own curiosity.

But it was hard to resist the temptation to wake him right now. He desperately needed access to a real library and if the Great Library still existed, it might have spell-books - spellbooks from Merlin! Who knew what infor-mation they could contain or what he could learn. He needed to find it.

Almost immediately after thinking it, a message popped up in his HUD.

> **You have received a new quest "Ruins of Camelot I"**
>
> **You have discovered that Camelot existed and may contain an ancient library of powerful books.**
>
> **Find the lost city of Camelot (0/1).**
>
> **Reward: 500 experience**
>
> **Accept quest (yes or no)?**

Ethan did a double take. Had he just given himself a quest? That was interesting. He couldn't remember that happening before. Maybe the journal had kicked off the quest?

Excited and unable to rest, Ethan paced the room for nearly a half hour before finally putting his clothes back on and taking a walk outside. Nia had still been sleeping and he didn't want to wake the foxgirl. Actually, part of him did want to shake her awake and tell her everything he'd learned but he resisted. He wasn't sure she'd appreciate it anyway.

No, King Arthur was a legend from Earth. A legend that had somehow made his way to this world. No one but him could really understand what that meant, and he wasn't even sure he fully knew what it meant.

Ethan walked around the entire village several times before finally becoming tired enough that he thought he could sleep. He went back to his home, stripped down and slipped into bed with Nia.

It took what seemed like hours before he finally faded off into a troubled sleep.

5

The next morning Ethan woke up early and, despite being tired, jumped out of bed. He was excited to go talk to Michalus and find out more about the area that Merlin had mentioned in his journal.

No sooner had he gotten out of bed than he heard a pained groan from the bed. He looked down to see Nia was still in bed. She growled at him and pulled the sheets over her head. "Why is it so bright?"

Ethan couldn't help but grin. He briefly wondered if this was the foxgirl's first hangover. Unfortunately, most of the cures he knew of involved coffee, which they didn't seem to have in this world. At least, not in this area of the world.

"Headache?" Ethan asked, sitting down in the bed. He was a little too familiar with the effects of a hangover. His job hadn't always been the most enjoyable. Occasionally, he'd been screamed at by customers and his boss on the same day. His remedy to that was either gaming with his friends or drinking rum and coke or jack and coke until he finally passed out.

"My head is on fire," the foxgirl moaned. "And there is too much light."

"Let me get you some water," Ethan told her. "It will help."

Nia moaned something unintelligible from underneath the covers which Ethan thought could be agreement. He quickly dressed and grabbed a couple mugs. He left his house and then paused.

Was it really his house anymore? Should he start calling it THEIR house? After all, if he was married to Nia, she owned half of it, right? Actually, he had no idea. He needed to ask Fearghas what the marriage laws were in the area. For all he knew, maybe the women owned all the land.

Quickly walking down to the river, he filled the mugs and brought them back to Nia. Helping her to sit up, he gave her the mug and told her to drink as much as she could. The foxgirl groaned but did as he told her.

She winced and squeezed her eyes shut. "Too cold."

Frowning, Ethan used a bit of *Fire* to warm the water slightly. "Is that better?"

Sipping the water again, she nodded. "Better. Thank you."

The foxgirl leaned her head into him, groaning some more. It was the first time he'd seen her so vulnerable. Normally, she was a stoic towards hardships and even pain. It was almost one of her defining characteristics.

"Have you ever been hung over?" he asked her, stroking her hair.

"Hung over?" she muttered, taking another sip of her water.

"It's what we call the day after drinking too much alcohol," he explained. "Have you ever experienced anything like this?"

Nia became quiet for a moment and then he felt her nod against his chest. "Just once."

Ethan was about to ask when, but she looked up at him and continued. "I drank very much the night of my marriage...

"I mean, my first marriage," she amended and gave him a coy smile. "My father had been killed and the new alpha had taken me, and I became Cha'to'mir'ta. I drank everything I could find."

"I'm sorry," he told her.

She wrinkled her brow. "You have no need to be sorry. You are not responsible."

Ethan chuckled. "My people say that. It means, I feel bad that you had to go through that."

"It is our way." Nia shrugged. "I just... did not expect it to be my fate. I thought I would be Tal'Cha one day."

"And now you are," Ethan reminded her.

She smiled up at him. "And now I am."

She finished up the water and then stood up and stretched, giving Ethan a bedside view of her firm body. Suddenly, the questions about Camelot and maps could wait. Grabbing her hand, he pulled her down to their bed.

~

LATER, the two of them entered the inn to see if there was any breakfast left. They'd stayed in bed much longer than either of them usually did but Nia was feeling much better. Truth be told, so was Ethan.

His companions were still at the table, though it appeared most of the food was already gone. The group looked up at the two, several of them giving the pair smiles and knowing looks.

"Sleeping in late?" snickered Ainslee. Her emphasis on the word "sleeping" told Ethan the dwarf didn't believe for one second that the two of them had been sleeping.

Elspeth stood up with a smile and started walking towards the kitchen. "I saved some food for you two, so a certain someone didn't eat it all."

Ainslee's head snapped to the innkeeper's wife. "Wait?! There was more food?!"

Rolling his eyes at the dwarf, he and Nia went over to the table and joined their companions. In a minute, Elspeth came back with some rolls, eggs and sausage and placed a plate before each of them.

Despite not eating "prey food" like vegetables, Nia did occasionally eat bread and baked goods. Today was not one of those times and she slid the biscuits to his plate. Despite really wanting sausage, he slid two of the three links to her despite her objections.

"Do as your alpha commands," he joked. When she gave him a sour look, he just smiled back. "Seriously, it's too much food with the extra biscuits."

"I'll take the biscuits," Ainslee offered. Nia and Ethan both glared at the dwarf. "What?! I'm still hungry."

The two of them ate their breakfast while the others

talked of what needed to be done around the village. When they were finished eating, Ethan turned to Michalus.

"I was reading more of the journal last night," he told the elven wizard.

The old elf raised an eyebrow. "Learn something?"

"You could say that. Do you know anything about the area south of here?" he asked, getting right to the point.

"The south?" Michalus asked, scratching his chin. He looked thoughtful for a long moment before continuing. "I explored down south a few hundred years ago. I expect it's changed since then."

"How far south did you go?" Ethan prodded. "Maybe nine weeks' horse ride south?"

Michalus chuckled. "Nine weeks? That's very specific."

The old wizard considered Ethan's question, seeming to go back in time inside his head. He muttered some noises before finally nodding. "Yes, I believe I went about that far, maybe even further. Down to the city of Avalon, though that's a dangerous city now."

"Avalon?" Ethan asked. He remembered something about an Avalon in Arthurian lore but couldn't remember the significance. He cursed under his breath. Where was an internet search when he needed it?

"Oh yes. The Order had a great library there. Well, until it was destroyed by the orcs. Burned all the books, I heard. Such a tragedy," the wizard lamented.

"Did you go east at all when you were down south?" Ethan asked hopefully.

"East?" the old elf chuckled. "Thor's hammer, no. Sherwood Forest is to the east. No one goes into Sherwood Forest."

Ethan rolled his eyes. Had he heard the old elf correctly? There was a Sherwood Forest on this world too? What about Robin Hood? Was he here too?

"You're serious?" Ethan asked. "There's a Sherwood Forest here?"

"Quite serious," Michalus replied sternly. "Those who invade Sherwood Forest rarely make it out alive."

"Why? What is it?" Ainslee asked. "Dragons?"

"There are all sorts of rumors," the wizard replied. "Strange lights, weird creatures, bandits... Heh... even trees that move and talk."

"Trees that move and talk?!" Yuliana chimed in suddenly. "They are here, on this world?"

"My dear," the wizard chuckled. "Those are just idle rumors. The talk of delusional, half-starved people who became lost in the forest."

"But they could be there?" Yuliana pressed.

"Well." The old elf scratched his head. "I mean, I suppose it's possible."

"I want to go to Sherwood Forest," Yuliana blurted out to the group. "I must go!"

"Weren't you listening?" Ainslee snickered. "People go in and they don't come out. Seems like a good place to avoid."

"You don't understand," the green-haired elf said impatiently. "These may be caretakers, the treefolk. These are the trees we tended in the groves. The trees that talked to us."

Ethan was suddenly having flashbacks to that movie

with the halflings and the ring of power. Were the talking trees like the ones in that movie? That would be something to see.

But he had his own reasons for going south and then into Sherwood. Somewhere, in Sherwood Forest, must be Camelot.

He looked around the room. "I want to go to Sherwood too."

"For Odin's sake," Ainslee growled. "Why?"

"I think that's where Camelot is," he answered.

"What is a Camelot?" Yuliana answered.

"It's a city. The city where King Arthur lived," Ethan replied. "If it still stands, it might have the largest library in the world."

"Oh?" Michalus perked up, eyebrows raised. "How do you know that?"

"It's in the journal," Ethan told him.

"A journal that may or may not be authentic," the old wizard pointed out.

Ethan shook his head. "Too much of it seems true. Things that I know are true and I'm not sure how anyone else would know."

"Like what?" Michalus asked, his curiosity showing on his face.

Biting his lip, Ethan debated on how much he wanted to tell the old wizard. If he let Michalus read the journal, the old elf would learn about the Fountain of Youth and the Holy Grail. Could he be trusted? He needed to speak with the others before they revealed that secret to him.

"Stop by this evening," Ethan told the elf, "and I'll show you."

By then, Ethan should be able to talk with the others. If they agreed that Ethan should share the secret, then he would. Otherwise, he'd have to make some excuse.

"Very well," Michalus agreed with a raised eyebrow. "I will stop over this evening."

"Until then," Fearghas said, looking around at the group. "There's a lot of work around the village that needs to be done!"

6

There were no barn raisings or roof raisings that day, so Ethan decided to go from farm to farm and then circle back to some of the village homes. Leaving Hawkshead behind, he began to walk down the road that led to the homesteads on the outskirts of Hawkshead.

Physical labor wasn't the type of work he was used to. Ethan had eschewed more physical work in favor of more technical and cerebral work a long time ago. And he'd never looked back.

Despite not being skilled in any physical labor, having magic gave him options in this world. He could use <u>Air</u> magic to lift things several men couldn't lift. Using *Earth* magic, he was able to mold stones into useful shapes, tools or even dishes for people to eat from.

But magic couldn't do everything. At least, Ethan couldn't make magic do everything. Sometimes, he just had to roll up his sleeves and help the people - which wasn't always a bad thing.

"Mayor! Mayor!" a woman's voice called frantically from down the road.

Looking down the road, Ethan saw a bloody woman running down the road holding her pregnant belly with one hand. He thought he recognized her from one of the farms. Yes, her name was... Amee. Sprinting towards the woman, he met up with her a hundred yards away.

"Are you okay? What happened?" he asked. The woman was bloody but there were no wounds immediately visible. The woman didn't answer so he repeated the question. "Are you okay?"

"I'm.... okay... it's... it's... eating... our livestock," she gasped, bending over. She was breathing hard and Ethan was afraid she'd have the baby right then and there.

"Do you need help?" Ethan asked, gesturing to her belly.

"No... I'm... fine... help Dill," she said. "The... monster... has him... trapped."

Ethan nodded. He opened his mouth to ask her which farm was hers, but he realized the farms were all along the road. Duh! Hers would be the one being attacked by a monster.

He squatted down so he could look her in the eyes. "I'll go see what I can do. You rest a bit, then try to make it to the village and tell my companions."

"I'll.... I'll come... with you," she insisted.

"No!" he retorted, louder than he meant to. He lowered his tone. "No. If I have to fight a monster and save Dill... wait... is Dill your husband?"

Ethan suddenly had visions of him running into danger to save her favorite chicken or pig, which she had named Dill.

"Husband...and father," she replied, pointing to her belly.

"Okay," Ethan said, relieved that he wouldn't be fighting a monster by himself to save a chicken. "I'll go help Dill. What kind of monster is it?"

"Gryph....Gryphon," she replied.

Ethan took a step back. He knew what a gryphon was in Earth legends. In stories, Greek he thought, it was a creature with the body of a lion but the head and wings of an eagle. That was also how they were portrayed in most of the MMORPGs and RPGs he had played. Not something he wanted to deal with alone. Not that he had a choice.

"I'll save Dill," he told her. "You, run into town and find my friends."

Not waiting for the woman to reply, he sprinted down the road, towards the farms. After a minute, he glanced back and saw the woman running to the village. Good. Amee would be safe and hopefully his friends would arrive in time to help him.

He didn't get far before he had to slow his pace. While he'd done a lot of walking and was now in decent shape, he hadn't exactly been keeping up with his cardio. He slowed to a jog and tried to push himself to continue. He knew time was critical but showing up out of breath and out of *Stamina*, might just mean a quick death.

Within five minutes of jogging, he came to the first farm. He tried to remember who lived there but he was so out of breath, he couldn't think. A man came running up to him. In the background, Ethan saw a woman and two children peeking out of the window of their house.

"Mayor!" the man said and his Analyze showed his name was Kal. "You gonna help Dill?"

Too out of breath to answer, Ethan nodded. He felt faint and he checked his HUD.

Stamina: 2

He cursed, or tried to, but he was breathing too hard.

Kal gave him an apologetic look. "Amee came and told us what was goin' on at the farm. I would have helped... but I wouldn't be no good against no gryphon. And I need to be here with my family in case it comes here next."

Ethan nodded. "I... I'll... take... care of... it... you... stay here... keep... family... safe."

"Thank you, mayor." The man nodded and then, taking a wary look at the sky, he hurried back to his house.

Ethan walked off but once he was out of eyeshot of the house, he turned off the road and went through the trees, to the river. Squatting down, he gulped down handfuls of water until his *Stamina* was topped off at its halfway point - the maximum he could restore it.

He sighed. He'd also managed to catch his breath but now he needed to jog again. Keeping his pace slow, he jogged back to the road and down it for another ten minutes before reaching the outskirts of the next farm.

As he approached the fenced area, he heard the screech of what resembled that of a large eagle. A very large eagle. It sounded like he was at the right farmhouse.

Ethan came to a stop and moved quickly to a nearby tree as he fought to get his breathing under control.

He peered around the tree trying to catch a glimpse of the monster or Dill, but there were too many other trees in the way. Ethan needed to get closer.

Hopping the fence, Ethan began going from tree to tree to get closer to the house he knew was there. He stopped at each tree and peered around both sides. He also kept an eye out towards the sky but with all the trees, he didn't think a gryphon could make it through the branches.

After several minutes, he finally caught a glimpse of the open farmyard and the barn. And the gryphon. He frowned. There was definitely a creature there with the head of an eagle. It even had white feathers on its head, like an eagle. The wings were like that of an eagle too, but they were brown to match the body.

It was the body that was wrong, at least, according to legends. Gryphons were supposed to have the body of a lion. This creature had the body of a horse covered in short, mottled brown fur. But even that was wrong. The back legs were definitely horse legs, but the front legs were like the taloned legs of an eagle. Despite lacking the lion's body, it was still a majestic-looking creature. Maybe that was what gryphons looked like on this world.

Whatever the creature was and whatever it was called, it was clearly agitated. It stalked back and forth in front of the barn, furling and unfurling its wings. It would flap its wings several times and then screech at the barn.

Tearing his eyes off the gryphon, Ethan scanned the rest of the farmyard he could see. There were several bloody bodies of animals - lambs he thought. Listening, he thought he heard more sheep baying from inside the barn. Was that where Dill was? He needed to find out.

Keeping his distance, Ethan moved parallel to the barn, along the trees and then circled around to the house. He wanted to go into the house, but there was too much distance between the tree he was hiding behind and the door to the house. The creature would see him.

Ethan grinned as he recalled Michalus's invisible shield. With a thought, he willed himself invisible, using *Air* and *Water* to bend the light around him. He looked at his hand to make sure he was invisible.

He couldn't see his hands until he moved them, then it looked like that movie with the predators that could turn invisible. Ethan remembered Michalus's warning about the spell not quite working perfectly when the hidden object was in motion. Great. Just great. He sighed and then slowly walked to the front door and slipped in.

He dropped the invisibility as soon as he was inside. No use in wasting *Mana*. He kept his voice low. "Anyone here?"

The place was as small as the first house he'd woken up in so long ago with only three rooms. He quickly looked in each one but found no one. Just great.

Ethan moved to the window and peeked out. The gryphon was still stalking around the barn. He took a better look around the yard and saw a few more dead sheep but didn't see anything that resembled a human body. Hopefully, that meant Dill was alive.

Making himself invisible again, Ethan ducked out the door and made it to a tree on the side of the house before dropping the spell. He moved from tree to tree until he was at the back of the barn. There was a door on this side of the barn too and, after making sure the gryphon couldn't see him, he bolted for the door.

He pulled the door open and a man inside jumped and screamed out before seeming to realize Ethan wasn't the gryphon. The man slumped back down and on the other side of the barn, the creature screeched again.

"Mayor!" the man breathed, relief washing over his features. Ethan saw that the man had a piece of cloth, possibly a shirt, tied around his leg. It was soaked with blood. His Analyze identified him as Dill, the woman's husband.

"Thank the gods it's you," Dill said and slumped to the ground. He saw Ethan looking at his leg and motioned to the creature outside. "The thing was killing my sheep. I barely got these inside, but it caught me with one of its talons."

"You're lucky to be alive," Ethan told the man. He looked around the small barn and saw the sheep in a pen in the corner. They shifted nervously and jumped each time the gryphon screeched.

The man was safe - for now. But Ethan would need to deal with the gryphon. He began to think of the best way to deal with the creature. He could fireball it or use the flamethrower effect he'd used on the spiders. Maybe he didn't even have to kill it. Maybe he could scare it away.

He sighed. If he scared it away, it might come back or just fly around and find another farm to bother. No, he had to kill it. Given its proximity to the barn, fire was probably not a good idea.

Grimacing at the idea of killing something so majestic-looking, Ethan looked around the barn for something he could use as a projectile. "Are there any tools in here?"

Dill shook his head. "Tools are in the tool shed."

Ethan frowned, remembering a small shed between the house and the barn. He'd actually thought it was an outhouse.

He was wondering if he should sneak back out and get to the toolshed when movement caught his eye. The gryphon peeked around the corner of the barn. Seeing Ethan in the doorway of the barn, it screeched and lunged at him.

Grabbing the door, he slammed it shut just in time to avoid the gryphon getting its beak inside. Ethan felt and heard the creature scratching at the door with its talons and beak.

"Bar it, quick!" Dill said, tossing Ethan a board.

Ethan noticed the brackets that would hold the bar and keep the door from being opened. He levitated the board over to him and slid it into place. The door continued to rattle as the creature pawed at the door.

Cursing, he looked around the room for something he could use. He moved to one corner and looked through some hay, trying to see if there were any stones or anything he could shape into a spike.

"What are you looking for?" Dill asked, flinching as his leg spasmed.

"Something I can use as a weapon," Ethan replied. He looked down at the man's leg. "Just hold on, my friends are on their way and one of them can heal."

Walking over to the opposite corner, he bent down to

look through the hay when Dill squirmed. "Mayor... you don't have to..."

The man stopped as Ethan, who had already started shifting the hay, stopped suddenly as he uncovered a large round stone. No. Not a stone. An egg. Much too large to be a chicken egg, the truth quickly dawned on him and he turned to the farmer. Dill's guilt was written all over his face and the farmer's eyes dropped to the floor.

"Please tell me this isn't what I think it is," Ethan said, eyes narrowed.

"Mayor," the man croaked, "gryphon eggs are worth a lot of money. I just thought, you know, with the baby on the way."

Ethan groaned and shook his head. It was one thing to kill a creature that was attacking him or a friend. But to kill what was probably a mother just trying to get her baby, he wasn't sure he could do that.

"I know it's worth a lot of money," he told the man. "But look what it's done to your sheep...."

"I can buy new sheep," the man argued, his voice stubborn.

"By taking a mother's baby from her," Ethan said. He remembered Dill's pregnant wife. "Is that how you'd want someone to treat your child?"

"That's different..." the man said but trailed off under Ethan's glare. He lowered his gaze again. "I just thought it would help with the baby."

"I don't know how much these eggs are worth," Ethan told him. "I'll do my best to help you any way I can, but I don't want to kill a mother trying to get her baby back."

Dill sighed in defeat and nodded. "I guess I didn't really think of it like that."

Ethan gingerly picked up the egg with two hands. It was large, over a foot long. And heavy. He carried it over to the front door and, using *Air*, pulled the bar off the door and pushed it open.

As the door opened, Dill looked over at him, defeated. "Mayor. Can you... uh... not tell my wife about the egg... please?"

Ethan snorted and then heard footsteps coming from the side of the barn and the gryphon came shooting around the corner.

Holding up the egg so the gryphon got a good look at it. The creature slid to a stop, its eyes locking onto the egg. It looked from the egg to Ethan and took a step forward and screeched. The message was loud and clear: Give me my egg.

Keeping his eyes on the creature and ready to block and attack with a shield of *Air*, Ethan slowly lowered the egg to the ground. As he did, he took the opportunity to scan the creature.

Hippogryph
    Level: 8

Hippogryph! It wasn't a gryphon after all. Now that he read the name, he remembered a creature like that from Greek mythology. The body of a horse and the head and wings of an eagle. The stories didn't do it justice. Of course, maybe that's because he had a beak the size of his forearm about two feet from his head.

Carefully setting the egg on the ground, Ethan slowly stood up and backed away. The hippogryph watched him warily until he stopped about ten feet away. It looked from him to the egg several times. Finally, it screeched at him before stepping forward and taking the egg gently in its beak.

The hippogryph then backed away, turned and trotted off towards the open field. As soon as it was clear of the trees, it flapped its huge wings and launched itself into the sky. Ethan followed it, watching it circle several times before flying off south.

As it disappeared into the distance, he heard a commotion behind him and turned to see his friends coming. Nia was almost a hundred yards ahead of the others.

"Did you kill the beast already?" Nia asked. The foxgirl had probably run the entire time and seemed barely winded.

Ethan looked back to the south, no longer able to see the creature in the sky. He turned and smiled at Nia. "I took care of it."

7

————

After Yuliana healed Dill, the group headed back to town. Ethan was tired and sweaty from his run, as well as the stressful situation with the hippogryph. All he wanted to do was take a dip in the river and then chill out for a bit.

Once they returned to Hawkshead, Ethan did just that. He found an isolated place in the river, stripped off his clothes and then jumped in the river. The water was cold, but at the moment, he didn't mind. He washed the sweat off him and went back to his house only to find Nia waiting for him in bed. He looked at her with a raised eyebrow.

"You fought a gryphon. You need to have your mana restored. Besides. You don't stink as bad at the moment," she said with a grin. Rolling his eyes, he joined his wife in bed. No point in passing up an opportunity.

Afterwards, Ethan thought about the farms he'd passed. Some of those farms had been severely damaged by the kobolds. Through hard work - and a little magic - most of them had been repaired. It reminded him that he needed to check on the progress of the village. Thinking of his HUD, he brought up the information on Hawkshead.

```
Hawkshead
   Town Rank: 1 (18%)
   Town population: 25
   Town morale: 53%
   Town total buildings: 19
   Town active buildings: 17
   Town Output:
   Food: 27
   Metal: 0
   Leather: 2
   Wood: 1
   Income from Taxes: 0
   Income from Trade: 0
```

They'd lost two people since the kobold raid. One had been to a fever that Yuliana could not heal and the other to a bear attack. At the same time, he'd restored some of the buildings, bringing his total buildings to 19. Not only that, but now 17 of the 19 were in use.

Now that the animals had returned and Odelina had access to the haversack he made, she was doing more hunting and also tanning some leather. This boosted both the food and the leather output.

He still hadn't managed to fill any of the other positions. Either no one was qualified, they didn't have time, or they simply didn't want the position. Ethan realized if he wanted to fill them, he'd need to fill them from outside the village. But that task could wait.

Remembering he needed to talk to his friends, Ethan gathered his companions before lunch to talk over the issue of sharing information with Michalus. He explained the pros and cons and then asked for their input.

"It really boils down to," Ethan concluded, "do we trust him?"

"He did take the elven children to Moonpoint," Yuliana pointed out.

"Yeah," Ainslee agreed, arms over her chest. "But that just means he likes children of his own kind. Doesn't mean he can be trusted."

Yuliana looked offended but Ethan jumped in before the elf could reply. "Has he treated you badly in any way?"

"Well, no," the dwarf admitted. She shrugged her shoulders. "Actually, he's been nice to me. I'm just saying, that's not necessarily a reason to trust him."

"Par'karr like elf wizard," the little kobold added. "Par'karr trust him. He help kill ogres. Not run away."

"True," Ethan agreed.

"He could have just been saving his own skin," Ainslee countered. "Just sayin'."

"What do you think?" Ethan asked Nia, turning to look at his wife.

Nia shrugged. "You are the alpha. I will abide by your decision."

Ainslee rolled her eyes but kept quiet and for once, Ethan agreed with the dwarf's sentiment. "Nia, I trust and value your opinion. After all, you are Tal'Cha, right?"

"Very well." Nia's expression didn't change but Ethan saw that she did stand up a little straighter. "I do not see a reason not to trust him. He has not smelled of deception and he kept his word to take the children..."

"We're taking his word at that," Ainslee interrupted. "He could have eaten them for all we know."

They all turned to look at Ainslee. She bristled under their concerted stares. "I mean, we don't have any proof. He did seem to get back pretty quickly."

Nia rolled her eyes at the dwarf and turned back to Ethan. "When he said he took them to Moonpoint, I smelled no deception...."

Ethan raised an eyebrow. It was the second time she'd mentioned smelling deception. "Wait. Are you saying, you can smell when someone lies?"

"Of course, it is obvious in their scent," the foxgirl said nonchalantly. Her expression became mischievous. "I can smell many things about a person."

Feeling suddenly embarrassed, he quickly tried to remember if he'd ever lied to her. If so, it seemed like she would have known. Ethan grimaced as he realized that he couldn't even tell a little white lie to his wife or she'd know.

"Wait." Ainslee screwed up her face. "You're saying you can tell when people lie. By the way they smell?"

Nia nodded.

The dwarf scrutinized her. "You're serious?"

Nia nodded again, a small smile creeping to her lips.

"Par'karr is a bird!" the kobold said suddenly. "Is Par'karr lying?"

Nia gave Ethan a "is he serious?" look. Ethan just

shrugged and the foxgirl stifled a giggle before answering the kobold. "Yes, Par'karr. You are lying."

Par'karr's eyes went big. "It true! She tell Par'karr is lying!"

Ethan bit his lip to stop from laughing but Ainslee rolled her eyes. She huffed and then put her hands on her hips and faced the foxgirl. "Try this one. My da's name was Marrog?"

"It is a lie," Nia said immediately.

Ainslee smirked. "Actually, his name was Dremur."

"Another lie," the foxgirl responded.

The dwarf was taken back. She narrowed her eyes. "Kaldern."

"Lie."

"Moulon."

"Lie."

"Sengun."

"Lie."

"Bramdon."

Nia cocked her head. "That is truth."

"Loki's balls!" the dwarf exclaimed, throwing her arms up. "Either you're really lucky or you really can smell the truth."

Nia crossed her arms over her chest with a satisfied smile. "I can smell the truth."

"How come you did not tell us of this ability before?" Yuliana asked. The elf didn't seem accusatory, simply curious.

"It has not come up," the foxgirl answered.

"You don't expect us to believe that, do you?" Ainslee

retorted accusingly. "And you just never bothered to tell us?"

Nia shrugged and maintained a neutral expression. "It is the way among my people. I did not realize until later that none of you could smell deception."

Ethan understood why Nia would have kept the ability to herself. He also respected her right to do so. After all, he hadn't told every little detail about his life to the group. Of course, that was mostly because they wouldn't understand the technology of his world.

He was a little hurt that she hadn't told him about the ability. She was supposed to be his wife, after all. Ethan would have thought that she would have let him know. Or had she kept it to herself to give her an edge?

Now that he did know, Ethan made a mental note not to tell outright lies to the foxgirl. He wasn't sure if she could tell half-truths or only part of the truth. He'd have to find a way to test the limits of her ability.

Not that Ethan planned to lie to his wife. Or cheat on her. Even if that was in his nature, there was no chance he'd get away with it. If she could smell a lie, she would certainly be able to smell another woman's scent on him. Then again, weren't multiple wives a thing where she was from? That gave him some interesting ideas, but, sadly, he wasn't in one of those trashy harem novels that seemed so popular.

Ethan realized everyone was looking at him. He'd lost track of the conversation. "What?"

"I said," Ainslee growled. "Did you know your wife could do that?"

"No," Ethan replied truthfully. "I didn't. But I haven't lied to her, so it didn't come up."

"You have lied," Nia corrected, crossing her arms over her small breasts. "Many times."

Ethan knew he must have a deer-in-the-headlights look on his face and realized everyone was looking from him to Nia. He cleared his throat. "I have?"

"Oh yes," Nia replied with a straight face. "At first, you lied by saying you did not want me. You have also lied when I caught you looking at my tail. Many times."

A small smile crept across her lips as she spoke, and Ethan felt relieved that those were the only lies he had told to her. Or were they the only lies she was bringing up.

"Well..." Ethan cleared his throat again. "You have a great body. I like looking at you.... And your tail."

Nia's smile broadened and she nodded. "As it should be now that I am your wife. You are not entirely bad on the nose either..."

"Freya's pale breasts," the dwarf gagged, rolled her eyes. "We get it! We get it! He likes to stare at your arse. Get a room, already."

"Ahem," Ethan cleared his throat loudly. "So, we've established that Nia can smell deception and she's smelled no deception from Michalus. Is that right, Nia?"

"That is correct," the foxgirl replied.

"Listen, wizard-boy," the dwarf said. "You're the one who made us all swear not to tell anyone. You made some good points and I agreed. Now, you want to share it with someone. Are you sure you want to do that?"

"He does seem trustworthy," Yuliana chimed in.

Ethan agreed but he realized there was a way to tell

whether or not the old wizard could be trusted. He grinned. "And we can tell whether or not he can be trusted to keep the secret."

"How?" Ainslee frowned.

"We can ask him," Ethan pointed out and then gestured to his wife with his head. "And Nia will be able to tell whether or not he's lying."

Ainslee looked skeptical. Her frown became a scowl and her forehead creased. "And just how are you going to find that out, without you actually telling him?"

"Nia and I will talk to him tonight and tell him we have a secret that we need to tell him, but he must keep it a secret. We'll ask him if he will keep it secret. If he lies, Nia will know and we won't tell him," Ethan replied.

"That good idea," Par'karr grinned.

"Yes," Yuliana agreed. "I'm sure he'll agree."

"Agree to something before actually hearing it?" Ainslee said doubtfully. Then she sighed. "It's up to you, wizard-boy. That might work and he might even mean it - unless he hears what it is. I imagine a wizard setting up shop selling immortality could earn quite a bit of money. Just sayin'."

She looked at him with a serious expression and gestured around to the village. "Are you sure you want to risk all this for the chance to find some old city?"

Ethan raised an eyebrow at the dwarf, who shrugged. "What, wizard-boy. This is the only home I got at the moment. I'm all for protecting it too."

"Fair point," Ethan conceded. "We'll do our best to test him before we actually tell him the secret."

She looked between Nia and Ethan. She gave them a curt nod. "You'd better."

"Then it's decided," Ethan told the group. "We will talk with Michalus tonight. If he passes our test, we'll talk to him and tell him the secret and see what he can make out of the journal."

There were muttered agreements from the other members of the group.

"Fine," Ainslee growled. "It's decided. Can we go eat lunch already?"

8
____

Michalus lowered Merlin's journal and looked over at Ethan. He opened his mouth to say something, then closed it. His brow was furrowed, and he looked deep in thought for a long moment. Finally, he spoke. "And you're saying, this is real. You actually found the Holy Grail and the Fountain of Youth?"

"Yes," Ethan answered.

Nia and he had quizzed the old wizard earlier and had him swear not to reveal the secret they would entrust to him. The elf had debated for some time, mostly over agreeing to not reveal something before he heard it. Finally, he had relented. He'd sworn not to reveal it without Ethan's permission and Nia had detected no deception.

He had relayed their adventure in the tomb and exactly what they had found and how they were now immortal and would never age. Michalus had been dubious but Ethan had given him the journal to read.

"This all seems so... fantastical," Michalus said. "Is there any way I can see it for myself?"

Ethan had anticipated Michalus's request. It's the same thing Ethan would have asked. He was a computer tech at heart, and he would want to see proof - see it with his own eyes. And he'd convinced Nia to help him charge up a couple of Chymera crystals so he could open a portal back to the tomb.

Ethan smiled. "Yes, as long as you don't mind traveling through a portal."

"Portal? You're not serious, are you?" the old wizard started, eyes opening wide.

"Nia and I have done it before," Ethan replied. He hadn't really had time to tell the wizard about their escape from the library and exactly how he'd done it. "In the library. I created a portal from the library to just in front of the library. Oh... and the actual library was on another planet."

"Another planet?!" the wizard exclaimed. He chuckled. "Surely, you're joking."

Michalus looked from Ethan to Nia. The foxgirl shook her head. "It had a huge red sun. It was not this world."

"Wait a minute," Michalus said, his eyes wild. "Are you saying that you created a portal from another planet to this planet."

Ethan nodded.

"He did," Nia confirmed. "I was there. We went through the rainbow bridge."

"The Bifrost." Ethan nodded.

"How is this possible?!" the old elf screeched. The wizard stood suddenly and started pacing around the room. "I've never even heard of anything like this... I mean, Merlin did say he thought it was... But no, it couldn't have been the same Merlin..."

Ethan nodded. "You read the journal. Merlin, Arthur and the knights all drank from the pool. They would not have aged. The Merlin you met could have been the same Merlin who wrote the book."

"That's.... That's just not possible," Michalus mumbled. He returned to his chair and sat down. The wizard stared down at the book in his hands. "Not possible."

"You have to admit," Ethan told him, "that you may actually have gotten to know THE Merlin."

Michalus shook his head as he looked down at the journal and then looked up at Ethan. "And you're positive you can open a stable portal to this tomb?"

"I'm 100% positive," Ethan said. "But I've opened two portals, plus I created the portal bags."

"Yes," Michalus agreed. "Which I have to confess, still astounds me how you figured it out on your own."

"I realized it was kind of like programming," Ethan said. "Or maybe like building a circuit."

The old wizard looked confused and Ethan shrugged apologetically. "Things from my world."

"I thought you said your world didn't have magic."

"It doesn't. But I think some of the same concepts for the science and technology of my world apply to the magic of this world."

"Interesting," Michalus said, rubbing his chin. "Perhaps there's some sort of universal law that governs all worlds."

"Possibly." Ethan shrugged. It was starting to get late and if he was going to use portal magic, he wanted to do it before he got too tired. He stood up and moved to an open area of the front room. "You ready to travel by portal?"

The old wizard bit his lip for a moment but then nodded. "Well, I suppose if it doesn't work, dying from experimenting with magic isn't the worst way to go."

"I will go first," Nia told the two wizards. She patted the pommels of her scimitars. "In case any of the spiders have returned."

Michalus started to open his mouth but Ethan shook his head. "Don't bother trying to talk her out of it."

"Very well," the old wizard chuckled. "I guess I will go second. I assume you have to go last to keep the portal open, correct?"

"Correct," Ethan confirmed. He looked at Nia and gave her a wink. "You ready?"

She gave him a toothy grin, hands on her swords. "I am always ready."

Ethan focused on the runes he'd left at the tomb. The same runes his portal bag used to get to the Grail. He hadn't thought he'd be making the trip back to the tomb so soon, but things seldom seemed to work out the way he expected.

"Alright," he told them. "Here we go."

Focusing his will on the place he wanted to go, he started to draw *Mana* from the crystals. Before he could do so, the portal opened up in front of Nia.

Taken aback by the suddenness of the portal's appearance, he almost lost focus and the portal flickered for just a moment. He regained his focus and brought up his HUD.

Mana: 23
Skill increase: Aether Magic +1%.

How was that possible? He'd opened a portal on his own without even tapping into the *Mana* in the crystals. The last time, he'd not only had to pull *Mana* from the crystals, he'd shattered a couple of them as well. Now he'd just opened a portal without even using up all of his own *Mana.*

Nia crouched down and crawled through, followed by Michalus. Ethan waited until they were both through and could see that they'd cleared the way before diving through himself.

Once again, Ethan found himself in the swirling vortex of colors. The Bifrost. He watched the colors swirl around him as he rocketed through the tunnel. Then he was suddenly crawling in the tomb.

Nia sprang to her feet, looking around in the illumination of her light stone. She hadn't drawn her weapons but her right hand was on the hilt of her scimitar while the left one held the stone.

Michalus got to his feet more slowly, groaning as he did. He caught Ethan giving him a concerned look and smiled. "Just old bones."

Ethan stood up and summoned two of his light orbs, illuminating the rest of the room. Nia's eyes scanned every corner and she sniffed in all directions before he saw her relax. "The spiders have not returned. We are alone."

Michalus looked around in awe, staring at the stone carvings on the walls and then letting his eyes come to rest on the sarcophagus and the golden chalice that sat atop it. His eyes then went down to the pool of sparkling water that surrounded the tiny island that held the sarcophagus.

"That's the Grail." Ethan pointed at the Chalice. "We used it to heal you."

"Remarkable!" the old wizard said, leaning closer to the Grail. He moved around, taking in the golden cup from every angle.

Ethan reached into a pouch and pulled out the necklace he'd made for Yuliana to prevent her from being affected by the Grail's high-pitched sound. He handed it to the old wizard. "If you're going to remove the Grail, you'll want to wear this. I made it to protect against the high-pitch sound it produces when removed from the tomb. Apparently, elves and foxlings can hear it, but not dwarves or humans."

"Thank you," the wizard said. He took the necklace and, after looking at it briefly, he put it around his neck. "Won't removing it cause the animals in and around the village to flee again?"

"I don't think so," Ethan said, remembering when they'd used it on the old wizard. "I think it starts off mild and then grows in volume the longer it's away from the tomb. Now that I read the journal, I think Merlin did it to make sure that Mordred couldn't keep it, even if he managed to take it. Eventually, it would just be too much for him to take."

"A short time away from the tomb will only cause a sound in this area?" Michalus asked.

"That's my theory at the moment," Ethan said and then grinned sheepishly. "But we probably shouldn't push our luck."

"That seems like a wise precaution," the old wizard agreed.

Michalus looked from the golden chalice to the pool and then back to the chalice. "I wonder if I might try some of the water."

Ethan shrugged. "Why not? We all did. Nia, you're wearing your necklace, right?"

The foxgirl reached under her armor and pulled out the necklace to show him.

"Go for it," he told Michalus.

"And you've had no adverse effects?" The old wizard raised an eyebrow.

Looking at Nia for confirmation, he shook his head. "Nothing that we've noticed. If anything, maybe I've felt more energetic lately."

"Much more energetic." Nia gave him a sly smile.

Michalus licked his lips and then took the chalice from the sarcophagus. The old wizard's eyes darted around, as if he expected something to happen. When nothing did happen, he looked down at his necklace and then slowly lifted it over his head.

"I wouldn't..." Ethan began but just then the old elf winced and dropped the necklace back down over his head.

"That was... remarkably unpleasant," the wizard muttered.

"So I've been told," Ethan agreed and Nia nodded her confirmation.

"That would certainly prevent me from keeping the Grail," Michalus stated. He licked his lips again and looked down at the pool of sparkling water.

Kneeling down, the wizard scooped up some of the water in the Grail. Standing up, he looked at the chalice and then looked at Ethan.

"Go ahead," he told the wizard.

The elves already had such long lifespans, he wasn't sure what benefit the Fountain of Youth would really grant him. And without a HUD, Michalus wouldn't be able to actually see the ability like Ethan and the others could.

Nodding to himself, Michalus brought the cup to his lips and took a sip. He lowered the cup and looked at Ethan. "I don't feel..."

Michalus suddenly doubled over, the cup falling from his hands. He groaned in pain as he moved his hands to his abdomen.

Ethan started to move forward but he stopped as he noticed the change happening with the wizard. Michalus's gray hair was turning brown and the liver spots on his hands were fading away. Stunned, Ethan could only watch as the wizard convulsed and seemed to be growing... younger.

The process was over in less than a minute, leaving Michalus gasping in a fetal position. He groaned and rolled over, revealing a much younger-looking version of the wizard who drank the water.

"Michalus?" Ethan asked. "Are you... okay?"

"And I thought... the sound was unpleasant," the elf replied, pushing himself to his feet. As he stood up he seemed to realize something was different. He looked at his hands, turning them around to see both sides. Then he stuck his head over the pool to look at his reflection in the water.

Nia moved alongside Ethan, holding the Grail she had retrieved after Michalus had dropped it. She offered it to Ethan.

He smiled. "I think we're done with it."

The foxgirl nodded and replaced the golden cup on top of the sarcophagus. Once done, she slid up next to Ethan again and looked over the formerly old wizard, who was still looking at his reflection in the pool. "He is young again."

Ethan nodded. "Yes. And this is going to be very difficult to explain to the villagers."

"Very," Nia agreed.

9

———

"Why did the waters of the pool not make us younger?" Nia asked as the younger version of Michalus took the time to look over his new body.

Ethan shrugged, completely at a loss. He hadn't expected the pool to make the old wizard younger. "I have no idea."

The foxgirl bit her lip. "Is it because we are already young?"

"Could be," he replied, looking over at the wizard as he gawked at his face in the water's reflection. "It is called the Fountain of Youth, after all. Maybe it returns you to your body's optimal age."

He thought back to his own experience. He'd been unconscious when they'd poured the water down his throat, probably nearly dead. Had it made his body younger? What was his optimal age? It must be fairly close to his current age since he didn't really look any different, at least to himself.

"There may be some truth to that," Michalus said, standing up from the pool and facing them. He held up his hand and looked at it. He wiggled his fingers and shook his head. "I can't believe this is my body. I haven't looked like this for hundreds of years."

"Now you'll look like that forever," Ethan pointed out. "At least, I assume so."

The formerly old wizard bent and stretched, grinning as he did so. "Oh, to be able to do this and not feel pain or aches. This is truly a miracle."

"You understand now why this has to be kept a secret?" Ethan asked.

Michalus sighed, looking down longingly at the pool. His brows furrowed before he finally looked up and nodded. "It could help so many people."

"Yes, it could," Ethan agreed. "But it would destroy many more. You know people's nature. As soon as one of the princes finds out about it, there will be outright war to control it."

Ethan was really guessing, but he didn't think he was wrong. He'd seen how Castlehaven had reverted to slavery and human sacrifice. How could he realistically believe they would be magnanimous with something like the pool.

He thought back to Merlin's journal. "Merlin knew it and so did Arthur. I suspect that's why they kept it a secret. To prevent the wrong people from using it and becoming tyrants forever."

Michalus nodded. "As much as I hate to admit it, you

are right... and so was Merlin. Something like this would tear the world apart."

The wizard stared down at the sparkling water. "I don't even know if this was somehow enchanted or if it's some sort of naturally occurring phenomenon. Oh, I would love to study it."

"The answer to that question and more," Ethan said, seeing his opening, "might be in the library of Camelot."

"I may look young now," Michalus said, narrowing his eyes at Ethan and tapped his head. "But I'm still old up here. I see what you're doing."

Ethan grinned. "I want to get to see what's in that library. Merlin created this tomb and there is magic here that I don't think anyone living understands. There might even be answers about how we got here."

The elf nodded, stroking his chin. "You do have a fair point. I still find it hard to believe that it is the same Merlin but if it was, I always suspected he knew more than he let on."

"You've been to the south. We could use your help getting there and if we find the library, we would all benefit," Ethan stated.

"Fine. Fine. You've convinced me." Michalus looked around the room, nodding. "I have to admit, this whole situation has me intrigued."

"Excellent!" Ethan exclaimed and did a little fist pump.

"That's assuming you can get us back," the elf said, gesturing around. "You can get us back, my boy?"

"Yes." Ethan smiled. "I just need to restore my *Mana*."

He saw Nia perk up but then her smile faltered when he grabbed the Grail, filled it with water and took a sip.

He didn't notice any differences, but his stats immediately jumped up to maximum. Replacing the Grail, he gave the foxgirl a wink. "You can help me refill my mana later."

She brightened and grinned.

"Ahem." The wizard cleared his throat, his face blushing slightly. "Perhaps we could get back and then you can... you know... do what you two do..."

"Fine." Ethan smirked, giving Nia another wink. "Let me open a portal."

Ethan hadn't left any symbols at the house. He'd been meaning to, but just hadn't gotten around to it. But he did have symbols already in the village. There were symbols on the chest that his portal pouch led to and also symbols in the stone "refrigerator" in the river.

He chose the latter, since theoretically it would be dark and no one would see them. Plus, his portal pouch chest was still with Elspeth. He guessed appearing in the inn out of thin air would not win him any points with the innkeeper's wife.

Focusing and keeping a careful eye on his *Mana*, Ethan opened a portal about half the height of a person. Judging by the size of the portal he'd created before and the amount of *Mana* he'd used, he guessed he could increase the size by about 25% without going into the negative. And he was right.

Looking at his HUD, Ethan grinned. He'd been right, but just by a hair.

Mana: 4

The portal appeared in the air next to the tomb.

Looking through it, he could barely make out the moonlight on the river beyond. Nia moved quickly, ducking through and hopping onto one of the larger rocks. Michalus followed quickly, also hopping onto a stone but with much less grace than the foxgirl.

Taking one last look around the tomb, Ethan hopped through and into the swirling colors of the Bifrost. He moved forward through the tunnel, seeing the colors speed by and then he was suddenly on a rock in the middle of the river.

Michalus was shaking his head. "You opened that portal without drawing magic from the crystals! How did you do that?!"

Ethan shrugged. "I have no idea. Unless my specialization in portal magic reduced the cost."

"You specialized in portal magic?" the wizard asked. "In what way?"

"It's something in my HUD I told you about earlier," Ethan explained. "I gained a level and received an ability called Specialization. It then allowed me to choose which magic skill I wanted to specialize in. I chose portal magic, or technically, I guess it's aether magic."

"It seems I need to find out more about this HUD and how it works," the elven wizard said. He looked around. "But it's late and we'll have plenty of time to talk on the road. I'll bid you good night."

"Michalus," Nia said sharply as the wizard started to leave. "Have you forgotten?"

"Forgotten?" The wizard turned, brows furrowed, and faced the foxgirl. "Forgotten what?"

"You are young now," the foxgirl retorted, gesturing

from his feet to his head. "If you return like that, there will be questions."

"Maybe you can tell them you cast a spell on yourself," Ethan suggested. "Some sort of illusion spell?"

The wizard looked dubious. "There is no spell that would make me young."

"You don't know any illusion spells?" Ethan asked. From his tabletop roleplaying days, he remembered using illusion spells to great effect. Perhaps those just weren't a thing in this world.

"Wizards who can do illusion spells are very rare," Michalus retorted. "It requires mental magic, something very few wizards ever learn, and fewer master."

"Is that another magic skill?" Ethan asked curiously. He hadn't seen any sort of mention of mental magic on his HUD. But then again, he didn't find out about Portal magic until he accidentally did it.

"It is," the elven wizard confirmed. "Just very rare."

"So not a spell, not an illusion," Ethan growled. "Any other bright ideas so people won't ask questions?"

"He is sick," Nia said.

"What?" Michalus asked, taken back. "No, I feel fine. Actually, I feel better than fine."

"No." Nia shook her head. "You must be sick, and you will stay in our house until we leave."

Ethan raised an eyebrow. "Our house?"

"We can control the avenues of approach to our house," the foxgirl explained. "And prevent curious eyes from spotting him."

"Yuliana will want to heal him," Ethan pointed out.

"We can tell the others tomorrow," she replied. "But only them."

"Makes sense," he agreed. An idea came to Ethan and he smiled. "When we come back, assuming you come back with us, we can say you are your son or nephew."

"What?" The wizard frowned. "I don't have a..."

Michalus trailed off as he understood what Ethan was suggesting. He cocked his head, considering. Finally, he nodded. "That just might work. A little play acting."

"Exactly," Ethan said. "Since no one knows of any magic that can make a person younger, they won't suspect you. We can call you Mickoli or Mike or something."

"How about Mykall," the elf suggested. "I actually did have an uncle named Mykall."

"Fine." Ethan nodded. "When we come back, we'll make sure everyone calls you Mykall and you'll have to come up with some story about why you're here instead of your uncle, father or whatever the relationship will be."

Michalus nodded. "We can think about that on the road. We'll have some time to think about it. It's a long journey south."

"Yes, it is." Ethan nodded. "Now all I have to do is convince the others to come along too."

The wizard looked surprised. "You haven't even asked them yet?"

Ethan shrugged. "Not yet. Hopefully, I can talk them into coming with us."

"You can," Nia said confidently. "You are the alpha."

Ethan chuckled. "Yeah, sure."

"She's right, my boy," Michalus agreed. "They look up

to you and follow your lead. I don't think you'll have any problems convincing them."

He nodded, but Ethan wasn't so sure. Par'karr would come along. The little kobold was loyal to a fault. Yuliana wanted to come to find out more about the living trees. He didn't think she'd be difficult to sway.

Ainslee would be the tough one. Despite the dwarf's gruff exterior, she seemed to prefer town life - or village life, as the case may be - instead of adventuring. Yes, she'd be the most difficult to convince.

"Come. It is late. You can figure things out tomorrow." Nia came and took his hand and pulled him towards their home. The foxgirl looked at Michalus. "You come too. We must prepare the ruse."

10

The next two days in the village went by in a blur. As expected, Par'karr had immediately expressed his interest in coming. The little kobold seemed to actually prefer to be on the road rather than in the village.

Yuliana also agreed to come along as soon as he asked. The elf was fascinated by the stories of living trees and desperately wanted to see the treefolk, or caretakers as she called them. She and Luna had quickly signed onto the proposed journey.

Then there was Ainslee. As expected, she hadn't been interested in another adventure. She was quite content to hang out at the village and work on getting the forge in order.

"Listen, wizard-boy," the dwarf said. "I've had enough of ogres, trolls and giant freaking spiders. I just want to get a forge going and start working metal again."

"We need you," he told Ainslee. "You're our tank."

"Ha," the dwarf snorted. "Most of the stuff, you just magic to death. You don't need me."

"We do," he replied, though he realized there was some truth to her statement. He remembered back to the tomb. "If it weren't for you and Nia, I'd be dead right now."

"Maybe," Ainslee said begrudgingly.

Ethan did believe they needed the dwarf. He didn't want to split up the party. He thought of her earlier statement about the forge and that gave him an idea.

"The caravans will start coming to town again," he told her. "If you come with us, I'll figure out a way to order you an anvil."

The dwarf looked hopeful, eyes bright. "You mean it?"

"Cross my heart and hope to die," Ethan shot back.

"What in Loki's balls does that mean?" the dwarf said, screwing up her face in confusion. "You're expecting to die?"

"Uh," he said, realizing it didn't translate well. "I promise."

"Fine," the dwarf said. "But I'll hold you to that."

During the two days, Michalus had hidden out in Ethan's home. Luckily, it was a large place since it wasn't just a home. It had actually been the general store when he'd taken over the building from Cuthbert. Unfortunately, most of the stock had been given to the bandits the treacherous mayor had hired. Ethan hadn't had the time or money to order more. That meant there was a good deal of extra room.

They'd only allowed Yuliana, Ainslee and Par'karr to see Michalus, telling everyone else he was sick. The villagers had been disappointed, since that meant only one wizard was helping them, but they'd accepted the story and wished him a speedy recovery.

Part of Ethan felt guilty for lying to them, but he knew it was for their safety more than anything else. He guessed whatever prince ruled Castlehaven wouldn't hesitate to kill everyone in the village to have the Fountain for himself.

Michalus kept a low profile until they left, busying himself with reading and re-reading Merlin's journal. Even when they finally rode out, he kept his hood up and coughed often to keep up the ruse. Once they got past the last farm, he was free to reveal his new, younger self.

Ethan didn't think he was a particularly observant person when it came to human interactions. It was the curse of being a techy, he had a certain lack of social skills and picking up on subtle social cues. But there was nothing subtle or hard to miss about the way Yuliana had begun to stare at the now-younger Michalus.

THE GROUP TRAVELED east for a week before reaching the coastal highway. Once again, he and his companions gawked at the enormous waterspouts. Despite having seen them before, it was still a sight to behold. And just as before, flocks of large pteranodons flew around them, diving in and out of them to emerge with the fish carried up in the spouts.

"We turn south now," Michalus told them as they continued to stare at the spouts. "There aren't many villages for almost a week, but then we'll see a few every few days until we reach the city of Highshire."

The wizard looked thoughtful. "That's assuming it's still there. I haven't been south for over a hundred years. Things change in a century or two."

Ethan nodded, remembering that he was immortal now. Provided he didn't get killed, he'd live for a hundred years or more. And he'd stay the same as he was now.

"Highshire is the last city that is part of the Northern Alliance," Michalus continued. "At least, it was back then."

"The northern alliance?" Ethan asked.

"It's a loose confederation of city states here in the north. Castlehaven, Moonpoint, Grayhorn, and Dragonmere, and then Highshire, of course."

"Are they like a country of something?" Ainslee asked.

"No." Michalus shook his head. "More like trade partners with an uneasy alliance."

"Is there another alliance to the south?" Nia asked. "Enemies, perhaps?"

The wizard looked thoughtful and stroked his chin. "It used to be Britannia, over a thousand years ago. But, if the journal is to be believed, that was when King Arthur ruled. Before the Doemenagg.

"For the past few hundred years, it's been nothing but a collection of warring city-states who can't stop fighting long enough to accomplish anything," Michalus told them. "Other than an occasional attack on Highshire."

"And we're going to be traveling through their territory?" Yuliana asked, her face concerned.

The wizard nodded grimly. "That's really my only

concern with this journey. Well, other than the forest itself."

"Sherwood Forest," Ethan thought aloud.

"Yes, Sherwood," the wizard repeated. "I'm still not too keen on the idea of entering that forest. Like I said, nothing but bad tales from those that have visited that place. At least, those that actually managed to come back out."

"Well, that doesn't sound ominous at all," Ainslee growled, leveling a hard stare on Ethan.

Ethan grinned. "I doubt the people who went in had two wizards and a battle-hardened dwarf with them."

Ainslee narrowed her eyes at him and then snorted. She turned to the south, but Ethan heard her mutter, "I am battle hardened."

"We should keep moving," Nia interrupted. "It will be dark soon and we must find a suitable camping spot and I must hunt."

The group spurred their horses and continued riding south. Once on their way, Ethan dropped his back, so he was next to Michalus. "You mentioned Avalon. Is that the next city past Highshire?"

"It is," the wizard replied. He shook his head. "Assuming it's still there. Because it's the northernmost city in the southern wastes, it is constantly changing hands so one of the factions can use it to launch attacks on Highshire."

"But we don't need to go that far south, right?" Ethan asked.

"No," Michalus confirmed. "We should be cutting into Sherwood a week before we would reach Avalon. I can't quite remember if Highshire is on the north or south side of Sherwood."

"That's still weeks away though," Ethan sighed.

"It is," the wizard agreed. "But you'll be surprised at how quickly it passes."

"You're probably right," Ethan said hopefully and moved his horse into position just behind Nia.

The companions stopped for the night about an hour before dark. Nia had spotted an adequate camping spot along the treeline. It was a large, flat area with multiple fire pits and Ethan guessed it was used regularly by one of the merchant caravans.

They all began getting the campsite ready while Nia went out hunting. Ethan still had the portal pouch linked to the chest back with Elspeth, but he hadn't been about to ask the innkeeper's wife to continue to make them food during their journey.

It was one thing when he was trying to save the village and had no access to food. It was another to ask her to keep making food while he was on his own mission. He wasn't about to abuse her kindness.

That said, he had asked her to check the chest regularly, in case Ethan and the group were in dire straits and needed something urgently. Ainslee had been with him and asked Fearghas to put Dwarven Spirits in as often as he could. In the end, Elspeth had agreed to check the chest every few days, so they had at least some safety net.

Nia returned just after dark with three pheasants. They quickly plucked and gutted the birds and set them to cooking.

"Are they done yet?" Ainslee asked for the fifth time in the last ten minutes.

Nia growled. "Asking if they are done over and over does not make them cook faster."

The dwarf made a face. "I'm hungry!"

"We are all hungry," Nia told the girl.

"You mean," Ainslee grumbled. "All of us except for Yuliana. She got food!"

Ethan looked over at Yuliana, who looked slightly embarrassed. Ethan had made her a small portal pouch that linked to a stone container in the water, similar but smaller than the one he'd made for the village.

Since the green-haired elf was the only vegetarian in the group, he wanted a way to keep any berries and nuts they found from going bad. A small portal pouch to a refrigerated stone chest was the best he could do currently.

Ainslee continued to grumble until Nia finally announced that the pheasant was done, and they all began to cut slices off and eat. All of them except Ainslee, who took one of the sticks with a whole bird and began eating it.

"Now you know why I got three," Nia whispered to him.

Ethan chuckled and Nia moved her mouth closer to his ear. "Tomorrow evening, you must come to hunt with me."

He looked at the foxgirl, who had a sultry look in her eyes. Somehow, he didn't think hunting was what she had in mind. He grinned. "I thought you said I was too loud."

"You will come with me," she whispered in his ear

before giving it a playful nip. "And we will both be loud. I miss my mate."

Ethan swallowed hard, heart thudding in his chest. He was getting very excited but there was nothing they could do at the moment. That was the way it had been since they started the journey. No alone time.

The prospect of "hunting" with Nia tomorrow night made his breeches uncomfortably tight and he had to shift his position. He smiled at her and winked. "I'd be glad to join you for a hunt."

She returned his smile and then leaned away, taking another bite of her bird. Ethan looked across the fire to see Yuliana blushing and pretending to be interested in Luna's fur. Sitting next to her, Michalus was looking at him with a sly smile. The wizard gave him a knowing wink and a nod of acknowledgement.

Ethan cursed to himself. Darn those elves and their super hearing. They'd both heard exactly what they had planned. It was a bit awkward and he almost felt embarrassed. But it had been a week since he'd been with his wife and he was missing it too.

He looked into the forest. How far would they have to go to be out of earshot of the elves? Ethan grinned as he realized he didn't care. It had been too long since he'd been intimate with Nia and after several times a day, the last week had been torturous.

He grinned again. Let the elves listen.

11

———

They continued south along the coastal road for three days. The group rode the horses during the day, each night retreating into the forest to prevent the pteranodons from bothering them. In the mornings and evenings, Ethan had gone out "hunting" with Nia. The two of them would walk a good distance before Ethan felt comfortable enough for, he and the foxgirl to have a little fun.

Each time, once they'd both been satisfied, Nia promptly told him to stand still and be quiet while she hunted. He was still too noisy for her to do any real hunting. In fact, his only real job on the hunt was to carry whatever she killed back to the camp.

Still, it wasn't a bad situation since he did get to spend some intimate time with his wife. And although he was certain everyone in the group knew what they were doing, no one said a word - not even Ainslee.

When they stopped for the evening of the fourth day,

Nia and Ethan went into the woods to hunt again but Nia stopped a few hundred yards in. She sniffed the air in all directions, looking about the forest as if expecting to see something.

"Everything okay?" Ethan asked.

Nia held her hand up to shush him and continued sniffing. She walked from tree to tree, looking up and down each.

Unsure what was going on, Ethan followed her. As he did, he kept quiet and looked around the forest too, trying to discern whatever had the foxgirl spooked. He brought up his HUD and checked his *Mana*.

Mana: 72

He was at maximum and ready to use magic to attack or defend if something suddenly jumped out at him. But nothing did.

The foxgirl walked around to the other side of a tree and then stopped and frowned. "We may have entered something's territory. Or perhaps a pack's territory."

"A pack of what?" Ethan asked, feeling the hairs on the back of his neck stand up. He glanced around the forest again, straining to see any sign of a monster or animal.

"Wolves," Nia replied.

"Wolves?!" Ethan snapped his head back to look at the foxgirl. "How many wolves?"

They'd heard howling the last few nights, but Ethan hadn't thought anything of it. Neither had anyone else. Having lived in a rural area, the night sounds of wolves and coyotes were not uncommon to him.

He knew wolves didn't usually bother humans, despite the way movies and books portrayed them. They tended to give humans a wide berth. At least, that's how they were on Earth. Were they the same on this messed-up world?

Nia was still frowning, and she reached up and ran her hand along the tree. Ethan walked around to the same side of the tree to see what she was doing.

As he spied what she was touching, he blanched. Gouged into the bark of the tree were claw marks. Large claw marks. And given their height, Ethan knew these couldn't be regular wolves. These wolves had to be much larger.

Ethan swallowed involuntarily. "That was made by a wolf?! How big would they have to be to put claw marks up that high?"

"Large," the foxgirl replied, running her fingers along the grooves the creature's nails had left. "Nearly as tall as the horses."

"Almost as tall as the horses?!" Ethan repeated loudly and then, catching himself, lowered his voice. "They're as tall as horses?!"

"That is how it appears," she replied, pointing out the tallest mark. "See how high the marks are. The creatures must be the size of our horses, perhaps slightly smaller."

He glanced nervously about the forest again. "Can you smell them nearby?"

The foxgirl shook her head. "I smell their urine. They have marked this area many times. The last time maybe a few days ago."

"Can you tell which way they left?" he asked.

She bent down and examined the ground. The foxgirl

took a stick and used it to move around small vegetation. Finally, Nia shook her head. "No, the ground is too hard. The tracks are unclear."

Ethan cursed quietly. "Do you think it's okay to camp around here tonight?"

Nia sniffed the air and bit her lip. "I don't know. Their scent is strong, but it is old.

"There is no sign of prey," she told Ethan, glancing around the forest. "And with the wolves marking their territory like this, the prey will avoid it."

"And we don't want to venture further into the forest," Ethan added.

"We could," the foxgirl replied. "But we would need to go much further than normal."

He looked up through the tree canopy to the fading light of the suns. The last thing Ethan wanted was to be out in the dark with a pack of giant wolves who could probably see better in the dark than he could. "We still have some of the wild boar we froze. Maybe we'll just eat that tonight."

"Ethan," Nia said, still glancing around, forehead wrinkled. He could tell she was worried. "I think we should continue through the night."

"You think there is a risk they will return?" he asked.

"Wolves are nocturnal," the foxgirl told him. "They will be on the move tonight. They may come back this way."

If Nia was worried, Ethan was worried. The foxgirl was not one to cower from a fight nor was she one to exaggerate danger. That was one of the things Ethan admired about her. She was very pragmatic. If she was worried, it was for a reason.

"Let's get back to the others," Ethan told her, reaching out and taking her hand. "We'll tell them what we found and see if we can convince them to keep moving."

"Ainslee will not be happy," Nia pointed out.

Ethan chuckled. "Ainslee's never happy."

"Except when she's eating or drinking," the foxgirl replied with a grin.

He returned her grin. "And when she's snoring."

The two shared a chuckle and quickly retraced their steps back to their companions. When they stepped into the clearing, all eyes turned to them. Looking around, Ethan saw the group had already unsaddled the horses and unpacked their bedrolls, as well as made a fire.

Ainslee looked them up and down, craning her head to look to each side of them. "You two forget something? You know, like food?!"

"We need to pack up and leave," he said.

"Pack up?!" Ainslee scoffed, screwing up her face. "Are you daft, wizard-boy?"

"What is it, my boy?" Michalus asked, standing up from in front of the fire.

Ainslee's face suddenly went pale. "It's not the dragon, is it?"

"It is not a dragon," Nia answered. "It is wolves."

"Wolves?" The dwarf rolled her eyes at the foxgirl. "We're packing up because of wolves?"

"Wolves the size of horses," Ethan added.

Mouth dropping open, Ainslee snapped her head to look back at the horses and then back to Ethan. She worked her mouth, but nothing came out. After a moment, she found her voice. "Are you serious?"

"Worgs," Michalus said grimly, massaging his temples. "And they're not quite the size of horses, but very nearly so."

"Worgs?" Ainslee swallowed.

Ethan looked at the elven wizard. "Are they aggressive?"

Michalus was already bending over and packing up his bedroll. He looked up, his expression deadly serious. "Very."

"Great! Just great!" Ainslee growled. She squatted down and began rolling up her own bedroll. "Giant wolves. Just what I needed."

"At least it not spiders," Par'karr offered happily. Ainslee shivered and gave the kobold a glare.

Ethan, who hadn't unpacked his own bedroll, grabbed his saddle and began to fasten it on his horse. Nia came over and grabbed her saddle and followed his example.

The others cast glances at the forest and then busied themselves with packing up and preparing to leave.

"We're not planning to ride at night, are we?" Michalus asked, saddling his own horse.

Looking over at the suns dipping into the horizon, Ethan nodded. "We can ride until it's too dark to see. Then we'll have to walk the animals."

"Walk?" the dwarf growled. "Why do we have to walk?"

"It'll be too dark," Ethan retorted. "We don't want one of the horses to stumble and break a leg."

"We have light stones!" The dwarf let out an exasperated breath. "You're a wizard. He's a wizard. You guys can make some light too!"

"You want to attract the attention of those things?"

Ethan asked, pointing up to the pteranodons that continued to circle the waterspouts towards the ocean.

Ainslee looked back to the ocean and growled. She muttered something under her breath, but Ethan couldn't make out her words.

A few minutes later, the others had gotten their own horses ready and Ethan extinguished the fire before starting to lead his horse down to the road. His companions followed his lead. When they reached the coastal highway, they mounted and pushed the animals into a gallop to put some distance between them and their camping site.

The group continued at that pace until Yuliana said the animals needed a rest. Par'karr voiced his agreement as well. Like most animals, the druid seemed to have an innate understanding of the horses and sensed how they were feeling.

Par'karr also seemed to have a good rapport with the horses. Given his small stature, Ethan thought the little kobold might make a good jockey. A tiny, purple-scaled lizardman jockey. That would be an interesting sight.

Trusting the green-haired elf and his kobold friend, Ethan called the group to a halt. It was nearly dark anyway and they had already put several miles between them and the campsite. They could afford to let the horses rest for a bit.

"Let's dismount and walk them," he told the group.

There was some grumbling from Ainslee, but they all did as he asked. Taking the horses by the reins, they began walking them along the road.

As they walked, the group continued to glance from

the waterspouts to the forest and then back to the ocean. Ethan frowned as he realized they could have enemies on both sides. It was going to be a long night.

At least, that's what he was thinking all the way up to the moment he heard the first howl cut through the air.

12
____

Everyone in the group froze. They'd been hearing wolf howls during the previous nights but somehow, knowing the size of the wolves, tonight was different. It seemed to fill all of them with a sense of impending doom.

For a moment, there was no other sound, other than the waves from the ocean and clomping of the horses as they stirred nervously. Then another howl answered the first, this one closer. Almost immediately, another howl split the air even closer.

"They are looking for prey," Nia hissed quietly.

"By prey, you mean us?" Ainslee demanded.

"Yes," the foxgirl responded impassively. "They have caught our scent and are now hunting us."

"Loki's balls!" Ainslee growled.

"What do we do?" Yuliana asked, her tone nervous and eyes darting around the forest.

To the north of them, the way they had come, more howls split the night.

"We keep moving," Ethan answered. He turned to look between Yuliana and Michalus. "Can you hear them?"

Both elves tilted their head, listening, and Yuliana brushed her green hair back from her tapered ears. They cocked their heads one way and then another. After a moment, both elves shook their heads.

"I don't hear them," Michalus said. His tone was such that Ethan heard the implied 'yet' at the end.

Ethan nodded. "I don't think we can outrun them in the dark..."

"They will not be running," Nia interrupted. "They will lope after us until one of them spots us. Once they do, they will signal the pack. The pack will run to that wolf and then they will run to catch up with us."

"Good to know," Ethan commented. And it was good. If the wolves were running, they would have no hope of outrunning them without the horses. And with wolves that large, their gait might make it impossible to outrun them even with the horses.

But, if the wolves were basically walking quickly, maybe even normally until they picked up the scent, then they might just have a chance.

"Okay," Ethan said. "Unless anyone has any better ideas, we pick up our pace and try to at least keep the distance between us at a constant. If we can keep ahead of them during the night, we might be able to put real distance between us during the day."

He looked at Nia. "You said the wolves are nocturnal, right? They should stop and rest for the day?"

More howls sounded in the distance. It was hard to know if they were the same wolves howling or different wolves. Even the distance was difficult to gauge.

Nia shrugged. "Normal wolves should. But these are not the wolves of my world."

"Then we have to hope they stop for the day," Ethan told the group. "But just in case, if we spot a very defensible position, we can think about making a stand."

"Why we run? Why not Ethan and Michalus magic them?" Par'karr asked hopefully.

Ethan exchanged a look with Michalus, both of them understanding the limits of their magic. "We have no idea how many of them there might be and how effective our magic might be on them. Plus, they could ambush us and take out one of us before we can even use our magic."

"The horses," Nia said with a gesture back to her own mount. "They will probably go for the horses."

"Why the horses?" Yuliana asked. The night was pierced by an additional chorus of howls. This time, Ethan could swear they sounded closer.

"More meat," the foxgirl answered pragmatically. "At their size, we will not offer much of a meal."

Ainslee scowled. "Well that's comforting."

"We stick to my plan unless someone has a better one," Ethan interrupted, trying to keep them focused. "Let's pick up the pace and see how far we can get."

"We're all tired," Ainslee complained. "How are we going to keep going through the night and the day?"

Ethan smirked. The comment about being tired was rich, coming from the dwarf. He wasn't sure of her exact total *Stamina*, but he guessed it was at least 50% more than his own and certainly more than anyone else in the party.

"We keep marching and drink as much water as we can," Ethan told them. "Once we get to the point where we can't restore stamina..."

Ethan paused, wondering if his next suggestion was really what they should be doing. Unfortunately, they didn't have much of a choice. He glanced down at the larger portal pouch on his belt. "Once we can't restore any more stamina from water, we'll pull out the Grail."

"The Grail?!" Ainslee furrowed her brows. "The magic cup? Are you serious? We're not wounded!"

"It doesn't just heal," Ethan retorted. "It also restores all of your stats - stamina included."

Ainslee looked thoughtful. "I didn't know it did that. So, we can go forever then!"

He sighed. Did anyone read the magic item descriptions? "Not quite. It's only usable by a person once per day."

"Loki's balls!" Ainslee growled. "What good is it then?!"

"It'll give us the equivalent of an extra night's sleep, once a day," Ethan explained, trying to keep his voice steady. He was a patient person, but he was tired too and his patience was wearing thin with the dwarf. "That's more than the wolves have."

Ainslee mumbled something under her breath but Ethan could hear what she said.

"We must go!" Nia told them. "Come!"

Nia began walking again, faster than before, and pulled her horse after her. The others watched her for a moment and then Ethan resumed his walk as well, followed by the others.

They walked for what seemed like hours, the howls of the wolves to the north urging them on. They moved as quickly as they could by the moonlight, allowing Nia and her superior night vision to warn them of any holes or obstacles that might impede the horses.

There was almost no talking and they only stopped at streams they found to fill their water bottles and let the horses drink. They continued this until according to his best guess, it was around 2am in the morning. That was when Yuliana said her *Stamina* was in the single digits and water no longer restored it.

All of them stopped then and, after moving the horses a hundred or so yards from Ethan, he reached into the pouch and pulled out the Grail, allowing the elf to take a drink. Yuliana flinched at the high-pitched sound from the magical cup, but it hadn't yet grown in intensity. She took a sip of the water and then he replaced the cup back through the portal and onto the sarcophagus.

The howling continued as they walked, getting decidedly closer the further they went. Slowly but surely, the wolves were gaining. Ethan caught both elves casting furtive glances backwards and wondered if they could tell how close the wolves were. Then he decided he didn't want to know, as long as they warned him in enough time to get ready.

They then continued on until first Michalus, then Ethan and finally Nia and Ainslee all needed a sip from the Grail. They even gave the horses a sip. They all felt instantly better after the magic of the golden chalice restored their stats, and they pushed on until daybreak.

The first sun appeared on the horizon. Ethan felt both elated and exhausted at the same time. They'd managed to keep ahead of the giant wolves all night and there was no sign of them.

"Do you think they stopped for the day?" Ethan asked Nia.

The foxgirl, like the rest of them, had bags under her eyes and her eyelids drooped. She looked back towards the north and then at Ethan. "I hope so. But I do not know, with these wolves."

"How will we know?" Ainslee asked. Of all of them, Ainslee had been the one who had complained the most. And yet, she also seemed the one least affected by walking through the night.

"They're not howling as much. That could be good," Michalus chimed in, "or that could be bad. It could be good, if they are, in fact, stopping for the day."

"Right! What could possibly be bad about that?" Ainslee growled.

"It could be bad if they are not stopping for the day because we will no longer have any clue how close they are," the elven wizard concluded.

"Oh," Ainslee grumbled. The dwarf looked north. "That's not good."

"Precisely," Michalus said tiredly. "We must all be on our guard."

Ethan wanted to groan. He was tired and despite the extra *Stamina*, he was mentally running on fumes. Apparently, the Grail would not cure sleep deprivation.

He swore silently as he once again wished he could just grab a large coffee from a McDonald's drive thru. Even a Diet Coke would be welcome at this point. Ethan wanted to ask Michalus if there were any beverages on this world with caffeine, but he wasn't sure the formerly old elf would even know what caffeine was.

Steeling himself, he walked back and mounted his horse. "Let's mount up and see how far we can get today. Maybe we can outdistance them, and they'll give up."

He looked at Nia for confirmation but the foxgirl's expression was grim. The message was clear. Don't count on the wolves giving up.

"What about breakfast?" Ainslee grumbled. "We are going to eat, right?"

Ethan frowned. His own stomach was growling but he knew they couldn't afford to take the time to hunt. "We'll stop around noon and hunt if we can but keep an eye open for anything that looks edible."

"Lunch?!" Ainslee exclaimed. "So, no breakfast at all?!"

Ethan bit back the retort he wanted to say and instead gestured to the forest to the east. "Do YOU want to hunt in that forest and possibly run into a wolf or a pack of wolves as big as these horses?"

The dwarf looked from Ethan to the forest and then down. She bit her lip and mumbled something, but Ethan couldn't make out the words. She looked back up at him. "But we are stopping and hunting at lunch, right?"

"I think it should be safe to venture into the forest by lunch," Ethan replied and looked at Nia.

The foxgirl just shrugged.

He sighed. "But keep an eye open for anything edible

between now and then. Maybe we'll get lucky and find some nuts or berries."

"I will keep my eyes open," Michalus said aloud as he mounted his horse. "There may be a few plants I recognize that you offworlders may not."

"Fair enough," Ethan said. "Now, let's get moving."

Without a word, the others mounted their own horses. They rode up next to Ethan and, at his command, the group urged their horses into a trot. It was going to be a long day.

13

———

The group pushed the animals to a gallop and almost immediately they heard crashes in the forest. Luna sprinted alongside Yuliana's horse. Ethan looked east to the woods and saw large shapes moving through the canopy. He swore.

"Wolves!" he yelled, letting go of the reins long enough to point east towards the forest. He heard similar curses from the others as they caught sight of the large shapes as well.

Cursing loudly, Ethan urged his mount on. "They were right on top of us!"

"They were probably about to attack when we started riding the horses!" Nia shouted back. "The wind is coming in from the ocean, so I did not smell them!"

"Great! Just freaking great!" he replied, trying to make his voice loud enough to hear over the galloping horses.

Craning his head back, he looked from Michalus to Yuliana. "You didn't hear them sneaking up on us?"

Both elves looked chagrined. Yuliana gave him an apologetic look, while Michalus just shrugged. "Sorry, my boy."

"They were probably stalking us!" Nia yelled to him. "Very stealthy when they want to be!"

Ethan glanced back up at the treeline and saw the large shapes keeping pace with them. "How long can they keep up this pace?"

"Wolves can only run in bursts," she shouted. "A mile! Maybe less!"

Ethan didn't really know much about horses, other than the few times he'd gone horseback riding with a former girl-friend. She was a country girl he'd met at the local grocery store and she lived on an actual farm - with her family, of course. The only alone time they'd had was when she came over to his place or when they went out on the horses. He tried to remember her name, but it escaped him at the moment since he was possibly about to be eaten by wolves.

He thought back to their rides through the country. How long had they galloped with the horses? How long could the horses keep up the pace before they gave out? They'd just have to push them as long as they could and see.

A minute ticked by and then another and Ethan saw that the wolves were starting to fall behind. Nia noticed it too. "They cannot keep up!"

"Good!" he shouted over the thundering horses. The group was definitely pulling ahead now. But how long could the horses keep up this pace?

Ethan kept them at a gallop for what he guessed was

about two miles. That was when Yuliana cried out. "Luna cannot take any more!"

Looking back, he saw that the mountain lion was starting to lag behind and looked like she had pushed herself as far as she could. He signaled the group to drop the horses to a trot. He cursed silently. The horses could keep up the pace longer than Luna could.

His heart sank as he realized they had no hope of outdistancing the wolves. Not with the big cat along. Her endurance was about the same as the wolves and she was only able to push herself a little further because of whatever bond she shared with Yuliana.

He realized that if the wolves continued to hound them, they'd need to do something. They would have to fight them.

Looking up at the trees, he tried to think about how big the wolves were. They had fought bigger things, but never many bigger things at one time. Ethan's thoughts went back to the ogres. There had been only two of them, but his group had been hard pressed.

"How many wolves do you think there are?" he asked Nia.

The foxgirl pulled her horse up alongside Ethan. "I do not know. At least half a dozen." Nia glanced back at Luna. "You realize we cannot outrun them."

"Yeah," he replied, lowering his voice. "Not with Luna slowing us down. She can't keep pace with the horses."

Even with his voice lowered, he caught Yuliana's eyes darting to him. He silently cursed her hearing and quickly continued. "Since we can't leave her behind and we can't outrun them, we'll need to find a defensible position to fight them - or scare them off."

Nia didn't look confident with his last suggestion. "They have stalked us for almost a day. I doubt they will be scared off easily."

"Wishful thinking," he admitted. He glanced down at the beach and then up towards the trees. "We need to find a place where we can make a stand. Someplace defendable."

"What're you two yapping about?" Ainslee called out, pulling her horse parallel to theirs. "We should be galloping and not walking the horses."

"The cat cannot continue at the horses' pace," Nia told the dwarf.

"So, leave it." The dwarf shrugged.

"No one gets left behind," Ethan said, giving the dwarf a hard look.

Ainslee shrugged again. "Just being practical. If those wolves catch us, the cat's a goner too."

"We don't know that we can't hold them off," Nia said. "We are capable fighters."

"Listen, foxy," the dwarf retorted. "Capable or not, there's probably more of them than there are of us. And while MAYBE each of us can handle one, I doubt any of us can handle two at the same time. Well, except maybe wizard-boy and Michalus."

Nia looked defiant but didn't correct Ainslee. Ethan realized the foxgirl must be thinking the same thing. Deep down, Ethan realized it too.

If the wolves were as large as horses, Par'karr's rabbits would have little effect on them. Yuliana could do nothing but heal and Luna would be no match for a wolf that large. Ainslee might be able to hold her own against one, Nia too. But against two? And wolves were pack hunters. They'd work together to bring down their party. Ethan wasn't even sure how he and Michalus would fare.

No, they needed a place where they could defend. A choke point, like back during the attack on Hawkshead.

"Michalus!" Ethan called. "Is there a cliff along this road or does it pass through a ravine at some place?"

The elven wizard pursed his lips and shook his head. "It's about the same as you see here all the way to the villages."

Ethan swore.

"But," Michalus continued. "There is a fairly decent-sized river not too far from here, if I remember correctly."

"A river?" Ethan perked up.

"With a stone bridge," the elf added.

Ethan grinned, realizing the wizard and he were thinking along the same lines.

The first time they'd met, it had been right after Ethan had defeated an ogre single-handedly with his magic by using the stone in the bridge as a weapon. His *Earth* magic allowed him to shape stone nearly instantly. He'd trapped the ogre first, then skewered it with spikes of stone.

But that had been a single ogre and the thing had taken the easy path across the river - the bridge. Would the wolves do the same? Would they swim across the river? He assumed it was deep enough to warrant a bridge and the wolves couldn't just trot across the water.

"It might work," he told the others. "If we can bottleneck them on the bridge, we might be able to hold them off, maybe even prevent them from following us."

"You really think you can hold off a pack of giant wolves on a bridge?" Ainslee scoffed.

"I did kill the ogre on the bridge," he reminded her. "And it was bigger than the wolves."

"That was one ogre, wizard-boy," she reminded him.

"Yes, but it was a choke point that I could control - just like the bridge," Ethan retorted. "And this time, we have two wizards."

Ainslee glanced back at Michalus before turning to face Ethan. "You really think you can hold them off? Even with bean-pole back there?"

"You know I can hear you, right?" Michalus harrumphed.

Ethan nodded. His mind was already thinking of ideas and strategies that they could use to fight off the wolves. Yes, if they had a chokepoint and they could control how many wolves came at them at once, they just might be able to do it.

"I think we can," he told them. "Between Michalus and I, I think we can hold them off. If we inflict enough damage, they'll retreat. They might be big, but they're still wolves."

"I hope you're right, wizard-boy," Ainslee said.

"Me too," Ethan said quietly. "Me too."

He turned in his saddle to face to Michalus. "How far to the river."

"A half-day's ride," the wizard replied.

Ethan cursed. "Half a day?!"

"Sorry, my boy," the elf replied. "That's how far I think it is... and that's just a guess."

Swearing again, Ethan looked behind them along the forest treeline. He couldn't see the wolves yet, but he knew they were back there. Back there and getting closer most likely.

"Fine!" he shouted, so everyone could hear him. "We're going to make for the bridge Michalus mentioned. We'll go in sprints. Push the horses... and Luna, then walk, then sprint. We'll keep that up until we reach the bridge.

"Michalus, Yuliana," he told the two elves. "Keep an eye out and an ear out. Let me know if the wolves are catching up."

Both elves gave him affirmative nods of their head.

"Good," he told them and turned to face forward. "Then let's ride!"

He urged his mount into a gallop and the others did likewise. Luna bounded alongside them, trying to keep pace.

Ethan's eyes were on the road in front of them, but his mind was formulating plans on how they could survive their forthcoming encounter with the wolves. He and Michalus were going to need all of their *Mana* - and a lot of luck.

14

The wolves continued to follow them for the next few hours. As soon as one of the elves would see or hear them approaching, they would break the horses into a gallop to stay ahead of them and try to put some more distance between them.

Everyone was exhausted. Despite the earlier drink from the Grail and the fact that they were riding, Ethan's *Stamina* had been slowly declining. He could see it in the others too. They were tired and their nerves were shot.

So far, Luna had been able to keep up with them, but the mountain lion was tiring quickly. Then again, so were they all. He just hoped the big cat could keep up.

Looking up to two suns and the ever-present black hole, he guessed it was almost noon. Still there was no sign of the river and bridge the elven wizard had mentioned.

They'd passed several tiny streams and even a small river with a stone bridge. Unfortunately, none of them had been nearly large enough to make a stand. The river they'd passed might have been deep, but it was only a dozen feet wide. That wasn't nearly wide enough to prevent the giant wolves from jumping over it and flanking them.

They pushed on. Another hour passed. Then another. Several times, Ethan had yelled to the wizard to see if he recognized anything or had a better idea of when they'd reach it but each time the answer was the same.

"It's been a long time," Michalus had answered. "But it should be any time now."

And then, an hour or so after noon, they crested a hill and saw the river in the valley below. Unlike the smaller one they'd passed, this was a large, fast-moving river. It had to be at least fifty feet across. And spanning the river was a large stone bridge, just as Michalus had said.

"There it is!" Ethan yelled. "Full gallop!"

Unfortunately, the wolves had just caught up to them. This is when they normally would have gone into a gallop to put some distance between them. As it was, the river was only a half a mile away. They wouldn't be able to establish much of a lead before the wolves reached them.

Yelling a curse, Ethan urged his mount forward. His companions did likewise, and the group raced towards the bridge. They raced to the place where they'd have to make their stand.

The sounds of howls and a glimpse of movement caught his eye and as Ethan looked eastward, he saw the wolves breaking cover. The pack sprinted out of the trees, on an intercept course. He swallowed involuntarily as he saw the sheer size and number of them. Then his eyes bulged as he realized what he was really seeing.

Nia hadn't been exaggerating when she said they might be nearly as tall as a horse. But the mistake the foxgirl had made was thinking these were giant wolves. They were not.

Up until now, the "wolves" had stayed in the shadows of the trees, never really showing themselves. The group had seen movement and vague shapes but hadn't gotten a good look at them. Now, with the creatures out in the open, Ethan could see what they truly were.

The creatures that ran towards them might pass for wolves at a quick glance. They had the canine head, the fur and even a canine tail. But they didn't look like true wolves, nor did they move like true wolves.

As Ethan scrutinized them, he realized that they were more like man-shaped wolves, running on four legs, instead of two legs. They looked like werewolves!

"What in Odin's good eye are those things, wizard-boy?!" Ainslee yelled, her eyes like saucers. "They sure as Loki's balls aren't wolves?!"

Ethan had no idea what the creatures truly were, but they certainly looked like the worst combination of a human and a wolf he could imagine. No werewolf movie he'd seen had done justice to the creatures he was looking at.

"Keep riding!" he yelled.

He counted twelve, maybe thirteen, of the werewolves as the pack sprinted towards them. And not only were they not real wolves, there were two werewolves for each of them. Not good odds - especially if they had more than animal intelligence.

"Werewolves!" Michalus yelled.

Shooting the elven wizard a sharp look, Ethan cursed. "Those are a real thing on this world?!"

"Yes!" he yelled back. "Fascinating really..."

"Later!" Ethan snapped. "Can they only be harmed by silver?"

When the elven wizard looked at him like he was crazy, Ethan guessed that part of the werewolf legend wasn't true. At least, not on this world. Thank goodness for that since he doubted they had any silver on them, except maybe a few silver coins.

They bolted towards the bridge and Ethan calculated that they'd make it before the werewolves, but just barely. He cursed. They wouldn't have time to set up defenses or prepare for an attack. He cursed again.

The group reached the bridge and thundered onto the stone structure. He turned to the group. "Keep going to the far end! Michalus, you and I will stop in the center!"

The elven wizard nodded and the two of them reined in their horses in the middle of the bridge just as the werewolves reached the bridge.

"What's the plan?" the wizard asked.

"I'm going to block off the bridge," he told the wizard. "Watch for any trying to cross by jumping in the river."

Ethan stretched out his hand, more to focus his thoughts than for any magical need to do it. Several feet in front of the werewolves, he caused stone spikes to erupt from the bridge. He created a wall of spikes ten feet tall with jagged, pointed ends. He had some spikes shoot out diagonally on the sides of the bridge as well to prevent them from just slipping around them.

Unable to stop in time, the front line of werewolves slammed into the stone spikes, piling up in a heap. Ethan felt the bridge shudder.

Michalus looked over at him. "Not bad. You know, you could have angled those spikes, so they ran right into them."

He nodded. Ethan thought of Par'karr. The little kobold had started out as an enemy but had become one of his friends. Things weren't always black and white. "I could have. But I don't know that these things are evil. I don't know anything about them."

"They may not be evil," the wizard retorted. "But they are driven more by instinct than reason, though they still possess reason."

"Is it a disease, then?" Ethan asked, watching as the werewolves untangled themselves.

"Transmitted by bite or scratch," Michalus confirmed. "It doesn't affect all who are bitten and some who are bitten go mad or simply die."

"Great," Ethan mumbled. "Just great."

The large black werewolf, which Ethan guessed was the alpha, stood up on two legs, looking the spikes up and down. Behind it, the other wolves growled and snarled.

"The big one is the leader," Michalus said quietly.

Ethan nodded, having come to the same conclusion. "Anything special about the leader? Any special abilities?"

"None that I'm aware of," the wizard replied. "Though I haven't really studied them much."

"Great," Ethan mumbled.

The werewolf alpha seemed about to jump over the ten-feet spikes, so Ethan made them grow another two feet. The alpha halted, looking directly at Ethan.

"Uh." Ethan swallowed. "Can they sense magic?"

"I don't remember reading that they could," Michalus replied, rubbing his chin. "But as I said, I haven't really studied them much.

"We could burn them all to a crisp, you know," the wizard said, gesturing to the tight group of werewolves at the end of the bridge. "With them grouped up like that."

Before Ethan could answer, the large black werewolf snapped its head around at the other werewolves and literally barked an order. The others immediately fanned out onto the bank, putting lots of room between themselves and the others.

"Did they just..." Ethan started but Michalus held a hand up.

The wizard leaned over and whispered into Ethan's ear. "It appears that they can hear and understand us."

The alpha werewolf turned back around and stared daggers at Ethan and Michalus. While he did, Ethan brought up his HUD and checked his *Mana*.

Mana: 61

Manipulating all of the stone had cost him a good portion of his *Mana*. He needed to reserve it. Maybe there was some way to communicate with it. First, he needed to know the extent of its hearing so he knew whether or not he and Michalus could make any plans.

"I'm going to impale it with a giant spike from underneath it," Ethan whispered and watched as the black were-wolf immediately leaped back.

Ethan sighed. He hadn't really been about to do that, but now he knew the extent of the creature's hearing. The werewolves' hearing was as good as the elves. Whispering was useless.

"Even whispering, it can hear us," Ethan said aloud.

"Yes, well," the elf said in a normal conversational tone. "No need to whisper then."

The black alpha looked from Ethan to Michalus. Then it barked something to the other werewolves and the group split into two groups and fanned out on either side of the bridge, near the water's edge.

"If any of them jumps in," Ethan yelled. "I'll freeze the water and lock them in place. Not to mention there are plenty of stones beneath the water that I can make into spikes."

The werewolves along the bank shifted nervously, looking at their leader. It was clear they were concerned, but they most likely feared the alpha more.

The big black werewolf growled and moved near the bars. For a moment, Ethan thought the creature might try to break the stone bars with sheer strength.

Instead, the thing leaned closer to the stone bars and stuck its snout part of the way through.

"Give us the female," the creature growled.

15

Ethan was too surprised to respond at first. He'd guessed the creature could hear and understand him, but he hadn't expected it to be able to speak. Judging by Michalus's open-mouthed stare, the wizard was surprised too.

Getting over his shock, Ethan mulled over the were-wolf's words. What had the creature said? Give them the female? Which female? Without thinking, he glanced over his shoulder at the women. Nia, Ainslee and Yuliana were at the end of the bridge with the horses. Safe for now.

"Which female?" Ethan asked, eyes narrowing. Although he did briefly daydream about handing over Ainslee, he quickly dismissed the thought. He wasn't about to give any member of his group up to a bunch of werewolves, let alone one of the women.

The alpha werewolf snarled at Ethan. "The foxling! Give her to us!"

Ethan's head snapped around to glance at Nia and

then rebounded to stare daggers at the werewolf. Without consciously even thinking about it, his *Elemental Armor* activated, wrapping his body in flame.

"You cannot have my wife!" Ethan hissed through clenched teeth. Feeling the anger boiling up from inside him, he reached his hand out, again more for show and to help him focus than anything else. Using *Air*, he grabbed the black werewolf by the throat and squeezed. Hard. Then he lifted it several feet off the ground.

The alpha's eyes bulged and the creature clawed at the invisible force around its throat. The other werewolves started forward, but Ethan created a wall of fire in front of them, cutting them off. It used up much of his *Mana*, but he didn't care. No one was taking Nia from him.

"Ethan!" Michalus said from behind him. "Stop! I don't think..."

Too angry to listen, Ethan tightened his grip on the alpha's neck, even as the werewolves began circling around his wall of fire. He needed to finish the big black werewolf off first and then he'd figure out what to do about the others.

"Ethan," came Nia's voice from right behind him. "Please put her down."

Eyes wide, Ethan cast a quick look back at Nia, who had come to stand behind him. "Her?"

"Ethan!" Nia snapped, giving him a meaningful look.

The werewolf had gone limp and its skin was bubbling and moving in a very weird way. Not only that, but its fur was starting to fall away. Ethan had seen enough werewolf and horror movies to know the thing was transforming out of werewolf form.

He wasn't sure whether he had killed it - or was it really a "her" like Nia had said. Lowering the transforming form to the ground, he released it from the bonds of *Air* he'd created.

The other werewolves ran over to the prone form. Some of them bent down to sniff or prod the alpha while others bared their teeth and snarled.

Ethan took the time to not only look at the transforming alpha, but also the other werewolves. That's when he noticed that all of them seemed to have breasts - or extremely large pectoral muscles. As he looked from werewolf to werewolf, he realized they were all females. An all-female pack?!

The alpha had finished transforming and was now a very naked human woman, whose face was growing increasingly purple. The woman was tall, broad and muscular. Other than her pale skin and dark ebony hair, she could have been a larger version of Ainslee.

"You've killed her!" snarled one of the werewolves, a grey and white one, as it shot its arm through the bars in an attempt to claw him.

He was too far away for it to reach but he nevertheless flinched back a step. Looking down at the human woman, he realized he'd probably crushed her windpipe and she was suffocating. She would die without healing.

Ethan swore. He hadn't meant to kill her. Well, maybe for a second. She hadn't actually attacked him but the thought of losing Nia had momentarily made him see red.

Cursing, Ethan dismissed his *Elemental Armor*, fumbled with his portal pouch and pulled out the Grail. He heard Michalus groan and Nia yelped as the high-pitch sound hurt their ears. The werewolves also reacted, yelping and snarling while trying to cover their ears with their hands.

Ethan reached out with his *Water* magic and pulled some river water into the golden chalice. He approached the bars but several of the werewolves snarled and clawed through the bars despite the pain.

"I can save her!" he growled. "But only if you let me give this to her now!"

The werewolves went quiet and looked around at each other. The grey and white one sniffed at him and then barked at the others. Then, the werewolves took a step backward.

Rushing forward, Ethan reached through the bars, grabbed the woman's head and pushed the chalice to her mouth. Tilting the Grail, he poured the river water into her mouth. He kept tilting the golden cup back until the woman finally snapped her eyes open and began coughing.

He snorted in amusement. Ethan knew exactly how the woman felt. It wasn't that long ago when he'd been on death's door and had woken up the same way.

He retracted the Grail and his arms through the stone bars and backed away out of their arms reach. He carefully put the Grail back through the portal pouch and set it on the stone sarcophagus back in the tomb, ending the high-pitch sound.

The woman on the ground blinked and looked around. Holding up her hand, she looked at it and frowned. Then she turned to Ethan, a look of pure hatred in her eyes. "What have you done?!"

"I just saved your life," Ethan retorted. He shrugged. "After I almost killed you."

He was sorry, now that he knew it was a woman. It was probably sexist, but that was the way he'd been raised. Men protected the women and a real man never struck a woman. Old fashioned, for sure, but that had been his upbringing. Of course, he doubted that when his dad had told him not to hit a woman, that his old man had been thinking of a six-foot werewolf with five-inch claws.

The raven-haired woman looked around at the other werewolves and then stood up, seemingly unconcerned by her nudity. She glared at Ethan for a long moment. "We still want the foxling."

"I don't think you and your... friends are in any position to make demands," Michalus said coolly.

The naked alpha looked Ethan up and down. "I know a thing or two about wizards. He can't have much magic left without resting."

"Ah," the elven wizard said, holding up a finger. "But I'm a wizard too and I can assure you, I have quite a bit of magic left. So, I would suggest that you all turn around and go back home... wherever home is."

"We will not leave a sister enslaved to a man!" snarled the grey and white werewolf.

Ethan rolled his eyes, causing some of the werewolves to growl and snarl. "She's not my..."

Nia interrupted him, stepping forward with her hands on her hips. "I am no one's slave! I am Tal'Cha!"

The werewolves stared at her blankly, then looked at each other in confusion. The alpha screwed up her face. "What is... towel cha?"

"First wife!" the foxgirl snapped, chin held high.

The raven-haired woman and werewolves looked from Nia to Ethan and then back. The alpha looked beyond Ethan to Yuliana and Ainslee, still by the horses. She screwed up her face even more. She practically spat out her words. "First wife? All three of them are his wives?"

The foxgirl glanced back at the other two women and shook her head. She gave the alpha a hard look. "No. I am the first and only wife. For now."

"For now?!" the raven-haired woman and Ethan said at the same time.

Nia shrugged.

"You wear a collar!" the alpha snarled. "You are his property."

"I asked her to wear it," Ethan explained. "Not because she is my slave, but to prevent us from having to kill anyone who came around trying to enslave her. Apparently, that idea didn't work as well as I thought."

The raven-haired woman ignored Ethan and looked expectantly at Nia. The foxgirl nodded. "He does not wish unnecessary conflict. But I will defend my own honor."

The alpha snorted. "How do we know you are telling the truth?"

Nia raised an eyebrow. "Can you not smell the truth on me?"

Looking back at the werewolves, the dark-haired woman snickered. "He's a wizard. You cannot trust his scent."

The foxgirl cocked her head and looked at Ethan curiously. "Can you control your scent?"

"Not that I know of," Ethan said. He looked at

Michalus. "Can we?"

Michalus rubbed his chin. "It's funny you say that. I remember reading a book by... I can't recall the wizard's name... who did hypothesize that we could control..."

"You can tell me later." Ethan held up his hand to the elven wizard. He looked to Nia and shrugged. "Maybe. But I don't know how, and I don't think Michalus does either."

Snorting at Ethan, the alpha looked at Nia. "Do you really trust a man?"

"I trust Ethan," Nia replied adamantly. The steel in her words surprised even Ethan. "I trust him with my life."

"Then you are a fool," the dark-haired woman spat. She looked to the werewolves. "She does not wish to be saved from the bonds of men. There is nothing for us to do here."

The werewolves began retreating away from the bridge, but the alpha stayed, looking at Nia. "You will find that men disappoint and betray you. When you grow tired of their abuse, come back to these woods. We will find you. We will bite you and give you the gift of Nott, goddess of the night."

Without another word, the raven-haired woman spun and trotted away. As she did, hair grew from her body and her arms and legs began to elongate into the shape they'd previously seen. The shape of a werewolf.

By the time she reached the forest, she was completely transformed and no longer recognizable as a human woman. She vanished into the woods with the other werewolves following her, barking and howling.

"A pack of female werewolves," Ethan muttered to himself. "This world is crazy."

16

———

With the werewolves gone, Ethan suggested the group set up camp on the opposite side of the river, along the treeline. Everyone was exhausted, so none of them objected. Everyone, even the horses, were mentally and physically on the point of collapsing from pushing themselves through the night.

Once camp was set up, Nia grabbed Ethan and practically dragged him into the forest to "hunt" for lunch. Ignoring the snickers from Ainslee, he followed the foxgirl several hundred yards into the forest. Out of eyeshot, the two of them quickly made up for their lost time. And recharged Ethan's *Mana* to maximum at the same time.

The foxgirl padded off to do the actual hunting as soon as they were done, leaving Ethan to think about the pack of female werewolves. Only a half hour later, she came back dragging a gutted deer. Ethan ran up to her and immediately began helping her drag it back to the camp.

Once the deer was cleaned, cut up and roasting over a stone grill Ethan had shaped for them, he sat down next to Nia, across the fire from Michalus.

"I take it you never encountered werewolves on your previous journey south?" Ethan asked the elf. Looking across at the old elf in the young elf's body, it was easy to forget that the 20-something-looking elf was over 800 years old.

The elven wizard looked up at him and appeared thoughtful for a long moment. "I've run into a few werewolves in my day, but I don't recall running into one on my journey south."

Ethan nodded and then remembered something the alpha had said. "Who is that Nott they spoke of?"

"Nott?!" Ainslee interrupted. The dwarf had been relaxing against a stone but sat up and looked between Michalus and Ethan. "She's the dwarven goddess of the night. Not sure what all that gift of Nott was, though. She's kind of spooky though - not many worshippers on my world."

He cocked his head. Ethan had heard the dwarf use the names of what he believed were Norse gods and goddesses over the last few months. He'd never asked her about it because, in truth, it wasn't a big concern. Plus, there always seemed to be something else on his mind. But perhaps now was a good time to ask.

"Who is Thor and Odin to you?" he asked the dwarf.

Relaxing back against the rock, Ainslee grinned. "Odin be the father of the dwarven gods, sometimes called the

All-Father. Thor be his son and the god of thunder and craftsmen."

"And they're both dwarves?" Ethan asked.

Ainslee shrugged. "They're gods. But they appear to us as dwarves."

"You've seen them?" Yuliana asked wide eyed. "Gods?"

"Well," the dwarf sputtered as her face flushed, "not me personally. But they've appeared throughout our history from time to time. The last time they showed up in force was in the Last Giant War, about 3000 years ago. Before my time."

Yuliana looked disappointed but nodded. "We have never seen Gaia, the earth mother, though she manifests in all living things. It is a great honor to meet your gods."

"Ahem," Ainslee cleared her throat. "Well, I suppose it is. But like I said, I haven't done it personally."

The dwarf turned her attention back to Ethan. "Why do you ask about my gods, wizard-boy?"

"The names you use," he replied, taking some time to choose his words. "They are also the names of some of the gods on Earth. Well, legends of gods. No one alive has ever claimed to have actually seen any of the Norse gods."

"Norse?" Nia asked. "What is a norse?"

"It's actually a place... Norway," he answered, trying to remember. "Actually, I think it's Norway and Scandinavia, two countries on my world."

"And these countries worship dwarven gods?" Ainslee questioned, brows furrowed.

"Not exactly," Ethan replied. "In Norse legends, they aren't dwarves. They look like men... er... humans."

Ainslee shrugged. "They're gods. They can take whatever form they want."

"Why the sudden interest in the deities and demigods?" Michalus asked with a faint smile.

"It's just something else that is similar between our worlds," Ethan explained. "Merlin, Arthur and the knights, those are all part of Earth myths. Thor, Odin and the other Norse gods are too."

Ethan pointed up to the twin suns and the black hole between them. "I'm, who knows how many million, billion, trillion miles from Earth, speaking what I think is English. Not only that, but Ainslee's world knows of Norse gods and goddesses and apparently, King Arthur and Merlin were real people who lived on this world."

Pausing to catch his breath, he looked around the faces of his friends. "I just don't understand how all of that's possible."

"It does seem extremely implausible," the elven wizard admitted with a nod.

"On my world, there have been rumors of alien abductions," Ethan blurted out, working out things in his own mind. "There's even speculation that aliens visited the earth thousands of years ago and helped the Mayans and the Egyptians."

"Who is Egyptian?" squeaked Par'karr, sitting up from his bedroll. The little kobold had appeared to be sleeping but had apparently been listening.

"The Egyptians were a culture of people from my world who were very powerful thousands of years ago, they built great stone pyramids that are considered one of the seven wonders of my world."

"Stone pyramids?" Michalus perked up. "Like the western pyramids of Ahhotep?"

"There are pyramids on this world?" Ethan asked, interest piqued. That might be yet another similarity between the two worlds.

"Oh yes." The elven wizard nodded. "In Sobat, the land of the beast people."

"Beast people?" Ethan raised an eyebrow. "What kind of beast people?"

Michalus looked thoughtful. "I've never been there myself, of course. That would require traversing the river Styx and that can be a dangerous game. But I've read that the beastmen of Sobat have the heads of beasts, like cats and jackals, and the bodies of men. Not completely unlike the werewolves we just met."

"Huh." Ethan nodded but his mind was whirling again. He was remembering the Egyptian hieroglyphs from the various museums he'd visited. Hadn't most of the Egyptian gods had the heads of beasts and the bodies of men or women?

Then there was Michalus's casual mention of the river Styx. Ethan remembered from Greek mythology that there was a river Styx and it separated the land of the living from the land of the dead. How and why were there so many crossovers in the mythology between his world, this world and some of the other worlds?

Was it the aliens? Had the aliens brought knowledge of other worlds to Earth? If they had, why? What would be the point in sowing the seeds of the mythology of other worlds?

Ethan was still thinking about aliens, mythology and

gods when Ainslee stepped over him and knelt down by the fire. "I think they're done."

Remembering Yuliana's aversion to meat, and feeling guilty it had taken him so long, he turned to the green-haired elf. "Did you find something to eat?"

The elf shook her head. "No. There does not appear to be anything edible in this area."

Frowning, Ethan nodded and gave her an apologetic look. "Sorry, let me eat a steak and I'll go with you to look for plants."

"Actually," the elf replied, her eyes darting to the ground. "I thought maybe Michalus could come with me." She blushed and then looked up. "I mean, he said he might recognize plants we did not."

Michalus straightened almost comically, his chest puffing out. "I would be delighted to help you find plants. I'm quite familiar with..."

Smiling, Ethan tuned out Michalus's ramblings about plants. They each brought out the stone dishes Ethan had crafted out of rocks and began eating their steaks with their knives. After they had eaten their fill, Ethan froze the remaining steaks and put them into his portal pouch for later.

When they were completely done, Ainslee lay back down on her bedroll. "We're staying here until tomorrow morning, right, wizard-boy?"

"Yes," Ethan replied. He'd seen how ragged his companions had become, not to mention the horses. A little time to recoup would do them all good. "Let's stay here until tomorrow morning."

"Good!" the dwarf mumbled and then, lying back on

her bedroll, she promptly shut her eyes. Par'karr was also curled up on his own bedroll.

Ethan looked at the two and then watched Yuliana and Michalus disappear into the forest. He smiled. A little nap didn't seem like such a bad thing at the moment. He started towards his own bedroll when he felt a hand on his arm.

Turning, he saw Nia looking up at him questioningly. At first, he grew excited, thinking maybe she wanted to "hunt" again. Then he saw the training swords in her hand.

"You are not going to waste an afternoon, are you? Not when you could be training," the foxgirl said innocently.

Suppressing a groan, Ethan shook his head. As tired as he was and as much as he wanted a nap, he knew the foxgirl was right. He'd been neglecting his weapons training lately and it was time to get back into the practice.

Putting a smile on his face, he took one of the practice swords and began walking towards an open space near the horses. "Sounds good to me. I can't think of a better way to spend my afternoon."

The foxgirl stared at him for a moment and then snickered. "You do remember that I can smell when you're lying."

17

Ethan was sore when they left the next morning. And every morning after that for the next two weeks. Each night, when they stopped for the evening, Nia trained him hard with staff, sword and even dagger.

If he thought the foxgirl would go easy on him just because they were "hunting" in the mornings and evenings, he had thought wrong. If anything, she pushed him to the point of exhaustion nearly every evening.

But the training had paid off. After the first week of continually training with the sword, he had gained a skill:

You have gained: Longblades.

After two weeks of continual training, he'd managed to gain ranks in his staff skill, Two Handed Crushing, as well as Shortblades and his new Longblades skill. Those rank increases earned him a point in *Strength* for the new rank in *Two Handed Crushing*. The two Blade skills earned him two more points of *Agility*.

The changes didn't just show on his character sheet either. For the first time in his life, he had toned muscles in his arms, legs and chest. Even his stomach was flat now. Holding a practice sword while sparring, doing forms and practicing footwork had done its job well.

And still, despite being exhausted, Ethan continued practicing his magic during his time on watch. He especially focused on his Portal magic. It was the one skill he had the least amount of practice with but also one with huge potential. He just had to be careful not to overexert himself.

Over the weeks, he'd managed to raise the skill and gain another point in *Intellect*. His stats were starting to look impressive in his character sheet.

Strength: 11
Agility: 15
Hardiness: 16
Intellect: 31
Intuition: 15
Charisma: 12

Ethan was proud of his accomplishments, but each time Nia beat him in their sparring, he realized how much more he still needed to learn.

FOUR MORE WEEKS of travel saw Ethan gain several more ranks in his weapon skills as well as a rank up in each of his magic skills. He'd also talked Nia into teaching him the bow, though he still let her do all the hunting.

And it wasn't just him training any longer. After

watching Ethan training each night for a couple of weeks, Ainslee had asked to be trained as well.

"If we're gonna keep fighting stuff," the dwarf had grumbled. "Might as well get better at whackin' it!"

Par'karr had joined them a few nights later. Then, even more surprisingly, Michalus and Yuliana had asked to join in their training sessions.

The two elves had been engaging in longer conversations during the journey and now went out on their own "berry hunting" trips. Ethan wasn't the most observant person, but even he could tell the elves were much more disheveled when they returned. Combined with the big grins they had when they returned, he didn't have to have mental magic to know what was going on.

But the biggest surprise and accomplishment Ethan made during the time was realizing that between his additional *Mana* and his new ranks in Portal magic, he could open a human-sized portal without resorting to pulling *Mana* from a crystal. Unfortunately, doing so required nearly all of his *Mana*, but he could do it.

It was only two days after making that discovery that things changed for them. They'd noticed the forest getting thicker for days but then they came upon another wide river.

This river, Michalus named it the River Maun, was much wider than the one where they'd faced the werewolves. It was fast-moving as well. Like the river near the werewolves, this one had an ancient stone bridge, though this one was wider and a bit taller.

The river wasn't what got their attention, however. It was what was on the other side of the river. A forest. A forest with giant trees, like the Sequoioideae - or redwoods - of Earth, these trees towered over everything.

"Loki's balls, those are some big trees!" Ainslee marveled.

Michalus gestured to the huge expanse of forest ahead of them. "Welcome to the eastern fringe of Sherwood Forest."

Ethan gaped. He'd never seen the redwoods in real life back on Earth - just pictures. Seeing these enormous trees close up was impressive. Impressive and intimidating.

"These are like the trees of my grove!" Yuliana exclaimed happily. She reached out and shamelessly took Michalus's hand. The wizard held it and grinned back at her.

"Those biggest trees Par'karr ever see!" the kobold squeaked from his saddle.

"That's how I felt the first time I saw them," Michalus told the group. "Quite impressive. Books just don't do them justice."

There was silence for a minute while everyone soaked in the sight of the giant trees. Finally, Nia broke the silence. "What dangers are there in these large trees?"

"We shouldn't have anything to fear," the elven wizard explained, his voice resembling that of a college professor lecturing his students. "As long as we stay outside the forest."

"Oh?" Ethan raised an eyebrow.

"For reasons that have yet to be satisfactorily explained," Michalus replied, "the creatures that live in the forest do not come past the boundary of the forest."

"Truly?" Nia asked, forehead wrinkled. "Not even to

hunt?"

"When I passed this way last time," he said, looking off into the distance. "I was not bothered at all. From what I read, this seems to be the normal behavior. Whatever creatures live in Sherwood, stay in Sherwood."

"What does live in there?" Ethan asked. The trees were huge and blocked out most of the light a hundred yards into the forest, turning day into night - or at the very least, twilight. If ever there was a forest that screamed "DO NOT ENTER" - it was this forest.

"The reports of people who have made it out have been... sketchy," the wizard admitted. "It's not really clear what is in there."

"Great!" Ainslee complained. "Just great! And let me guess... that's where we need to go?!"

Ethan nodded. "Not yet but yes, in another week or so, we should cut into the forest and head west."

The dwarf muttered unintelligibly under her breath and, looking at the majestic but foreboding forest, Ethan couldn't help but agree with her sentiment.

"I'd say four or five more days," Michalus agreed. "According to the journal you let me read, that would be about the spot where Merlin cut west toward Camelot."

Nia turned to face him. "And this Camelot is worth the danger?"

Ethan sighed. He thought it was. If the Great Library was somehow still intact, he might be able to learn all sorts of things. Things about magic, portals, maybe even more about this world and the aliens that had brought them here. He got excited just thinking about all of the knowledge.

Then there was Excalibur. According to the journal, Merlin had embedded the sword into a stone in Camelot. He felt compelled to find Camelot and the Excalibur. It seemed irrational, but it was like those two things were part of history. Earth's history. It was like they were a little piece of Earth.

He almost laughed at himself. He rarely thought of home at all anymore. And now he desperately wanted to find some link between this world and his former world. Yet, despite the absurdity, he still felt like he needed to do it.

"I think it's worth it," Ethan replied. "But no one needs to come with me. It sounds like anyone who stays outside Sherwood should be safe until I return."

"I am Tal'Cha," Nia said in a tone that did not invite argument. "Where you go, I go."

"Par'karr go too!" The kobold bobbed his head and gave Ethan a toothy grin.

"The trees that move, that talk," Yuliana said, looking at Michalus. "They are... in Sherwood?"

"Those are the rumors," Michalus confirmed. "But as I've told you before, they're just that... rumors."

"I must see for myself then," the green-haired elf replied, a rare passion filling her voice. "I must find them."

"Well," the wizard said with a lopsided grin. "If you're going, then I'm going."

"So, everyone else is going?!" Ainslee growled. "Well, I sure as Freya's white arse ain't stayin' out here by myself!" She mumbled something. "I guess that means I'm coming too."

Ethan nodded. He'd expected as much, though he

hadn't been completely certain that Yuliana, Michalus and Ainslee would go with him. He felt both elated that the whole party was coming and responsible for them all.

If anything happened to his companions on this quest, adventure, sight-seeing tour, or whatever it was, it would be Ethan's fault. This whole thing was his idea. He'd just need to make sure that didn't happen - somehow.

Even knowing that, he felt compelled to go. It was hard to explain, even to himself. He just felt like all the answers would be waiting for him in Camelot.

"Now that it's decided that we're all going along," Ainslee huffed. "Can we break out the food and eat some lunch?"

They chuckled. Despite their long journey, the dwarf's appetite had not changed. Which was to say, Ainslee was always hungry.

Ethan looked up at the double suns and the patch of blackness between them. It was noon and as good a time as any to eat.

"That sounds like a plan," he said. Looking across the river, he added, "Let's cross the river and make a fire on the other side."

"Fine, wizard-boy," the dwarf grumbled. "Let's get moving then!"

Ainslee dug her heels into her mount and began crossing the bridge. After a moment, Ethan and the others followed.

It wasn't until they were halfway across that the water suddenly began bubbling and huge tentacles burst from the water on both sides of them.

18

———

"What in Hel's underskirt is that thing!" Ainslee yelled, yanking her hammer from her belt.

It was a testament to their training that the group reacted as quickly as it did. Rather than panicking, they drew their weapons almost as one.

Unfortunately, the horses hadn't been training. They bucked and reared back, whinnying in fear and knocking their riders from saddles. Free of their riders, the horses bolted for either side of the river at full gallop, avoiding the reaching tentacles.

Yuliana and Par'karr managed to hang onto their horses but were powerless to stop their fleeing animals as the horses carried them across the bridge and out of the melee. Luna hesitated only briefly before racing after Yuliana and the fleeing horses.

Ethan was thrown from his horse, nearly cracking his

skull on the hard stone. His magical practice paid off and he was able to cushion his fall a bit with tendrils of air. He hit his head, but not enough to crack his skull or, hopefully, give him a concussion. It still hurt though.

He managed to reach out with *Air* and catch Ainslee and Michalus just in time. He could have grabbed Nia, but the dexterous foxgirl did something that could have been a backspring or somersault before coming to rest on her feet, scimitars in her slender hands.

A tentacle from his blindside smacked Ethan across the side of the head, sending him skidding across the bridge.

Sollasina crushes you for 14 damage.

Coming to a rest, Ethan blinked to clear the stars in his vision. His vision swam and he didn't see the next tentacle until it was too late. Before he could roll out of the way, it smashed into his chest, driving him back to the stone of the bridge.

Sollasina crushes you for 13 damage.

Dazed, Ethan felt the tentacle starting to wrap around him.

"Ethan!" he heard Nia's voice cry out but from his vantage point flat on his back he was unable to see where she was. Luckily, he maintained the presence of mind to activate his *Elemental Armor.*

Immediately, flames enveloped his body. And then

winked out as the tentacles tightened around him just as fast.

Elemental Armor (Fire) is dispelled by Sollasina.

"What the - ?!" Ethan gasped in stunned disbelief as the tentacle began to tighten around him.

"It's a Sollasina!" came Michalus's panicked voice from somewhere to his right. "They cannot be touched by magic!"

"Now he tells me," growled Ethan. He tried to grab his shortsword but the tentacle squeezed his arms too tightly for him to wiggle it free.

Frustrated by the sudden loss of his *Elemental Armor* and unable to get his shortsword, Ethan began to pull free his dagger when daggers began to hammer at his mind. Images and sound began to pummel his mind threatening to drive him into unconsciousness.

Ethan wasn't sure what a migraine felt like, he'd never really had a true migraine, but suddenly he felt a piercing pain in the front of his skull! He imagined the sensation he was experiencing was the worst migraine ever.

Pain stabbed into his brain from behind his eyes, making it impossible to keep his eyes open. But then it got worse. Even with his eyes shut, images began to bombard his mind, images of terrible things.

In one scene, he was being dismembered by his friends while they laughed. In the next scene, he dismembered his friends while he laughed. And the images only got worse as every terrible thing he'd read or saw in a movie began to slam into his consciousness.

Then there were the emotions. Things he had never remembered ever feeling suddenly began to overpower his mind. Pure terror, such as he had never felt before, invaded his mind like a red-hot poker suddenly thrust into the middle of his brain.

He thought he heard himself scream. He thought he was moving his arms and legs, trying to get away. But he couldn't be sure. He couldn't be sure of anything.

Part of him knew he was moving. Knew that wasn't a good thing. The tentacle had him and was probably going to drop him into some huge gaping maw of whatever beast the tentacles belonged to.

Ethan knew this, but the terror and the pain pushed it to the side. He couldn't bring himself to care. It was almost as if he wanted it to happen. He wanted it to be all over, just to make the pain and the terror end. At least then it would be over.

Through everything, he thought he heard a scream. His scream? No. It was a woman's scream. He knew that voice. Nia. It was Nia's voice. She was screaming. She was in pain too. He had to help. He had to help! Letting this tentacle thing eat him was one thing but he had to save Nia. He had to.

He tried to force his eyes open, but the emotions and the pain doubled, as did the horrific images. He saw himself killing Nia and doing other terrible things to her over and over, all while laughing and enjoying it.

"No!" he screamed. Or rather, he thought he screamed.

He wasn't sure if he had done it for real or just in his mind.

It was hard to think, but Ethan realized this was some sort of mental attack. It had to be. The creature, the Sollasina, was somehow able to get into his mind. It was doing this to him - creating these emotions and images in his mind.

Summoning all of the willpower he could, he forced his eyes open. The light momentarily sent shards of pain throughout his eyes and into the front of his brain. He wanted nothing more than to close his eyes. No! Ethan gritted his teeth and forced his eyes to stay open.

Images continued to pummel his brain even as he tried to focus on his surroundings. The idea of keeping his eyes open was suddenly terrifying and he nearly shut them. No! This was the creature. The Sollasina. It was putting these thoughts in his head.

Keeping his eyes open, Ethan looked around. He was suspended in the air in one of the giant tentacles. With supreme effort, he forced his head to turn until he could see the others. They were caught in tentacles too, their bodies limp and slightly glowing. The creature was doing something to them - probably to him too!

With supreme effort, he forced his HUD open. There were messages waiting for him.

```
Sollasina     drains     1     point     of
Intellect from you.
   Sollasina     drains     1     point     of
Intuition from you.
```

```
    Sollasina    drains    1    point    of
Charisma from you.
```

Even as he watched, the messages repeated.

```
Sollasina       drains    1    point    of
Intellect from you.
    Sollasina    drains    1    point    of
Intuition from you.
    Sollasina    drains    1    point    of
Charisma from you.
```

He cursed. The Sollasina was "feeding" off his party's mental energy - like some sort of psychic vampire. And he guessed reaching zero in any of the mental stats was a bad thing.

More images bombarded him, combined with more terror and fear, causing his HUD to wink out. He grimaced.

Wasn't there a creature like this in one of the wizarding books he'd read? A creature that caused you to experience your worst fear? Yes. He remembered it now, through the haze of pain and blinding emotion.

What had they done to defeat it? He tried to remember but it was hard while he was being assaulted with the terrible images of him doing unspeakable things.

Humor! That was it. Laughter. That had warded them in the book. But would it work in this case?

Ethan began to pull up every funny memory he could. He thought of every hilarious cat video his friends had ever sent him. Every funny meme. Every hilarious scene from his favorite comedy movies.

And it worked. The feelings of terror began to recede and while the images came, he kept replacing them with funny images and scenes from funny movies. Ethan laughed aloud at the absurdity of creating a mental wall around his mind - with memes and cat videos. But it worked. He was able to bring his HUD back up.

```
You have gained: Mental magic.
    Sollasina    drains    1    point    of
Intellect from you.
    Sollasina    drains    1    point    of
Intuition from you.
    Sollasina    drains    1    point    of
Charisma from you.
```

Blinking, Ethan regained some of his awareness. He saw the messages in his HUD but couldn't really register them in his mind.

```
Skill increase: Mental magic +1%.
```

He saw his friends in the tentacles, fifteen or twenty feet above the water. The tentacles were swaying gently back and forth as the Sollasina fed. Forcing himself to look down, he saw a huge brain-like shape just below the surface of the water.

```
Skill increase: Mental magic +1%.
```

The thing's brain shape appeared to have dozens of eyes surrounding it, all rolled back into their sockets - possibly at the ecstasy of feeding off its victims. Or perhaps that's the way the eyes always looked - he had no way of knowing.

```
Skill increase: Mental magic +1%.
   Sollasina    drains    1    point    of
Intellect from you.
   Sollasina    drains    1    point    of
Intuition from you.
   Sollasina    drains    1    point    of
Charisma from you.
```

He did know he needed to stop it. And he needed to stop it now, before it did any more ability damage to him and the others.

Magic wouldn't work on it. He already knew that and he remembered Michalus yelling something similar. That meant his magic was useless against it. Or was it? Looking at the shore, he grinned.

```
Skill increase: Mental magic +1%.
```

Ethan reached out with *Air* and picked up the largest boulder he could. It was tough and he saw his *Mana* depleting quickly. Still, he lifted the boulder up while moving it towards him.

His *Mana* continued to plummet and he realized as the creature sucked away more of his *Intellect*, it was in essence sucking away his *Mana* too.

Skill increase: Mental magic +1%.

Just in time, he got the boulder into position about fifty feet above him. He looked down at the brain shape below him. Through gritted teeth he hissed at the creature, "Don't like magic? How about gravity?"

He released the boulder.

As expected, the boulder plummeted downward - straight towards the brain mass in the water. It covered the distance between where it had been and the creature in less than a second and hit the thing with the force of a car moving at 70 mph.

Like a deer hit by a high-speed car, the huge rock pulverized the brain, sending a spray of red across the river and turning the water crimson.

You critically crush Sollasina for 491 damage.

   Sollasina dies.

   You gain 200 experience.

Experience to next level 4,160.

The tentacles that held Ethan and his group spasmed and went slack, loosening their grip and dropping them towards the river.

His *Mana* was too low, but Ethan burned *Stamina* to reach out with *Air* and grab his companions and himself, dropping them all onto the bridge before collapsing himself. He crawled over to Nia and checked for a pulse. She was alive. So were the rest of them.

Groaning, Ethan reached down to his belt. He pushed

open his portal pouch and pulled out the Holy Grail. He was about to will *Water* from the river into it, but he remembered the crimson, bloody water he'd just seen.

Thinking better of it, he grabbed his water bottle and began the process of healing himself and his companions. He wasn't sure what a Sollasina was, but he wasn't about to put water mixed with its blood into the Holy Grail and then give it to his friends.

19

E than drank first, restoring him instantly to perfect health. At least, that's what his character sheet said. His brain still felt like it had been shaken, not stirred and he would get sudden intense flashes of one of the horrific scenes the creature had been feeding him.

Despite the flashes, he began to revive his companions, starting with Nia. She was startled and wide-eyed when she came to, head darting from side to side. Her eyes seemed wild and it was almost as if she looked right through him before blinking several times.

Finally, her eyes seemed to focus, and it was as if she was seeing Ethan at least. Her eyes narrowed. "Is... this... real?"

"Yeah." Ethan nodded and held up the magical chalice. "I just gave you water from the Grail."

The foxgirl bit her lip, looking up and down at Ethan. "I...I..."

"I had dreams that I was killing you," he told her, assuming she'd had similar dreams. "And dreams of killing the others. I also had dreams of you all killing me - and each other."

Still biting her lip, Nia nodded. Her eyes still had a wild look to them. It was as if she was about to bolt at any moment. He went to put a reassuring hand on her shoulder, but she flinched away and stared at it like he was on fire.

"You okay?" he asked, withdrawing his hand.

Eyes still wild, she looked around the bridge. "I... I don't know... Things... happened to me. And I... did things..."

Ethan shook his head. "They weren't real. The creature was attacking our minds. I think it was feeding on our energy somehow. Maybe even our terror. I need to ask Michalus."

"Michalus," Nia repeated but without any real recognition.

The entire time he talked with Nia, images kept flashing into his mind. They were starting to give him a splitting headache. He rubbed his temples, trying to keep those happy thoughts in his head to counteract the vile images that kept appearing. It was only partially working.

Leaving Nia, he scrambled over to Michalus. Ethan held the cup up to his lips and forced some water from the Grail down the elf's throat. Coughing and sputtering, the wizard's eyes fluttered open.

The elf's eyes went wild and he burst into flames. Ethan yelped in pain as the hand holding the back of

Michalus's head was burned and he snatched his wounded hand away too slowly.

`Michalus Moor burns you for 11 fire damage.`

Ethan swore and backed away. "What the heck, Michalus?!"

The wizard stared at him with wide eyes, though Ethan got the impression that he was actually staring through him.

"The images," Ethan said through clenched teeth. He cradled his burned hand. "They're not real!"

He saw Nia crouch down, a low growl in her throat. She had pulled a dagger from her boot and looked like she could be ready to either attack or bolt at any second.

Swearing again, Ethan prepared to defend himself - if it came to that. Part of him, a part that hadn't been there before, told him to strike first and strike hard. It wanted no mercy for them.

Ethan shuddered. Those weren't his thoughts. Or, at least, they hadn't been his thoughts until the Sollasina had mentally attacked him. Now, things weren't as black and white. Were they his thoughts, or weren't they? Perhaps they were something from deep in his unconscious? Yet, part of him didn't accept the thoughts as really his.

Nia and Michalus had retreated to opposite sides of the bridge, pressed up against the low walls. Their eyes darted from Ethan to each other like cornered animals.

Ignoring his headache, he started to crawl between

them to get to Ainslee. Both Michalus and Nia flinched, and Ethan stopped. He sighed.

"I'm not going to hurt either of you," he said with raised hands. His left hand was red where he'd been burned, and it hurt. Unfortunately, he couldn't heal it with the Grail since he'd already used it once today. He'd need to wait until Yuliana came back. He looked from Nia to Michalus. "I'm just going to go heal Ainslee."

Neither of his companions said anything in response. Ethan sighed heavily and started forward. Both of his companions watched him pass between them and then watched him give the dwarf a sip of the water from the Grail.

"What?! Who?!" Ainslee's eyes fluttered open and she looked around. "Where'd the beastie go?!"

Ethan looked down at the dwarf, brows knitted. "Are you... okay?"

Ainslee patted herself down and then shrugged. "I think so. You kill the tentacle monsters?"

"Yeah," he answered. The dwarf didn't show any of the symptoms of the other two. If anything, she seemed... normal. At least, normal for Ainslee. "You sure you're okay?"

The dwarf's eyes suddenly went wide. She glanced around with a horrified expression. She looked over the short wall of the bridge at the river with a look of horror. "Odin's good eye! I think I lost my hammer!"

Relaxing slightly, Ethan shook his head. "But otherwise you're fine?"

"I guess so." Ainslee frowned. "But I liked that hammer."

"What about images?" Ethan asked her. "Are you getting any images flashing in your head?"

The dwarf shrugged. "I was. Nasty stuff. Like a nightmare. But it's gone now."

Ethan sat back and slipped the Holy Grail back through the portal pouch and onto its resting place back in the tomb. It had served its purpose and if the horses came back, it would only unsettle them. Then he turned to his other companions.

Flinching as the burns on his left hand gave him a flash of pain, he looked between Nia and Michalus. Both were now darting their eyes between Ethan, Ainslee and each other.

"What's wrong with them?" Ainslee asked, watching the pair.

"Remnants of the creature's psychic attack," Ethan replied. At least, that was his working theory. He thought back to that series of Nightmare movies with that guy who wore a bladed claw. Hadn't he invaded people's dreams too?

Remembering what Ainslee had said about her hammer, Ethan looked over his other two companions and saw that Nia's scimitars were missing, as was Michalus's staff. They'd all lost their weapons when the creature had captured them in its tentacles.

Looking over the side of the bridge, Ethan guessed the weapons were all at the bottom of the river or carried down the river. He cursed.

"What?!" Ainslee grumbled.

"It's not just your hammer," he retorted. "I think we all lost our weapons when the thing had us. I doubt we can just buy new ones at the villages. We'll be lucky if we can get new shoes for our horses."

Ainslee moved slightly and looked down into the dark waters of the river. The crimson blood had mostly washed down the river and the tentacles had sunk below the surface, along with the brainy mass. She looked up at Ethan. "Can't you just... you know... magic them back, wizard-boy?"

Ethan furrowed his eyebrows. He knew he didn't actually have to see something to interact with it. After all, it was how he channeled his magic through the Chymera crystals. He sensed where they were and channeled his magic without seeing them.

Using *Earth* magic, he could sense stone and manipulate it and bend it to whatever shape he wanted. Using the same *Earth* magic, he could even manipulate metal though it didn't quite bend to his will. Instead, cold metal tended to explode under the strain when he tried to bend it.

Still, the theory was sound. He might be able to sense the weapons and then bring them to the surface. Only one way to find out.

Casting a glance back at Nia and Michalus to make sure they were both still there, he closed his eyes and reached down with his *Earth* awareness. He went down into the river. There was nothing so he went deeper, then deeper yet.

He sensed nothing until suddenly he felt the bottom of the river. Dirt. Stones. And metal! Yes, he could tell the difference. There was definitely metal down there at the bottom. Lots of metal. More than would account for their lost weapons.

Reaching out with *Water*, he grabbed hold of some of the metal and brought it up to the surface.

Skill increase: Water magic +1%.

He got an increase in *Water* magic for his effort but when the metal came to the surface, he found that it was a rusted suit of armor. A suit of armor with a skeleton in it.

"What's that?" Ainslee gaped.

"One of the creature's previous victims," Ethan guessed aloud. Grabbing the armor in tendrils of *Air*, he moved to the side of the river and deposited it there. "This is too slow."

"What's too slow?" Ainslee asked.

"There's a lot of metal down there," Ethan replied, remembering how much he sensed. "It's going to take a long time to pick it up, piece by piece."

The dwarf frowned.

An idea came to Ethan then and he summoned a Lesser Elemental and chose a water elemental. The thing appeared as a four-foot watery dolphin and looked at him for instructions.

"What's that?!" Ainslee asked, mouth open as she stared at the shifting water elemental.

"It's like that fire weasel elemental," he explained. "But this is a water one."

The dwarf furrowed her brow. "How's that supposed to help?"

Turning to the dolphin, Ethan pointed to the river and

then to the shore where he'd deposited the armor. "Go to the bottom. Bring anything made of metal and toss it up on the bank, over there."

Without hesitation, the water dolphin hopped over the bridge's edge and disappeared into the water. Within a minute, it had pulled another suit of armor up to the surface and was swimming it to the shore.

Ethan smiled and looked at Ainslee.

The dwarf looked down at the water dolphin, pulling the armor in its mouth. "That works, wizard-boy."

20

While the elemental did its work, Ethan tried talking with Michalus and Nia. At first, they were too skittish to respond to him. Both simply retreated to their side of the bridge, watching Ainslee and him warily.

Ainslee, who seemed completely recovered, suggested knocking them on the head. Ethan didn't think it was a good idea to add actual head trauma to the emotional trauma the psychic attack had caused.

Ethan continued to get what he thought of as psychic aftershocks, or perhaps afterimages was a better description. Flashes of some of the more horrific images that stabbed into his consciousness. He met each one with a renewed wall of the funniest cat videos and memes he could think of.

Keeping an eye on his HUD, Ethan noticed that each time he received one of the afterimages, he also received a skill increase in his new *Mental* magic skill. Maybe his mental wall of happy things was fighting off whatever residual attack was happening.

Skill increase: Mental magic +1%.

As he did fight it off - whatever "it" was - each attempt increased his newly acquired *Mental* magic skill. Yet another type of magic he'd have to learn and practice with, especially if there were more creatures like the Sollasina.

Ainslee seemed either mostly immune to it or simply resilient to the psychic attack remnants. She was acting completely normal and didn't seem to have any of the lingering afterimages Ethan and the others were experiencing.

That left Nia and Michalus. Both were either still experiencing the same afterimages he was or had been psychically damaged somehow. Unfortunately, Ethan knew little about psychology and nothing about dealing with psychic attacks.

He thought of his own defense: blocking the bad thoughts with good thoughts. He wasn't sure if that was all there was to it or if, by gaining the *Mental* magic skill, he had some natural defense against it.

Hoping that his defense might work for the others, he started with Nia. He got as close as the foxgirl would allow. "Nia! Listen to me! These images aren't real. They're fake! You have to think of something happy. Use happy memories to block out the bad images. Try it!"

The foxgirl continued to look at him with wild eyes,

darting her gaze around the bridge from Ainslee, to Michalus and then back to Ethan. He sighed.

Turning and getting as close to Michalus as he dared, he repeated his advice to the elven wizard. Like Nia, he just glanced around, wide-eyed, like a trapped animal. If the wizard understood him, he gave no visible sign.

"No luck, wizard-boy?" Ainslee asked as she regarded their companions.

"No." Ethan grimaced. "Nothing I say to them seems to reach them. I don't know what to do."

The dwarf looked at him. For the first time in a long time, Ainslee's expression was concerned - sympathetic even. "You might be a wizard-boy, but you ain't a god. You can't do everything. I'm sure they'll get better. Probably just takes time. You know, like when you hit your noggin real hard."

Ethan nodded but he didn't really feel any better. He knew he wasn't a god. Not even close. There was so much he didn't know and couldn't do. Standing up, he swore under his breath. He wasn't sure what else to do to help his friends and he felt helpless. He didn't know what else to try with them. Unless...

Bringing up his HUD, Ethan looked at his skill list and saw his new magic skill in the list.

Mental Magic: 1

He had the *Mental* magic skill. If it were just like his other magic skills, could he use it to somehow help Nia and Michalus? Ethan bit his lip. He'd literally gotten the skill less than half an hour ago. He knew nothing about *Mental* magic. What if he somehow made things worse?

Ethan was debating what to do when he heard the sound of approaching hoofbeats. Looking up, he saw Yuliana emerge from the trees and bring her horse to a halt just before the bridge. A few moments later, the familiar shape of Luna padded out of the trees and stopped next to her.

"Is Par'karr with you?" Ethan called out.

Yuliana shook her head. "I was able to get my horse under control after a few miles but Par'karr could not. He kept going."

Nodding to the elf, he cursed under his breath. Splitting the party was never a good idea. Not in games, not in horror movies and definitely not on this world. Ethan hoped the kobold was okay.

He also hoped the horses were okay and that they could find them. If not, this was going to be a very long and slow journey until they found a village with horses for sale. And that was assuming there were any horses for sale at all, and that they had the money for them.

Ethan hadn't made a big deal of it so he didn't worry the others, but they were low on gold. He'd used nearly all of their money to hire the mercenaries to scout out the area around the village so the trade routes would restart.

There hadn't been any gold in Arthur's tomb, other than the Grail. Given what he'd read in Merlin's journal, he guessed Mordred had kept all of the riches of Camelot for himself and his designs of conquest.

"What is wrong with them?" Yuliana asked as she approached. The druid had dismounted and had been leading her horse towards Ethan and the others, who were still in the middle of the bridge. She had stopped a few yards away from the wizard, her forehead creased with concern.

Ainslee crossed her eyes and wiggled her fingers next to the side of her head. "They're a bit looney now."

Yuliana's eyes went wide. "What?"

Ethan gave the dwarf a glare of disapproval but Ainslee just shrugged and went back to looking at the elemental in the river.

"The creature we fought had some sort of psychic or mental attack," Ethan explained. "It may have caused them some sort of post-traumatic stress disorder."

"Post what?" The elf looked at him with furrowed brows, clearly not understanding what he was talking about.

He took a moment to think of how to phrase it in terms she would understand. "I think there might be some sort of mental poison that the creature left in their... our... minds."

"*Mental* poison?"

"Yeah," he confirmed. "I think its attack left residual things in our minds. Like really, really bad memories - but much stronger than a normal memory. And it might be playing over and over in their minds."

"Yul...Yuliana..." Michalus said, locking his eyes on the green-haired druid. "Is... that... you?"

"Yes," she answered and started to take a step towards him but his elemental armor flared to life again.

Gasping, the druid took a step back. "What is he... Why did he do that? It's me."

Ethan slowly let his fists unclench. He had very nearly clocked the wizard with a fist of *Air*. He had thought the wizard might be attacking Yuliana and had been ready to defend her. He saw that Ainslee had a rock in her hand and was staring at Michalus too. She had been ready to do the same. He cursed.

"I don't know what he sees," Ethan admitted. "He may not really recognize you or somehow the creature may have perverted his memories of you."

"Will he get better?" Yuliana asked, taking another step back. Her face was a mask of hurt and betrayal.

"I... I'm not sure," he told her.

"What about the magic cup?" the green-haired elf asked hopefully.

He shook his head. "I already gave them all a drink from it. I think it healed the physical damage - but not the mental damage or whatever memories the creature created."

Yuliana went silent. Ainslee kicked at the stones on the bridge before looking up. "Wizard-boy, we can't trust them like this. I mean, I certainly don't."

Ethan nodded. He felt the same way. Whatever the creature's psychic attack had done, it seemed like it wouldn't be going away any time soon. And the way Nia and Michalus were acting, they couldn't trust either of them.

He realized he had two choices. One, he could try to restrain the two of them until they were better. That was assuming he could even restrain Michalus. The elf was a wizard and more experienced than Ethan was. About the only thing he could do was to surprise the elf and knock him unconscious.

His second option was to try his *Mental* magic skill. That was potentially more dangerous, at least to Nia and Michalus, since he had no idea what he was doing.

"There is something I can try," Ethan blurted out, instantly regretting it as he saw Yuliana's face fill with hope.

"What? What can we do?" she demanded.

Grimacing, he looked around at his companions. "I can use something called *Mental* magic to try and help them. But I don't really know how it works and I could do more harm than good."

Yuliana bit her lip, forehead creased in concern. She looked at Michalus. Her gaze lingered on him before giving a quick glance at Nia. She breathed out. "If you can help them, you have to try."

Ethan sighed and nodded. He knew the elf was right. It was either help them or keep them unconscious or tied up until they got better - IF they got better. "I'll try."

"Good luck, wizard-boy," Ainslee said, her tone revealing nothing but sincerity for a change.

"Thanks," Ethan replied and took a deep breath. It took him almost fifteen minutes to decide on a strategy.

Magic worked on the principle of envisioning what he wanted and then willing it into being. He didn't necessarily need to know the specifics, somehow the magic filled in the gaps - most of the time.

The first hurdle he ran into was his lack of understanding of how the brain worked. Then, on top of that was how the actual MIND worked. It seemed like an insurmountable challenge to understand both.

Then, he put it into computer terms. The brain was the actual gray matter in a person's head. In computer terms, it was the computer hardware. It was the hardware that the operating system - in this case, the mind - ran on.

When he put it in those terms, he felt the issue would be more like an operating system issue than a hardware issue. The Sollasina had left a virus in their minds and it was causing havoc. Or, in computer terms, it was causing system crashes, or blue screens of death, as computer techs called them.

So, using his analogy, he needed to basically create a magical antivirus to find and remove the Sollasina's virus and quarantine the bad memories. That's what a real anti-virus program would do. Would the same thing work on a person's mind? Even with magic? There was only one way to find out.

Envisioning what he wanted to do, but keeping it in computer terms in his mind, he focused on Michalus first. He knew it was selfish, but he didn't want to try it on Nia first, in case something went wrong. He felt terrible for feeling that way, but if he screwed up Nia's mind, he'd never forgive himself.

Ethan locked in a picture of what he wanted to happen to the elven wizard's mind and then pushed *Mana* into his idea.

Skill increase: Mental magic +1%.

The result was instantaneous. He felt a chunk of *Mana*

go out of him and then Michalus blinked. The wizard looked around, eyes clear for the first time since the attack. He settled his gaze on Yuliana and he smiled.

Extinguishing his elemental armor, he pushed himself to his feet. He looked around and shivered. "I feel like I was in a very bad nightmare."

"In a way," Ethan told him, "you were."

The wizard raised an eyebrow. "You did something, didn't you?"

"A little *Mental* magic," Ethan grinned.

"You learned mental magic?!" Michalus asked in surprise.

Ethan nodded.

The wizard's shoulders dropped, and he rolled his eyes. He shook his head, but Ethan could see the small smile that played across his lips. "Of course, you did."

"One moment," Ethan replied, holding up a finger. Turning to Nia, he repeated the process, creating the same magical anti-virus in her mind.

Skill increase: Mental magic +1%.

Nia blinked and looked around. She looked from companion to companion before resting her eyes on Ethan. "Is that... you, Ethan?"

"It's me." He grinned and started forward.

"Wait!" she said, squirming back against the wall of the bridge. "Don't touch me. Don't come near me."

Ethan stopped immediately and he could feel the look of shock and hurt on his face. He tried to calm himself and remember she'd just gone through a very difficult thing. He caught the others looking at him, their own faces concerned.

"Nia," he said in a calm voice. "It's okay. The images you experienced weren't real."

The foxgirl shivered, bringing her arms up to hug herself. It was a gesture he'd seen many times back on Earth, but seeing Nia do it was the most vulnerable he'd ever seen the foxgirl look.

She looked up at him, eyes watering. "I just need some time... alone."

Feeling hurt and a bit numb, Ethan nodded and backed up a step.

"Hey, wizard-boy," Ainslee's voice cut through the tension. "You'd better take a look at this."

21

Ethan's gaze lingered on Nia but the foxgirl turned away. Not knowing what to say or what to do about her, he turned to Ainslee. The dwarf was sitting on the small wall of the bridge, looking over the side and chuckling.

Walking over to the dwarf he stopped and looked down at her. "What?"

"Look!" She pointed to the southern shore and grinned. "It's been at it this whole time!"

He followed the dwarf's finger to where she pointed and his mouth dropped open. Lying on the shore of the river were at least two dozen armor-clad bodies or just empty sets of rusted armor, along with a collection of metal implements - some weapons, some tools.

As he watched, the dolphin elemental emerged from the water with a rusted sword in its mouth and with a flick of its head, tossed the sword onto the grass of the shore. It turned but before it could move back into the water, it stopped. In a splash of water, the water dolphin winked out of existence.

"Where'd it go?" Ainslee demanded.

Ethan shrugged. "That's probably the duration of the summons."

"Summon another one!" the dwarf insisted. "There's probably more stuff down there!"

He looked at the collection of rusted junk and sighed. "It's just junk."

Ainslee shook her head. "I'm pretty sure I saw it pull out a small chest."

Brightening at the mention of a chest, he turned back to the dwarf. "Are you serious?"

"It was rusted," she replied with a nod. "But I'm pretty sure it was a chest. Probably with coins."

The dwarf's face suddenly went serious and her eyes shot to Nia before going back to Ethan. "How is she? I heard what she said, wizard-boy. She gonna be okay?"

Ethan flicked his eyes towards Nia. The foxgirl was looking off into the distance, eyes haunted and unfocused. He felt a lump in his throat, and he swallowed. "I don't know. I don't know what the thing showed her."

Ainslee punched him in the arm hard enough to make him flinch.

"Ow," he said, rubbing his arm.

"Don't worry, wizard-boy." The dwarf grinned. "I'm sure she'll be back to normal in no time. Now, summon another water thingy and let's see what else is down there. I still haven't seen my hammer!"

Shaking his head and seeing no reason not to, he checked his *Mana* and *Stamina* and summoned another water elemental and gave it the same command. Without comment, the dolphin dove under the water.

Hoofbeats in the distance caused Ethan and the others to look to the south. Within a few minutes, a small rider came through the trees, leading four other horses. It was Par'karr and he had recovered their horses.

As they got closer, Ethan saw several large demon rabbits running alongside and behind the horses. He chuckled. Were the rabbits "herding" the horses? Rabbits herding horses. That was a new one for him.

The kobold rode up to the far end of the bridge and reined in the horses. Hopping down from the saddle, he tied the horses off.

Running over, Par'karr looked around. "Where monsters?"

"It's dead, small-fry," Ainslee answered. "No thanks to you."

Ethan gave the dwarf a hard look but she ignored him and kept her gaze on the kobold. "Where'd you go? Why'd it take you so long to get back?"

The kobold's countenance fell and he looked down at his feet. When he spoke, his voice was soft and full of guilt. "Par'karr's horse not stop for long time. Par'karr try to make it stop but it keep running. Finally, Par'karr summon rabbits. Rabbits stop horses. Par'karr grab all horses. Bring them back but come back too late."

"You're fine," Ethan said and forestalled what Ainslee was about to say with a hard look. He spoke to Par'karr but kept his gaze on the dwarf. "You brought back the horses. At least we don't all have to walk."

Ainslee rolled her eyes and went back to watching the water elemental.

Ethan turned and gave the kobold a grin. "And that means we have our packs too, so we don't have to sleep on the ground."

Par'karr shrugged. "Par'karr not mind sleeping on the ground."

"I know you don't, buddy. But I think the rest of us are thankful we have our packs," he told the kobold with a grin.

Par'karr returned the grin and then surveyed the area. He looked from Michalus and Yuliana to Ainslee and finally let his gaze linger on Nia. The kobold cocked his head. He looked up at Ethan. "Nia hurt?"

Ethan's smile faded as he looked over at his wife. She was still staring out into the distance and didn't appear to have moved. "I'm not sure, Par'karr. I'm not sure."

He knew she wasn't physically hurt. The Grail had seen to that. It would have healed any physical wound she had. But whatever the Sollasina had done to her - done to all of them - hadn't been physical. It had been mental and emotional.

Of all of them, it appeared that the creature had affected her the worst. Ethan's *Mental* magic had helped her but hadn't completely healed her. He briefly thought about trying it again but decided not to. He really had no idea what he was doing with *Mental* magic. What if he made it worse?

"My hammer!" the dwarf yelled and pushed herself to her feet. Ainslee bolted past Ethan and Par'karr and nearly bowled them over.

"She really like hammer," Par'karr commented, rubbing his shoulder where the dwarf had smacked into him.

Ethan grinned down at Par'karr. He made sure he spoke loudly when he replied. "Almost as much as she likes dinner."

"I heard that, wizard-boy!" the dwarf yelled without turning.

Par'karr and Ethan shared a chuckle before the situation with Nia stole away his mirth. He started towards her but stopped. He craned his head so she would see him. "Is there anything I can do for you?"

Nia didn't respond at first but finally looked up, almost as if waking up from a dream. She looked up at him and shook her head before turning back around and staring out towards the forest.

Not knowing what else to say, he let out a frustrated breath. He turned to Par'karr and lowered his voice to a whisper. "Can you keep an eye on her for me?"

Par'karr stood up and puffed out his chest but he kept his voice low too. "Par'karr watch Nia for Ethan!"

"Thanks, buddy," he replied. Turning, Ethan walked towards the far end of the bridge. Thinking about Nia was causing him to get all twisted up inside. He needed to busy his mind with something else.

Walking to the end of the bridge, past Michalus and Yuliana and then past the horses. He continued down to the shore where he found Ainslee wiping off her hammer with a cloth.

She looked up at him as he approached and grinned. "Good as new!"

He forced a smile, though he knew it didn't reach his eyes. It was hard to be happy at the moment, knowing Nia was not all right.

Ainslee gestured with her hammer to a small pile of metal chests and coffers. Most were rusted and mud caked, but they looked intact. "Hopefully some coins or something good in them."

Ethan nodded mutely. He looked around for Nia's scimitars and found one of them lying near the shore. He took a step towards the sword, but the dwarf held the hammer in front of him and shook her head. She gestured towards her boots which were caked in fresh mud. "I wouldn't. I almost got stuck in the mud. Disgusting stuff. Sucks you down."

Nodding again, he reached out and grabbed the scimitar with *Air* and floated it over to him. He caught the blade by the grip and whirled it around several times. It was a motion that was familiar to him from his practice sessions.

Thinking of the practice sessions made him think of Nia and then his insides began to twist up again. Ethan set the scimitar down on the ground and went over to the small pile of coffers and chests.

He spent a half hour prying them open with rusty blades or using *Earth* magic to make the locks explode into metal fragments. Some were so rusted, they didn't even explode but just crumbled into rusty pieces.

None of the containers were waterproof and he found soggy and mostly destroyed parchment, along with rotten leather pouches containing coins of all sizes and denominations. There were mostly silver and copper, but several coffers contained dozens of gold coins.

Two of the smaller metal boxes were actually made of silver and hadn't rusted. Cleaning them revealed several gems embedded in the boxes. He opened them to reveal several pieces of jewelry - some gold, and some silver.

"Not a bad find," Ainslee whistled from behind him.

His mind had been on the cases and on Nia and he started, very nearly conjuring a fireball. He let the feeling drain away and turned to the dwarf. "Worth much?"

"Good craftsmanship." The dwarf nodded. "Clean it up and I'm sure some rich lady would fancy it."

Ethan chuckled mirthlessly. There would be no place to sell them unless he went back to Castlehaven. It wasn't like any of the villages they would run into would have the money to buy them. He'd just have to store them away until then.

"That thing must have been there for a long time," the dwarf said matter of factly.

Ethan creased his brow. "Why do you say that?"

"Some of this stuff is rusted completely through," Ainslee replied, pointing to several objects that looked to be nothing but bundles of rust. "That takes years, decades... maybe even hundreds of years sometimes."

"So that thing was lurking there, feeding on people for decades or even a hundred years," Ethan said sullenly, remembering the lingering effect it had on Nia.

Sensing his dark mood, Ainslee let him be. Unfortunately, his solace didn't last. Fifteen minutes later, Michalus squatted next to him.

"Are you okay, my boy?" the wizard asked, concern lining the eyes that were now too old for his young face.

Ethan gave Michalus a thin smile. "I'm okay."

"Humph, sure you are." Michalus snorted. Ethan opened his mouth but the wizard waved away his words. "I'm not here to argue. I came down to suggest we camp here for the night. I don't think any of us are feeling up to traveling today."

Ethan nodded numbly. He didn't feel like traveling and was perfectly content to camp nearby. "That's fine."

"Uh, wizard-boy," Ainslee called from behind him. "If we're camping here. Let's camp as far away from the water as possibly. You know... just to be sure."

Ethan shivered at the thought of another one of those creatures popping out from the river in the middle of the night. "Good point."

Pointing to a small incropping of trees about fifty yards from the river's edge, Ethan turned to his companions. "Let's camp there. And hope that, if there are any more of those things, they can't leave the water."

22

They moved to the spot he had picked out and set up camp. Nia came along with them but kept her distance from Ethan and the others. As soon as the foxgirl unsaddled her horse and tossed her pack onto the ground, she grabbed her bow and started into the woods. Ethan started after her but she twisted and held up her hand.

"I will hunt alone. You will only slow me down." Not waiting for a response, Nia spun and stalked into the forest.

Ethan tried not to let the hurt show on his face as he watched the foxgirl disappear into the trees. He felt a hand on his shoulder and looked over to see Michalus. The wizard gave him a sympathetic look.

"The girl just needs time," the wizard told him. "I've read that the Sollasina's mental attacks can be quite severe."

Ethan turned to the elf. "So you know what that thing was?"

"A demon," Michalus replied grimly, looking over Ethan's shoulder toward the river. "Or some poor channeler who succumbed completely to the change. Either way, something that should not be in our universe."

"Wait!" He blinked and did a double take. "That thing could have been a channeler?!"

The only other channeler Ethan had met had been Mertin from the Order of the Scroll in Castlehaven. He still remembered the man's horns and tail. He knew channelers' bodies changed to match the demon they drew power from, but he had no idea it could be so extensive. He was suddenly VERY glad he hadn't chosen channeler as his class.

The wizard nodded sadly. "You know that channelers slowly change to become more like their demon patron."

"Yes." Ethan nodded, remembering what he'd learned. "The more channelers use the magic of their host - or whatever you call it - give them, the more they physically transform into a semblance of the host."

"Correct." Michalus smiled as if he were a teacher hearing a correct answer from his student. "That is absolutely correct. But that's not the entire story."

Ethan arched an eyebrow. "Oh?"

"It's not just a physical change," the wizard revealed. "It's a mental one too. Some scholars even theorized that the channelers become a version of the host and thus, in some way, allows the host to enter our universe."

Furrowing his brow, Ethan let the disgust show on his face. "Why would anyone do that?!"

"Power, my boy. Power," the wizard answered. "Wizards, like us, take for granted the enormous power we have at our command. We can burn things to the ground, lift up heavy objects, freeze things, shape earth and stone - some of us can even create portals."

The wizard was right. He'd gotten so used to his power that he did take it for granted. He shook his head as he realized that it was only a few months ago that he was a computer tech, working an eight to five job for a computer repair company. Now he was wielding power that only fictional characters in comics, movies and TV shows could wield.

Ethan nodded. "You're right. It's become second nature to me now."

"As it should be," Michalus chuckled. "As it should be. You're a wizard. A new wizard, but you've developed your power remarkably fast. Frankly, faster than anyone I've known or even heard about."

If Ethan detected a hint of jealousy in the wizard's voice, it was gone in an instant. Michalus was too good-natured to be jealous of others. Plus, he suspected the elf was just as interested in the study and theory of magic as he was in actually performing magic.

"But imagine if you didn't have that power and someone offered it to you," Michalus suggested. "Imagine being a farmer with the ability to plow a field with a thought. Or a guardsman who can catch criminals in bonds of air. Or even a soldier who can burn his enemies to ash. What would you give to go from a no-name commoner to someone of power?"

"I still don't think I would," Ethan said. He thought he

meant it to. He knew he wasn't the type to go after power at any cost. He thought back to some of his buddies. At least one of them would have jumped at the opportunity in an instant - consequences be damned.

Michalus eyed him for a moment. "You know, my boy, I don't think you would. I'd like to believe I wouldn't either. But there are people who would. Some of them are tricked and don't understand what they're signing up for. Others stop using the power once they realize how far the transformation has gone. Others don't, or can't, stop."

"And they transform all the way?" Ethan asked.

The wizard shook his head, his eyes sad. "Most of them die. Our bodies just weren't meant to handle that amount of... change."

Ethan furrowed his brow in confusion. "Then..."

"Then how do you get something like that?" Michalus chuckled, gesturing at the river. "Some demons, very few thankfully, grant their channelers not only their normal magical energy. The most powerful demons can also grant them a secondary power, like a limited form of regeneration."

"What?" Ethan thought of one his favorite comic book characters with a metal skeleton and claws who could regenerate from any wound almost instantly. "Like a healing factor?"

The wizard shrugged. "I suppose you could call it that. The demon lords have that power innately, along with whatever elemental power they possess. They grant it to their channelers not out of any kindness, but so that the transformation will have a greater chance of success."

Ethan whistled. "And a part of the demon enters this world."

"Exactly," the elf confirmed.

A terrible thought made Ethan start. He turned towards the river, eyes straining. "Do you think the creature is regenerating?"

Michalus chuckled. "Oh, I don't think it will regenerate from your boulder to the brain. If the brain dies, the body dies. The body has to receive signals from the brain in order to regenerate. And I don't think there was enough of its brain left to regenerate anything."

Letting out a breath, Ethan let his body sag. He'd had visions of the creature suddenly bursting out of the river and crawling towards them - intent on vengeance.

Thinking of the creature and Michalus's statement, Ethan turned to the wizard. "You said the thing had regenerative powers, right?"

"Yes," he replied.

"Would those regenerative powers have given it long life?" he asked the wizard. He was thinking again of the superhero mutant with regeneration powers. In the comics, his regeneration allowed him to live for an exceptionally long time. He was also thinking about the comments Ainslee had said about some of the items being decades or even hundreds of years old.

Michalus rubbed his chin for a long moment before nodding. "That's very possible. I've read some theories about that. The regenerative nature of the power has been hypothesized to be able to extend life. Though I don't remember reading any conclusive evidence."

Ethan gestured to all of the items lying around the

riverside. "This thing had to have been here for a very long time."

"Very possible," the wizard said, rubbing his chin again. "Very possible. Once it fully transformed, it might have had whatever lifespan the creature would have had in its own dimension. Or perhaps it did not age at all."

Ethan rolled his eyes and let out a frustrated breath. "You'd think that, if there was a giant Cthulhu-like monster living under a bridge, someone would have thought to put a warning sign!"

The wizard chuckled. "Perhaps. But it might have slumbered for years between feastings. Who knows how long the energy it drains from its victims can sustain it. It could have slept for ten, fifteen or even twenty years between attacks. Enough time for the locals to believe it was only a rumor or legend."

"Still," Ethan muttered. "A sign would have been nice."

"Yes, it would! Unfortunately, in life, there are very few warning signs of what's ahead." Michalus chuckled again and clapped Ethan on the back before going and checking on Yuliana.

Left by himself, Ethan stared off into the forest where Nia had disappeared. He wanted to go after her, but he knew she didn't want him to. She needed time alone. He let out a heavy sigh. He hoped she didn't need too much time alone. He hoped that whatever was bothering her, she'd share it with him.

Walking back to the pile of items on the shore, Ethan began going through the items. He didn't really care about them, but it was something to take his mind off of Nia.

By the time Nia returned, just before dark, Ethan had

collected several pouches worth of gold coins and even more silver and copper. It was a small fortune. And yet, he felt no joy in it.

The only thing that even partially lifted his spirits was a bag of crystals he'd found inside one of the metal coffers. Chymera crystals. Enough for him to make a few more portal pouches, maybe even some more interesting items.

When he saw Nia return, he left the remaining stuff and walked back to the campsite where Ainslee already had a fire going. He was hoping the time alone would have made the foxgirl feel better. But that didn't seem to be the case.

He watched as Nia dropped to her bedroll, legs tucked in and arms around her knees. She was just staring at the fire while Ainslee cut off strips from the deer the foxgirl had killed.

But the food wasn't what caught his attention. Ethan couldn't help but notice that Nia's bedroll was on the opposite side of the fire from his. They'd been sleeping next to each other for weeks. The message was clear. Stay away.

Ethan was muttering a curse under his breath when Ainslee looked up at him with a grin. "Hey wizard-boy, can you make one of those gr... gor... gorilla things to cook on?"

Unable to help himself, Ethan chuckled softly. "A grill?"

"Yeah... that's what I said... a grill," the dwarf replied without missing a beat.

23

Nia was already gone hunting when Ethan woke the next morning. She returned with two of the reptilian turkey creatures called cockatrices, that tasted, more or less, like chicken. The foxgirl gave them to Ainslee, packed up her belongings and then announced that she would be scouting around the area for enemies before disappearing back into the woods.

It all happened so abruptly that he was still staring at where Nia had disappeared into the woods before Ethan thought to say something. When she was out of sight, all heads turned to him. Embarrassed, hurt and a little angry, he just shrugged. "Probably not a bad idea."

He wanted to go after the foxgirl and talk out whatever was bothering her, but Nia's abrupt actions made it very clear she didn't want to talk with him. She didn't even want to be near him.

Ethan raged inside, but not at Nia. He had no idea what sort of things the Sollasina had done to her. Or how it had affected her. Ainslee seemed to have some natural resistance to it and she was over a hundred years old. Michalus was similar. The wizard was hundreds of years old. He had the experience to balance the insane images the creature had shown him.

Even he was different. Exposure to horror movies, news, and TV shows in high definition had possibly numbed Ethan to the creature's mental attack - to a certain degree. Though it had been the thought of hurting Nia that had really knocked him out of the thing's mental grip.

Nia was different. She was nowhere near as old as either Ainslee or Michalus. She was young, despite the relative age of her species. She didn't have hundreds of years of experiences to fall back on. Nor Ethan's desensitization from modern media.

Turning away from the forest, Ethan faced the river. Growling in anger and frustration, he closed his eyes and clenched his fists. He felt the anger surging through him, but he didn't fight it. He wanted to put his fist through something!

He wanted the Sollasina alive so he could kill it again, over and over. He heard a noise, but it was a buzzing in the back of his head as he imagined a number of ways to destroy the creature over and over.

"Ethan!" came Michalus's shouted voice, his tone insistent - almost panicky.

Ethan spun around, hands still clenched. Everyone was looking at him. "What?!"

The wizard gestured to Ethan's body. "You are channeling magic and not using it! You must stop!"

Ethan looked around and saw energy of all sorts was radiating from his body. His skin was literally glowing in swirling bands of color. For a moment, it reminded him of the Bifrost with its rainbow tunnel effect.

"Stop channeling, Ethan!" Michalus yelled again.

Taking a deep breath, Ethan consciously willed himself to let go of the magic. He held up his hand and watched the colors slowly fade until his skin was its usual color. As it did, he felt drained and tired.

He pulled up his HUD, almost afraid to look at it.

Mana: 11

Ethan blinked and read the number again. He was down to 11 *Mana* from his maximum of 84?! Had he really used up over 70 points in less than a minute? "What the -- ?"

"Are you okay, my boy?" Michalus asked, hurrying over to him. Ethan saw that neither Ainslee nor Yuliana made a move towards him. Even Par'karr just stared, open-mouthed at him.

"I'm fine," Ethan replied. "Just a little drained."

"Drained?!" snorted the wizard. "You're lucky you're not dead! Never channel magic into yourself without using it!"

Looking at his hand, which was normal again, Ethan frowned. "Was that the rainbow colors on my skin just now?"

Michalus nodded, his expression serious. "That's just the external manifestation of it. The power builds up inside you. It can literally burn you from the inside out!"

Ethan looked over his body again. He shrugged. "I don't feel any different. Though I used up almost all of my mana!"

The wizard shook his head. "You're lucky that's all you did. Your body can't take the strain of so much magic for that long!"

He suddenly remembered his experience in Arthur's tomb, where he'd absorbed more *Mana* than his body could handle. It had nearly killed him and the only thing that had saved him was the Holy Grail. He definitely didn't want a repeat of that.

"I wasn't trying to do it," Ethan told Michalus.

"You're so powerful." The wizard shook his head. "I forget how inexperienced you are."

Ethan opened his mouth to object but Michalus held up a hand to forestall him. "Most wizards take years to learn what you seem to master in days or weeks. That's both good and bad."

"Oh?" Ethan asked, curious why learning things faster would be bad.

"It's bad because most wizards are overcautious because our masters give us so many warnings," Michalus explained. "Perhaps a tad too many, in my humble opinion."

"But," the elven wizard continued. "It's good because it gives us wizards the time and discipline, we need to control the magic fully."

"I can control..." Ethan started but once again, Michalus held up his hand.

"You have remarkable control," he assured Ethan. "Much more than I would expect from someone of your age and limited experience. But what just happened shows you haven't fully mastered controlling your magic when you're extremely... emotionally.... distraught, shall we say."

"I was distraught," Ethan echoed with a chuckle. "I guess that's true enough."

"As I said," the formerly old wizard said grimly, "you're lucky you didn't burn up from the inside out."

"Spontaneous human combustion?" he replied with a raised eyebrow. "That's a thing here too?"

"More like wizard combustion," Michalus replied. "It doesn't just happen to human wizards. Wizards of all races have fallen victim."

"Fine," Ethan said. "I'll be more mindful of my emotions."

The elven wizard harrumphed. "See that you do! Burning up from the inside out seems a terrible way to go."

Ethan swallowed, once again remembering the pain he'd been in back in the tomb. If that was any indication, it would be a terrible way to go.

"The...uh ... cockatrice will be done soon," Ainslee announced, gesturing to the reptilian turkey carcass, cooking over the fire.

Nodding, Ethan turned back and walked down to the bridge. He sat down on the short, stone wall and stared down into the fast-moving waters below until Par'karr appeared with a leg of cockatrice.

"Ethan okay?" the kobold asked, handing Ethan a hot lizard-turkey leg.

It was almost too hot for Ethan to hold and he pulled

some of the heat out of the bottom portion with his magic. He looked at the little kobold and put on a smile. "I'm fine."

Par'karr shook his head. "Ethan not fine. Ethan sad. Ethan sad about Nia."

"You're right," Ethan admitted. "I am sad about Nia."

"Nia not same," the kobold said. "She not sleep next to Ethan. Not take Ethan hunting."

Ethan nodded dumbly, unsure whether the kobold's words were making him feel better or worse.

"Nia still like Ethan," the kobold told him.

Lowering the arm with the cockatrice leg, Ethan cocked his head at the kobold. "How do you know?"

"When Par'karr on watch, he see Nia looking at Ethan. She look for long time when she think Par'karr not watching. She have sad eyes. But she keep looking," the kobold related.

Unsure what to say, Ethan brought the cockatrice leg up to his mouth and took a bite. If Par'karr was telling him the truth, then Nia had been watching him. But what did that mean?

He gave the kobold a more genuine smile. "Thanks for telling me that, Par'karr."

The little kobold grinned and hurried back to the fire, leaving Ethan alone with his thoughts. At least for a time.

Before he knew it, the others were packed up and ready to go. Even Nia had emerged from the woods and saddled her horse.

Ethan stood up and walked back to the camp. Par'karr, who had packed up his bedroll, handed him the bundle.

He took his gratefully and, saddling his horse, tied his pack to the horse.

Once done, he mounted up with the rest of them, taking his place at the head of the line. Normally, Nia would have been right next to him, but he saw her starting to lead her horse to the back.

When the foxgirl caught him looking, she looked at him with no expression. "I will guard the rear."

Turning, she led her horse past the others, to the back. Ethan took a deep breath, remembering to control his emotions, and turned to the road.

Ainslee rode up next to him. He turned to look at the dwarf, who turned towards him with a big grin. "You look lonely up here, wizard-boy. Don't worry, I'll keep you company."

She turned her head towards Par'karr and gave the kobold a wink. The kobold grinned back.

Not waiting for him, Ainslee dug her heels into her mount and urged it forward, forcing Ethan to do the same to keep up with her. Behind him, the rest of the party followed.

Ethan quickly caught up to the dwarf and pulled his horse next to hers. She glanced back over her shoulder at Par'karr.

"Silly little kobold. Offered me his lunch if I'd ride up here with you." The dwarf snorted. "You know what they say, the way to a dwarf's heart is through her stomach."

24

The group traveled for two more days along in the shadow of the great trees of Sherwood Forest. The forest seemed to grow denser the further they went. That wasn't unexpected or surprising.

What was surprising were the Pteranodons. While the waterspouts in the ocean to the east were still as large and plentiful as any other stretch of ocean they encountered, the prehistoric reptilian birds began to quickly thin out. By the second day, there wasn't a Pteranodon in sight.

"Why do you think the lizard birds are gone, wizard-boy?" Ainslee asked, as she glanced out at the ocean.

Ethan shrugged on his horse. "I'm not sure."

"Maybe no fish here," Par'karr offered.

"Maybe." Ethan shrugged again. He looked into the dark, thick trees of Sherwood, then looked back at Michalus. The wizard was riding next to Yuliana and the two were talking quietly.

"Michalus," he called out, getting the elf's attention. "You said the forest is dangerous, right?"

"Oh yes," the wizard replied. "Few people who venture far into the woods return."

Ethan nodded and turned to Ainslee and gestured at trees. "My guess is, they can't nest in the forest for whatever reason."

"Monsters," Par'karr said quietly.

"Maybe," Ethan admitted. Though none of them had seen any monsters. They hadn't seen the talking, moving trees either but Ethan guessed they wouldn't be hanging out on the fringes of the treeline. "Or maybe they can't nest in these large trees for some reason."

"Because monsters!" Par'karr bobbed his head.

Ethan chuckled as he looked back at the little kobold but then he caught sight of Nia in the back and his mirth died.

The foxgirl had barely spoken to him since they left the river. For that matter, she'd barely talked to anyone. Ethan had tried to start up a conversation with her but she seemed to get nervous and agitated whenever he tried. After an awkward minute or two, she would make some excuse and leave.

He desperately wanted to know what was going on inside her head. He couldn't do that without having a real conversation with her. Unfortunately, that seemed impossible at the moment since she'd rebuffed the few attempts he had made. It made him feel helpless and he hated feeling helpless.

Helplessness was a feeling he was familiar with. He'd often felt a sense of helplessness about his life back on

Earth. But since he'd been dropped off on this world and had discovered he could do real magic, it hadn't haunted him like before.

Unfortunately, this time magic didn't appear to be the answer. At least, he had no idea how to apply the magic he knew to help Nia. Perhaps there was something he could do with the *Mental* magic skill, but it seemed too dangerous to fool around with.

Ethan sighed guiltily. He had actually considered using *Mental* magic on the foxgirl once or twice, even if he didn't know what he was doing. She was obviously in pain. At least, he assumed it was pain. Whatever it was, it was clearly bothering her. And if he could help...

He swore silently. No. He wasn't going to risk using *Mental* magic on Nia. At least, not until he knew what he was doing. That meant, he needed to practice. But how did he practice *Mental* magic?

Looking up at the sky, Ethan realized it was lunch time. He called a halt to their procession and dismounted his horse. "Let's take a break for lunch!"

The others followed his lead, dismounting and stretching their legs. Ethan found a log and tied his horse to it before facing the ocean.

"You gonna thaw some meat for us?" Ainslee asked, coming up beside him. The dwarf licked her lips. "I'm starvin!"

Ethan didn't answer. Instead, he looked out over the ocean, less than a mile away. Glancing up and down the shore, he looked closely for any Pteranodons. When he didn't spot any, he rubbed his chin. "Actually, I think I'm going to try fishing."

"Fishing?" Ainslee asked, giving him a look that clearly indicated she thought he was crazy.

Ethan grinned and started walking towards the shore. As he did, he used *Summon Lesser Elemental* and summoned an air elemental. Immediately, a large bird-like distortion appeared in the air near him.

While he'd summoned the minor version of his air elemental many times, this was the first time he'd actually summoned the more powerful lesser air elemental. Like the smaller version, the larger elemental was nearly transparent, appearing as only a distortion of light in the vague shape of a bird-like creature. A very large bird-like creature.

The elemental began flapping its wings, hovering a half dozen feet from him, at eye level. Its head turned his way and although Ethan couldn't see its eyes, he knew it was looking at him.

He pointed out to the waterspouts. "Fly out to the waterspouts but be careful. When one rises, fly into it and grab some fish. Bring the fish to me and drop them here at my feet. Then do it again."

The bird elemental continued to flap its wings while staring at him. Just as Ethan was getting uncomfortable, it turned its head to the ocean and then flew off amazingly fast.

"What in Loki's balls are you doing?" Ainslee asked.

"Ethan make bird go fish. Like lizard birds," Par'karr said enthusiastically.

Ethan turned to see everyone had gathered around him on the sandy beach - everyone but Nia. The foxgirl remained back with the horses. She was looking their way but when she saw Ethan looking, she turned away.

Growling quietly with frustration, Ethan turned back to the ocean. He looked for his elemental but against the moving waterspouts and ocean waves, he couldn't pick out the creature's distortion.

"You're having your elemental hunt the same thing that the Pteranodons hunt," Michalus observed with a nod. "Fascinating."

He grinned. "I actually thought of this before. But I wasn't about to try it with any actual Pteranodons near, in case they chased it. They seem territorial."

Par'karr bobbed his head. "Lizard birds go after dragon!"

"That's right!" Ethan remembered. When they had been on their way to Castlehaven, a dragon had flown overhead towards the ocean and a group of Pteranodons had come out to battle it. They'd been no match for the dragon but it did prove they were either territorial or suicidal.

"Not many things in this world can stand up to a dragon," Michalus noted gravely. "They are incredibly strong and durable creatures. Very magical."

"Magical?" Ethan asked with a raised eyebrow. He hadn't seen the dragon do any magic.

"Oh yes," the elven mage replied. "They can use magic, like us, and they live for thousands of years. If their sheer size and strength can't overcome an opponent, their magic can."

"Great," Ethan said, rolling his eyes. "Super powerful magical dragons, just one more thing to worry about."

He cocked his head as he saw a distortion coming at him. It was his air elemental and in its talons, it held two wiggling fish. The elemental swooped down near him and dropped the fish at his feet. Its task complete, the elemental hovered a few feet from him.

Ethan looked down at the two large fish wiggling on the ground in front of him. Before he could do anything, Luna bounded forward and grabbed one in her mouth. With her paw, she ripped it in half and crunched down on the head. After a few chews, the mountain lion finished off the rest of it.

The group watched the cat quickly finish off her fish and then look down at the remaining fish. Par'karr chuckled. "Big cat hungry!"

The cat looked from Ethan to the remaining fish, as if asking permission to have the second one. He shook his head. "Go ahead, Luna."

"Sorry," Yuliana said as the big cat happily grabbed the remaining fish and quickly finished it off. "She must have been really hungry."

"Or she like fish," Par'karr offered.

Ethan shrugged. There were plenty of fish in the sea, as the saying went. He commanded his elemental to go get them more fish.

"If we're having fish," Ainslee said, rubbing her hands together in anticipation, "I'll go get a fire going."

Ainslee and Par'karr went back to the horses to look for wood for a fire while Michalus and Yuliana stayed for a few minutes to await the next catch. When a few more fish had been caught by the elemental, the two of them carried the fish up to the fire to begin cooking them.

Ethan stayed on the beach until the elemental had caught over a dozen fish and then dismissed the air elemental and carried the remaining fish up to the others. When he reached them, he looked around for Nia but the foxgirl was nowhere to be seen.

"Where's Nia?" he asked.

"Ow!" Ainslee yelped as she took a bite of steaming fish. "She said she would scout around."

"Did she eat before she left?" Ethan asked, concerned for the foxgirl.

The others looked around at each other before giving little shrugs. He sighed and looked at Ainslee. "Make sure you save her some!"

Ainslee managed to give him an indignant look, but it was ruined by the fact that she was stuffing another large bite of fish into her mouth. "Wha-? Why ju luukin' at mey?"

25

———

After eating lunch and freezing the few extra fish fillets they didn't eat, the group got back on the trail. They rode until an hour before sundown and then found an area to set up camp. Once Ethan said he would use his air elemental to get more fish, Nia immediately announced that she would go look for berries and nuts. Before anyone could question her, she had ducked into the trees and disappeared into the forest.

Ethan was concerned about Nia going into Sherwood Forest alone. After the stories Michalus had told him, he didn't feel it was safe - even for someone with Nia's skills. When he mentioned this to the elf, the wizard told him not to worry, that she was staying close to the edge of the forest. It was the deep forest people didn't return from.

Mollified, at least for the moment, Ethan walked down towards the ocean and summoned his lesser air elemental. He set the creature about the task of fishing and sat down on the sand. He'd been thinking all afternoon of how to test his *Mental* magic and had a few ideas he wanted to try.

He checked to make sure the others were back up at the campsite. Once he was confident no one was around, he looked around for his first victim. Unfortunately, there wasn't much to choose from. The only things he spied were crabs near the water and the ever-present seagulls.

One of the seagulls was the closest, being only ten feet or so away from him. It was pecking at a small crab that had been unfortunate enough to garner its attention. Ethan nodded. The seagull would be his first victim.

Still unsure exactly what *Mental* magic was, Ethan had decided to experiment with various mental powers from various mutants from some of the comic books he'd read and TV shows he'd seen. First on the list, mental command.

His timing seemed impeccable because at the moment, the seagull finally managed to seize the small crab by one of its legs, lifting the crustacean off the sand. Ethan focused on the seagull, willing it to drop the crab and then pushed some *Mana* into his suggestion.

Skill increase: Mental magic +1%.

The seagull dropped the crab. Ethan frowned, unsure if it had been his magic or if it had just done it on its own accord. Then the seagull turned its head and looked directly at Ethan. It began squawking loudly and launched itself into the air, circling until it met up with the other seagulls flying overhead.

Ethan looked at where the seagull had been. Had it

actually worked? Or had it been a coincidence? He looked at his HUD and saw the skill increase. He checked his *Mana* level.

Mana: 70

He'd been at his maximum *Mana* of 84 when he walked on to the beach. Ethan had used 10 *Mana* to summon the lesser elemental, which would have dropped him to 74. Since he was at 70 now, that meant his mental command had cost him 4 *Mana*.

Only 4 *Mana* for a mental command wasn't bad, but it hadn't been a complex command and seagulls weren't very intelligent creatures. At least, he didn't think they were. Still, just because he'd used *Mana*, did that mean it actually worked? He wasn't sure. But it was promising. He needed more testing.

The seagull was gone and the crab had disappeared into a nearby hole, so Ethan glanced around for another victim. He walked a few dozen paces until he found another seagull near the water.

Reaching out with his mind, he commanded the thing to walk towards him and then pushed some *Mana* into the command.

Skill increase: Mental magic +1%.

The seagull stopped in its tracks. It stayed frozen for a second before turning towards Ethan. Then, slowly it began walking towards him.

He sent another message: Stop and don't move.

Skill increase: Mental magic +1%.

The seagull froze, though its eyes looked panicked. Ethan wasn't sure why. Did it KNOW he was manipulating it? If so, how? Did the bird somehow sense its will was being overwritten?

The seagull suddenly flapped its wings and took off into the sky, squawking loudly. Ethan briefly considered giving it a command to return, but he was starting to feel uncomfortable with his powers.

It wasn't like in the comic books, where someone could be made to do something, and they didn't even know they were being manipulated. If these seagulls were any indication, then the creature knew they were being controlled. And given how both seagulls had stared at him, Ethan thought they knew he was doing it.

The air elemental dropped more fish at his feet, startling him. Ethan looked up at the large bird-shaped distortion. He meant to say "Thank you" but since he'd just been playing with his *Mental* magic, he thought it instead. Unconsciously, he put some *Mana* behind it.

Thank you, he sent, looking down at the wiggling fish.

Skill increase: Mental magic +1%.

You are welcome, master, the air elemental's "voice" echoed in his head.

Skill increase: Mental magic +1%.

Ethan nearly jumped out of his skin when he heard

the elemental's voice in his head. It was a strange voice, deep and monotone, but he instantly knew it wasn't his voice. And yet, he was communicating mentally with another creature!

You can... understand me? Ethan thought at the elemental.

Skill increase: Mental magic +1%.

Of course, it replied. *I am here to serve.*

Skill increase: Mental magic +1%.

That was an interesting response. The air elemental was here to serve. But it was here from where?

Where are you from? he asked it.

Skill increase: Mental magic +1%.

I am from a world much different from this, it replied. It was beating its wings to maintain its altitude but had lowered its head to be level with Ethan's.

Skill increase: Mental magic +1%.

Ethan was starting to get a bit freaked out. He'd thought the elementals were just constructs, made of magic and an element. This seemed almost like the summoning that Par'karr did. The summoning of rabbits from the demon world. That begged a question.

Skill increase: Mental magic +1%.

Are you a demon? Ethan asked the elemental cautiously.

Skill increase: Mental magic +1%.

No. My kind are not demons, though we know of demons, the elemental replied.

Skill increase: Mental magic +1%.

Ethan hoped it couldn't read anything but the thoughts he sent because at the moment he wasn't sure he could trust its words. After all, would a demon admit it was a demon?

He decided to change topics. *Why do you come when I summon you?*

Skill increase: Mental magic +1%.

We serve the Elder Gods, it replied. *A pact was formed long ago between the wizards of this world and the Elder Gods of my world. We come when we are called and help how we can to prevent the Fall. If this world falls. All worlds fall.*

Skill increase: Mental magic +1%.

Feeling suddenly drained, he brought up his HUD.

Mana: 26

His *Mana* was draining rapidly with this telepathic conversation. He knew he'd have to end it soon. He left his HUD open so he could monitor his levels.

I am running out of Mana, he told it. *Perhaps we can speak later.*

Skill increase: Mental magic +1%.
   Mana: 22

Perhaps, the elemental replied. *But it may not be me who answers next time.*

Skill increase: Mental magic +1%.
   Mana: 18

It's someone different each time I summon you? he asked. His *Mana* was getting dangerously low and he knew he had to end the conversation very soon. Yet, the revelation that it wasn't the same elemental each time was something he wanted to explore.

Skill increase: Mental magic +1%.
   Mana: 14

Yes, whoever is closest to the portal, it replied.

Skill increase: Mental magic +1%.
   Mana: 10

Ethan realized he was out of time, or more appropriately, he was out of *Mana*. He cursed silently, knowing he had to let go of the conversation.

Perhaps we'll talk again, he told it.

```
Skill increase: Mental magic +1%.
   Mana: 6
```

Perhaps, it replied and Ethan cut the connection. He wasn't sure exactly how, but he felt the connection sever.

```
Skill increase: Mental magic +1%.
   Mana: 4
```

Feeling mentally drained, Ethan nonetheless looked at the elemental. He smiled at it. Then, remembering the fish, he did a quick count and looked back at the elemental.

"Before you leave, if you could grab a few more fish, I'd be grateful," he told the elemental aloud.

The elemental inclined its translucent head and then flapped and flew back towards the waterspouts. It obviously understood him. He might even be able to send his thoughts to it through the normal summoning spell. It just had no way to communicate back to him.

Ethan watched the translucent shape disappear among the motion of the spouts and the ocean. He was mentally fatigued, but he had managed to increase his skill in *Mental* magic. He'd also learned that the air elementals were sentient beings from another world - or universe - or maybe a completely different dimension.

The revelation was exciting, but it made him reconsider how he was using them. If they felt pain, like any other sentient creature, that really changed how he could ethically use them. He checked his *Mana*.

Mana: 4

He wasn't getting any more answers at the moment. His *Mana* was too low to do any more telepathic conversations.

While Ethan was caught up in his thoughts, the elemental obediently brought a half dozen more fish and dropped them on the ground in front of him.

"Thanks again," Ethan told the elemental. Once again, the creature inclined its head, once again proving it could understand him. Ethan inclined his own head and then dismissed the elemental to return to its own world.

He'd learned much today, even if it wasn't what he'd set out to learn. Still, it was fascinating, and he wanted to talk over what he learned about the elementals with Michalus later that night.

Reaching down, he picked up the fish and began walking back to the campsite. He thought about his practice session. Ethan had managed to increase his skill though he wasn't quite sure how increasing his skill might help him.

Ethan still needed to do more experimentation once his *Mana* regenerated. He needed to understand the skill and how it worked. Most importantly, he needed to master *Mental* magic and help Nia get back to normal.

That night Ethan used his time on watch to practice *Mental* magic on the horses. He wasn't sure if it would work but he'd been able to communicate with them on a very basic level. Very basic. Their conversations consisted of asking about apples and asking if it was time to go. Still, he managed to get some additional skill increases before his *Mana* ran out.

The next morning, he went "fishing" again with his elemental. He tried communicating with it again, only to learn that it wasn't the same elemental he'd spoken to before. This one didn't seem very interested in talking, it just wanted to do its task and go home.

Ethan explained the fishing process to the elemental and then let it go about getting fish before dismissing it and making fish for breakfast. Nia, who had been gone when he woke, came back with a pouch full of nuts for Yuliana.

The elf accepted the nuts and thanked the foxgirl but

Nia barely acknowledged her. Instead, she began silently packing her bedroll and then began saddling the horses.

While she was saddling Ethan's horse, he walked over. "Nia..."

The foxgirl stiffened, her ears going back and tail freezing in place. She didn't verbally acknowledge him but was still.

"...if you want to talk, I'm always here." He waited but she didn't move and didn't respond.

Feeling like an idiot, Ethan struggled to think of something else to say. It was obvious he made her uncomfortable and it was equally obvious that she didn't want to talk. He turned and, seething, stalked away.

Ethan was angry, but not at Nia. Well, mostly not at Nia. This wasn't her fault. It was that creature and whatever it had done to her head. But what HAD it done? Why was Ainslee, Michalus and he okay now and Nia still affected? And she wasn't just mildly affected. It was almost as if she were a different person.

He frowned as he repeated his last thought. She really did seem like a different person now. But what could the Sollasina have done to her that would have affected her so deeply?

He cursed silently. It was almost like a computer virus affecting a client's hard drive. The symptoms were obvious - the computer was doing weird things that it didn't usually do. But to find out exactly what was wrong, he would normally run a virus scanner on the computer, find what virus was infecting it. Then it was just a matter of quarantining the infected files.

It all sounded logical when he put it in computer

terms. The problem was, Nia wasn't a computer and he didn't have any anti-virus software for her. He scratched his chin. Or did he?

He'd practiced communicating with the animals and could get a general feel for their minds even without expending any *Mana*. Could he somehow "scan" minds without actually initiating a link?

There was only one way to find out - he needed to practice on someone. And the only person he was certain would agree was Par'karr.

"Par'karr," he said to the kobold as he was getting his pack ready.

Par'karr looked up and grinned. "You need something from Par'karr?"

"Actually," he smiled, "I do. Can you take a walk with me on the beach? I want to see if we can use your rabbits for spearfishing."

The kobold gave him a quizzical look. "Par'karr rabbits fish?"

Michalus looked up at Ethan with a raised eyebrow. Ethan didn't want to tell anyone what he was doing. At least, not within earshot of Nia. He gestured to the water. "If we're going to be in a Pteranodon-free area for a while, we might as well have as many fishers as possible. I'm certain your elemental can do the same thing my does. I want to see if Par'karr's rabbits can fish or if it will just be us two."

"Oh, yes." The wizard nodded. "Any time you want me to help with the fishing, you just let me know."

"Thanks, this shouldn't take long," Ethan replied and

then, gesturing for Par'karr to follow him, walked out onto the beach.

Par'karr, and his rabbits, followed Ethan out onto the beach. He led them as close to the beach as he dared, then walked along the beach until the camp was out of sight. The elves' hearing was sharp, so he hoped the distance and the sounds of the ocean would drown out their conversation.

Stopping, he bent down and lowered his voice. "Can you send your rabbits towards the water and see if they can spear any fish on their horns and then bring them back to us?"

The kobold bobbed his head up and down and the rabbits took off towards the ocean. Ethan watched them run off for a second before turning back to Par'karr. "That's not the only reason I wanted you to come out here."

Par'karr gave him a quizzical look.

"Have you noticed that Nia isn't acting like her normal self?" he asked.

The kobold nodded sadly, his grin turning into a frown. "Nia not like Par'karr any more. Nia not talk to Par'karr."

"It's not just you," Ethan said with a shake of his head. "She doesn't seem to like me, either."

"She not sleep next to Ethan," the kobold blurted out. "Par'karr notice. Everyone notice."

Ethan sighed. He knew in the back of his mind that everyone noticed but hearing it aloud didn't make him feel any better. Quite the opposite. He put on a smile for the kobold. "That's right. She doesn't sleep next to me. But that's not all. I think the creature did something to her mind."

Par'karr just blinked at him. "Nia mind?"

"Yes," he confirmed. "I think it did something to her mind and I want to help her."

"Par'karr want to help too!" the kobold exclaimed, and Ethan put a finger to his lips.

"You can," Ethan said softly. "But this has to be a secret. The elves have good hearing, so we'll talk really quiet, okay?"

The kobold looked around conspiratorially before nodding. "Par'karr be quiet."

"I have an idea of how to help Nia. I want to use magic to scan her mind to see if I can find what is... broken," he said and looked at the kobold for confirmation he understood.

Par'karr nodded. "You use magic to heal Nia?"

Ethan frowned. "I'm not sure yet. First, I have to know what's wrong. That's what I want to practice. But I need someone to practice it on. Someone who can keep a secret."

While he didn't necessarily mind if the other members of the party knew, he didn't want Nia to know. It would be hard enough to scan the foxgirl when she wasn't aware. If she knew and resisted, Ethan had a feeling it might be impossible. At least, impossible for someone of his skill level.

"Par'karr good at keeping secrets!" The little kobold grinned.

"I know you are," Ethan said. He said it, but he didn't

know for certain. He'd never asked the kobold to keep a secret before. But he didn't really have a choice.

"I need you to let me scan your mind," Ethan told the kobold. "But you can't tell anyone that I'm practicing it on you."

"Scan Par'karr mind?" Par'karr blinked at him. "It hurt?"

"No." Ethan smiled. "It doesn't hurt. I've done something similar with the horses and with my elementals. If it does hurt, just let me know and we will stop."

The kobold bit his scaly lip. "Par'karr not mind some pain if it help Nia. Nia is Par'karr's friend."

He put his hand on the kobold's shoulder and gave it a squeeze. "She's my friend too."

Glancing around to make sure no one had followed them, Ethan let go of the kobold and backed up a step. He checked his *Mana* level.

Mana: 15

His *Mana* had regenerated slightly and he had enough to give his "mind scan" a try. "We can try now and you can tell me if it hurts, okay?"

"Okay," Par'karr agreed. "What Par'karr do?"

Ethan grinned. "Nothing. You can just stand there. I'll do all the work."

The kobold bobbed his head happily. "Par'karr do that."

Taking a breath, Ethan focused on the kobold. He reached out with his mind, as if he were about to push some *Mana* into a connection. He felt the kobold's... something. He didn't know exactly how to describe it. It was an... awareness... of the kobold's consciousness.

Skill increase: Mental magic +1%.

Ethan looked up at his HUD and saw the skill increase. He checked his *Mana* level and saw that it hadn't changed. That was interesting. He could get skill increases without actually expending any *Mana*. That could be a good thing. A very good thing.

He looked at Par'karr. "Did you feel anything?"

Par'karr shook his head. "Par'karr not feel anything. Ethan start yet?"

Grinning, Ethan nodded. "I did. I think that's the first step and something I can practice."

"Par'karr glad it not hurt," the kobold admitted.

"Me too," Ethan agreed. "I want to try different things, but not right now. I think I can focus enough while the horses are moving. If so, I can practice while we travel. Once I get the basics down, I'll want to go deeper."

"Deeper?" Par'karr said with a little trepidation.

Ethan gave him a reassuring smile. "It shouldn't hurt at all, but it will allow me to scan your mind - hopefully. That's what I need to do to Nia. Scan her mind so I can see if the creature did something to it."

The kobold nodded grimly. "Par'karr help. Par'karr and Ethan help Nia."

"That's right, buddy," Ethan told the kobold. "Hopefully, together we can figure out what's going on inside her head."

He'd just finished speaking when two of the three rabbits bounded into sight. Ethan looked at Par'karr. "Where's the third?"

"Third one crushed by wave. Boom!" the kobold said,

slapping his fist into his opposite hand. Then he shrugged. "Par'karr will re-summon."

As the other two got closer, Ethan saw that they had something on their horns, but it wasn't fish. Both rabbits had managed to spear medium-sized crabs with their horns.

"What that?" Par'karr said, craning his neck to get a better look at the impaled crustacean.

"A crab," Ethan chuckled. "It's not fish, but it's edible."

The kobold made a face. "Look too hard."

"You crack the shell, then eat what's inside," Ethan explained.

Par'karr made another face. "Too much work."

Ethan chuckled again. "I've heard some people say that."

"Come on," he told the kobold, pulling one of the crabs from the rabbit's horns. "Let's get back and tell everyone the good news."

27

Ethan and Par'karr returned and told the others about the rabbits' ability to spear crabs. He was surprised to learn that none of them had ever eaten crabs. He understood Yuliana never having them since she was vegetarian. Ainslee said her world didn't have crabs, though they had some crab-like, land-based creatures in the mountains but they tasted foul.

Michalus said he'd never had them either. Given the perilous nature of being so close to the waterspouts, they were much too dangerous to catch for average people. He did point out that crab was considered a rare delicacy among the rich merchants and princes.

Nia kept her distance during the entire conversation, busying herself with packing things up and tending the horses. As far as Ethan could tell, the foxgirl didn't look over once at the group. Her behaviour reminded him that he needed to do whatever he could to be able to help her.

Ainslee insisted on cooking the crabs before they left.

Ethan had intended to freeze the remaining fish fillets but found that Michalus had already done it.

"You're not the only wizard, my boy," the elf chuckled when Ethan had given him a curious look. "I'm not above doing my part."

Michalus, Ainslee and Ethan tried some of the grilled crab before leaving. As far as he could tell, it tasted like an Earth crab. Afterwards, the group mounted their horses and continued on their way.

During the trip, Ethan alternated between letting his *Mana* recharge and probing Par'karr's mind. As before, he was able to probe what he referred to as the "surface" of the kobold's mind without using any *Mana*. Not only didn't it cost *Mana*, Par'karr didn't seem to be able to detect that sort of probing.

Sometimes, especially at first, Ethan would probe too deeply and he'd use *Mana* to establish a connection. When that happened, Par'karr would cough. The cough was their agreed-on signal to let Ethan know the kobold could sense the connection.

When the connection happened, Ethan would usually sever it immediately, though sometimes he would telepathically "talk" with the kobold. Par'karr seemed to get a kick out of the telepathic communication and told Ethan it made him feel like a wizard.

By the time they stopped for lunch, Ethan received a welcome message in his HUD.

```
You have reached Rank 2 in Mental
Magic.
    +1 Intellect.
```

Ethan wasn't sure if the increased rank would translate into any additional abilities, but he looked forward to trying it after lunch.

Lunch consisted of more fish and a few crabs that Ethan and Par'karr caught and then it was back on the road.

While Ethan and Par'karr were out "fishing," he and the kobold discussed the next step, which was a deeper probe of the kobold's mind. While he wasn't sure what to expect, if comic books and movies were any indication, Ethan might be able to read Par'karr's thoughts and he made the kobold aware of that possibility.

For his part, Par'karr was excited at the possibility. The kobold enjoyed the telepathy and felt good that he was doing his part to help Nia.

Ethan was thankful that the kobold felt that way, though was still cautious about probing too deeply. Everyone had thoughts they wanted to keep buried. He didn't want to go digging around in things that shouldn't see the light of day.

The group ate their "seafood buffet" and then continued south along the road. During that time, Ethan probed the kobold's mind. At first, he tried the shallow approach but noticed that it was now only giving him skill-ups every fifth or sixth time.

Next, he tried the deeper probing and, as they agreed, Par'karr coughed when he felt the connection. Although he did send a few telepathic messages to the kobold, he focused on reading surface thoughts and then trying to go deeper and pull out memories.

The process was much more difficult and intense than it was portrayed in the comics and movies whenever they showed someone with mental powers. It was also exhausting. Or perhaps he should say, it was mentally fatiguing, since it didn't affect his *Stamina*.

By the time the group stopped for the evening, Ethan was ready for the break. He and Par'karr went "fishing" again and the kobold chatted excitedly about sensing Ethan in his head.

Listening to Par'karr relate how it felt, Ethan became frustrated. How did a wizard with *Mental* magic ever get away with anything if everyone could feel them in their head? Was that why *Mental* magic was so rare? Wizards didn't pursue it because people sensed when you were in their head?

It seemed so limiting. He thought about the principles of magic he'd learned so far. Michalus had said that the magic happened because the wizard willed it and that it was will that shaped the effect.

That made sense to him from an elemental magic standpoint. Think of a fireball, will it and get a fireball. Think of an air shield, will it and you get an air shield. It seemed straightforward and he thought he had a good grasp on it.

So why was *Mental* magic different? Why did people realize you were in their heads? Hadn't Michalus said that *Mental* magic allowed illusions? How would an illusion work if you felt someone in your mind?

Ethan stopped suddenly as realization hit him. *Mental* magic wasn't any different from elemental magic!

Everyone SAW the effect of elemental magic - with the possible exception of *Air* magic, which was naturally invisible. But the point was, just like *Mental* magic, people did know that elemental magic was happening because of the effect.

Since *Mental* magic had no visible effect, people couldn't see it, but they did feel it. And why could they feel it? Because Ethan was making no attempt to conceal his attempts. He wasn't trying to be stealthy about it, he was just trying to do it.

Excited, he looked down at Par'karr. The kobold had stopped when Ethan had stopped and was staring up at him.

"Ethan okay?" the kobold asked.

"Better than okay," Ethan replied excitedly, "if my theory is correct!"

"Theory?" The kobold tilted his head and looked at Ethan quizzically.

Ethan brought up his HUD and checked his stats.

Mana: 23

His *Mana* had regenerated a bit and he thought he should have enough to test out his theory. He looked at Par'karr. "I think I may have figured out a way to probe your mind without you knowing. Is it okay if I test it?"

The kobold bobbed his head up and down enthusiastically. "Ethan can test!"

Giving Par'karr a grin, Ethan focused his will. Like he'd done many times that afternoon, he started to probe at the kobold's mind but this time, he willed it to be undetected. Then he fed some *Mana* into it.

As had happened previously, Ethan began picking up on Par'karr's surface thoughts. He looked down at the kobold to see if he would give Ethan a sign but Par'karr just continued to look up at him expectantly.

Experimentally, Ethan delved deeper, bringing up a memory of earlier in the day when they were riding. He looked down at Par'karr but there was still no reaction. Starting to feel tired, Ethan brought up his HUD.

Mana: 6

Ethan cursed and severed the connection. He'd just gone through 17 *Mana* in less than a minute. Apparently, getting into someone's mind without them knowing it was more *Mana*-intensive than doing it without the subtlety.

"It not work?" the kobold frowned.

"You didn't feel anything?" Ethan asked.

Par'karr shook his head. "Par'karr not feel Ethan."

He grinned. "I was in your head! But it took a lot more mana than I thought."

"It work?!" the kobold asked with wide eyes.

"It did!" he replied, his smile slipping.

Ethan thought about Nia and using his *Mental* magic on the foxgirl. He wanted to help her, but he didn't think she would agree to it. That meant, if he wanted to help, he had to do it stealthily - without her knowledge.

The idea of going into someone's mind without their consent seemed wrong. After all, he certainly wouldn't want someone going into his mind without his permission.

"What wrong?" Par'karr asked, concern etched on the scaly face.

"I think I could look inside Nia's mind," he told the kobold. "But I don't know if that's the right thing to do without asking her."

"Nia not talk to anyone," the kobold said sadly.

"I know," he replied. "But I don't think I should try to help her without her permission."

The kobold scratched his head. "If Par'karr knocked out, Ethan ask permission to heal Par'karr?"

Ethan blinked. That was an angle he hadn't considered. There were times when you had to help people, even without their permission. But still, going into someone's mind was different. It revealed things - private things.

"It's not quite the same," he said. "I could see things that she doesn't want me to see."

"Ethan care about Nia?" Par'karr asked.

"Of course," Ethan replied instantly.

"Nia care about Ethan?" the kobold followed up.

Ethan was seeing where the kobold's line of reasoning was going. "Yes, but..."

"Why Ethan not help Nia then?" Par'karr asked.

Ethan nodded, not knowing how to answer the kobold's question. For Par'karr, it was simple - if he could help, he did. There was no hesitation or worry about offending the other person. The kobold would just do it.

Despite the kobold's words, Ethan still felt going into someone's mind would be a violation of the person's privacy. After all, what would be more private than a person's thoughts.

And yet, if the situation was reversed and Ethan was the one who was going through some sort of mental trauma, wouldn't he want someone to help him - even if he hadn't given them permission? It was a tough call.

"Let's head back," he told the kobold. They had enough fish and crabs and Ethan had a lot to think about.

28

E than gave the food to Ainslee who had taken over as "master griller" for Nia. It was hard to go wrong with the stone grills he'd shown Michalus how to make. Just lay the meat on the grill and flip it over when it was ready. Even the dwarf could do that. Plus, she liked to tear pieces of the food off - to test, of course. Or so she claimed.

After they'd eaten and it was Ethan's turn to take watch, he stared at the sleeping form of Nia for a long time before finally deciding to do what he could. He'd start with the surface-level scan that he'd been practicing on Par'karr. It didn't require any *Mana* and she wouldn't detect it. At least, that's what he hoped.

He took a deep breath. Summoning his will, he ran his magical sense across her mind - and instantly recoiled as he felt something "slither" away from his mental touch. It had just been a brief contact, but it felt so wrong that he'd pulled away instantly.

Breathing heavy, he stared down at the foxgirl as she stirred in her sleep. She made a little noise and her brow furrowed.

Frowning, Ethan tried to figure out what that strange mental slithering had been. Was that simply how Nia's brain worked? She was an alien after all. Obviously, her mind would be different from Par'karr's mind.

Still, something about it had felt wrong. Very wrong. And yet, there was something familiar about it. Something Ethan couldn't quite place.

He wiped his sweaty palms on his breeches and looked back at Nia. Ethan knew he had to try again. He hadn't gotten anything the first time. Nothing except that weird slithering feeling.

Focusing on the foxgirl again, Ethan reached out with his *Mental* magic. This time, there was no slithering, just a jumble of surface thoughts. He furrowed his brow. This was more like what he'd encountered with Par'karr. It seemed normal. Had he imagined the slithering?

Taking another deep breath, Ethan prepared to go deeper using the "stealth" technique he'd tried with Par'karr. He just hoped he was doing the right thing. Gritting his teeth and summoning up his will, he fed *Mana* into his thoughts and plunged in.

Immediately, something seized at him. Something slithering. It tried to wrap around him and pull his will in. At the same time, Nia's eyes snapped open and she snarled. The foxgirl stared daggers at him but Ethan felt like he was looking into the eyes of a stranger. There was nothing looking back at him that was familiar.

The slithering tried to tighten itself around him.

Feeling it closing around his own will, Ethan panicked. With effort, he pulled free and, channeling more *Mana*, slapped the mental tentacle away.

Ethan's blood went cold. *Mental* tentacle. Yes, that's what it had felt like. A tentacle... or mass of tentacles. And the sense of familiarity he'd had earlier - he realized where he'd felt it before. The Sollasina!

He stared into the alien eyes of Nia and realized he was right. Some way, somehow, the Sollasina - or its mind - was INSIDE the foxgirl.

Nia smiled without humor, the blank eyes looking at him, burrowing into him. She spoke but her voice was strange. "You will not stop me!"

The foxgirl pounced at him then and he barely had time to catch her in *Air*. At the same time, the tentacles lashed out at him and his will, trying to grasp him - trying to reach into his mind.

Ethan gritted his teeth as he fought back the invisible tentacles that tried to wrap around him. He could feel his *Mana* draining away with the exertion of maintaining the *Air* bonds around Nia's body while also fighting the mental war against the Sollasina.

The tentacles continued to reach around his mind, poking and prodding to find a weakness it could exploit. It was all he could do to keep it at bay. It was like a computer virus trying to infect a system and he didn't want to think what would happen once it got inside his mind.

"Michalus!" he growled but the elf didn't stir.

Even that little bit of distraction calling out to the elf had cost him a little bit of mental ground as the tentacles tightened their grip. Ethan was actively fighting it off, but he was wasting *Mana*. He needed a different strategy.

He thought back to his virus analogy. What stopped a virus from invading a system? Virus protection. Or a firewall! That's what he needed, a mental firewall.

Solidifying an image of what he wanted, he formed a mental wall around his mind and channeled some *Mana* into it. Instantly, the pressure on his mind eased and he felt anger and frustration from the mental presence.

Ethan also felt it trying to penetrate the wall and he wasn't sure how long it would last. After all, no firewall was perfect. He'd only bought himself a short reprieve.

Nia twisted, growled and spat in his bonds of *Air*, trying to get to him. Or maybe the Sollasina was just trying to get him to waste more *Mana*.

"MICHALUS!" he yelled, now able to focus his thoughts a little more.

This time, the elf stirred and so did everyone else. The wizard sat up and looked around. The others did likewise, their eyes taking in Nia and Ethan.

"Help me!" Nia said in a voice that sounded more like the old Nia. "He's hurting me!"

"What're you doin', wizard-boy?" Ainslee growled, rubbing sleep from her eyes.

Everyone looked at Ethan and he gritted his teeth as the tentacles clamped down on his firewall and squeezed, trying to crush his will. "The Sollasina... it's... in... her mind! Hold her... with <u>Air</u>!"

"He's hurting me!" Nia whined, her tone pitiful.

The group looked from Ethan to Nia and back.

Ainslee stood up and slapped a fist into her open hand. "Let her go, wizard-boy!"

Ethan growled as the tentacle onslaught continued. Splitting his *Mana* between the *Air* and the *Mental* magic was taxing him quickly and he knew he had to be getting low.

"Does that... sound like... Nia?" Ethan said through gritted teeth. "Has she... ever... asked for help... like that?"

Ainslee frowned and looked at the foxgirl. "Now that you mention it, she ain't ever asked for help before."

Nia gave them a pitiful look. "He's hurting me!"

"She... never... admits... she's in pain," he gasped as the tentacles pressed even more tightly. "It's not... Nia... it's the Sollasina. It's... in... her head."

Michalus looked at Ethan and then at Nia and seemed to make up his mind. Grabbing his staff, the Chymera crystal at the top of it glowed with blue light. He nodded to Ethan. "I have her. You can let go."

Letting the Air slip away, Ethan focused all of his will on the mass of mental tentacles bombarding his firewall. It was still holding, for now, but he couldn't keep it up indefinitely. No. In this case, the best defense might be a good offense.

Leaving his firewall in place, he pushed his will back along the tentacles and into Nia's mind. He caught fragments of memories and emotions as he followed the trail deeper into the foxgirl's consciousness. He followed it until he reached the core. At least, that's what he thought of it as. It was the mental core of the Sollasina.

The Sollasina seemed to realize he'd reached it and was raising its own defenses. But it was weak, overconfident or simply hadn't expected him to find it, and the mental creature wasn't fast enough.

Reaching out with a mental claw, Ethan seized the core with all of his anger and frustration. He felt it squirm as the Sollasina Cthulhu tried to wriggle out of his grip. But that wasn't happening.

This thing had invaded his wife. The woman he loved. And it was going to pay. He grinned manically. "Time to play operation - the wacky wizard game!"

With as much will and *Mana* as he could muster, he pulled the squirming entity from Nia's head. He heard the foxgirl screaming but he focused on the squirming mass of mental tentacles. The tentacles, which had been trying to break through his mental firewall, retracted and instead tried to desperately find purchase in the foxgirl's mind.

Sensing what they were doing, Ethan became even more infuriated. He channeled what he thought of as mental fire and burned the tentacles away, as they tried to latch onto portions of her memories and emotions.

Part of him knew he might be hurting Nia, but he now knew that if he didn't kill or destroy this thing, it would completely consume the foxgirl. It might even be able to somehow transform her into a new Sollasina. No matter what, Ethan knew he had to destroy it.

"Kill... it..." Nia gasped. "Whatever it... takes...kill it!"

Ethan looked into Nia's eyes and saw pain and anger there. More importantly, he saw Nia. The creature's struggles with Ethan had loosened the thing's grip on her and he was talking to the real Nia. He nodded to the foxgirl.

Then, turning his full attention to the Sollasina, he pulled with everything he had while at the same time, bombarding it with mental fire. The combination seemed to do the trick and he felt the mental mass weakening.

It was like trying to pull something out of thick mud. It was barely moving, barely moving and then with a mental "pop," he ripped the Sollasina free of Nia's mind.

He held it there, suspended in nothing, with no mind to latch onto. He felt it raging and struggling but without any mind to feed it energy, it quickly withered. Ethan could sense it growing smaller and smaller as it consumed its own energy to stay alive for a few more precious seconds.

And then it was gone. Just like that, it was there one second and then completely gone the next. He felt around for it, trying to make sure it hadn't latched onto someone else but there was no sense of it at all.

The Sollasina Cthulhu was really dead. Still smiling, Ethan collapsed onto the ground.

29

When Ethan woke, he was lying on his bedroll with his blanket over him. The first thing he noticed was the ache in his head. Pain throbbed in his head and he felt like he had a bad hangover.

Ethan groaned quietly. He seemed to wake up feeling like he had a hangover way too frequently considering. Wasn't there supposed to be a fun part before the hangover? That was always the part he seemed to miss out on.

Looking up, he saw it was dark. Judging by the moons, it was near midnight. If it were still the same night, then he'd been out for hours. Remembering his fight with the Cthulhu-like creature, Ethan shot up into a sitting position. Heart racing, he looked around, startling Michalus.

"You're awake finally," the wizard commented with a yawn.

As things came back to him, Ethan glanced around

until he saw Nia lying on the opposite side of the fire. He looked back to Michalus. "Is Nia...okay?"

The elf gave him a sympathetic look but shrugged. "From what we could tell, she seems physically fine. She passed out about the same time you did and you're the first one awake."

Head still throbbing, Ethan rubbed his temples and summoned up his HUD.

```
Strength: 10
  Agility: 16
  Hardiness: 15
  Intellect: 30
  Intuition: 10
  Charisma: 8
  Health: 30
  Mana: 70
  Stamina: 48
```

He was a bit out of it, but he instantly recognized that he'd taken stat damage. Reading back through his messages, he saw that his mental battle with the Sollasina Cthulhu had caused him to deplete his *Mana* faster than he'd thought. His *Overchannel* ability had kicked in, burning up his stats when his *Mana* had run out.

It had left him weak but luckily, he had a cure for that. Ethan reached into his portal pouch and pulled out the Grail. Grabbing his water bottle, he poured some water into it and took a sip.

Immediately, he felt better as the golden chalice's power worked its magic on him. His headache vanished and he felt clear-headed and more energetic. Flipping back to his HUD, he checked out his stats again.

    Strength: 12
       Agility: 27
       Hardiness: 15
       Intellect: 36
       Intuition: 15
       Charisma: 12
       Health: 30
       Mana: 85
       Stamina: 60

Ethan frowned. His *Hardiness* had been at 16. Why hadn't it healed back up to normal? He thought about taking another sip from the Holy Grail but remembered it could only be used once a day per person. It was no big deal. He could always drink again tomorrow and finish healing himself.

He pushed the chalice through his portal pouch and set it back on its perch, inside the tomb of Arthur. Ethan started to ask Michalus a question but stopped and furrowed his brow. Something didn't seem right.

Previously, the Holy Grail had completely healed him of everything: wounds, stat damage, scars... everything. It also completely restored his *Mana*, *Health* and *Stamina*. So why didn't it heal all of his *Hardiness*?

Starting to have a sinking feeling, Ethan opened up his HUD. Bringing up the log, he scrolled through until he saw a message in red.

Using Overchannel has caused the permanent loss of 1 point of Hardiness.

Ethan cursed loudly before remembering everyone was asleep and lowering his voice.

"What's wrong, my boy?" Michalus asked, giving him a concerned look.

"I permanently lost a point of Hardiness," he retorted angrily, clenching and unclenching his fists. He looked around for something to kick, but there was nothing but trees and rocks - unless you counted Ainslee. He half grinned as he thought of kicking the dwarf but immediately dismissed the idea.

He swore again but kept his voice low. Ethan worked hard for that point of *Hardiness*. And since *Health* was twice your *Hardiness* and *Stamina* was four times your *Hardiness*, he'd lost 2 *Health* and 4 *Stamina* too!

Michalus nodded solemnly. "Channeling your own life force into *Mana* is a very dangerous proposition. And the more you use it, the more likely it is to cause too much strain on your body or mind."

"I've used it before though," Ethan countered. "And the Grail is supposed to heal ANYTHING."

"Some things can't be healed," the wizard replied and looked down at Nia. "Didn't you give us all a drink from the Grail after the Sollasina?"

Remembering back to the fight on the bridge, Ethan nodded.

"And yet, Nia became infected with a piece of the creature," Michalus pointed out.

Ethan let out a breath. The wizard was right. After seeing the miraculous things, the Grail could do and how it seemed to heal everything, Ethan hadn't really thought it had any limitations. Now he knew better. And it had cost him a point of *Hardiness*.

"You're right. I should have been more careful." He cursed again but then looked down at the sleeping form of Nia.

He had no idea what the Cthulhu creature would have done to Nia, but he knew it wouldn't have been pleasant. Ethan had a feeling, maybe something he'd learned from the creature's mind, the Sollasina would have destroyed Nia's consciousness and taken over her body. It had wanted to do the same with Ethan.

Ethan had fought the creature with everything he had - and then some. To save himself, sure, but also to save Nia from having her mind crushed. If all it cost to save his wife was a point of his *Hardiness*, then it was something he'd do again in a heartbeat.

Looking at it from that perspective, Ethan felt better. He smiled down at the sleeping foxgirl and then looked up at Michalus. "I saved her and that's the important thing."

"Indeed, it is. But I'm sure you'll earn back your Hardiness." The wizard nodded approvingly. He looked from Nia to Ethan and held his gaze. "You'd never earn another Nia."

"Good point." Ethan nodded and bit his lip, feeling his eyes moisten slightly. Michalus's words made him think about how close he'd come to actually losing Nia. He cleared his throat. "Very good point."

Thinking back to Nia and the Sollasina, Ethan looked around at Michalus and then to his other companions, sleeping near the fire.

"You're asking yourself whether or not it infected anyone else," Michalus said, catching Ethan off guard.

"That's exactly what I was thinking." Ethan narrowed his eyes and looked up at the elf. "Do you have mental magic too?"

The elf chuckled. "Boy, I don't need mental magic. I have many of your lifetimes of experience. It was written all over your face."

Michalus looked around at the others, his expression turning grave. "Plus, it's what I'd be thinking about now."

"You think I should scan everyone?" Ethan asked, though he was certain he already knew the elf's answer.

"Everyone." The wizard nodded. "Myself included."

"I can ask them tomorrow..." Ethan started but the wizard shook his head gravely.

"If anyone else is infected," he said. "They know what you can do. They could kill you in your sleep tonight, kill us all for that matter. Or, they could run off so the Sollasina can finish its work without your interference."

Ethan let out a heavy sigh. He really felt like invading a person's mind was a violation but considering what had happened with Nia, he felt he had no choice. He'd drunk from the Grail and would be at his strongest right now.

"Just be ready to help if I need you," Ethan told Michalus.

"You'd better start with me," the wizard said. "Just in case."

"Yeah, but wouldn't you have just not helped before? I mean, if you were infected?"

"Who knows what a Sollasina thinks. It's not human nor elven. It's hubris to think we would know how a creature like that thinks."

Nodding, Ethan prepared a very powerful <u>Air</u> to the head spell to throw at Michalus if he, or the Sollasina, tried anything. Hopefully it would be enough to knock out the wizard without actually snapping his neck. "Alright, let's get this party started."

Without hesitation, Ethan delved into the wizard's mind. Michalus's long life had given him so many memories that the elf's mind was vast - so much vaster than Nia's mind. Still, Ethan scanned through images, feelings and memories, looking for any trace of the Sollasina. Thankfully, there was none.

Next, Ethan scanned Ainslee. Her mind was not as vast as Michalus's had been, but it was much more structured and orderly than he would have given the dwarf credit for. Was that why she had not been affected as much by the Cthulhu? She came up negative as well.

"They're clear," Ethan announced but Michalus's expression didn't change. "Scan Yuliana, Par'karr, Luna and the horses."

Ethan frowned. "Why? They weren't even there when the thing attacked."

"They've been around Nia," he said simply. "And she was infected."

He glanced down at Nia and shuddered. Could the Sollasina really have used her to infect others? It was a frightening thought.

Taking the wizard's suggestion, Ethan scanned the others, including the horses. Luckily, none of them had any traces of the alien's mental presence.

"They're all clean," Ethan told the wizard as he stifled a yawn. The mental probing had drained his *Mana* and he was ready to catch some more shut eye.

Michalus let out a breath and seemed to relax. "Good. I'll sleep easier knowing I'm not going to have my mind stolen from me while I sleep."

"Speaking of sleep," Ethan yawned. "I'm going to try to get more sleep."

"Go right ahead," the wizard replied. "You've earned it."

Lying back down, Ethan shut his eyes and almost immediately fell asleep. Unfortunately, it was not restful and once again he had dreams of being chased. This time, there were insects coming for him. Despite running, hiding and all of his attempts to avoid them, the insects seemed to always find his trail and he was barely able to keep ahead of them.

30

Ethan awoke later to something pressed against him. He didn't have to open his eyes to know it was Nia. Her back was against him, her tail down near his feet. She was sobbing quietly.

"You okay, Nia?" he whispered, opening his eyes. He could only see the back of her head and the glow of the fire.

The foxgirl went still and she didn't reply, so Ethan put his arm around her and gave her a squeeze. Nia stayed rigid for a moment and then pressed herself more firmly against him. With her hand she took his and pulled his arm all the way around her, like a blanket, before resuming her quiet sobbing.

Unsure what to say, Ethan remained quiet and held the foxgirl. He had a lot of questions for her, but he knew this wasn't the right time. He'd wait until she was feeling up to talking. For the moment, he enjoyed the feeling of

Nia against him and, quite unintentionally, soon fell back to sleep.

When he awoke next, he could tell it was light out without even opening his eyes. He also didn't feel Nia next to him. Groaning, he opened his eyes and saw Ainslee and Par'karr huddled over the fire.

Par'karr looked over at him. "Michalus say let you sleep. Ethan okay?"

Yawning, Ethan pushed himself up and looked around. "Where's Nia?"

"Down by the beach, wizard-boy," she said, looking over at him. She nodded towards the beach. "You might want to go check on her."

Stifling another yawn, Ethan blinked and turned around to face the beach. Glancing around, he saw the foxgirl's red and cream tail flapping in the wind not too far from the water.

"Par'karr catch crabs," the kobold said.

Ethan was going to make a wisecrack but realized no one would understand it and gave the kobold a smile. "Good job."

"But you can thaw some of those fish," Ainslee suggested as he stood up. "The crabs might not be enough."

"Sure," Ethan said and went over to his backpack. He found several of the frozen bundles and, with a little *Fire* magic, thawed them enough that they could easily grill them.

"Where's Michalus and Yuliana?" he asked, tossing the fillets down on the grill.

"Elves look for berries," Par'karr answered.

Ainslee snickered. "Is that what we're calling it now?"

"What?" Ethan raised an eyebrow and Par'karr looked confused.

The dwarf just gave him a knowing smile. "I ain't got an anvil for a brain, wizard-boy. I see what's going on... even when I can't see what's going on."

"Uh," Ethan started but then realized he didn't have a good retort and shut his mouth. After all, he hadn't really thought the rest of the group wouldn't figure out what he and Nia were doing on their "hunting" trips.

Knowing he was probably turning red, Ethan spun and grabbed his shirt and his boots. "I'll go check on Nia."

He already wore his pants, so slipping on his boots and sliding his shirt over his head didn't take long. Thus dressed, he walked over the dunes and down onto the beach towards Nia.

"Mind if I join you?" Ethan asked as he got closer to the foxgirl.

Nia didn't look away from the ocean but patted the ground next to her. "You are always welcome, my alpha."

As he sat down, Nia grabbed his hand and pulled his arm around her shoulders. Then she leaned against him.

He shook his head. Nia was never this affectionate. At least, not unless they were making love. The poor foxgirl must have been through a terrible mental ordeal. He squeezed her tight. "I'm sorry for whatever you went through."

Nia stiffened slightly but didn't say anything. Then she began to sob.

"It'll be okay," Ethan said softly. "Whatever it did to you, it wasn't real."

She sobbed for several more minutes before lifting her head to look at him. "I woke up last night.... And... everything was different...."

Ethan furrowed his brow. "Different? How?"

He saw the foxgirl bite her lip before answering. "Everything was...gone."

"Gone?" Ethan said, even more confused. "What was gone?"

"Everything we had was gone," she repeated. "THEY were gone."

"They?" he asked. He had no idea what the foxgirl was talking about. Did she mean the creature's presence was gone?

Nia looked over at him. "Ethan, Ainslee told me what had happened since the creature attacked us. But I remember nothing of it. I was... somewhere else..."

"Somewhere else?" Ethan asked cautiously. Nia had been with them the entire time, so he wasn't sure what she meant.

The foxgirl looked around the beach, bottom lip trembling. "For me, it feels like a year has passed. Perhaps more."

"A year?!" he repeated incredulously. "But it's just been a few days."

"Not for me, Ethan," she said. "Not for me. I lived... a different life. You and I, we..."

The foxgirl looked out to the ocean and took a deep breath. "You were a great alpha and ruled all of the cities. I had your children. Two girls and a boy. They were strong. We were happy... so happy..."

Ethan realized his mouth was hanging open and

closed it. He'd thought the foxgirl had been mentally tortured - and maybe she had, just not in the traditional sense. The Sollasina hadn't shown her terrible images to torture her mind into submission.

It had been much more insidious. It had shown her happiness, maybe even bliss. A perfect fantasy world in her mind to keep it occupied while it slowly took over. Like dreams, whatever mental fantasy the creature had created distorted her sense of time. What was a few days in the real world was a year or more to her. And now it was all gone.

"I'm sorry," he told her and squeezed her against him.

"I miss them," she sobbed into his shoulder. "Braiden, Jade and Paige. I miss them, but they were not real."

Ethan continued to hold her until Par'karr yelled that if they didn't come quickly, Ainslee would eat their food.

"I am not hungry," the foxgirl told him.

Standing, he reached down and took her hand. Gently, he pulled her to her feet. "Maybe not, but you need to keep up your strength. You've been through an ordeal - even if it seemed pleasant at the time."

"Everything was so perfect," the foxgirl said sadly, a far-off look in her eyes.

"I'm sure that was its intention," he told her. "Create a perfect world. Give you everything you wanted so that you were so satisfied with it that you didn't resist. Then it slowly took over your mind."

Nia shivered. "I think... I think part of me knew it wasn't real. That it was too good. But it was just so..."

"Perfect," Ethan finished.

"Perfect." She nodded.

It was hard for Ethan to imagine what it would feel like to lose what she had thought were real children. Especially after a year, or however long it had been in her mind. It would be like losing real children. He silently cursed the Sollasina.

He thought about her perfect world. A world where she had his children. Part of him bristled at the idea. He'd never really thought about kids. Actually, that wasn't true. He'd thought about the concept of kids. But since he hadn't had any long-term relationships, it had never really been a possibility.

Ethan glanced at the foxgirl. She might want children, but she would never have his children. They were different species. It just wasn't possible. It would be like a cat trying to have children with a dog.

Unsure if she knew they couldn't have kids, Ethan decided to keep that to himself for now. There was no reason to add that burden on her at the moment. Especially not considering what she'd just experienced.

"This isn't perfect. But it's real." Ethan gave her a smile and gestured around.

After he said it, he almost regretted it. There was still some part of his own mind that wondered if he was in some alien simulation and none of this was actually real. But he'd keep that to himself for now. She'd just lost one reality. He wasn't about to strip another one from her.

He gave her a lopsided grin. "And you still have me."

"I do still have you," she said with a small smile. "That is the only thing that makes this bearable. At least you are real."

Not knowing what to say to that, Ethan took her by the

hand and gestured to the campsite. "Come on, we'd better grab our food before Ainslee has second breakfasts."

"Do not tell the others," Nia told Ethan as they walked. "It is not something I wish to share... for now."

"No problem," he replied. "It'll be our little secret for now."

"It is no secret," she replied. "I just do not wish to discuss it. It is still too... painful."

"I understand," he said, though he was sure he didn't really. Waking up to find the world he'd been living in had all been a dream would really mess with his mind.

He glanced around at the strange world he was wandering around in, with its multiple suns, black hole and gas giant. Was he in a dream world too? Would he wake up one day to find out all of this was nothing but a dream? Or some virtual simulation?

For now, it didn't matter. Ethan would keep going like this was reality. It wasn't perfect - far from it. There was way too much pain for it to be perfect. And perfect worlds didn't have monsters like the Sollasina Cthulhu.

Reaching the others, the two of them ate their breakfast fish fillets. By the time they were finished, Michalus and Yuliana had returned. Both of them asked Nia how she was doing, and Yuliana gave the foxgirl a long hug.

He smiled, looking at Nia and the others. For the moment, at least, things seemed back to normal. At least, it seemed normal until the fishmen attacked.

31

Their first warning that something was about to happen was Luna's growl. The next thing he knew, a dozen hissing creatures were jumping over the sand dunes at them.

The sudden appearance of enemies startled Ethan as the creatures seemed to almost materialize out of nowhere. The monsters were roughly bipedal but had four arms and walked hunched. To him, they seemed fish-like, with webbing between their long, clawed fingers and toes.

While they were roughly humanoid in shape - despite the four arms - their aquatic qualities marked them as sea-dwelling creatures. Large fins jutted from their heads, as well as their forearms and shins. Looking closely, Ethan thought he saw gills on the side of their necks, which seemed to also indicate they were ocean monsters.

Further supporting his assumption, was the fact these creatures were garbed in what appeared to Ethan to be some sort of coral breastplates that still had seaweed hanging from it. Even the tridents and bucklers they wielded looked to be made of coral.

Ethan wrinkled his nose. They also smelled like fish. Or rather, they stank like dead fish left out in the sun too long.

Without really thinking about it, he scanned the closest fish-man, analyzing it with his HUD.

```
Reef Clan Raider
    Akugyo
    Ranger 5
```

He'd never met a ranger before on this world, so he had no idea if they had any special class abilities or not. He hoped not, since the creatures outnumbered his group 2 to 1 - and they had two sets of arms.

Luna and Nia reacted before any of the others. As always, Nia wore her scimitars strapped to her waist and in an instant, she had them unsheathed and had jumped in front of Ethan. Luna, didn't attack but moved protectively in front of the still-surprised Yuliana and growled a warning at the newcomers.

Like Ethan, the rest of his companions were slower to react to the surprise attack. Trying to buy them some time, Ethan tried reaching out with his *Earth* magic to turn the coral armor and weapons against the Akugyo.

And, it didn't work! There was some small part of the coral he could latch onto with his *Earth* magic, but he couldn't get a firm grip to manipulate it. He remembered the stone in the tomb and how it had been enchanted to resist magic. Ethan started to worry that somehow the armor and weapons of the fish-men was the same, but then he remembered that although coral looked like stone, it was an organic substance created by sea creatures. He cursed for wasting the time and effort and tried a different approach.

While he was trying his *Earth* magic, Michalus had reached his staff and the blue light of his Chymera crystal flared as the sand suddenly sprang up in a blinding sandstorm between the group and the Akugyo.

Yuliana, eyes wide, was glancing around, looking unsure what to do. Or, perhaps the elf was waiting for someone to get hurt so she could heal them. Ethan cursed himself again for not reviewing everyone's abilities. There just always seemed to be something else going on. Something else to do. He needed more time. But at the moment, time was the one thing he didn't have.

As suddenly as Michalus's miniature sandstorm had sprung up, it disappeared, and the elven wizard's eyes went wide. He glanced around, finally resting his gaze on the one fish-man who was still at the top of the dune. This one's trident had a blue glow around it and Ethan cursed. A wizard. A fish-man wizard. Just freaking great.

The Akugyo wizard was glaring at Michalus, probably recognizing him as a wizard from his glowing staff, just as Ethan had recognized the fish-man as a wizard from his Chymera crystal. Ethan unconsciously thought of his own crystal, in the pouch on his belt. He needed to ask Michalus if there was some advantage to having it out or if it unnecessarily marked the person as a wizard.

Looking up at the fish-man wizard, Ethan realized he

had never fought a wizard. He hadn't even really fought a warlock. When he'd defeated Charmine in Patheos, it had mostly been through trickery. He hadn't faced her in an all-out magical battle. He suddenly found himself unprepared, like a student who hadn't studied the material and was suddenly being given a surprise test. Only a fail here meant death.

Despite their apparent ability to sneak up on the group, the Akugyo moved awkwardly on land. Ethan cringed as he thought of the old saying, like a fish out of water. Cheesy saying or not, he was glad it was true.

The creatures had stopped when Michalus's sandstorm sprung up and were slow to restart their charge. Luckily, this allowed Ainslee to grab her hammer and shield and the others to get ready.

Two of the fish-men fell to the ground as Par'karr's rabbits sprang forward, leaping up and burning their horns into the thighs of the lead Akugyo. Because of their awkwardness on land, the Akugyo behind the two injured fish-men tripped, tumbling to the ground and buying them a bit more time.

The third rabbit tried the same trick, but the fish-man managed to knock the demon-bunny aside with one of its bucklers. Unfortunately for that fish-man, it couldn't deflect the two stones that Par'karr shot from the enchanted shotgun. Both hit the creature, one in the neck and one in the head and it fell lifeless to the ground.

Ethan saw the Akugyo wizard's head snap around to look at Par'karr, but then it quickly returned its attention to Michalus.

The fish-men that weren't on the ground lumbered

forward. One went for Ainslee, two came for Ethan and Nia, while three of them went right for Michalus. Ethan swore. These creatures were intelligent. They were trying to take out the wizard first. They just didn't know there were two wizards.

"Yuliana," he yelled to the druid. He pointed at the Akugyo on the ground. "Use the reeds to entangle them!"

The druid, who always seemed to look like a deer in the headlights during combat, nodded. Gesturing with her hands, she was briefly enveloped in green light and then the long grass around the Akugyo grew and wrapped around the fish-men's arms and legs.

The fish-man wizard pointed its trident at Michalus and a stream of what Ethan thought might be steam shot out. It forked, targeting both Michalus and Yuliana.

At the same time, Nia danced between the two Akugyo that came for them. There was a clatter of steel on coral and he saw yellow blood splatter the ground.

Trusting his wife to handle the two fish-men, Ethan reached out with *Air* and grabbed the legs of the three fish-men going for Michalus. Yanking, he sent all three tumbling to the ground.

Ethan guessed the fish-wizard's attack was trying to keep Michalus busy until the other Akugyo reached him. At least, that's what he would have done.

While he was tripping the Akugyo, Michalus held his staff out in front of him. The torrents of steam were directed up, then turned back on the fish-wizard. The enemy wizard was forced to cease its spell just before the steam hit it.

Yuliana saw the other fish-men on the ground. She

was once again surrounded by the green glow of her magic as she started to entangle the other Akugyo. Before she could complete the magic, her head was rocked back as if struck by an invisible force and she collapsed onto the ground.

Ethan cursed the enemy wizard as he realized it must have struck out with *Air* at the druid. Michalus glanced at the fallen elf with concern and the enemy wizard took advantage of his distraction.

A beam of fire shot from the fish-wizard's staff, directly at Michalus. Ethan wasn't sure whether or not his friend even saw it coming and acted on instinct. He grabbed one of the fallen fish-men with <u>Air</u> and raised him into the path of the beam.

The Akugyo made a high-pitched sound that hurt Ethan's ears as the fire burned a hole in its chest.

Reef Clan Raider dies.
    You gain 25 experience. Experience to next level 4,135.

As he let the body drop to the ground, he saw the fish-wizard looking around the group until his eyes rested on Ethan. It appeared that his secret was out. The Akugyo wizard knew he was a wizard too. The fish-man narrowed its bulbous fisheyes. Ethan swallowed.

Michalus seemed to realize it too. "Feel the magic from the wizard, Ethan. Counter it any way you can."

Breaking out in a cold sweat, Ethan had no idea what the elven wizard meant. He never really sensed any magic but his own. Okay, that wasn't really true. He sensed the enchantments. But that was different. Or was it?

Ethan looked at the crystal on the fish-wizard's staff. He'd sensed enchantments from crystals. Could he sense the spells the wizard was using through the crystal? Is that how it worked?

Reaching out to the crystal, he felt the *Mana* filling it. He also felt something else. Yes, it was... air. Air directed at Michalus and him!

Just in time, Ethan used his own magic to block a strike of Air that was aimed at his head. The fish-wizard had tried the same trick it had used on poor Yuliana, but Ethan had deflected it.

Fine. Two could play at that game. He gathered his own ball of Air and sent it at the fish-man's face. It got within a foot before it was blocked. Ethan thought he actually saw the Akugyo grin, displaying rows of needle-like teeth. At the same time, Michalus tried to throw a bolt of fire at the creature but it was similarly blocked.

Nia had killed one of the fish-men but had taken a gash along her leg during the fight. It didn't look life-threatening, but it was slowing her down and allowing the other Akugyo to keep pace with her.

Par'karr's rabbits were leaping and retreating at the entangled fish-men and it looked as if they might have caught one in the eye. It lay next to the other dead Akugyo, unmoving. Another whooshing sound from behind him and two stones slammed into another of the fish-men. One cracked a piece out of its coral breastplate but the other hit in the shoulder, causing the arm to go limp.

Ainslee barreled into the fish-man she was fighting, shield first. The Akugyo was knocked back, momentarily stunned and she brought her hammer down on its knee, crushing it. The creature staggered forward, trying to hold itself up on one good leg, leaving it open to a follow-up swing that caught it in the head, twisting its neck around at an unnatural angle. The fish-man collapsed on the ground.

"Ha! Take that, you overgrown trout!" she bellowed as it fell to the sand.

Unfortunately, Ethan didn't have time to celebrate the dwarf's victory as he sensed magic gathering in the wizard's crystal. It was some sort of water magic, but he didn't know what kind until suddenly his head was enveloped in water and he started to choke.

Ethan barely managed to stop himself from taking a breath and even though he clawed at the water, it continued to stay around his face. The fish-wizard was trying to drown him!

You are suffocating.

Fighting down the rising panic, Ethan realized he could still sense the Akugyo's magic. It was having to concentrate to maintain the effect. He needed to think of a way to distract it and fast.

He hadn't known the water spell was coming and hadn't taken a deep breath. Already, Ethan could feel his lungs burning and he was constantly fighting the urge to take a breath. He knew he couldn't. The moment he did, it would be over. He'd start drowning.

Through the distortion of the water bubble, he could see the same thing happening to Michalus. Apparently, the elven wizard hadn't been any luckier than Ethan in blocking the spell. That meant he couldn't expect help from his friend. He was on his own.

You are suffocating.

He needed to think of something, some way to distract the wizard and break his concentration. Ethan threw an *Air* bolt at the fish-wizard but the creature deflected it without losing its concentration.

Cursing, he realized this wizard was more experienced than Ethan and could probably block anything Ethan threw at it. Where did that leave him? No place good.

Ethan began to see spots before his eyes and knew he didn't have long. It was getting harder to think. He needed air and he needed it quickly. He just needed a quick distraction. But this fish-wizard could counter anything he did.

You are suffocating.
   Reef Clan Tide-caller suffocates you for 11 damage.

Cursing as he read the new message, Ethan really began to panic. He was taking damage. He didn't have much time. He needed something the fish-wizard couldn't counter.

Unfortunately, the fish-wizard could counter any of the regular magic Ethan threw against it. That gave him an idea. Not all wizards knew all magic. Hadn't Michalus said that *Mental* magic was rare, and few wizards had it? Could a wizard counter magic he didn't know? It was time to find out.

Reaching out like he'd done with Par'karr and Nia, he targeted the Akugyo's mind. With as much will as he could muster, he slammed his own will into the fish-man's mind like a sledgehammer.

You blast Reef Clan Tidecaller for 21 mental damage.

The bubble of water surrounding Ethan's head lost cohesion and fell to the ground and he gasped for air, allowing it to feed his lungs. Oxygen had never felt so good before and he took several deep breaths before looking up on the dune.

The fish-wizard was staggering to its feet. It was bleeding from its eyes and its attention was completely on Ethan. He hadn't had time to be subtle and the Akugyo knew where the mental attack had come from.

The fish-wizard pointed its trident at Ethan and a beam of fire shot out at him, aimed right for his head. Acting on pure instinct, Ethan opened up a portal right in front of his head. The beam disappeared into the portal and re-emerged on the other side of the portal, which Ethan had created just behind the fish-wizard.

The Akugyo arched its back as its own fire beam burned a hole into it. The beam died out at the same time the fish-wizard fell face first into the sand, a smoking hole in its back.

Reef Clan Tidecaller dies.
You gain 70 experience. Experience
to next level 4,065.

Another blast from the shotgun ended one fish-man's struggles and Michalus blasted one with a bolt of fire, even as Ainslee brought her hammer down onto the head of another fish-man.

Nia had killed the Akugyo she'd been fighting and was limping towards the two fish-men who were near Michalus. She had only taken a couple of steps when the elven wizard slammed the two with a series of *Air* blows before hitting each with a fire bolt. They didn't get up.

The remaining fish-man became the sole target of Par'karr's rabbits. They were too quick for the Akugyo to block and one of them scored a lucky blow on the crea-ture's throat, ending its struggles for good.

32

———

After making sure there were no other fish-men nearby, the group searched the fishmen corpses. The creatures had their coral armor and tridents but that was about it. Ethan briefly considered trying to use some of the armor, but it was heavier than it seemed. Most likely meant for use underwater, where the weight wouldn't be as noticeable.

The tridents the creatures carried were crude, but still sharp. Despite that, none of them seemed interested in using a trident. At least, none of the regular tridents.

When he came to the Akugyo wizard, Ethan decided to keep the creature's trident. The piece of crystal in it was larger than any of the Chymera crystals he'd seen. He thought he might be able to pry it out and use it for something.

"You're going to use a staff like a proper wizard?" Michalus joked.

Ethan grinned, holding up the staff. "I might."

"Can we leave," Ainslee grunted. "They ain't got no money, their armor is terrible, and I don't want one of those pitchforks."

The dwarf's stomach rumbled as she looked down at the fish-man, and Ainslee rubbed her chin. "You think we can cook one of these things and eat it?"

THEY TRAVELED for two more days before they reached a large clearing. During the two days, Nia hadn't hunted because there were still no signs of pteranodons and Ethan and Par'karr were able to fish.

On the second morning, Nia had asked to take a long walk on the beach. Ethan had thought the foxgirl might want to talk about her experience but instead she had pounced on him as soon as they were out of earshot of the elves.

Ethan had never made love to a woman on the beach and, not expecting it, hadn't brought a blanket. He quickly found that sand seemed to get everywhere and was quite abrasive. Not that it stopped either of them. He just made a mental note to bring the blanket next time.

During the sex, Ethan couldn't help but keep an eye on the waves. He half expected fish-men to be standing over them at any moment. Nia seemed to get frustrated with his distraction.

"I have their scent now," she told him. "I will know before they come."

He trusted the foxgirl and tried to relax. It mostly

worked. Then, after their lovemaking, they returned to the camp and ate breakfast with the others.

It wasn't until later that day, a few hours after lunch, that they reached an interesting, ruin-filled clearing. Ethan called the group to a halt. He turned to the wizard. "Michalus, do you know what this is?"

The clearing had a river that ran through it. On their side of the bank was what appeared to be the ruins of a white stone tower that was now very overgrown. Large pale stones lay scattered around the tower, having fallen from the main structure.

Even more interesting than the tower was what Ethan guessed was the remains of a very old paved road that paralleled the river and led into Sherwood Forest. The stones of the road were mostly overgrown with weeds and other vegetation, but it was clear that it had been a road at some point.

"Ah," the wizard said, pulling his horse up to Ethan. "The Sherwood road. Also called the Devil's Road, or sometimes the Witch's Walk."

"The Sherwood road?" Ethan asked with a raised eyebrow.

"Devil's Road," Ainslee repeated, giving the road a sour look. "Just great."

"Witch's walk?" Par'karr whispered and then swallowed hard.

"It's been here for hundreds of years," the elf explained, pointing towards the road. "And supposedly leads to the heart of Sherwood itself. According to rumors, many people have followed it, hoping it leads to some treasure or riches. Almost no one returns. Most sane people avoid it like the plague."

"The survivors," Yuliana said excitedly, "are they the ones who speak of the moving trees?"

"Yes, my dear." Michalus nodded, but his expression was grim. "But keep in mind, VERY few people who go into these woods return. Especially on this road."

"Ha, he said SANE people avoid it," the dwarf snorted. She turned a pointed look on Ethan. "I'm guessing you want us to go in there."

Ethan shrugged, thinking of the library that awaited him. A library full of books that would help him survive on this crazy world. "I need to go. I need to know if Camelot is in there and I need to find that library. The rest of you can wait here for me. If I'm not back in a week or two, go back to Hawkshead."

"I go with you," Nia said adamantly.

"Um," Par'karr said giving the road a wary look. "Ethan Par'karr friend. Par'karr go too.... Unless Ethan change his mind..."

"I need to go too," Yuliana said quickly. "I need to know if the moving treelings are the same as the treelings from groves that I tended."

"You tended a grove of moving trees?" The dwarf gave the elf a skeptical look.

"And spoke with them. They are very ancient and very wise. They were the caretakers of the world, and we were their caretakers," she replied with a sigh, looking into the forest with a sense of longing.

"You all will need my knowledge," Michalus said, but Ethan noticed the wizard looked at Yuliana when he said it. Ethan realized that Michalus would no more let the druid go into the forest alone, than Ethan would let Nia go in alone.

Ethan nodded to the wizard and then turned to Ainslee. "What about you?"

"I sure as Loki's Balls ain't staying here by myself!" The dwarf rolled her eyes. "I guess I'm coming."

"It wouldn't be the same without you," Ethan told Ainslee with a grin.

"Yah, yah," the dwarf muttered. "We going in now or what?"

Ethan looked up at the sky, noting the position of the two suns and the ringed planet. They had a few hours of light left but they wouldn't get far before they'd need to stop for the night. "Let's camp here tonight. We can go tomorrow."

"Fine! Let's have an early supper then!" the dwarf stated and slid off her horse.

The group tied off and unsaddled the horses, then made camp. Ethan checked on their stores of frozen fish and found that they had over a dozen of them.

"We should thaw and eat the frozen fish," he told the others.

"No fresh fish?" Ainslee asked.

Ethan shook his head. "Between tonight and tomorrow, we can use up all of the frozen fish we have at the moment. Par'karr can get some crabs to throw in with the meal, so those will be fresh. But anything I catch today and tomorrow, I want to freeze and take with us."

"Why?" Michalus asked. "Do you not think there will be game in the forest?"

"I'm sure there will be game in the forest," he answered, thinking back to stories of living trees from folklore and roleplaying games. In nearly all of the stories, the living trees were protectors of the forest. If Ethan and company went in and started killing creatures in the forest, he doubted the living trees would appreciate that.

He thought back to what Yuliana had said. The trees were the caretakers of the world and she had been their caretaker. If that were true, then the living trees wouldn't take kindly to a bunch of people coming into their forest and upsetting the natural balance.

"I think we should avoid killing animals in the forest, if we can help it," Ethan told them. When most of the group looked at him like he'd grown two heads, he held his hands up. "Just hear me out. If there are these living, moving trees and they are like the ones Yuliana cared for on her world, then they might get a bit upset if we waltz into their home and start killing their animals."

Yuliana nodded and Ethan felt a bit more confident in his assumption. He gestured to the ocean. "Par'karr and I can do some extra fishing sessions today and tomorrow. I'll freeze as many fish and crabs as possible to take with us. We can store them in my portal pouch, so they don't bog us down."

Ethan patted his second portal pouch. It was the one that led back to the chest back in Hawkshead. The same chest that Elspeth had stocked full of food and water while they were in the tomb.

He hadn't asked the innkeeper's wife to do the same this time, since he'd known they'd be able to hunt, so right now, it only contained the items Ethan would put in it.

The chest was a decent size and should hold nearly a week's worth of fish. The only bad part would be having to refreeze all of those fish each day.

"That sounds like a wise precaution," Michalus agreed. "We don't want to end up as one of those people who don't return. We can use my portal pouch to store some food as well."

"Exactly," Ethan agreed.

"Par'karr like to return," the kobold agreed.

The dwarf threw up her hands. "Fine! Whatever! Can we just have an early dinner now?"

"We might also consider avoiding a campfire while we're in the forest," Yuliana said quietly.

"Say what?" the dwarf said, head snapping around to look at the elf.

"In the forest, I mean," the green-haired elf clarified. "The caretakers will not like us creating fires in their home."

"No fire?" Ainslee grimaced. "You're serious?"

"Yuliana has a point," Ethan said, causing the dwarf's head - and ire - to focus on him. "How would you like it if someone walked into your home and just started a fire in your bedroom or living room."

"We can be careful," the dwarf protested.

"The caretakers, or living trees, or whatever they are called," Ethan replied, "are wood. That means, fire is one of their natural enemies. They're probably afraid of it." A thought struck Ethan. A memory of the tomb and the dwarf's arachnophobia. "How would you like it if someone came into your house and started laying spiders all over the place..."

"Fine! Fine!" Ainslee said with a shiver. "No fire. But it's going to get cold.... Especially at night!"

"Maybe not," Ethan said with a smile. An idea for a magic item was already forming in his head. "Let me think about it."

"Fine!" Ainslee huffed. She licked her lips. "So, about that dinner..."

Ethan brought out the frozen fish and unwrapped them from the cloth that he'd wrapped around them. He looked to Michalus. "Can you warm these up so we can cook them?"

"Certainly," the wizard replied.

"Ainslee," he said, turning to the dwarf. "Can you gather some firewood and make a fire so we can cook the fish. Par'karr will have some crabs later."

"Yuliana, can you and Michalus scout around for berries and nuts," he told the druid. "Find as many as you can and store them. We may not find some inside and if we do, they may not like it if we take them."

"I do not think the caretakers would mind us taking berries and nuts," Yuliana told him. "It is natural, and it is a way to spread the seeds."

Ethan rubbed his chin. "Let's still take as much as we can with us. Just to be on the safe side."

"What about me?" Nia asked. "Should I hunt?"

"No," Ethan replied quickly, glancing at the overgrown road that led into Sherwood. "I don't want anyone going into the forest alone at this point."

The foxgirl followed his stare and shrugged. "What do you want me to do then?"

"You can come with me to get some more fish," he said.

"You and I can fish to the north, while Par'karr fishes to the south."

Nia gave him a knowing smile, but he caught Ainslee snickering. He ignored the dwarf and motioned to the kobold.

"Come on, Par'karr," Ethan said, taking Nia's hand. "Time for us to catch some fish."

"And crabs," Par'karr said happily.

Ethan and Nia began to walk towards the beach when Ethan remembered something. He let go of Nia's hand, rushed back to his horse and then returned with two blankets under his arm.

Ainslee snickered again. "Have fun... fishing..."

33

———

Ethan lay with Nia on one of the blankets he'd brought, his eyes shut. For a moment, lying on the beach with the sun beating down on him and the sound of the thunderous surf in the background, he could almost imagine he was back on Earth. Almost.

Unfortunately, as soon as he opened his eyes and saw the double suns, the black hole and rings of the gas giant that this world orbited, the illusion was shattered. And of course, Nia herself spoiled the illusion. Not in a bad way, but there were no women like her back on Earth.

The foxgirl turned towards him and propped her head up with her hand. "It is nice to lie in the sun with you, but we must get back."

"I know," he grumbled. "It was just... for a second, it felt like Earth."

"Earth, your home?" she asked.

"Yes," he said and turned to face her, propping his own head up. "Sometimes I miss it. Do you miss your world?"

The foxgirl scrunched up her face in thought for a long moment before answering. "Sometimes. But I like this world too. Especially now that I am Tal'Cha to a mighty alpha."

Ethan snickered. "Oh, yeah. That's me. Mr. Mighty Alpha."

Nia cocked her head at him. "Did you not destroy the tentacle creature single-handedly? And then free me from... whatever it was doing to me."

"Well." He grinned. "When you say it like that, it sounds pretty impressive."

"It is truly impressive. No alpha on my world could have done so," she said sincerely and then shivered despite the warmth. "Not against such a creature. There is nothing like that on my world. Not even in our nightmares."

Ethan nodded. The Cthulhu creature was the stuff of nightmares. Despite killing it and having *Mental* magic now, he hoped that had been the only one of those creatures on this world. He had no desire to battle another one.

Looking at the position of the suns and the ringed gas giant, he guessed they'd been out for an hour. Nia was right. They needed to get back. And he hadn't even summoned his elemental to go fishing.

He smacked his head. A thought occurred to him then that he was surprised hadn't occurred to him before. He'd been fixated on the way the pteranodons hunted the fish. It hadn't occurred to him until that moment that there might be a more efficient way.

"Are you okay?" Nia asked.

"I'm fine," he said, grinning and reaching for his clothes. "I just thought of something that I should have thought of days ago!"

Pulling on his pants, he grinned at the foxgirl. "I had originally summoned an air elemental to hunt the fish because that's what the pteranodons did."

"The lizard birds." Nia nodded.

"Yes," he continued and slid his shirt over his bare chest. "But I think there's a better way."

Nia buttoned her blouse and arched an eyebrow at him. "Better way?"

Ethan shook his head for not thinking of it earlier. Especially after using a similar technique at the bridge where they'd fought the Sollasina Cthulhu. "Water elemental."

"Water elemental?" she repeated, pulling on one of her boots and furrowing her brow at him.

"The water elemental seems to be able to move through water with no problem and is strong enough to haul a skeleton wearing rusted plate mail," he said, and yanked on his own boots. "It should be able to bring me a half dozen fish at a time - easy."

"Truly?" she asked. Nia strapped on her weapon belt and adjusted it, so the scimitars fell to either side.

"There's only one way to find out." He grinned. He grabbed his own belts and strapped them on. They contained his regular portal pouch and the pouch that led to the Grail. There was no way he was going anywhere without them.

Finally, he reached down onto the blanket and retrieved

the three Chymera crystals he'd charged. Later, he would try to make them into some sort of heating magical item. How exactly, he didn't know yet. He was still working on ideas.

"Let me get closer to the water and I'll summon it," he told Nia and started towards the edge of the water.

He didn't get too close, since the water from a collapsing waterspout could splash out over a hundred yards. Instead, he stopped at about the same distance that Par'karr did when sending his rabbits to get crabs.

Ethan knew his *Mana* would be full, but he double checked his *Stamina* to make sure he had enough.

Stamina: 23

That was plenty, so he used *Summon Lesser Elemental* and chose water.

Water flowed from the ground and formed a large dolphin made of water. The elemental looked at him, waiting for orders.

"I want you to go into the water," he told it, pointing at the edge of the ocean. "Grab as many fish as you can, bring them here and drop them in front of me."

The water elemental gave him no acknowledgement and since he hadn't established a mental link using his magic, he couldn't communicate with it telepathically. Instead, it simply turned and sped towards the ocean and then disappeared into the water.

It seemed only a moment later that the elemental emerged from the ocean. The dolphin had no hands to grasp fish with and Ethan didn't see any fish in its mouth.

Then he saw the moving shapes INSIDE the water elemental.

Looking closely at the elemental as it approached him, he saw numerous shapes swimming inside the elemental itself. When the thing got close to Ethan, it stopped and one by one, the fish were expelled from the watery body of the elemental. Then, the elemental turned and slid back towards the ocean.

Nia bent down and counted them. "Five fish."

The foxgirl gathered them into the sheet they'd brought along to hold the fish. It was the same one they'd been using for days now and it was now unusable for anything other than carrying fish since, no matter how many times he washed it in the rivers they'd passed, it still stank of fish.

After only ten minutes, the water elemental had brought them just over fifty fish. That was twice as many fish as he would have gotten from the air elemental in the same time. He felt a little proud of himself for thinking of it - finally.

With their cache of fish, the two of them returned to the camp. Nia and Ainslee began gutting and cooking the fish. Par'karr was back and playing with his rabbits but Michalus and Yuliana were still out "looking for berries."

That gave Ethan some time to sit down and figure out how to make a magical heater - that didn't use fire. This, unfortunately, proved to be much more difficult than he thought.

He tried several failed experiments before finally coming up with a viable solution. His final attempt involved two different enchantments. The first generated heat in a stone core inside a chest-shaped "heater" made of stone that he'd created. The chest was hollow except for the "core" that went through the middle.

When the trigger crystal was touched, the spell toggled from active to inactive, or vice versa. Just that bit had taken him nearly an hour. *Fire* magic heated up the core very quickly and kept it hot. Unfortunately, by itself, that did very little as the heat didn't radiate out far.

A second crystal turned on an <u>Air</u> enchantment that would suck air into the "chest heater" from holes in the top. The enchantment sent the air down around the core, and then expelled it through holes in the side.

It worked, but it was limited. First, neither the temperature of the core nor the amount of air coming in or going out could be changed. It was basically an on or off heater. Second, the air coming out of the heater didn't go very far. They'd need to be close to it to feel any warmth.

But it was better than nothing - he hoped. After all, it worked in theory, but they'd need to test it to find out whether or not it was even viable.

Looking around at his companions gathered around the campfire, he stood up and got their attention. He explained what he had made and how it worked, demonstrating it and letting everyone feel the warm air coming out.

"It won't be as warm as a real fire," Ainslee pointed out, giving the heater a skeptical look.

"I know," Ethan agreed. "But it's better than getting on the bad side of any tree-men, or tree-women... ah... tree-folk, we meet."

The dwarf shrugged and looked around at the tall

redwood-like trees. "Yeah, you're probably right about that."

"You'll have to show me how you did that... what did you call it... toggle switch," Michalus said, eyeing the heater. "I have a few ideas of how I could use that."

"Sure." Ethan grinned. The wizard had been the one who taught him the basics of making magic items. To hear him ask Ethan to show the wizard how to do something made him feel good.

"Alright," he told his companions. "Get some sleep. Tomorrow, we're going into Sherwood and it sounds like we're going to need to keep our wits about us."

At Ethan's request, they put out the campfire so they could test the heater. Given how dark it was, he suggested they put out the light stones in a circle so those on watch could see something.

The others muttered acknowledgements, set out their light stones and went about their evening rituals to get ready for bed. Ethan did his own ritual, which was really just going out and relieving himself and then coming back and taking off his boots. He lay down on his bedroll and after a few minutes, Nia slid next to him.

Yawning, he put his arm around the foxgirl. Before he knew it, he was asleep and dreaming of being chased by insect-like monsters.

34

The next morning the group packed up their gear, ate breakfast and began their journey into Sherwood Forest. The remnants of the road were too uneven to ride on, so they walked along the side of it, leading the horses after them.

The first thing Ethan noticed was that the forest wasn't as dark as he thought it would be. Probably due to their size, the trees were spaced a good distance from each other in most cases, allowing light to filter through the leafy canopy high above.

He also noticed how much foliage there was on the forest floor. The pictures he'd remembered seeing of the redwoods in California always seemed to have very little foliage around them. That wasn't the case in Sherwood. There were plenty of plants of all sorts - even smaller trees in between the larger trees. Was that because of the proximity to the river?

"This is so much like the groves on my world," Yuliana said as she looked around, a large smile on her face.

"You see any of those moving trees?" Ainslee asked warily, her eyes darting around the forest.

"No," the druid replied. "But you cannot see them in a forest unless they wish to be seen."

"That's a bit of good news," the dwarf mumbled sarcastically.

As the group walked on, Ethan also saw forest creatures of all sorts - deer, squirrels, chipmunks, rabbits, and even a few foxes. This forest was teeming with life, more so than any of the other forests he'd been in on this world.

Nia seemed to notice the abundance of game as well. She walked her horse alongside Ethan. "Are you sure we cannot hunt in this forest?"

Ethan looked around and caught a pair of rabbits hopping through the bushes on the far side of the river as the group got closer to them. It was tempting. They'd been eating fish and crabs for several days in a row now. He grinned. A nice brace of coneys would taste nice. Especially with some taters.

He shook his head, looking up at one of the huge trees nearby before glancing back to Nia. "If there really are living trees in this forest, I don't think it's in our best interest to upset them in any way."

"But isn't one animal hunting another a natural thing?" Nia protested. "The strong hunt the weak - predators and prey."

"True," Ethan admitted. "And you may be right. I just don't want to provoke something that could be as large as a tree."

Nia looked around at the huge trees around them and then shrugged. "Could you and Michalus not burn them with your magic?"

"We COULD," Ethan replied, giving the foxgirl a disapproving look. "But I'd prefer to make friends of them, rather than enemies."

Nia shrugged. "You are the alpha."

"You really want to fight something that is potentially a hundred or more feet tall and made of wood?" Ethan asked. "It would make those ogres we faced look like kobolds. And what if there are several of them... dozens, even."

Nia let out a frustrated breath. "Perhaps you are right."

The foxgirl lapsed into silence and they continued to walk along the trail until noon, when they stopped for lunch. Ethan and Michalus used magic to warm up some frozen fish fillets and they sat next to the river.

"Any sign of the tree people?" Ainslee asked Yuliana, biting off a chunk of the fish. "I ain't seen no moving trees."

"I have seen nothing so far," the green-haired elf replied, looking around the forest. "If there are caretakers in these forests, they are either not here or chose to remain hidden."

"They can do that?" Nia asked. "Be unseen?"

The elf shook her head. "If they are not moving, they are indistinguishable from normal trees. On my world, I could sense them, but I do not know if I can sense tree-folk from this world."

"And what do the tree-folk do on your world?" Michalus asked, nibbling on his own fish. "I'm not sure if I fully understand it."

"They care for the forests and maintain the balance," the druid replied.

"I thought you cared for the forest," Ainslee said, furrowing her brow and taking another bite from her fish.

"I care for the grove," the elf replied with a shake of her head. "Not the forest."

"Grove not forest?" Par'karr asked.

"No," she answered. "The forest is vast, and the tree-folk manage it. We manage the groves - the homes of the tree-folk."

"You're housekeepers for trees?" Ainslee asked skeptically.

"They do not have houses," the elf said. "They come back to the groves to replenish their energy. Every tree-folk must return to a grove to touch the earth at least once a moon cycle."

Ethan, who had just finished up his own fish, turned to the elf. "Then the tree people use these groves to recharge their energy every so often?"

Yuliana nodded.

"What happens if they don't recharge?" he asked.

"They can no longer share their energy with the forest and the forest will start to wither," the elf replied as if this were something everyone should know.

"What kind of energy do they share?" Michalus asked. "Is it magical energy?"

"It is not magical." Yuliana shook her head. "It is the energy of the earth. The caretakers absorb it from the earth and then spread it throughout the forest."

Michalus frowned. "But it's not magical?"

"No," the druid responded. "It is simply the energy of the earth."

"Sound like magic," Par'karr interjected.

Michalus nodded. "I have to agree with Par'karr. It does sound magical, though what kind of magic I cannot say."

"But, it's not..." she started.

"If you grew up with it," Ethan cut in, "it may seem perfectly normal and natural to you. But I've never heard of anything absorbing energy from one spot and then distributing it to other things. It does seem... magical."

Yuliana bit her lip and looked at her hand. As she did, it glowed green with healing magic. It did that for a second before fading away. "Perhaps it seems like magic to you because you did not grow up with it, but it is simply the way things are in my world. And it is nothing like the type of magic here."

Ethan nodded. He could accept that he didn't understand it, but just because he didn't understand it, didn't mean it was magical.

All of his companions, except Ainslee, came from a pre-industrial society with no schools. Even Ainslee's grasp of advanced technology like computers and microchips would be extremely limited. If he showed a cellphone, an automobile, a microwave or any of hundreds or even thousands of modern inventions to anyone in the group, they'd think the items were magical. But that was just because they didn't understand the science behind them.

Michalus rubbed his chin before asking another question. "Do you think there are any of these... groves... on this world?"

"I do not know," the druid said, a tone of sadness to her voice. "My people can sense the groves, but I have not sensed one since I arrived on this world."

Ethan arched an eyebrow. "You think there might be groves in Sherwood?"

The wizard shrugged. "If they were going to be anywhere, Sherwood seems like a likely place."

"If the tree people-thingys do make things grow," Ainslee said, looking up at one of the nearby redwoods. "Seems like they've been puttin' some overtime in around here."

Ethan looked around at the giant trees. Could Ainslee be right? Could these huge trees be a result of energy being fed to them from these tree-folk creatures? Or, like back on Earth, was this just a forest of this particular variety of tree?

After all, there were redwoods back on Earth. It was just a different species of tree. And there were no tree-folk caretakers there and no sacred groves. He chuckled to himself. Unless Bigfoot was a caretaker.

The group lapsed into silence as they finished up their lunch. Once they had finished their meal, the group filled their water bottles, let the horses drink and then set back off down the trail.

They continued down the trail until it became too dark to keep going and they stopped for the night.

"It get dark quick," Par'karr said, looking up at the sky.

Ethan nodded. "The canopy is going to block most of the moonlight, so it will be dark tonight."

"And cold," complained the dwarf. "Your heating contraption had better work."

Shivering involuntarily, Ethan couldn't help but agree. It was definitely colder in the forest than it had been along the beach, even accounting for the wind on the shore. Was that because of the proximity to the river? Or just lack of sunlight filtering in during the day?

"Okay," he said, pulling the heater off his horse. He carried the magical space heater to a nearby stone and set it on top. He turned to his companions. "We'll have to set up our bedrolls as close as possible. Maybe we can set the light stones nearby so it's like a campfire."

"No," Nia said. "Set the light stones to set up a circle of light around us. That will give us maximum visibility if any enemies try to sneak into the camp."

Ethan looked around the area and nodded. "Good idea. Set up the stones and let's break out dinner."

"About time," Ainslee said. "I'm starving!"

35

After eating, Nia collected all of the fishbones and took them near the river, about a hundred yards away. When she returned to their camp, Ethan gave her a quizzical look.

"Why'd you move them over there?" he asked.

"They stink," she told him. "I do not wish to smell them all night. Plus, if predators smell them, they may wander into our camp."

He nodded and insisted they set double watches for the evening. Considering the wizard's warning about people not coming back from the forest, he thought it was prudent. Ainslee grumbled - as usual. Yet, in the end, everyone agreed that it was the right thing to do.

Ethan and Par'karr took the first watch. As he hoped, their watch was uneventful, and they woke Michalus and Yuliana for their turn. He lay down next to Nia and, putting an arm around her, quickly fell asleep.

After what seemed like only a moment, Ethan awoke

to someone shaking him. Then he felt Nia spring up next to him. "Wha-? What's going on?"

"We have company, my boy," Michalus said quietly, standing up and staring out into the darkness.

Blinking, Ethan pushed himself up from his bedroll and looked out into the darkness where Michalus was staring. While he couldn't see much beyond the light of their magic stones, he could make out several sets of yellow eyes staring back at him.

"What are they?" Ethan whispered as he pulled on his boots.

"Barghests," the wizard breathed. "Carrion eaters. We heard them coming but wasn't sure we'd attracted their attention until they began crunching on bones."

Ethan looked out again and realized where the barghests were. They were near where Nia had dropped the fish bones. He whispered a curse and looked to the foxgirl. She gave him an "I told you they stink" look and drew her scimitars.

"Can we scare them away?" Ethan asked. Looking around, he saw that Yuliana had woken Ainslee and Par'karr. The kobold's rabbits were already hopping around him nervously while he pulled out the shotgun.

"They're not afraid of much when they're in a pack," Michalus commented.

Yuliana came to stand beside Michalus with the big cat following her. Luna was crouched down low, head moving from side to side. He could hear the mountain lion's low growl as the cat looked out in the darkness.

His first thought was to use fire to scare them away, but he suddenly remembered where they were. Sherwood

Forest. He had no idea if the tree-people or tree-folk, or whatever they were called, might be watching and whether they might take his use of fire as a bad thing. He was certain if they were watching, they wouldn't appreciate him lobbing around a few fireball spells so close to the redwoods.

He cursed. Michalus seemed to read his mind. "Too close to use fire?"

"Best not take a chance. The tree-people might be watching," Ethan replied. "No fire... unless absolutely necessary."

The wizard didn't look happy but nodded. "It won't be easy without fire. And there are more out there than I can see. I can hear them circling."

"They are surrounding us," Nia confirmed, sniffing the air. "They will attack soon."

"How many?" Ethan asked.

"At least ten," she said. "There may be some that I cannot smell."

Ten enemies out there. That was a lot, but they'd faced worse. There had been twelve of the fish-men and they'd managed to survive. And one of them had been a wizard. Surely ten or so wild creatures wouldn't pose too much of a risk.

Just then a howl sounded from the side and Ethan's head pivoted towards the sound. Then another howl sounded on the opposite side and his head snapped toward the new sound. Then a chorus of howls joined in and the creatures charged.

Par'karr's rabbit dashed out towards one of the advancing creatures. As it came into the light, Ethan could see that it appeared to be a cross between a wolf and a hyena. The head was similar to a wolf, except the jaws were larger.

Like a wolf, the head had thick black fur, but the thick fur ended at the shoulders, except a long black patch that ran down its spine. The rest of the canine was spotted, gray short fur, except at the lower parts of its legs, which were also covered in thick, black fur. The barghests were unlike any creature Ethan had ever seen and they moved fast.

He managed to Analyze one as it got closer.

Barghest
    Level: 6

They were level 6 and there were a lot of them. His mind raced to think of a good strategy, but the creatures were closing too fast. Just as he got an idea, the barghests reached them. He heard the snap-hiss of Michalus's energy-blade appearing right before one of the large canines leapt up and slammed into him.

Ethan was knocked backward and barely managed to get his arm up in time to prevent the barghest from burying its teeth in his neck. Instead, the creature locked its mouth around his arm, biting down like a vice. Without meaning to, Ethan screamed as the creature's teeth punctured his skin and snapped the bones in his arm.

Barghest bites you for 17 damage.

Screaming, Ethan struck out at the creature with *Air*, pummeling it from different sides.

```
You strike barghest for 7 damage.
  You strike barghest for 6 damage.
  You strike barghest for 8 damage.
```

The creature didn't let go, but instead began to shake its head, sending excruciating pain through Ethan's entire body. He shouted a curse and, pushing through his pain, buried his fist in the creature's chest and summoned his own energy-blade.

With a snap-hiss, the blade appeared in his hand. With the angle his hand was at, the blade burned through flesh and emerged out of the creature's back.

```
You burn barghest for 17 damage.
```

The creature yelped and jerked back. Unfortunately for it, the energy-blade was pure energy. It offered no resistance to the creature as it pulled its body back. Instead, the barghest's movement caused the blade to slice through its chest and head.

```
You burn barghest for 25 damage.
  Barghest dies.
  You gain 60 experience. Experience
to next level 4,005.
```

The creature toppled over, dead. Ethan looked down at the bloody mess that was his forearm. It hung at an unnatural angle and he guessed it had been broken in multiple places. When he tried to move it or even wiggle his fingers, intense pain shot through his arm and straight into his brain.

Looking around, he saw the others in his group weren't faring well either. A barghest lay dead at Nia's feet while she kept two others at bay with her scimitars.

As he looked, Par'karr unloaded the shotgun at near point-blank range. The barghest he had shot had two demon-rabbits buried in its side. The rabbits struggled but didn't seem to be able to get their horns free of the creature. The barghest staggered a step and collapsed on its side, trapping the rabbits underneath.

Ainslee seemed to be holding her own. One of the barghests locked its large jaws on her shield and started shaking its head, trying to pull the dwarf's arm off or pull the shield off her arm. It didn't seem to be working.

Ethan knew from experience that the dwarf was much heavier than she looked. Combined with her low center of gravity and tremendous strength, the dwarf managed to keep hold of the shield. Not only that, but she brought her hammer down on its head. Once. Twice. Three times and the creature went limp and slid off her shield.

"Next!" he heard her shout as Ainslee looked for another enemy.

Michalus was holding his own. One of the canines lay on the ground, half of its head missing. The wizard fended off another one with his mana-saber. He kept himself between the other barghest and Yuliana.

The druid was keeping herself behind Michalus but her eyes were on a rolling bundle of fur and teeth. Luna was rolling around the ground with one of the barghests as both of them struggled for dominance. They scratched, bit and rolled around, howling and growling.

Movement caught his eyes as two more barghests trotted out of the shadows, growling and moving to either side of him. He checked his *Mana*.

Mana: 53

Even as he looked, it dropped another point. He cursed. The energy-blade was going through his *Mana* quickly. He needed to make his move and make it quickly.

Just then, he heard Par'karr scream. He glanced back to see what had happened and the two barghests rushed him.

Anger flared inside Ethan at the possibility that his friend was being mauled by one of these creatures. Without really thinking about it, he used *Air* to seize both barghests in mid jump. He felt a lot of *Mana* leaving him, but he ignored the sensation and slammed the two creatures together.

You crush barghest for 11 damage.
You crush barghest for 14 damage.

Still holding the two barghests with *Air*, he took a step forward and, snarling, lopped off both of their heads.

You critically burn barghest for 65 damage.
Barghest dies.

You gain 60 experience. Experience to next level 3,945.
You critically burn barghest for 59 damage.
Barghest dies.
You gain 60 experience. Experience to next level 3,885.

Ethan released the two headless barghest corpses and spun to look for Par'karr. He saw the kobold on the ground with a barghest atop him. Ethan started to reach out with <u>Air</u> to pull the creature off his friend but then saw that the canine wasn't biting Par'karr, it was gnawing on something in the kobold's hand.

As he looked on, the kobold twisted the item in his hand and yanked back on the trigger. The barrel was lodged in the barghest's mouth and when the whooshing sound went off, the back of the creature's head exploded in a shower of blood and brains. The dead barghest slumped to the ground, pinning the poor kobold underneath.

He was about to lift the dead creature off his friend when Ainslee yelled. "Ethan!"

In an amazing move of strength and dexterity, that Ethan hadn't known the dwarf was capable of, Ainslee hurled her hammer directly at him. At least, that's what it looked like to Ethan. It flew so fast that he didn't even have time to grab it with *Air*.

But it wasn't aimed at him. The steel hammer flew past his head - WAY too close to his head - and he heard a yelp behind him. Spinning, he saw a twitching barghest lying on the ground near the headless ones. Its head was smashed in from the dwarf's hammer.

He turned back around. "Thanks for that."

"No problem." She grinned, then looked impatient. "Can you get me my hammer back?"

"Right," Ethan said and picked it up with *Air* and sent it back to her, just in time for her to snatch it back and pummel a barghest she'd just smashed with her shield.

Nia had finished off hers and also finished off Luna's barghest. Both Luna and Nia were bloody, but the cat appeared to have gotten the worst of it.

Three of the creatures lay at Michalus's feet, though the wizard's right leg was dripping blood from what looked like a bite on his thigh. Yuliana was healing him as he kept a wary eye on the forest.

"It sounds like the rest are running off," Michalus said to Ethan and Yuliana nodded.

"Do you think they will be back?" Ethan asked, levitating the canine corpse off of Par'karr.

Michalus shrugged. "I've seen pictures of them and read a little about them, but I'm afraid I'm no expert."

Ethan looked to Nia. "What do you think?"

"Their pack has been decimated," she said, gesturing around the clearing with her bloody scimitar. "But they are carrion eaters. They will return to eat their dead."

He winced as pain shot through his broken arm. He released the mana-saber and it disappeared with a hiss. The others seemed to notice the extent of the damage to his arm and Nia gasped. "Your arm!"

Yuliana started towards him, but he held up a hand.

"The bones are broken. If you heal me, they'll just heal wrong like they did that time in the forest."

The green-haired elf stopped and bit her lip. Her eyes took on a faraway look and he guessed she was remembering the time they'd fought two ogres. They'd killed them but the ogres had broken Michalus's leg and Nia's ribs.

Both of them had been healed by Yuliana but even though the wounds healed, and the bones fused, they hadn't fused correctly. Whatever magic she had might knit flesh and restore bones, but it didn't do it perfectly.

"The Grail?" Michalus asked with a raised eyebrow.

Grimacing, Ethan nodded to his right side where his arm hung limp. "If someone could just reach into my pouch and pull the Grail out. I can't quite reach across and get it."

Nia came forward quickly and retrieved the Grail. As always, she winced from the sound - as did the elves - but they each quickly drank and returned the chalice before the noise began to be too painful.

When it was Ethan's turn, he sipped from the cup and then dropped to his knees as agony rocked his right arm. There was popping sounds and lots of pain for what seemed like eternity and then everything was fine.

Hesitantly, he looked down at his arm. It was still bloody but there was no pain. Tentatively, he wiggled his fingers. They moved easily and he seemed to have a full range of motion with them. Ethan flexed his arm several different ways before he was satisfied that it was fully healed. He grinned at the others. "Good as new."

36

At Nia's insistence, they dragged the bodies away from the camp before trying to get some more sleep. Thankfully, the barghests did not return and nothing else bothered them for the rest of the night. Only Ainslee managed to actually fall asleep, so they were all tired the next morning.

His magical space heater did work. Unfortunately, he wouldn't go so far as to say it actually kept them comfortable - and certainly nowhere near as warm as a fire. Ethan would need to think of a better design. He was sure he could do it, he just had to figure out how.

Breaking out fish for breakfast, Ethan sat down by Michalus. He gestured to where they'd piled the barghest bodies. "First those fish-men, now barghests. Is this all because of Sherwood?"

"I'm not sure, my boy. This area has always been dangerous, but I don't remember anyone mentioning fish-men." The wizard looked thoughtful. "Then again, I doubt anyone has tried fishing like you do - with the water elemental, that is."

"You think that's what attracted the fish-men?" Ethan asked. If that were the case, he could have been responsible for them being attacked.

Michalus shrugged. "I wouldn't worry overly about it. We have no idea what their motivation was or why they attacked us. Perhaps they were hunting - and we were their prey."

Ethan nodded, once again wishing he knew more about the world. Hopefully, if the Great Library still existed in Camelot, he'd learn more very soon. He felt excitement at the prospect of the library and all the books and knowledge it would hold.

It was strange. He'd never gotten so excited over a library on Earth. Now, he felt an almost obsessive compulsiveness to find the library. Then again, back on his world, the knowledge a library contained didn't mean the difference between life and death.

After eating breakfast, they followed the overgrown path until shortly after lunch time. During their morning travels, they came to a spot where the river they were following was revealed to be a fork off a larger river that split in two. The main river, now wider, continued west, while the branch ran south. They followed the larger river westward until they saw something that made them stop.

Just up ahead, there was an open, white stone bridge that crossed the large river and the path led over the bridge and west along the other side of the river. On either side of the entrance to the bridge were the remains of statues, carved out of the same white rock.

The statue on the right had broken in half and the part that had hit the ground was shattered. The one on the left was still mostly intact and looked to have been the carving of a knight, complete with a bucket-style helmet, similar to the carved reliefs in the tomb.

"I think we're on the right trail," Ethan said, pointing at the left statue. "That looks like one of the carvings from Arthur's tomb."

"Is this what's left of the city?" Ainslee asked. "It ain't much."

Ethan looked around the area. There was nothing but trees and foliage, with the occasional forest animal scampering around the forest floor. Listening, he could only detect the sound of birds and the roaring of the river. Other than the bridge, there was nothing that remotely appeared to be remnants of Camelot.

"This might just be a bridge," he told the dwarf. "Or perhaps it's the entrance into the kingdom of Camelot."

"I take it, we keep going?" the dwarf grumbled.

"I think there's more to find," Ethan said, though it was mostly hope on his part. After all, a thousand years had passed. Who knew what would be left of the city - if anything. True, back on Earth there were buildings that had survived well over a thousand years - the Pyramids, the Parthenon, maybe even the Colosseum.

If those buildings had survived for at least 2,000 years, through two world wars, maybe there would be something left of Camelot too. Considering Arthur's tomb had been a thousand years old, it was possible - especially if the stone had been enchanted.

"Let's keep going," he said and started his horse forward towards the bridge.

The others followed him onto the stone bridge, the clopping of the horses' hooves echoing around them. The path they followed was overgrown with vegetation and masked the sound of the horses' hooves to a great deal. Not so with the bridge. There was some growth on either end of the bridge, but the middle was unmarred stone.

"If whatever's in the forest didn't know we were here," Michalus observed. "It does now."

Ethan frowned. "How far did people have to go into the forest before they disappeared?"

"Stories vary," the wizard replied. "For some it was a day, others two days, for some it was barely a hundred yards."

"Great," Ethan said, looking left and right across the bridge.

"Yuliana," he called back to the green-haired elf over the sound of the horses. "Have you sensed any of the tree-folk or one of those groves you were telling us about?"

"No," she called back. "Nothing."

Ethan made it to the far side of the bridge, and he felt the hairs on the back of his neck stand up. He stopped, causing the others to come to a halt behind him.

"What is it?" asked Nia, free hand dropping to her scimitar.

"I'm not sure," he said. "Michalus, can you come up here."

A moment later, the wizard stopped next to him on his right. His brow furrowed and he shivered.

"You feel it too?" Ethan asked.

"Yes," Michalus replied, looking around. "Magic. To the west."

"Is something wrong?" asked Nia, coming to stand on his left. Her free hand was on her scimitar's hilt.

"I don't... know," Ethan said. "There's something to the west. Michalus feels it too."

"What?" Nia demanded.

"Yeah, wizard-boy," Ainslee said from behind him. "What is it that's got you and Mikey spooked?"

Ethan looked to Michalus; this time he shivered as the feeling passed over him. It felt magical, but it also felt wrong. Plus, there was something familiar about it. He just couldn't quite put his finger on it.

"Any ideas what that is?" he asked Michalus.

The wizard was quiet for a moment, swaying left, then right. The elf tilted his head slightly one way, then another.

"Anyone going to answer me?" the dwarf asked.

"It's magic," Michalus said finally, "If I had to guess, I'd say it was either channeler magic or warlock magic."

"That's it!" Ethan snapped his fingers. That's why it felt familiar. He'd felt something similar when he'd been around Charmine, the warlock from the Order of the Scroll. She was the one who had sent him to the library of Daemonium to retrieve some lost tomes. The warlock had ended up trying to take the tomes from him, with the help of a priestess of Hel and her goons.

He nodded, remembering the feeling of wrongness and revulsion he'd gotten off the warlock. Ethan felt his forehead wrinkle as questions popped into his head. He looked to the west, where the feeling was coming from.

"Why are we feeling it?" he asked the wizard.

The wizard scratched his chin, squinting to the west. "That is a very good question. I've felt warlock magic before, but never this far away - and it does seem far away."

Ethan nodded again. That was his impression as well. It was distant. Strong but distant. What did that mean? And how powerful was the creature or creatures who were creating it? It was a disturbing thought.

"Why are you ignoring me?!" Ainslee demanded louder.

"Sorry, Ainslee," Ethan said, looking back at the dwarf and the others. He looked to Michalus, silently asking if he should tell them. The elf nodded gravely.

"Michalus and I sense something to the west," he told them. "We think it might be a warlock or channeler."

The others exchanged glances, then looked back to Ethan.

"Close?" Par'karr asked, glancing around the forest.

"We don't think so, it feels far away," Ethan answered.

"Is that... normal? You sensing magic from far away?" Ainslee squinted one eye at Ethan and then at Michalus. Her tone made it evident that she didn't believe it was.

Casting a glance at Michalus again, Ethan shook his head. "No. Neither of us have sensed magic like this from afar."

"So, there could be some big mean demon or dragon waiting for us?" the dwarf growled.

"I don't think it would be a dragon," Michalus answered with a fatherly smile that looked awkward on his now-young face. Then he looked thoughtful. "But a demon... you know, it could be a demon."

Ethan saw the dwarf blanch. The only other demon-type creature they had run into - other than the Cthulhu creature - had spit acid and scarred the dwarf terribly, blinding her in one eye. Only the healing power of the Grail had been able to restore her back to the way she was.

The dwarf recovered and turned a baleful gaze onto Ethan. "Wizard-boy, you didn't say anything about a demon."

"My dear, we don't even..." Michalus started but Ainslee cut him off.

"Don't 'my dear' me!" the dwarf growled. "No one said nothing about no demon. I have half a mind to turn around right now and go back to Hawkshead."

"We don't even know that there is a demon at all," Ethan protested. "Michalus and I just get a weird feeling. It could be some sort of residual magic from the city of Camelot. It was supposed to be a magical city."

"Can you promise me it's not a demon?" Ainslee demanded, though her expression was almost pleading.

Ethan sighed. "I can't promise, Ainslee. I don't know what's ahead of us. I do know that if we run into a demon, you don't have to fight it."

Emotions played across the dwarf's ebony features for several seconds. "I ain't no coward."

"No one thinks you're a coward," Ethan said. "You fought a giant queen spider, remember."

"Don't remind me." Ainslee shuddered and then shook

her head. "As I was saying, I ain't no coward. But demons aren't natural! They're all messed up! They... do things."

The dwarf ran a hand along the side of her face that had been scarred. It was clear she was remembering the incident where the demon lizard had scarred her with acid. They were terrible, disfiguring wounds that had only been healed by the power of the Grail.

"Very true," Michalus said. "In this world, they are abominations. That's why, for the longest time, channelers and warlocks were outcasts - even criminals..."

"I get it! I get it!" the dwarf interrupted. "I just don't want to go near another demon, if I don't have to."

Ethan bit his lip. He didn't want to lose the dwarf, but he didn't want to drag someone along against their will. "It's up to you, Ainslee. If you want, I think I can summon a portal back to Hawkshead. You can go back and wait for us to return."

The dwarf blinked, then turned to Ethan. "You mean it?"

"If that's what you want." Ethan shrugged. "I'll send you back."

The dwarf looked around to the others and then sighed and hung her head. "No. I ain't never run from anything - well, except those spiders. I ain't going to start now. I'll stay with you. At least for now."

Ethan smiled. "Anyone else? The offer is open."

No one else said anything and Ethan nodded. "Well then, let's see how far we can get before nightfall."

37

When the shadows deepened and it was too dark to continue their journey, the group set up camp next to the river. They set out their light stones in a circle, laid out their bedrolls and activated the space heater.

After two days in Sherwood, the animal sounds had blended into the background while they traveled. Once they stopped for the night and the horses were quiet, the cacophony of crickets, frogs, insects and animal sounds reminded them that the forest was teeming with life.

Despite the sounds of the forest, Ethan could still feel the far-off magic, though it didn't feel quite so far off as it had back at the bridge. Whatever it was, they were getting closer to it.

While they ate, Ethan sat alongside Michalus for a while and they'd discussed possibilities. Unfortunately, none of their hypotheses could be proven - not until they reached whatever the source of the magic was.

As he and Michalus finished talking, Ethan noticed Yuliana was looking around nervously and biting her lip. Michalus seemed to notice it too. He turned towards the druid. "Everything okay, my dear?"

The green-haired elf, who had been stroking Luna's head, looked up with a start. "Oh. Yes. I think. I mean... I'm not sure."

"What's wrong?" Ethan asked. His first thought was that she didn't have food. Unlike the rest of them, she didn't eat meat and so the fish didn't help her. But they'd all helped her pick some blackberries earlier and then found a nut tree near dark. So he didn't think she was hungry.

"I am not sure," she said. "I feel... anxious. Strange."

"Strange how?" Nia asked, looking around. "Do you hear something? An enemy approaching?"

Yuliana shook her head. "No, there is nothing but the sounds of small creatures scurrying around."

The druid glanced around, hands fidgeting, and forehead wrinkled. She looked back to the group. "It's hard to explain. I can sense groves. All my people can. And I feel something like a grove, but not a grove."

"Huh? A grove that ain't a grove?" Ainslee asked, screwing up her face in confusion.

Ethan noticed Nia sniffing the air, turning her head in different directions. She finished, turned back to him and shrugged. "I smell no enemies."

"As I said," the green-haired elf told them. "I am not sure what it is. It does feel like a grove, but not quite."

"Do you think you are somehow sensing the same magic we are?" Ethan asked and saw Michalus perk up.

"I... am not sure," the druid admitted, unconsciously scratching behind the big cat's ears. The mountain lion leaned into her scratching, letting out a satisfied purring.

"You've never sensed wizard magic before, have you?" Michalus asked.

She shook her head.

Michalus looked to Ethan. "It's very rare that someone who cannot work arcane magic can sense it. I would think that if she had that ability, it would have manifested sooner."

Ethan considered the wizard's words. "Yuliana, this feeling you have, can you point to the direction it's coming from?"

Yuliana nodded and pointed east. Ethan gave Michalus a pointed look. "That seems coincidental. That's where our feeling is coming from too."

The wizard scratched his chin and looked thoughtful. "It's still not conclusive. There could be more than one sort of magic at work."

"More than one sort?" Ethan asked. "You mean a lot of arcane and druid magic?"

Michalus smiled and shrugged. "It could be. She could be sensing the druid magic while we sense arcane magic at use."

"Can someone have both?" Ethan asked. He remembered in some of his role-playing games, people would dual class or multi-class, giving them access to the abilities and magic of two or more classes.

The wizard got a faraway look in his eyes, as if trying to remember something. Finally, he shook his head. "Not that I have ever heard or read about. But there are so many things we don't really know about..."

"Demons!" Ainslee blurted out. "You think it's demons?"

Ethan looked to Michalus, raising a questioning eyebrow. He knew nothing about demons of this world or their capabilities. The only thing he really knew was that warlocks and channelers got their power from them.

"It's rare that actual demons come to our world," Michalus replied hesitantly. "Although it has happened in the past. It's one of the reasons that channelers and warlocks were shunned before the wizards started getting murdered."

"And with good reason!" Ainslee said. Ethan wondered if the dwarf was remembering their battle with the warlock Charmine, outside the library in Patheos. She'd had tremendous power with fire and might have burned Ethan alive except that he was carrying the tomes she wanted.

Charmine had been a relatively low-level warlock too. Ethan imagined how strong a warlock or channeler would be if they were level 10 or even higher. What sort of power would they wield?

Michalus nodded to the dwarf. "Right you are, my dear. The good reason you refer to is the fact that eventually, either the warlock or channeler dies, or they become a puppet to the entity who grants them their powers."

Ethan and Ainslee exchanged looks. It was clear she was remembering the warlock's bizarre behavior and Charmine's habit of talking to something that wasn't there.

"The more a channeler uses magic," Michalus explained to the group, "the more they take on the physical attributes of their patron. Eventually, if it goes on long enough, they seem to take on the personality of their patron as well. They become a lesser version of their patron, here on this world."

"Not good," Par'karr chimed in. "That why Par'karr only summon rabbits."

"Indeed," the wizard chuckled. "It is not good at all. Warlocks, on the other hand, don't transform their bodies. Instead, their patron slowly exerts more and more mental influence over the warlock until they are little more than a hollow shell for the entity to work through."

Ethan furrowed his brow. "So channelers are worse than warlocks?"

The wizard shrugged. "In the end, they're both puppets. Warlocks seem to get the better end of the deal, because they retain their human form. They have more power at their command in the beginning. But their physical form limits them in many ways."

"Their humanoid bodies can only handle so much energy," Ethan guessed.

"Exactly right." Michalus smiled. "But if a channeler ever lives long enough to transform completely, their patron would be able to channel much more energy through them."

"Has that ever happened?" Nia asked.

"A few times in history," Michalus said with a thoughtful look. "Targon the Red was the last one and that was six hundred years ago. He managed to open up a portal and summon real demons. That was back when I was still a relatively young man and there were hundreds of wizards to stand against them. But despite an army of men, elves and dwarves, backed by wizards, he conquered dozens of cities to the south and left most of them in ruins."

"How did they stop him?" Ainslee asked.

"They didn't," Michalus chuckled mirthlessly. "The body finally gave out and he destroyed himself in a column of fire so high, they say you could see it for miles. When he died, the portal closed, and the armies managed to destroy the remaining demons."

"Not good way to die," Par'karr remarked.

Ethan nodded his agreement. He turned to Michalus. "I don't get it. This is common knowledge, right? Why do people become channelers and warlocks, knowing all of this?"

"Very few elves do," Michalus said. "Or dwarves. We have long memories. But humans and halflings, even foxlings, have short lives. A few generations go by and they forget. Or they think they can handle the power.

"But don't get me wrong," the wizard chuckled. "There have been bad wizards too. The lands of Arithgard, to the far east, are ruled with an iron fist by wizards."

"Oh?" Ethan raised an eyebrow. This was the first he heard of another country, especially one ruled by wizards - and bad wizards at that.

"It's too late to get into politics of Arithgard," the wizard chuckled. "Suffice it to say, it makes the current practices of Castlehaven look like a halfling holiday."

Ethan had no idea what a halfling holiday was, but he got the general idea. Arithgard was ruled by wizards and they were bad - worse than the slavery in Castlehaven. Wonderful.

"Why are you telling us all this?" Ainslee demanded. "You trying to give me nightmares or something?"

"Sorry, my dear," the wizard apologized. "That wasn't my intent. I'm afraid I went off on quite a tangent. Now I've gone and forgot what we were talking about to begin with."

Ainslee rolled her eyes. "You and Ethan sense magic. Yuliana senses magic. Is it the same magic?"

"Right," the wizard chuckled. "I think I just demonstrated that it is highly unlikely that they would be the same magic."

The dwarf rolled her eyes. "All I heard was talk of demons, channelers and warlocks!"

"Yes, but..." the wizard started but Ainslee held up a hand.

"I don't want to hear any more about it," the dwarf said adamantly. She looked from Ethan to Michalus. "Just answer the question: Are all three of you sensing the same thing?"

Michalus opened his mouth to speak but Ethan beat him to it. "The answer is: we don't think so, but we don't really know."

Ainslee threw up her hands. "Why didn't you just say that?"

"Yes, well," the wizard chuckled. "I thought I did. But you are right, enough about that. I think we should all get as much rest as possible. Who knows what tomorrow will bring."

Rubbing his chin as the others prepared their bedrolls, Ethan wasn't sure if Michalus's comment sounded reassuring or ominous.

38

The feeling of magic and of that "wrongness" continued to get stronger as the group traveled east the next day. Ethan checked with Michalus and with Yuliana. Both of them confirmed their own feelings of magic were growing stronger too.

And it wasn't just the feeling of magic and wrongness that was bugging him. Something else was growing stronger too. Ethan hadn't noticed it before, but the longer the day went on, the more he sensed... something.

Just before lunch, Ethan noticed it first as a buzz in the front of his head and at first he'd thought it was a headache, but fifteen or twenty minutes after it started, he received a notification in his HUD.

`Skill increase: Mental magic +1%.`

It was an increase in *Mental* magic. But why? He hadn't been practicing it since he'd helped Nia. Ethan stopped in his tracks and looked around. He felt himself breaking into a cold sweat. Was it some sort of mental attack? His eyes darted to the river. Was there another Sollasina?

Frowning, he looked up and down the nearby river. The fast-moving whitewaters and the boulders that littered the water appeared too tumultuous to hide one of the nightmare creatures. Then again, he really had no idea what a Cthulhu was capable of.

Stopping, he slid off his horse and walked a few steps closer to the river. He used his *Mental* magic to probe into the water, ready to slam his defenses into place.

"What is it?" asked Nia, who had moved up beside him. The foxgirl was sniffing the air warily and had her free hand on the hilt of her scimitar.

"I'm... not sure," Ethan replied. He'd scanned up and down the nearby river but didn't sense any sort of strong mind in there, just smaller sparks of mental energy - probably fish. His frown deepened as he looked around the foliage. "Something set off my mental magic."

"It did?" Michalus asked. The wizard left his horse with Yuliana and came to stand on Ethan's other side. "Some sort of mental attack, like the Sollasina?"

Ethan shook his head. "No, nothing nearly as strong. It's just a feeling in the front of my head. That and a message in my HUD."

"Interesting," the wizard said, glancing towards the river. Michalus pulled his staff from its place on the back of his saddle. "You're certain it's not a Sollasina?"

Ethan probed the river with his *Mental* magic again. He felt those few small flickers, which he assumed were fish. But there was no big presence and nothing as sinister as a Sollasina Cthulhu.

"What is wrong?" Nia asked, hands on her scimitars. She sniffed the air.

Nodding, Ethan looked from the river to the foliage and the trees. "You don't smell anything weird, do you? Some sort of enemy?"

He purposefully didn't say Sollasina Cthulhu since he didn't want to worry anyone. Especially not Ainslee, who already seemed spooked enough at the idea of possible demons.

"Why are we stopping?" Ainslee asked. She had walked her horse closer to them and was now immediately behind Ethan. The dwarf had her hammer out and slapped into her opposite hand. "Something out there?"

"We're not sure," Ethan replied. "I felt something."

"Like what?" Ainslee asked, eyes narrowing.

"Some sort of mental probe or attack," he said.

The dwarf's eyes opened wide. "You mean like that tentacle monster?"

"No," Ethan assured her, though he didn't know for certain. There wasn't a Sollasina in the river but could one live on land?

"You're sayin' no." The dwarf smirked. "But you don't look so sure."

Par'karr and Yuliana had joined them, and Ethan looked around at his companions. "None of you feel anything. No buzzing in your head?"

The group shook their heads or muttered negative replies.

Ethan looked to Michalus. He bit his lip, knowing that

his next question would get a reaction from the group. "Is it possibly another Sollasina? Can they live on land?"

The wizard rubbed his chin. "I've never read about one out of water. And I believe it actually needs to be in contact with you to use its mental attack. At least, from what I've read."

"It wasn't touching me when it was in Nia's head," Ethan protested, remembering how the thing had mentally attacked him.

"Ah, yes," the elven wizard said. "But you reached out to it, correct?"

Thinking back to the experience, Ethan nodded. "True. I did reach out mentally."

"Your probing might have opened some sort of mental conduit that it attacked through," the wizard suggested.

"That's possible," Ethan admitted. Silently, he made a mental note to be careful who and what he reached out to. If Michalus was right and probing someone opened up a conduit, then he could be opening himself up to being assaulted.

In computer terms, it was like adding a computer to a network. He remembered once when he and his friends had been playing a new multiplayer RPG game. They'd connected their computers in a sort of "virtual LAN" so they could all play at the same time. The problem was, Hunter's computer had been infected with a virus and it had infected everyone's computer.

At least, it had tried. Being the computer geek he was, Ethan had the latest firewall software on his computer. His firewall had blocked the attack, but Gage and Wyatt hadn't been so lucky. Their computers had been infected and they'd had to wipe their entire hard drives and reload all of their software. They had not been happy, and Hunter had been forced to buy pizza for the next several gaming nights as recompense.

The brief bout of nostalgia brought a smile to his face but also a bit of sadness. Ethan knew he'd never see Hunter, Gage or Wyatt again. Or his parents. The realization brought a sense of melancholy. Unfortunately, it wasn't a feeling he could indulge at the moment with the buzzing still in his head.

On the other hand, his computer analogy made him wonder what might be trying to "infect" his mind. Obviously, it wasn't a computer virus, but something was clearly trying to get into his brain, possibly into his friends' minds as well. But because they didn't have *Mental* magic, they couldn't detect it.

The question was: what was doing this probing?

"Michalus, any ideas what might be trying to get into our minds?" he asked.

"Our minds?" The wizard raised an eyebrow.

"I'm the only one with mental magic," Ethan explained. "I might be the only one who can detect it. That doesn't mean whatever it is isn't probing all of us."

The group looked uneasy. They glanced around the area, as if they could see whatever was mentally probing them.

Once again, Michalus rubbed his chin and looked thoughtful. Finally, he shrugged. "That's possible. But I can't think of anything. There aren't many things that have any sort of mental attack. The Sollasina, of course, but that was a demon, or a channeler transformed into a demon."

Ethan frowned. Being over eight hundred years old, Michalus was a treasure trove of knowledge. If he hadn't heard of anything, then there probably wasn't anything. At least, nothing natural.

The Sollasina had been a demon, or as Michalus had pointed out, a channeler who had completely transformed into its demon patron. But that was just one sort of demon. And if one sort of demon could have the ability, then it was logical to assume other demons might have the same or similar power.

He and Michalus both still sensed magic to the east, but it was magic tainted with a sort of wrongness. Was there some sort of demon to the east that had mental powers? *Mental* powers that didn't require touch. If so, how powerful was it that it could touch them from such a distance.

Thinking back to his memory of his friends and how their computers were infected, Ethan was reminded that his firewall had saved his computer. That made him remember the noise-canceling necklaces he'd made for Nia and Yuliana.

When the high-pitched noise from the Grail had hurt their ears to a point where it had nearly incapacitated them, he'd created magical necklaces that prevented high-frequency noises from reaching their ears and affecting them.

Could he create something similar to block out mental attacks? It seemed like the same concept but instead of sound, he'd block out mental attacks.

"I have seen that look," Nia said. She had narrowed her eyes, but she wore a smile. "You have an idea."

"I think I do." Ethan nodded.

"Does it involve turning around and going home?" Ainslee asked hopefully.

"Sorry, no," Ethan replied.

Ethan fished through his pouches until he found his bag of Chymera crystals. Opening it, he looked at the small collection. And, sadly, it was a small collection.

Between the portal pouches, the portal backpack for the villagers and some of his other items, he'd used up almost all of the crystals he'd taken from the library at Patheos. Creating the magic space heater had used up quite a few, as well.

"Do you have any Chymera crystals?" he asked Michalus.

The elf raised an eyebrow. "You're thinking of enchanting something?"

"Several somethings." He grinned.

"I do have a small collection." Michalus flashed him an apologetic look. "But they are back at my home."

Ethan cursed. Having created a number of items on his adventures, he always kept them with him. Maybe that hadn't been such a good idea. He'd become a little too cavalier with his creation of magic items and now he barely had any left.

"What are you planning to make?" the wizard asked.

"Firewalls," Ethan replied with a grin. When he received the confused looks from his companions, he continued. "I want to create a magic item that will block out the mental attack - or whatever it is."

The wizard rubbed his chin. "That's a very interesting idea. I've read about charm bracelets that wizards have created to block certain elements. Terrific in duels, I've read - so long as you have one for each element and there's enough mana to feed the effect! If the crystals are drained of mana, the enchantment fails, and it leaves the duelist vulnerable."

"You're saying enough of that element, say fire, directed at someone with the charm and the charm fails and fire gets through?" Ethan asked.

"Precisely," Michalus confirmed.

Ethan bit his lip. If they were feeling the mental attack this far away, how powerful would it be as they got closer? And if the attack was constant, how long would the *Mana* in the battery crystals last before it was exhausted?

"Let's set up camp," Ethan told his companions and received more confused looks.

"It's not even lunch time," Ainslee protested but then seemed to have a change of heart and brightened. "But we can have an early lunch!"

"What are you thinking?" Nia asked him.

"I don't want to get closer to whatever is creating this mental attack - or whatever it is - until I see if I can create some sort of mental shield for us," Ethan told the foxgirl.

"I will prepare the camp," she told him. Taking his horse and hers, she led them to a smaller tree by the edge of the river. The others went with her. All except Michalus.

"You might need my help, if you're going to be creating more magical items," the wizard said and then chuckled.

"Actually, I think you may have created more magical items than I have."

"Maybe," Ethan replied. "But they're all simple. You've created more complicated items - like your invisible shack and that portal detector."

Michalus nodded. "We'll then, let's put our heads together and see what we can come up with."

39

After explaining his idea several times to Michalus, the wizard sat back and thought about it for nearly half an hour. While the elf was contemplating the best way to enchant an item, Ethan began charging up some Chymera crystals.

He managed to fill two crystals before he needed to recharge. When he mentioned to Nia that he was out of *Mana*, she was only too happy to help him refill his supply. There had been no hunting since they entered Sherwood. That meant there hadn't been any opportunities to slip away for some alone time.

Ignoring the snickering from Ainslee and the slightly embarrassed look from Yuliana, Ethan and Nia walked back down the road the way they had come. The two walked just out of sight of the camp before ducking into the foliage.

Even where they were, Ethan still felt the buzzing in his head, and he found it hard to get into the mood with

Nia. It felt creepy, like someone was watching him. Someone he didn't know and who could have sinister intentions.

Nia, who had been stripping off her clothes, stopped and looked at him. "Is something wrong? Did you not want to 'recharge' your mana?"

He smiled at his wife. "I do. I just need to see if I can mask out this mental buzzing."

The foxgirl nodded and went back to stripping off her clothes. Ethan watched her for a moment, distracted by her nubile body before shaking his head and remembering what he had been about to do.

Focusing on it, he was able to mask it out by imagining a mental wall around his head and then feeding some *Mana* into it.

Skill increase: Mental magic +1%.

It worked. The buzzing stopped. Unfortunately, his Mana began dropping as well. He began counting to himself to see how long before another point dropped. That was when he noticed Nia had finished stripping off her clothes and had spread a blanket on the ground. She smiled invitingly at him. Suddenly, how long it took to use up a point of *Mana* with his mental shield didn't matter so much.

After he recharged his *Mana* with Nia, he tried something different. Ethan used his *Mana Siphon* ability to charge one of the crystals by pulling some of Nia's *Mana*. He then used his own *Mana* to fill up another crystal.

With the crystals charged, they had another love-making session. His *Mana* was full, as usual, but he was happy to learn that Nia's *Mana* was completely restored as well. He smiled that would make things much easier.

Ethan and Nia charged up six more crystals over the next hour and by the end, he needed to replenish his *Stamina* at the river. The river water was cool and refreshing but he still eyed it warily. He didn't sense a Sollasina in the water, but he was still new to *Mental* magic. For all he knew, the creature might be able to block his magical probing like he'd just blocked out whatever was probing him.

After drinking their fill at the river, Ethan and Nia went back to the camp. Par'karr was busy playing with his demon rabbits, while Ainslee leaned back against a tree with her eyes closed. Yuliana was sitting on the grass with Luna purring next to her as the elf rubbed the cat's belly.

He found Michalus sitting near the river's edge. The wizard looked up as he came over. He flashed Ethan a sly grin and winked. "Finished charging your crystals?"

Ethan returned his smile and shrugged. "I have ten crystals charged and 6 left over. I can use five of those as the control crystals."

"Good," the elf said and motioned Ethan to sit down next to him.

Ethan did so and the elf looked out at the river and rubbed his chin. "I've been thinking about your idea and it's very similar to protection charms that dueling wizards use. They can protect from one or more elements during a magical duel. Very helpful."

"Yes," Ethan said excitedly. "That sounds like exactly what we need - only for mental magic attacks."

"Ah," said the wizard, holding up a ringer. "And therein lies the problem. You see, the charms work - but only for so long."

Ethan started to ask why but then realized the answer. "The crystals."

"Very good." Michalus nodded. "As you know, once joined, a series of crystals can generate a charge and charge themselves back up over a period of time. Depending on the power of the enchantment, some enchantments run continuously."

"Like my light stones," Ethan said, thinking of the light stones he'd created in the tomb to shed light. The enchantment to make light used so little magic, the light effect was constant.

"Precisely," the wizard agreed. "But some enchantments are intensive and they use up the charge in the crystals much more quickly."

Nodding, Ethan looked over to Par'karr, who still carried his magical shotgun. At least, his attempt at a shotgun. It shot round stones using <u>Air</u> magic, but the enchanted weapon took almost a minute to recharge between shots.

Michalus followed his gaze. "Yes, your... what did Par'karr call it... oh yes, a boom-stick. It can fire once a minute, right?"

"Both barrels, yes. But technically, you can fire one barrel every thirty seconds or so." Ethan grinned. He was thinking of his favorite movie that he'd taken the idea from for the magical shotgun. He did miss his favorite movies.

"Ah yes, well," the wizard continued. "The concept is

the same for protection charms. You can protect against harmful magical effects - but there are limits."

Ethan frowned. He thought back to the "noise canceling" necklaces he'd created. They protected against the high-pitch sound constantly. They'd never run out of *Mana*. "I think you know I created a couple of necklaces that blocked out the high-pitch sounds from the Grail. They never needed a recharge time."

"Ah, that might be true," Michalus admitted. "But those sounds, while annoying or even headache-inducing, never caused damage. The amount of power that the necklaces were actually blocking was negligible. Compare that to trying to stop a torrent of flame from a powerful wizard or warlock."

The wizard gestured down to his portal pouch. "Then there are things like these. How did you get your pouch to operate all of the time?"

"I..." Ethan started to answer and realized the point Michalus was making. "Ah... so one way around that is to use more battery crystals."

"Battery crystals?" the elf cocked his head.

Ethan facepalmed himself as he realized they didn't have batteries in this low-tech world. "The crystals that store the mana."

"Ah, yes," the wizard retorted. "The mana crystals. Right you are. You can get a more powerful effect or a longer duration by adding additional mana crystals. Plus, the majority of the power of opening a portal comes from opening it. Not much is actually needed to keep it open."

"I see your point," Ethan said, and he did. Unfortunately, what the wizard said made sense. "You're saying the items we make will only protect from the mental attacks for so long. The only way around that would be to add more battery crystals."

"Or they will need a period to recharge," the wizard agreed. "But, if you are counting on them to provide constant protection, I would think of a mental attack as similar to a torrent of flame. Depending on the power of the mental attacks, it might last hours or only minutes. It all depends on how many mana crystals you have powering the enchantment."

"And we're down to our last batch of crystals." Ethan cursed. He'd thought he could make mental-protection items as easily as he'd made the noise-canceling items. It sounded like it wouldn't work that way.

As he thought about the magic items, he remembered his mental shield he'd erected earlier. He brought up his *Mana*, which had been at full after their last love-making session.

Mana: 84

He frowned. He was still at max *Mana*. Why wasn't it decreasing? Then he remembered he recharged a point of *Mana* about every minute. The draw from his *Mana* pool must not quite be a point per minute. He could maintain his shield indefinitely, but the cost of the shield would effectively negate his natural *Mana* regeneration.

Checking his messages, he noticed that he had a dozen increases in *Mental* magic. Did that mean it was some sort of ongoing attack? Or were the increases coming from maintaining the shield he'd erected.

He sighed as he realized that wasn't the case. Right now, this mental buzzing was barely a probe. It certainly wasn't an attack. How much *Mana* would his mental shield use to ward off an actual attack against the Sollasina? He hoped he'd never find out.

"Thinking of something?" the wizard asked, interrupting him from his thoughts.

"Sorry," Ethan said apologetically.

"No need to apologize," Michalus said, waving his hand. "I get lost in my own thoughts quite often."

"I've constructed a mental barrier for myself and right now, it's not using any *Mana*," he told the elf. "I assume that's because I'm regenerating it as quickly as I use it."

"Yes," the wizard confirmed. "We can sustain small enchantments indefinitely. But the more powerful enchantments will consume our mana much more quickly. And like the charms, the more magical energy you block, the more mana it will take to block it."

Ethan nodded, remembering the mana blade - the laser sword-like enchantment that caused an enchanted blade of energy to appear. Michalus had first used it against some ogres that had attacked them, but he'd later taught it to Ethan. It was a devastating weapon, but it consumed a lot of *Mana* to maintain.

Frowning again, he began wondering how much protection the necklaces would actually provide for his friends. Then again, wasn't some protection better than no protection?

He thought about his own mental wall and an idea came to him. "Can we make an item that taps into a person's *Mana* to recharge itself?"

Michalus rubbed his chin, staring out at the river. "It's possible, but rarely used on items with mundane use. Even wizards are careful about carrying items that consume the user's own *Mana*. Wizards have much more mana than an average person. While the drain on us might not be very noticeable, the item might drain a mundane's to unconsciousness. But even for a wizard, a powerful enchantment can consume a good deal of your mana."

Ethan thought of the Chymera crystal switch he'd created for the shotgun on the triggers. He grinned. "What if we added an on/off switch to the recharging?"

The wizard furrowed his brow and looked at Ethan. "An on/off switch?"

"I created a similar thing for the boomstick," Ethan explained. "The triggers have crystals on them that actually activate the air to shoot the stone. Until then, it just stores the charge. We should be able to rig up something that turns the recharge on and off. Then, the person could decide whether or not they wanted it to draw mana from them."

Michalus considered his idea for a moment before nodding. "That might work. But there are still some dangers."

"True," Ethan said. "But there are dangers if we run into some sort of Sollasina attack too."

"Right you are, my boy." The wizard shuddered, most likely remembering the Cthulhu encounter at the river. "Right you are."

40

Ethan found five stones near the river and shaped them into circlets with Earth. Since everyone's head was different, he had to shape them to fit each person correctly. The last thing he wanted was for them to be too tight to wear, or so loose that they fell off.

After shaping them and embedding the crystals, he enchanted them with Michalus watching over his shoulder. The wizard didn't say much, but the extra attention made Ethan feel like he was doing a test for a college professor or working on a computer while the customer watched him.

Finally, around dusk, Ethan was done, and he handed them out to his friends. They looked down at the newly created circlets and then at each other. Nia made a little shrug and slipped it onto her head. She cocked her head one way, then the other.

"I do not feel anything different," she told the group.

The others, apparently happy to let Nia be the scape-goat, nodded and then slipped their own circlets on.

"Not too bad, wizard-boy," the dwarf said. "Kinda plain though. Next time, maybe you could put some runes or patterns on the band. I can draw some up for ya, if you like."

Unsure how to take the dwarf's words, Ethan nodded. "I can try that. I can mostly make the stone do what I want, but I've never tried to make patterns in it before."

"That's the difference between a fair smith and a good smith," Ainslee said. "Little things like etchings and inscribed runes. They don't just add decoration, they also show the smith's skill."

"I'll give it a try next time," Ethan promised. He meant it too. He'd rather create cool-looking items than plain items. But in the end, he was more about the function than the form. After all, a cool-looking item that didn't work helped no one.

"Now that you have them, let me explain a bit about them. These are..." Ethan started and looked over to Michalus, since he'd forgotten what the wizard had called them.

"Protection charms," the elf supplied.

"Protection charms," Ethan continued. "They protect specifically against mental attacks..."

"Like the Solla-whatchamacallit," the dwarf added.

"Yes." Ethan nodded. "And whatever is generating the mental attack that we're all experiencing now."

"It is an attack?" Nia asked. "Even though we do not feel anything?"

"Who is attacking us?" Yuliana asked at the same time.

Ethan shrugged. "Attack or probe, I'm not sure which but I don't want to risk anything else getting inside our heads. I have mental magic, so that's why I can detect it. None of you do, so I assume that's why you can't feel it."

"Probe?" Par'karr asked, his scaly brow furrowing.

"A probe. Similar to what I was practicing on you," he told the kobold.

"That not hurt," Par'karr retorted.

"No," Ethan admitted. "But I never tried any sort of mental attack. I don't know enough about mental magic to know if the probe can be used as an attack. I just don't want us blind-sided with an attack like the Sollasina."

The group nodded almost as one.

"You do not have one," Nia said with a frown.

"I can protect myself with my mental magic shield," he told her.

"You are the alpha. You should have one," Nia insisted and removed her circlet. "You must use mine."

Ethan waved her circlet away. "I can't. First, it won't fit. Second, I need it protecting you. If you are under some sort of mental attack, it will take me a lot more mana to shield you than it would to shield myself. Trust me."

Thinking of his shield, he brought up his HUD and checked his *Mana*.

Mana: 37

It was still at the same level it had been from enchanting the circlets. It hadn't decreased, but it also hadn't regenerated either. The effort of keeping his mental shield in place was consuming the *Mana* as it regenerated, just as he had guessed it would.

The foxgirl held the circlet out for a moment longer before replacing it on her head. "Then I will wear it."

The group started to turn to go back to their bedrolls, but Ethan cleared his throat to get their attention. "One more thing. The crystals that power it only have so much energy. If you feel something in your head... like a buzzing in the front of your mind, then the crystals have run out of juice."

"Juice?" Par'karr asked.

"Uh, power," Ethan corrected. "If you feel the buzz, it's out of power. If that happens, you can tap the crystal in the front of the circlet, and it will start to draw on your own mana... like I did to open the dragon door in the tomb."

"Wait! What does that mean - draw on our own mana?" Ainslee asked.

"It means, it will start powering the enchantment with your own mana," Ethan answered. "If you do that, bring up your HUD and watch your mana carefully. If it goes too low, turn it off by touching it again."

Ethan turned to Michalus and then to Par'karr. "You two don't have HUDs, so you'll need to be particularly careful."

"After a few hundred years, I have a good feel for my mana, my boy," the wizard replied with a chuckle.

Par'karr didn't look too certain. He took off the circlet and looked at it, then put it back on his head. "How Par'karr know?"

Biting his lip, Ethan shrugged. "I'm not sure, buddy. Just be very careful with it."

The kobold nodded and Ethan hoped he would. He was pretty certain his enchantment wouldn't take someone below zero *Mana*, but he hadn't had any way of testing it. "Everyone be careful when using your own mana to power the circlet."

"You do not know what is attacking us?" Yuliana asked.

Ethan shook his head. "I have no idea. Until the Sollasina, I didn't even know that creatures could do mental attacks."

"There are some demons, and by extension some channelers," Michalus explained, "who can create mental attacks and use mental magic. It's very rare. The only one I know of for certain is the Sollasina. But it does stand to reason that there are others."

"Everyone be on guard. Watch each other for any behavior out of the ordinary," he said, purposefully not looking at Nia.

The foxgirl had been "possessed" by the Sollasina and her consciousness locked away in a sort of dream world while the Sollasina was controlling her body. If the same thing happened to any of the others, he'd have a mental fight on his hands - one that had permanently cost him a point of *Hardiness* when he'd freed Nia. He didn't want to go through that again.

"But your circlet should protect us, correct?" Yuliana asked, her eyes darting to Nia. Ethan noticed that the elf wasn't the only one who cast furtive glances at the foxgirl.

"It should," Ethan replied, "as long as it has power."

The green-haired elf nodded, her hand moving up to the circlet around her head.

"This is why I'm tired of these adventures, wizard-boy," the dwarf said. "No dwarf ever got attacked by tentacle creatures or werewolves or mental attacks out of nowhere, by working their forge."

He started to reply but the dwarf held up her hand. "I told you I'd come with you for this so I can get me anvil. But after this, I don't want nothing else to do with adventuring. I've said my piece. That's all I got to say about that."

Ethan nodded and the others went back to their bedrolls. He brought out some of the frozen fish and heated them up before handing them out to everyone. As he ate his, he thought about Ainslee's words.

The dwarf had been upfront with him back in the village about her thoughts on adventuring. He'd convinced her to come along with promises of an anvil for her forge. The dwarf's attitude hadn't changed, and he couldn't blame her.

Ainslee wasn't an adventurer. Neither was Yuliana. Their lives had been dedicated to their jobs before they had been abducted. The dwarf had been a smith, while the elf had been the caretaker of some sort of sentient trees that tended their world.

Even Par'karr and Michalus weren't adventurers. Par'karr had been a rabbit herder before a hostile tribe had wiped out his people. Michalus, despite being over eight hundred years old, had spent his life in the academic pursuit of magical knowledge. He was a scholar, not a warrior.

Only Nia came from any sort of warrior background.

She'd been trained as a chieftain's daughter to be a fighter - a very good fighter.

Ethan thought of himself then. He wasn't an adventurer. He was a computer technician. He fixed computers, printers, set up networks and did basic troubleshooting. Sure, he was a total science geek and had watched way too much discovery TV, but he was just a geek. Why was he having an easier time dealing with it than everyone else?

He thought about his magic. Was that why he was having an easier time? Because of his magic?

Thinking back to his conversation with Ainslee in the village, when he was trying to convince her to come along. What had she said? "Most of the stuff, you just magic to death. You don't need me."

The real question was, why wasn't he freaking out about the entire situation? Was it just because of the magic, or was it possible the aliens had done something to him? And if they had, why not do it to the others?

Ethan thought back to all the roleplaying games and MMORPGs he played back on Earth. Was that part of it? All of these monsters and magic, had he trained his mind to accept all of this with all of the games he'd played? Did part of his mind, even back on his own world, crave adventure?

He looked around his companions as they ate. None of them, except maybe Nia and Par'karr, looked like they wanted to be here. And he guessed Par'karr only wanted to be here because he was here. The little kobold seemed loyal to a fault.

He was still thinking about his companions when Par'karr screamed and disappeared into the bushes.

41

———

Ethan had been zoning out when he heard the kobold scream and it took him precious seconds to process what was going on. He started to jump to his feet when the vine he was sitting on suddenly snaked around his legs. The vine seemed to grow thorns, or perhaps the thorns had been flush against the vine until it attacked.

```
Thorny   Snare   pierces   you   for   1
damage.
    You have been poisoned.
```

Cursing as he felt the sting and read the message, Ethan nearly activated his fire elemental armor. Just in time, he stopped himself. Was this one of the tree-folk? If so, was there a chance they could talk their way out of this?

The main reason Yuliana had come was to meet the

tree-folk and see if they were like the caretakers back on her world. If this were one of the tree-folk, then burning it certainly wouldn't help her win any points with it.

He lurched as the vine began to pull him along the ground. As he did, he saw that some of his other companions had also been entangled and were being pulled into the bushes. Nia was slashing at the vines with her scimitars, but more vines sprang up around her. He giggled.

Ethan paused. Why had he just giggled? It wasn't funny. Or was it? He giggled again. Actually, it was funny. He laughed, even while he felt a very pleasant lethargy overcome him. As he was dragged into the bushes, he saw the vines grab Nia again, this time snaking around her legs. He giggled as he disappeared into the underbrush, feeling the pleasant warmness tingling throughout his entire body.

ETHAN SHOT up in his bed, grasping at the vines around him. He blinked, then his eyes grew open wide. He was in his bed. In his bed back on Earth. His head whipped from side to side, taking in the entire room. It was almost exactly as he left it.

How was this possible? Had the aliens returned him to his house? Why would they do that? Had he died on that world, or had it just really been a simulation and he had died in the simulation and the aliens had brought him back to Earth?

"Go back to sleep," came a voice from next to him. A familiar voice.

Glancing down, he saw the naked body of Nia tangled in the covers. Only, it wasn't Nia. At least, it wasn't his Nia. She had the same slim, athletic body as Nia - but this girl was human. A very attractive human with a mop of fiery orange hair.

He reached down and touched her arm. It was flesh, not the light, soft fur that his Nia had. He looked around and caught part of her bare buttocks sticking out from underneath the blanket. Human buttocks, with no fox tail.

What was going on?! Had she died too, and the aliens had made her human and dropped her on Earth too? And what? Made her human? That made no sense.

"Nia?" he whispered.

"Go back to sleep," she groaned. "We can go at it again in the morning."

"But your name is Nia?" he asked.

The woman did stir at that. She turned to look at him, frowning. "UH ...yeah. You get me confused with some other girl?"

"Yes..." he started but saw the dangerous look in her eye, her frown deepening. "I mean... no... I mean... I just had a dream about you... only you weren't... you."

The redhead's expression didn't soften. "A dream about me, only it wasn't me?"

Ethan shook his head. He still felt thick headed from just waking up. "No, I mean... in the dream you were a fox."

Nia raised an eyebrow. "As in a real fox or are you one of those guys who are into furrys?"

"Um..." Ethan couldn't think straight. He still felt so tired, but he had the presence of mind to know that whoever Nia was in this world, she was starting to get annoyed with him. He put on a grin. "I'm not really into furries, but in my dream you were a foxgirl - like in Japanese manga."

"You mean," she sighed, letting her head fall back into the pillow. "Like the foxgirl on my anime t-shirt? The one I was wearing tonight? Just go back to sleep. I have work tomorrow too, remember."

A foxgirl on an anime t-shirt she'd been wearing? What was going on? He had so many questions, but he didn't want to annoy this Nia. He had no idea who she was or what their relationship was, but he guessed he wouldn't score any points by asking things like "Who are you and how did you get into my bed?"

By this time, his eyes had adjusted to the dark and he looked around his room, taking in the details. He saw their clothes on the ground. He also saw an empty bottle of Fireball whiskey.

Was that why he was feeling lethargic? They'd polished off a bottle of whiskey? And then what? Had sex? Given the way the clothes were strewn about the floor and the fact that she was naked, it seemed a logical assumption.

Did that mean everything he'd experienced during the last several months had just been a dream? He shook his head. No, there was no way all of that was just a dream. He bit his lip. Or was there?

Ethan glanced around the room again. This was his room. He looked down at the end table. There was his phone and his clock. The clock read 3:31 am. That was way too early to be up. Maybe he should go back to bed.

He looked down at his phone and then over to Nia.

Her eyes were closed, and she was breathing regularly. Did that mean she was asleep?

Reaching over, he picked up his phone and used his fingerprint to unlock it. It was the same as he remembered. He brought up his text messages. They were all to and from his friends. He clicked on the last message in a group conversation to his buddies.

He scrolled down to a picture he had sent and opened it up. It was a picture of Nia and him in a booth. He stared at it, head still dull. He recognized that booth. It was at a Thai restaurant and bar not too far from his house. He'd gone there to eat dinner every now and then.

Scrolling down further in the texts, he started reading:

```
Hunter: Still on tonight right?
   Gage: We'd better be
   Ethan:  Still  on.  Gonna  stop  by
Uncle Rogers and grab fried rice. Be
on at 7
   Wyatt: 7 good for me
   Hunter: Me 2
   Gage: Same
```

He vaguely remembered that text exchange, though it seemed like months ago now. He looked at the time stamp, it had been today. Wait, it was after midnight. Technically, it had been yesterday.

```
Ethan: Really hot girl here. Gonna
talk to her.
   Gage: Ha sure you will
```

```
Wyatt: 20 he doesn't
Hunter: Yur on
Gage: Double dog dare you
```

There was almost twenty minutes before the next text. It was a picture he'd sent to his buddies. He brought it up. The picture was a selfie of Ethan and Nia next to each other, smiling. He read the remaining texts.

```
Ethan: No gaming tonight we're going
back to my place
    Gage: You go Ethan!!!!
    Wyatt: Dude! She's gorgeous!!!!
    Hunter: Pay up Wyatt
    Wyatt: Ha worth it if he actually
gets some
    Wyatt: Wats her name in case she
murders you and cuts your body into
pieces?
    Hunter: Axe-murderer!
    Gage: Or just cuts off 1 thing!
    Ethan: Nia
    Hunter: Full report tomorrow
```

That was the final message. Ethan looked at the picture again. In the picture, Nia was wearing a green shirt with a foxgirl on it and Japanese characters that he couldn't read. He'd really summoned up the courage to talk to her? Or more amazingly, she might have talked to him.

He glanced back at the sleeping woman. He'd just met

her, and they'd hit it off and then come back to his place and had sex? That never happened to him! And why couldn't he remember it?

His eyes fell on the empty bottle of whiskey. Had he really drunk so much he couldn't remember? He rubbed his temples. His head certainly felt like he was nursing a bit of a hangover.

Then what about the last several months on that planet where he was a wizard? That had really all just been a dream? He could still recall everything in such vivid detail. The kobold attack on Hawkshead, the library in Patheos, the tomb of Pendragon - even the Cthulhu tentacled monster that had attacked them. He remembered it all.

He bit his lip again and looked down at Nia again. Tentatively, he tried calling up his HUD. Nothing happened. He tried summoning a ball of fire. Once again, nothing happened. He suddenly felt stupid, and a bit disappointed. He shook his head. It really had just been a dream.

Ethan set his phone back down. It was so hard to think. His head hurt and he was tired. So tired. He yawned. Maybe Nia was right, and he needed to go back to sleep.

Lying down, he covered up with the blanket and closed his eyes. Maybe this would all make sense tomorrow and hopefully he wouldn't have a bad hangover.

THE SUN WAS STREAMING through the window when Ethan opened his eyes to light kissing on his back. They felt good and he shivered at her touch.

"I gotta run home and get dressed for work," she said, pulling him onto his back. "But I have time for a quickie."

Ethan's head was foggy, and he had a headache, but he still rose to the occasion. Their sex was fast and both familiar and strange. This Nia was so much like the Nia in his dream and yet, it wasn't her.

Nia hadn't been joking. Ten minutes later, they were done, and she immediately hopped off the bed and began dressing.

"Sorry, Ethan." She grinned. "Duty calls. Well, work calls at least. Give me your number and I'll call you later."

Ethan had been staring at Nia as she got dressed. At the mention of work and his phone, he turned and grabbed his phone. It was 6:53. He was going to be late.

Swinging his feet off the bed, Ethan stood up. At least, that was his intention. Instead, he collapsed to the floor.

He heard Nia's musical laughter and her head poked over the bed so she could see him. "Did I wear you out?"

Grinning, Ethan shrugged. "I guess so."

He tried standing again, but his legs wouldn't move. They were like jello. He began to panic. "I can't move my legs."

The smile faded from Nia's face and her brow furrowed. "Are you serious? This isn't some sort of joke, is it?"

Fighting the panic as he tried to move his legs again, Ethan shook his head. "No joke. I can't move my legs at all."

Coming around the bed quickly, Nia knelt down beside him. She looked him over, her face a mask of both concern and panic. "What do I do? Should I call 9-1-1?!"

Trying to move his legs and failing again, Ethan nodded. "I think you'd better."

Nia reached down and slapped him hard across the face. "Get up!"

Face stinging, Ethan raised his hand to his cheek and blinked. "What? Why did you..."

Nia slapped him again, harder and he tasted blood in his mouth. She looked down at him, her face dark. "WAKE UP!"

The girl brought her hand back for another slap and Ethan closed his eyes. He felt another stinging sensation and snapped his eyes open. Gorgeous or not, she needed to stop hitting him. "That's enough!"

Ethan snapped his eyes open and then blinked. Staring down at him were Yuliana, Par'karr, Michalus, Ainslee and Nia - his Nia. The foxgirl looked down with a smile. "He is awake!"

"See," said Ainslee with a grin, pulling her hand back from his face. "I told you. I just had to slap him harder."

Looking from face to face, Ethan asked the obvious question. "What the heck is going on?"

42

"Cup now," Ainslee said, "talk later!"

"What?" Ethan said, still disoriented. Nia helped him sit up and he had a momentary feeling of vertigo. He felt weak all over, as if he'd just had a really bad fever. He looked down at himself and saw that his clothes were stained with blood at various spots where his leather armor didn't cover. "What happened?"

He squinted as a familiar buzzing in his head seemed to cut through his brain. He made a pained face and remembered what it was. It was the mental attack he'd felt before. Ethan also felt the need to get to Camelot more strongly than ever. He wasn't sure why he felt so compelled. But then again, it was really hard to think at the moment.

Ethan threw up his *Mental* shield and the buzzing disappeared. At the same time, maybe because he was just thinking about it, he noticed that his strong need to get to

Camelot diminished too. He wondered why that was but then Par'karr answered his question.

"Plant attack us!" Par'karr told him, pointing to the left. Ethan saw spots of blood all over the kobold's scaly arms and legs too but no open wounds. Looking down at his own arms and legs, he saw no puncture marks. Yuliana must have already healed them.

Following the kobold's finger, he saw an enormous venus fly trap-looking plant with long, snake-like vines. Squinting, Ethan could see that some of the vines were coated red with blood. Their blood.

He was close enough to Analyze it and brought up its stats.

```
Thorny Snare
    Level: 10
```

The Thorny Snare was level 10. That put it about the same level as the ogres they'd fought. And it had caught them by surprise. Why was he still alive? Why were any of them still alive? He furrowed his brow. "How did we get away? I don't remember anything after it grabbed my legs."

Ainslee put her meaty hand on Yuliana's head and messed up her hair. "Our little elfy here can talk to plants! She asked it to let us go... and it did."

Ethan shook his head. "Wait?! What?!"

"This plant is like the caretakers." Yuliana nodded excitedly. "I can communicate with it!"

"You talked to it?" Ethan asked. He tried standing up

but his legs buckled, much like they had in the dream. "What's wrong with my legs?"

The group exchanged glances.

Nia frowned. "You were the last one it let go. It was sucking out our blood and you lost the most."

"It's a vampire plant?" Ethan asked. It looked a lot like a venus fly trap, but he didn't remember venus fly traps being vampires. They certainly didn't have vines that wrapped around people and dragged them to the main body of the plant.

"Not in the traditional vampire sense," Michalus replied. "The thorny snare, or datura stramonium, also called the devil's snare, is a carnivorous plant that supplements its nutritional needs by the blood of animals - or in our case, humanoids. The thorns on the vines inject a poison that causes powerful hallucinations while also giving the creature a feeling of euphoria, so it doesn't struggle while the plant... drinks."

The wizard looked troubled. "Some people have harvested the poison to sell on the blackmarket. But as you can imagine, that is a dangerous profession."

Ethan blinked at the elven wizard. It was like he was reciting an entry from Wikipedia. He tried to process it, but his brain was still fuzzy. Plus, the hallucination had been so real. He really had begun to believe he was back on Earth.

Nia dropped down to her knees in front of him and held him by the shoulders. She looked into his eyes to get his attention. "Ethan. Get the Grail. We still have the plant's poison in our systems."

He blinked again. His addled mind slow to understand

her. Then he realized what she was asking. That was right, Yuliana could heal wounds but couldn't cure poison. Reaching down, he pulled the Grail from his portal pouch. Nia flinched and the two elves grimaced. The elves fumbled for their necklaces, foreheads wrinkled in pain.

"Sorry," he said belatedly, remembering the high pitch sound the Grail emitted when removed from Arthur's sarcophagus. Normally, he gave them time to put on the special noise-canceling magical necklaces he'd enchanted. This time, he'd just pulled it out without waiting.

Nia pulled out her water bottle and poured some water into the Grail, then pushed the chalice towards Ethan's mouth. "You first."

Ethan didn't feel like arguing and took a sip. Immediately, his head cleared, and he felt better all over. Bringing up his HUD, he checked his stats.

```
Health: 30
  Mana: 84
Stamina: 60
```

His stats were back to normal. Ethan moved his legs and was happy to see that they responded normally. He handed the Grail to Nia and stood up.

Once everyone had taken a turn with the Grail, Ethan replaced it in the portal pouch, setting it back on Arthur's tomb. Then he looked at the Thorny Snare. "So, we're safe now?"

Yuliana nodded. "I convinced it that we are friends."

"Friends not food?" Ethan smiled, remembering a line from some animated fish movie.

No one reacted and he sighed. "Does this mean we can go back to camp without worrying about it?"

Ainslee shook her head. "Ah, I don't think I want to sleep anywhere near this thing."

"Par'karr not want to sleep near it either," the kobold said.

"The thorny snare will not bother us again," Yuliana told them confidently.

Looking around, Ethan could read the others' faces. No one but Yuliana was confident the plant wouldn't decide it wanted a midnight snack. Now free of the lingering effects of the poison, his mind was starting to work again. "Wait... what about the horses?"

Yuliana shook her head. "It did not go after them."

"Probably too heavy," Ainslee snickered.

"Whatever the reason, why don't we pack up and give the thorny snare some room," Ethan suggested and everyone but Yuliana nodded or muttered agreements.

The green-haired elf looked back at the Thorny Snare but then shrugged. "That is probably for the best. If we are near, we will scare off its other food."

"How do we know we won't just walk into another one of those thorny things?" Ainslee asked. "I don't know about you, but I didn't see it until it was wrapping itself around me."

Ethan looked at the giant venus fly trap plant. He opened his mouth to respond but closed it. The dwarf was right. It had been twenty feet from the camp and none of them had noticed it. Or maybe they'd seen the vines, but they hadn't rung any alarm bells.

"I don't know that we would see another one without

scouting the area around any camps we make," Ethan told them.

Nia shook her head. "I have its scent now. I will know if one is nearby."

"Very nice, fox-girly," bellowed Ainslee, slapping the foxgirl on the back and causing her to stagger a step.

Rolling her eyes at the dwarf, Nia looked at Ethan. "You wish to find another campsite for tonight?"

Ethan looked from the giant plant to Yuliana and then back to Nia. "I think that would be best."

The group returned to their camp, gathered up their stuff and started walking. The horses were skittish but hadn't broken the rope that bound them. With a little coaxing and soft words, they finally relaxed enough that the group could load their gear.

With horses in tow, they set off down the overgrown road. It was dark, so they used their light stones to light the way. Nia went first, sniffing the air constantly for any scent of more Thorny Snares.

After about two miles, they found another suitable clearing and stopped while Nia sniffed around the area. After a minute, she returned to the group. "I smell no thorny snare."

The group quickly began setting up their camp and placing the heater and light stones. As they did, Ethan turned to Nia. "Did you have a...uh... dream while the creature had you?"

Nia frowned and nodded. "It was like the dream I had when the creature was in my head. I saw our children again."

Ethan moved over to the foxgirl and gave her a hug. "Sorry it was just a dream."

He let go of the foxgirl and saw that her eyes were moist. He was trying to find some comforting words when Ainslee spoke up. "I dreamed I was back on my own world. I had a smithy and I owned a tavern! I would craft and then go drink as much as I wanted."

"Par'karr dream he was rabbit!" the little kobold told them. "Par'karr like being rabbit."

The rest of the group looked at the little kobold. Par'karr shrugged. "Par'karr likes rabbits."

"What about you, elfie?" Ainslee asked Yuliana. "Did you have a dream? Was it about your tree people?"

Yuliana shook her head. "The poison of the thorny snare did not affect me. That is why I was able to communicate with it."

"You're immune to poison?" Ethan asked.

She shrugged. "I was not affected by it. I had no dreams, nor any lethargy."

"Is that normal for your race?" he asked.

Once again, she shrugged. "We are not normally affected by plant maladies."

"Well," Ainslee snorted. "Whatever the reason, it's a good thing you weren't affected, or we'd all be plant food!"

The dwarf's stomach rumbled. "Hey! Speaking of food!"

"Fine," Ethan chuckled and reached into his portal pouch for some of the fish fillets. As he did, he looked over at Michalus. "I take it you're immune too?"

Startled, the wizard looked up. "I'm sorry, my boy, what did you ask?"

"I asked if you are immune to the poison too?" Ethan repeated.

"Oh...ah... no," he replied, his face flushing slightly. Ethan caught the wizard's eyes flick to Yuliana and then back to Ethan. "I wasn't immune. Which is fascinating that she was immune and I wasn't..."

"What'd ya dream about?" Ainslee interrupted.

Ethan saw Michalus's gaze flick over to the green-haired druid. "I... ah.. Dreamt about... a library. Yes, I was in a library, filled with books of all kinds. It was wonderful."

"A library?" Ainslee said, screwing up her face. "That was your big dream?"

"Yes," the wizard replied sheepishly. "That was my big dream."

Nia moved closer to Ethan's ear and he felt her hot breath on him. He felt himself get excited. "He is lying."

Ethan looked over to her, remembering she could smell lies, and nodded. He looked at the wizard, whose gaze had returned to Yuliana. He chuckled quietly. "I know."

43

———

Everyone was tired the next morning. Ethan hadn't slept well and even when he did, he'd had dreams of being back on Earth with a human Nia. The dreams were normal dreams and certainly not as intense as the poison-induced hallucinations, but it was strange to dream of Earth again after all this time.

Looking around at the others, it appeared no one had gotten a good night's sleep either. Even Ainslee, who seemed to be able to sleep through anything, looked tired. The group ate breakfast robotically then continued down the trail in silence.

The first part of the day was uneventful and just before lunch, Ainslee called up to Ethan. "Hey, wizardboy. How long are we going to follow this road? We ain't found nothing yet."

Ethan twisted his head to see the dwarf. He still felt the magic and the wrongness. It felt stronger - closer now. But trying to pinpoint it was impossible. "A day or two more, I think. At least, I think it shouldn't be a few more days."

Looking over at Michalus, the wizard nodded. He sensed it too and it was definitely getting closer.

"You think?" the dwarf retorted. "I don't want to keep going deeper into the woods with more of those plant things. Good dreams or not, being sucked dry by plants ain't my idea of a good death."

"We must find the caretakers," Yuliana insisted. She looked to Michalus. "How far were the tree-folk you spoke of?"

"Ahem." The wizard cleared his throat, looking slightly embarrassed. "I told you, those were just stories. I do not actually recall hearing where they saw them. The people who made it out were delirious."

Yuliana bit her lip and looked down.

"You still sense the grove... or whatever it was you sensed before?" Ethan asked the green-haired elf.

She nodded. "I feel it more strongly now."

Ethan turned back to Ainslee. "We're getting closer. But I've never felt anything like this, so it's hard to gauge exactly how far it is."

"Fine! Fine!" the dwarf growled. "Let's just watch out for those plant thingies!"

"Fair enough," Ethan agreed.

They continued walking in silence and that gave Ethan some time to think. He definitely sensed the magic ahead of him and the closer they came to it, the more powerful it seemed. Whatever it was, it was vastly more powerful than either Michalus or him.

While Ethan was curious as to what the magic was,

the sheer power of it worried him. If there was something so strong waiting for them, how would he defend himself and his friends? And what was the *Mental* attack that he was experiencing?

His thoughts went back to the Sollasina Cthulhu creature. Its attacks had been strong, and it had implanted... something... in Nia's mind. He'd defeated it, but at the cost of a point of one of his stats. What if there were more of them ahead and that was what he was feeling?

The thought was sobering. He'd barely defeated one of those creatures. What if there were dozens or even hundreds? Ethan didn't think he had the *Mana* to sustain a *Mental* battle against more than two of them.

Ethan checked his stats:

```
Health: 30
  Mana: 74
  Stamina: 31
```

The *Mental* shield was constantly draining his *Mana*, slightly faster than it regenerated. So far, he'd purposefully avoided practicing his *Mental* magic - any magic for that matter - since he'd put the shield up. He wanted to make sure he always had *Mana* if they were attacked and with the shield up, it wouldn't regenerate like it normally did.

Then again, they would be stopping for lunch soon. Maybe he could get Nia to help him recharge his *Mana* when they stopped.

Ethan debated the pros and cons for several minutes before finally deciding that the benefit of practicing his

Mental magic outweighed the risk of a surprise attack. After all, he would still have some *Stamina* to burn.

He remembered Michalus's warning about using *Stamina* to power his magic. Given what had happened with battling the Cthulhu in Nia's head, he was wary. Still, even losing another point of *Stamina* would be preferable to one of his companions dying or him dying. He'd have to cross that bridge when and if he got to it.

His decision made, Ethan began practicing his *Mental* magic. Since he had already practiced on Par'karr, he reached out telepathically to the little kobold. And nothing happened. There was a moment of panic before he realized his mistake.

Ethan cursed under his breath. He'd forgotten about the necklaces he'd created for them. At least he knew they stopped probing. Hopefully it would give them some protection if they actually came face to face with another Sollasina.

In the meantime, Ethan didn't have many choices. He didn't want to practice on the horses. The last thing he wanted to do was spook one of the horses and have to chase it a few miles. He thought for several minutes. In the end, the only thing he could think of was to scan the area for minds and see what he could find. So that's what he did.

He practiced about an hour before they stopped for lunch. He'd gotten several skill-ups in the skill as he scanned and prodded at little animal minds. He did manage to find some more sophisticated minds - probably something larger but not humanoid.

When that happened, if it were coming towards the

group, he gave the creature a mental nudge. It used more *Mana*, but the sudden *Mental* intrusion was usually enough to send the creature running.

When they did finally stop for lunch, he pulled out the fish fillets and gave them to Michalus to heat. Then he grabbed a blanket and whispered to Nia. She nodded and the two of them started to walk off.

"Really?!" Ainslee snickered. "Over lunch?"

"We won't be long," Ethan said.

Nia elbowed him.

"Okay." Ethan grimaced. The foxgirl had sharp elbows. "We might be a bit."

THE OTHERS WERE WAITING when they returned. Since the two of them hadn't really been able to find much alone time in the forest, Nia had wanted to make the most of it. Ethan was happy to oblige. In between sessions, Ethan warmed up some of the fish fillets and they ate them quickly.

When they were done, they washed by the river - after Ethan scanned it for anything large. Then they dressed and walked back to the others.

"About time," the dwarf snickered.

Ethan just shrugged. "Let's go!"

Michalus gave Ethan a questioning look. "Is your mental shield draining your *Mana* that quickly?"

"It's not just the shield," Ethan explained. "I've been practicing my mental magic as we go along. Just little things like probing animals but with the shield up, my *Mana* won't regenerate."

"Ah." The wizard nodded then his expression turned sober. "You're worried about whatever is generating these mental attacks."

It was Ethan's turn to nod. "If we can feel them this far away, whatever is generating them must be powerful."

Michalus rubbed his chin. "Perhaps. Not all magic works that way, though."

"Oh?" Ethan asked. This was news to him. "How so?"

"Well, take for instance, portal magic," he said. "If you are powerful enough to open a portal, it doesn't really matter how far away that portal travels, right?"

Ethan frowned. "Doesn't it?"

"Think about the portal pouches," the wizard replied, gesturing to his own pouch. "It takes the same amount of mana to open the portal to my chest from here as it does if I'm right next to it. You, who can actually open portals, it costs you the same mana to open one from here to the river as it would take to open one from here to the village."

Cocking his head, Ethan considered the elf's words. There was a certain truth to those words. But that was portal magic. It worked that way because it was targeted to a specific spot - the runes next to the Grail or the runes in his own chest back in his house.

Mental magic seemed different. He could only reach out to minds within a certain range. "I'm not sure mental magic is the same."

"To be truthful," Michalus replied. "*Mental* magic is very rare. Not much is known about it and what is known about it may be conjecture. It's hard to say. But there are stories of those with mental magic being able to communicate over long distances with people."

"Really?" Ethan asked.

"Thor's hammer!" Ainslee interjected. "So, people can get into our minds and we can't even see them?!"

"Or so the stories say," the wizard confirmed. "But I've often wondered if that ability worked similar to the portal ability."

Ethan started to ask what he meant but then it clicked. "Wait. Are you saying maybe they can communicate over long distances if they know the person? Sort of like how we can create portals over long distances by homing in on a unique pattern like the runes we make."

"It's just a theory," the wizard admitted. "But I think it's possible."

"But we still sense powerful magic," Ethan countered.

"True," the wizard admitted. "But are they the same thing? Is the magic we sense the same as what is causing the mental attack?"

That gave Ethan pause. He'd assumed the two were the same. It seemed somewhat logical: big magic ahead and as they get closer, they start getting a mental attack. Michalus was right. There was no proof the two things were connected.

Unfortunately, that brought up a disturbing possibility. "There could be two things where we're going. Whatever is generating the magic and whatever is causing the mental attack."

"Three actually," Michalus replied, glancing back at Yuliana. "The magic, the mental attack and whatever Yuliana is sensing."

The wizard gave him a pointed look and then took his horse's reins. "Something to consider."

Ethan took his own horse and moved to the head of the line with Nia. As they traveled through the afternoon, his thoughts were on Michalus's words and what that might mean. What would they be facing when they finally arrived at whatever they were headed for?

44

It was late afternoon the next day when they reached an area where the redwoods began to thin. During the morning, Ethan had once again practiced his *Mental* magic. He allowed himself to get low on *Mana* just before lunch. Then, like the previous day, he and Nia had recharged his *Mana* while the others ate and rested.

Sometime around midafternoon, he'd gotten a skill increase in *Mental* magic and another point of Intellect. He'd checked his new score.

Intellect: 37

That brought his maximum *Mana* up to 86 It was only 2 more points, but every point helped. The only problem was, now that he'd gained a skill rank, skill increases would come slower. He'd need to find a new way of practicing.

For the moment, his main concern was the sparseness

of trees. As the day had progressed, the redwoods had become noticeably more sparse.

"Why do you think the trees are thinning out?" Ethan asked Yuliana.

The green-haired elf stopped in her tracks and frowned. Glancing around, she tilted her head one way and then the other. "This area does not feel as... alive."

"What does that mean?" Ainslee demanded. The dwarf looked around the forest, as if expecting trouble. And she wasn't the only one.

"The smell of the plants is different here," Nia added. "There is more... decay."

"Decay?" Ethan asked. Now he was glancing around as well, taking a harder look at the trees and the foliage. He even sniffed the air, but nothing seemed different to him. Other than the trees further apart and maybe fewer ground plants, it seemed normal.

"Over there," Michalus said, pointing to their right. Ethan followed the wizard's finger and saw what he was pointing at. A fallen tree.

"Have we seen any fallen trees?" Ethan asked. He didn't remember seeing any, but then again, he hadn't been looking for them either.

"We have not," Yuliana said.

"Other fallen tree there," Par'karr barked, pointing off to the left.

Ethan looked back at the druid. "If we haven't passed any fallen trees before, any idea why we suddenly spot two of them?"

The elf bit her lip, looking from one fallen tree to the

other. "I... I'm not certain... but that feeling I have is much stronger now. It is close."

Everyone began looking around, as if expecting to see something. Not that any of them knew what to expect. Even Yuliana didn't know.

"So, what do we do now?" Ainslee growled. "All this talk of something up ahead or nearby is giving me the willies!"

Ethan shrugged. "We keep going."

"We just blindly walk into danger?" Ainslee snickered. "That's our plan?"

Sighing, Ethan looked at the others, who were all looking at him expectantly. "No. I think now might be a good time to do a little aerial recon."

"Huh?" Ainslee asked, her face screwed up in confusion.

"I'll scout the area around here with my air elemental," Ethan clarified. He turned to Michalus. "You want to take the right and I'll take the left?"

"Certainly, my boy," the wizard replied. He handed the reins of his horse to Yuliana and sat down by the road.

Ethan did the same, handing his reins to Nia and sitting near the wizard. He summoned his air elemental and sent it soaring to the sky. Using his clairvoyance, he shifted his awareness to the elemental and began to see through its eyes.

Briefly, he considered reaching out to it mentally, like he had done with the other elementals but he wanted to conserve *Mana*. Plus, he didn't really need it with the clairvoyance skill. It was almost like being in the elemental's head.

He flew up, circling around the giant trees. The trees here were sparser, so getting through the canopy of branches was no problem for the elemental. Once he cleared the trees, Ethan was treated to the full view of the afternoon sky.

As expected, he saw the twin suns and the black hole between them. There was also another moon visible, as well as the gas giant itself. It really was an amazing sight - especially from so high up. It reminded him that he really was on another planet, in another solar system and possibly in another galaxy.

The air elemental hovered, sensing his desire to take in the panoramic view but Ethan knew they needed to finish their task. The others were waiting for him. With a thought, he had the elemental circle the area, scanning the area with its sharp eyes.

Nothing caught his attention in the immediate area, so he flew along the road. The terrain had been mostly flat, with only a few steep hills scattered throughout their journey. Over the past day, it had gotten more hilly and thus the trees were at different levels and seemed to rise as they went further into the forest.

Ethan flew higher and then searched east through the elemental's eyes. Immediately a flash of sunlight caught his eye. Directing all of the elemental's attention to where he'd seen the flash, he spotted the source.

It was a city on the top of a hill. A city built from white stone. It had been the reflection of the sunlight off the stone that had caught his attention. Ethan would have grinned, but the elemental's beak didn't allow it. They'd found Camelot.

Looking at it more closely, Ethan realized it didn't look right. The scene of the city and the area was... wrong. He willed the elemental to fly closer, but it balked. He cursed silently. He was at the elemental's range. It couldn't go any further.

He cursed again. He wanted to get a better look, but this would need to suffice. He had the elemental fly back and forth, looking at the structure, so Ethan could get a look at the city from different angles.

The elemental's eyes were good, but the city was still two days away, so despite its excellent vision, Ethan couldn't make out much detail. Still, he took in all he could of the city and the area around it. Something about the area around the city looked off.

From this height, Ethan could see that the trees continued to thin out the further east he looked. But the area of the hill upon which the city stood was covered with trees. The river they'd been following wrapped around the hill, making it almost like a moat. A moat with no bridge. At least, none that he could see.

Why the strange lack of trees? Had the people of the city cut down the trees? Or was it due to some sort of siege against the city? But if that were the case, why leave the trees on the hill? It was odd and... unnatural. He made a note to ask Yuliana about it.

Focusing his attention and straining his vision, or rather, the elemental's vision, he zoomed in on the city itself. Or rather, what was left of the city. Now, it was mostly ruins with only a few small structures standing.

There was no vegetation in the city itself, only barren earth. Ethan wondered if the entire area of the city had been paved or cobbled back when the city stood. Or perhaps the footsteps of thousands of citizens had worn the vegetation down.

As he tried focusing on the various buildings, he could see that most of them were just piles of rubble. Whatever the city had once been, it had either deteriorated or been destroyed. Did that mean the library had been destroyed? Had time destroyed it?

Ethan remembered the passages from Merlin's journal. Once Arthur passed away, Mordred had tried taking over the kingdom. Was this destruction due to him? Mordred had been a channeler. The journal didn't mention what sort of demon the son of Arthur had bound himself to, but who knew what sort of powers it would have given him.

Then again, it could have been caused by the nobles who had fought against Mordred. Was that what happened? The nobles banded together and laid waste to Camelot? Was this where Mordred had met his final end?

Unfortunately, that might mean that the library had long since been destroyed or sacked by whoever slew Mordred. That meant the whole quest was a bust. Well, technically not a complete bust. He should at least get some experience for finding Camelot.

As he thought about the quest, he'd gotten back in Hawkshead, he wondered why it hadn't updated. He had technically found the lost city of Camelot. Or did he have to get closer? Maybe actually walk into Camelot? Maybe finding it through clairvoyance didn't count.

Ethan continued to scout around. As he looked at the ruins of Camelot, another odd thing struck him. Like

Castlehaven, Camelot was a walled city with an outer wall that encircled it. The strange thing was, despite the buildings in the city being mostly ruined, the outer city wall looked intact - almost pristine.

Catching sunlight glinting off the wall, he realized it was probably the wall that had first attracted his attention. That really was odd. Why were the buildings in the city in ruins while the wall was intact?

The answer was obvious. Magic. Ethan guessed the walls had somehow been enchanted - like the walls and floors of the tomb. It made sense. If you couldn't enchant the entire city, enchant the walls to protect you against siege.

Ethan couldn't even fathom how many Chymera crystals had to have been used to complete a wall that large. Between the tomb and the wall, Merlin must have used thousands of crystals, tens of thousands even. Maybe that's why they were scarce now.

He looked over the city several more times but wasn't able to make out any additional details. It didn't matter. Ethan had enough information for now and he could always scout it out more as they got closer. Letting go of the clairvoyance, his awareness shifted back to his own body and he dismissed the elemental.

Blinking his eyes, he looked around at his companions. Michalus was among them, so he must have already finished his scouting.

The wizard gave him a meaningful look. "I take it you saw what I saw?"

"What?!" Ainslee asked. "What did you see?"

"I did," Ethan replied, standing up.

"What was it?" Ainslee demanded with her hands on her hips. "Don't keep us in suspense!"

Ethan saw that the dwarf was just voicing everyone's curiosity. They all looked at Ethan expectantly.

"Go ahead, my boy," the wizard said. "Tell them."

Looking around at his companions, Ethan nodded.

"We've found Camelot," he told them.

45

———

After confirming his observations with Michalus, Ethan related what he'd seen, with some details filled in by Michalus. As he talked about the hillside with the city atop it, he mentioned the trees that surrounded it.

"But they were not redwoods," the wizard interjected.

Ethan blinked and looked at Michalus. "They weren't?"

"No, too small," he replied.

Thinking back, Ethan realized it was true. He'd been more intent on the city itself than the trees around it. But the wizard was right. The trees had been smaller than the redwoods. Much smaller. Otherwise, they would have obscured the city.

"What kind of trees were they?" Ethan asked.

Michalus looked thoughtful and rubbed his chin. "I'm not sure. Hard to say from so far away."

Nodding, Ethan continued relating the details of Camelot, from the ruined stone structures to the still-intact wall. When he was done, he sat back and waited for the inevitable questions that would follow. He didn't wait long. He saw Ainslee open her mouth, but Nia beat her to the punch.

"Did you see any enemies?" the foxgirl asked.

Ethan glanced at Michalus, who gave a small shake of his head. "No. There was nothing moving in the city. And I don't think we missed any. There's no tree cover for a good mile around the city."

"I don't even know if I would call it a city," Michalus interrupted. "I think it's more of a large keep."

Thinking back to the size of the walled area, Ethan mentally compared it to Castlehaven. He hadn't seen Castlehaven from the air, but he thought the wizard might be right. "Good point. Now that you mention it, it was smaller than I expected."

"If that is Camelot," Michalus said, rubbing his chin, "it's possible what we saw was just the keep itself. The city itself could sprawl out a mile or more in each direction."

Ethan furrowed his brow. "I didn't see any signs of a city."

"It's been over a thousand years, the smaller houses and other buildings may not have stood the test of time," the wizard chuckled. "I've been alive for over 800 years. You'd be surprised at how many towns and cities that I walked through in my youth are now nothing but open fields."

"Good point," Ethan conceded. He remembered various pictures of ancient towns from Earth that were very similar. Structures like castles endured, but houses and buildings of wood and thatch faded away.

"Whichever is true," the wizard said. "It's the source of the magic we've been sensing. And that wrongness."

Ethan perked up. He hadn't noticed that at all. Then again, he'd been more interested in the buildings and trying to see if there was still a library. "Are you sure?"

"Let's just say age and experience do have their perks," the wizard replied with a sly smile.

"I take it this means we're going to keep going?" Ainslee asked.

Ethan nodded. They had to. At least, he had to. He had a quest to finish and hopefully some books to find. Part of him just needed to see if there really was a library or not.

"Did you see any of the caretakers," Yuliana asked, looking between Ethan and Michalus.

"No," Ethan replied and Michalus shook his head. A thought occurred to him then. Michalus said the magic he and the wizard were sensing was coming from the ruins. What about the magic, or whatever it was, Yuliana was sensing?

"You're still sensing the... whatever it is you're sensing, right?" he asked the druid.

Yuliana nodded. "It's stronger now."

"Which way?" Ethan asked, glancing at Michalus. The wizard nodded, seeming to know what Ethan was driving at.

"That way," Yuliana replied and pointed directly at where the ruins of Camelot were.

Ethan and the wizard exchanged glances.

"What?" the elf asked, seeing their expressions.

"That's the same direction as Camelot, my dear," the wizard replied.

"What does that mean?" Ainslee interjected. "All the stuff you bunch have been feeling is all in Camelot?"

"It does appear that way," Michalus answered, "though we still do not understand exactly what it is you are sensing."

"It is like a grove," the green-haired elf replied. Her face beamed with excitement. "But more powerful now. I've never felt a grove this strongly. The caretakers must be close."

"I'm sorry, my dear," the wizard replied. "We didn't see any caretakers."

Michalus looked to Ethan for confirmation and he nodded. "Though, to be perfectly honest, I don't know that I'd know one if I saw it. I mean, they look like trees, right?"

"Yes," Yuliana answered, gesturing around the forest at the trees. "But not these trees. They were large, but not this tall."

"On your world," Ethan reminded her. "On your world they may not look like these trees, but on this world, they might look different."

Ethan almost added "if there are any caretakers here at all" but decided not to. They'd find out soon enough and there was no reason to discourage her. The caretakers really seemed the only thing she showed any passion for. No need to ruin that prematurely.

"So, we're going to Camelot?" Ainslee asked, putting her hands on her hips. "To look at a bunch of stones? I mean, that's what you said it was now, right?"

"That's all we could make out from that distance,"

Ethan retorted. "But there could be some intact structures."

"Did you see that library you've been looking for?" the dwarf asked with a raised eyebrow. "That is why we all came all this distance, right? That and that sword... X-cally-something."

"Excalibur," he replied. "And no, I didn't see it either, but you couldn't spot a sword from this distance. It would be far too small."

The dwarf rolled her eyes, then crossed her arms over her chest. "That's fine. This is my last adventure. I'll see it to the end."

Ethan nodded. He knew the dwarf didn't like adventuring. Now, between werewolves, fishmen and the Cthulhu, she seemed more adamant than ever that she wasn't going on another adventure. Not that he could blame her.

He blinked and realized everyone was looking at him. He realized someone had spoken to him. "Sorry, I zoned out. What?"

"Zoned?" Par'karr repeated, his scaly brow furrowed.

"Earth saying," Ethan explained. "It means I was thinking about something else. Sorry."

Nia rolled her eyes at him. "I asked if we are stopping for the night or moving on?"

Looking east, towards where he knew Camelot was, he then looked up at the twin suns and the black hole that lingered between them. "Let's see how far we can get before dark."

The others muttered their acknowledgements and the group resumed their marching order with Nia and Ethan in front. They led the horses down the road, even as Nia sniffed the air, trying to sniff out enemies, or plants in the case of the Thorny Snare.

As they walked, Ethan's mind went back to Ainslee's comment about this being her last adventure. He thought he understood how she felt. In his old life, he would have felt the same.

The question he kept asking himself was: why didn't he feel the same way now? Any sane person wouldn't want to keep running into monsters like they did. It was dangerous. That venus fly trap plant would have sucked him - all of them dry - if it hadn't been for Yuliana.

Ethan snickered. The obvious answer was, he wasn't sane. Or maybe, in his mind, he still thought of this all like a game - like the tabletop role-playing games or MMORPGs he'd played back on Earth.

Or was it something else. Were his magical abilities starting to give him a hero complex, or worse, an invincibility complex. He didn't think so, but he had to admit that, for the first time in his life, he felt truly powerful.

And yet, he wasn't. He had a very finite limit on *Mana*. He could do a lot, but he couldn't do everything. Ethan remembered his *Mental* battle with the Sollasina Cthulhu remnant in Nia's mind. He hadn't been invincible then. He'd permanently lost a point of *Hardiness* for exerting himself too much.

He frowned, remembering the tomb and remembering how close he'd been to dying. Up until they'd found the Grail, he had been sure he was going to die. And yet, he hadn't. The Holy Grail had saved him, and he'd made a full recovery.

And now, here he was, weeks from Hawkshead, on a crazy quest to find a 1,000-year-old library and he was dragging the only friends he had in the world along for the ride into unknown danger. When he thought of it that way, Ethan didn't feel so great about the quest.

Ethan felt the strong sense of magic up ahead, to the east, along with that feeling of wrongness. He knew the feeling was coming from Camelot. It was there, waiting for them. He just didn't know what "it" was.

46

———

He didn't sleep well that night. His dreams were troubled and the recurring dream of being chased by insects plagued him. In the dream, Ethan felt as if they were hunting him. Closing in on him. Several times they caught up with him, but he always awoke right before they pounced on him.

Ethan also had strange dreams about Camelot. In his dream, he had a ring in his nose, attached to a chain and he was being pulled into the city. It was as if he were a fish and was being reeled in by some unseen fisherman.

When he was finally pulled into the city, he went to look up at the person who had been reeling him and woke up. He managed to fall back asleep only to jump back and forth between the insect dream and the Camelot dream.

When morning finally came, he was both relieved and frustrated. Ethan was relieved because no more sleep meant no more dreams. He was frustrated because no more sleep meant no more rest. He was also sore in his chest for some reason. He checked his stats.

```
Health: 30
  Mana: 62
  Stamina: 35
```

Stifling a yawn, Ethan cursed under his breath when he saw the numbers. He hadn't completely regenerated his *Mana* or his *Stamina*.

"What's wrong?" Nia asked.

"Nothing," he lied. "Just tired."

She nodded. "It is no wonder. You moved around a lot in your sleep last night."

"Really?" Ethan asked.

"Yes," the foxgirl replied. "You woke me several times."

Ethan flashed his wife an apologetic look. "Sorry about that."

"It is fine." Nia shrugged. "I elbowed you until you woke."

He rubbed his still-tender chest. No wonder it hurt. He knew from previous experience, the foxgirl had sharp elbows. He didn't remember having dreams where he moved around. Then again, he lived alone most of the time so there wasn't anyone to tell him if he had. "Was I that bad?"

"Wizard-boy," Ainslee said, giving him a frown. "I almost came over and elbowed you myself. Between moving around and mumbling, you woke me up."

Ethan gave the dwarf an incredulous look. If there was one person in the group who shouldn't be complaining about waking people up, it was Ainslee. The dwarf snored like a bear.

Nia nodded. "You did mumble."

He was too tired to argue or even defend himself. Ethan just nodded and finished pulling on his boots, yawning as he did so.

The group ate and did their normal morning duties. Ethan had been refreezing the fillets in his portal pouch each morning but his *Mana* was already low, so he asked Michalus to do it. The wizard came over and Ethan pulled the fish fillets for him to refreeze.

That's when he noticed their supply was getting a bit thin. He did a quick count of the remaining. They had two days' worth of fish left in his pouch. Ethan looked at the wizard, who seemed to share his concern. "How many do you have in your pouch?"

"Three days' worth, with one or two extras," Michalus replied.

Ethan frowned. "You sure?"

The wizard nodded. "I refroze mine earlier, while you were still sleeping."

"We're not going to make it back to the ocean before we run out," Ethan told the wizard. "Unless we start rationing."

Michalus considered his words for a long moment. "The berries and nuts are plentiful here."

Looking around at the more sparsely populated forest, Ethan gestured around them. "It might not be that way for long."

The wizard glanced around and then nodded. "Right you are, my boy."

"Give me the fish in your portal pouch," he told the wizard. "We'll consolidate them in mine. Then, the next time we come across berries or nuts, we can store them in yours."

"Good idea," Michalus replied with a smile. He opened his own pouch and began handing him fish, which Ethan then put into his own bag.

As he put the last fish into his own bag, Ethan wrinkled his nose. "Your chest probably smells like fish now. Hopefully Yuliana won't mind her nuts and berries smelling like fish."

The wizard chuckled, shaking his head. "I'll clean it out."

"How?" Ethan asked, brows furrowed.

"Magic, of course," the wizard replied.

"But you can't do magic across portals.... Can you?" Ethan asked. He remembered when he'd tried casting a light into the portal in the library. It had vanished as soon as it entered the portal. The same thing with his elemental. The moment it had entered the portal, the elemental had vanished.

The wizard chuckled. "Good to see there are still a few things I know that you don't."

Wrinkling his forehead, Ethan gave him a confused look. Did the wizard really know a secret to casting magic through a portal? Or was he really that powerful?

The wizard settled into what Ethan thought of as his "professor lecturing" voice. "You are correct that you can't cast magic through a portal..."

"Right, I tried... back at the library of Patheos..." Ethan replied but the wizard held up a finger.

"You stood on one side of a portal and tried casting magic through the portal, right?" Michalus asked.

"Yes, I tried sending a light orb through and then an elemental," he replied. "I used clairvoyance with the elemental and saw the Bifrost. That's how I knew it was a portal."

"Ah." The wizard smiled and stroked his chin. "That was clever. I wouldn't have thought of sending an elemental through while using clairvoyance."

Accepting the praise, Ethan gestured for the wizard to continue. "So... about casting magic through a portal..."

"Ah yes, right," the wizard continued. "You are actually correct. You cannot actually cast magic through a portal."

Ethan's brow furrowed. "Wait. I thought you just said..."

"No." The elf grinned. "You are correct that you can't cast magic through a portal.... Unless... you are through the portal, at least... part of you."

He was confused briefly - probably because he was so tired - then he understood. "Wait. Are you saying, if I stick a hand through to the other side of a portal, I can cast magic on the destination side?"

"Precisely," the wizard said, giving him an approving smile. "As long as part of your body is on a side of a portal, you can do magic on that side."

"I can't believe I didn't think to try that," Ethan said.

"Believe it or not," Michalus continued, "a few hundred years ago, some wizards started becoming assassins. They used scrying to find their targets, then they'd open a portal to them, stick a finger through and kill them without ever leaving their towers."

"Wait," Ethan said, holding his palms up. "Scrying is a thing here? You can spy on people remotely?"

"Oh, not I," the wizard said. "I never really had any use for scrying. But there were wizards who made quite a bit of money either scrying for rich merchants or princes or creating devices that could scry."

"How does it work?" Ethan asked, excitedly. Scrying seemed like a particularly useful skill to have.

Michalus shrugged. "I don't really know. Because it was such a lucrative skill, barely any wizards wrote about it. They kept it a secret and shared it with scant few. There are...or I guess I should say...were... only a few alive today who knew it."

He already knew the answer to the question, but he asked anyway. "They were killed?"

The wizard nodded. "In the end, the scrying didn't help them."

"You guys done jabbering?" Ainslee called out loudly. "We're all ready to leave except you two!"

Ethan and Michalus looked around and saw that the dwarf was right. Everyone had their gear packed, loaded on their horses and were ready to go.

"Sorry," Ethan said. "Let me get my stuff."

"Ah... well, yes," the wizard said. "Me too."

The two of them quickly gathered their gear and packed it on their own horses. Ethan stifled a yawn and moved to the head of the procession, alongside Nia.

Before they started off, he needed to tell them about the food situation. He turned to the others. "We only have five days of fish left, so everyone keep your eyes open for any berry bushes, fruit trees or edible nuts. We'll need to supplement our diet with whatever we find, otherwise, we're going to go hungry before we get back to the shore."

Ainslee groaned but, surprisingly, didn't say anything. Ethan waited, thinking the dwarf would make some snide comment. When she didn't, he turned around.

"Let's get moving," he told the group. "Eastwards to Camelot."

47

The companions walked the horses along the remnants of the stone path. As he'd seen from the sky, the further they went, the sparser the trees were. Even the ground foliage was sparser, including growth on and around the path itself.

Trees and foliage weren't the only things getting sparser. There were fewer and fewer animals as well. The forest grew more and more silent, the closer they got to Camelot. Almost unnaturally quiet.

It was eerily similar to how quiet it had been in Hawkshead, when the Grail had been scaring off the animals with its high-pitched sounds. But that couldn't be the case here. The Grail was safely tucked away in the tomb and neither of the elves had complained about any high-pitched noise.

"The forest is very quiet," Yuliana muttered from behind him.

"No animals," Par'karr agreed. "No rabbits."

Nia stopped, causing everyone else to come to a halt as well. The foxgirl had been sniffing as she walked but turned to face the group. "The scent is wrong here."

"Wrong?" Ethan asked, eyebrows raised. He and the others glanced at the foxling. "Wrong how?"

"It is the scent of..." The foxgirl paused, struggling to find the right word. "Decay. It is the scent of death."

"Death? Decay?" Michalus asked. "What sort of decay?"

Now everyone was looking around the area, their hands hovering near their weapons. Ethan guessed they'd also noticed the strange quiet and they were on edge. Truth be told, so was he. Something just didn't feel right.

Nia's eyes darted around the area too, but she seemed less nervous than the others. "It is like the smell of leaves in the fall as they decay and rot away."

Ethan sniffed. He had never had a great sense of smell but now that Nia mentioned it, he did notice something in the air. It reminded him of mildew. "I think I smell it too."

"The trees here have a blight," Yuliana said, her face a mask of sadness. "They are dying slowly."

"You sure?" Ainslee asked, looking around at the trees. "They look the same as the trees we've been passing."

He was inclined to agree. To Ethan, the trees around them looked identical to the trees they'd been passing for days. "How can you tell?"

"I can feel it," Yuliana explained. "They are hurting. Dying."

Michalus walked over and put a comforting hand on her shoulder. Yuliana smiled up at him, but it didn't reach her eyes. Her eyes were sad as they glanced back to the trees around them.

Ainslee put her hands on her hips. "The trees are sick. What does that mean? Is there something killing them?"

Yuliana bit her lip and shrugged. "I do not know."

"If we don't know what's killing 'em, we can't do nothing about it." The dwarf shrugged. Ainslee looked around at the others. "Right?"

Ethan bit his lip, uncertain what his group could do. He certainly didn't have a green thumb. Even house plants died by his hand. "Yuliana, is there anything we can do to help them?"

The elf continued to bite her lip as her eyes darted around the forest. "I... I do not think so. It feels... it feels as if there is something wrong with the very ground. As if the ground no longer holds the nutrients the trees need."

Remembering back to the barren earth of the city, Ethan wondered if his guess had been right. Had the nobles fought back against Mordred and won? If so, had they done something to the countryside around the city?

"When I saw the city," Ethan said. "It was barren. Merlin's journal said that Mordred warred against the nobles - or the nobles warred against him. Either way, maybe during the war, the area around the city was ruined."

Michalus rubbed his chin. "I'm not familiar with any magic that would have such a profound effect on the earth - especially after a thousand years."

Ethan made a face as he tried to remember something. Something he remembered reading. Once again, he noticed how much more difficult it seemed to be to remember things about his past life - especially when he was actively trying to remember.

Salt. Yes, that was it. Salting the earth. Didn't the Romans salt the earth of enemies when they had conquered them? To prevent them from growing crops? He thought he should remember more, but it just wasn't coming.

"It might be something mundane," Ethan ventured. "Like salting the earth."

"Salting the earth?!" Yuliana gasped. "Why would anyone do such a thing?! The salt would absorb moisture so the plants could not get it. It would devastate plant life!"

"I think that might be the point," Ainslee said.

Nodding, Ethan looked apologetic. "A long time ago, people from my world would sometimes do things like that to prevent enemies they'd conquered from getting too powerful again. No crops, meant less food."

"Aye." The dwarf nodded. "And less food means less people."

"It's horrible," the green-haired elf said, and Ethan saw that her eyes were moist.

Michalus squeezed her shoulder and Yuliana put her hand atop his as she wiped her eyes with her other hand.

Ethan faced east. He still felt the sense of magic - powerful magic - as well as that persistent feeling of something wrong. Could the magic, or whatever it was, be affecting the trees?

"What about the magic that Michalus and I feel," he wondered aloud. "Could that be affecting the trees? Or whatever it is you feel?"

Yuliana, who appeared to have been deep in her own thoughts, looked up and blinked. "What did you ask?"

"The blight, or whatever it is," Ethan repeated. "Could

it be caused by the magic that I sense or the magic you sense?"

The elf blinked again and then looked east. She cocked her head one way and then the other. "It still feels like a grove... but not quite. The closer we get to it, the more it feels... strange."

"We ain't gonna figure it out standing here yappin'," Ainslee said.

"True," Ethan said. "Let's keep moving. Maybe we'll find some answers."

After a moment, the party agreed, and the group once again started down the path. They traveled in silence until lunch when they ate their fish and a few nuts and berries they'd managed to find. They made some small talk, but their lunch was almost as quiet as the journey.

After their meal, they set off in silence again. Each person was either lost in their own thoughts or just uneasy about the unnatural silence of the forest.

The group kept going until just before dark when they were forced to stop. And not because the twin suns were setting. One of the giant redwood trees had fallen across the road and the tree was completely blocking it.

The river was still on their right and the tree, although lying across the river, wasn't actually blocking the water, which continued to flow underneath it. But it did effectively block them from going around the tree to the right - unless they wanted to cross the river.

On its side, the tree was nearly thirty feet tall. Even if one of them were able to climb up it, there was no way the horses would. Ethan doubted even he and Michalus, working together, would be able to lift all of the horses over the tree with magic.

"We'll have to go around," Ethan stated.

"Just figured that out, wizard-boy," the dwarf snorted. She looked at the tree and whistled. "That is one large tree."

When upright, the tree had probably been well over 500 feet tall. They had to go off the path almost two hundred and fifty feet to circle around the enormous tree. When they rounded the fallen tree to the left, Ethan and the others stopped.

They were at the crest of a hill that looked down upon a valley. In the middle of the valley was a raised hill, surrounded by trees. They had found Camelot.

```
Quest Complete.
   Ruins of Camelot I
   Find   the   lost   city   of   Camelot
(1/1).
   Reward: 500 experience
   You gain 500 experience.
   You gain +1 Fame.
   You   have   received   a   new   quest
"Ruins of Camelot II"
   You   sense   disturbing   magic   from
inside   of   Camelot.   Investigate   the
ruins   and   find   the   source   of   the
corrupted magic.
   Find   the   source   of   the   corrupted
magic (0/1).
   Reward: 1000 experience
```

Accept quest (yes or no)?

Ethan looked at the new messages in his HUD and the new quest he'd just received. He glanced around at the others. "Did any of you just get a quest?"

There was a chorus of no's and Ethan frowned. Why had only he gotten the quest? Most of the time, it was a group quest, and everyone got it.

"What quest do you have?" Nia asked.

Ethan looked sheepish as he realized he didn't remember actually telling the group that he had a quest to find Camelot.

"It was called Ruins of Camelot I and the goal was to find the lost city of Camelot," he replied and then pointed to the hill. "And I think we just did."

"And you say you have another quest?" Michalus asked with a raised eyebrow.

"Yes," he confirmed. "It's part 2. Now I have to find the source of the corrupted magic."

"Bad magic?" Par'karr asked, swiveling his little reptilian head from Ethan to Camelot and back.

"Interesting." The elf rubbed his chin. "If your quest is to be believed, then there is actually something corrupting the magic in Camelot. That does beg the question - what is in Camelot that could be doing that?"

Almost as one, the group stared across the valley to the tree-covered hill. The whole castle and surrounding hillside suddenly took on a more sinister overtone. It was as if something waited for them down there.

This new realization was made even more disturbing by the fact that Ethan sensed magic from the city - the same sense of magic and wrongness he'd been feeling for days. Whatever was down there was the source.

"Good question," he told the wizard, looking at the walled city. "What is in Camelot?"

"One thing I know," Ainslee said, putting her hands on her hips. "I ain't going down there in the dark."

Gazing down into the valley and seeing how much of it was already in shadow, Ethan agreed with the dwarf. "Me neither."

48

The group retreated back around the tree for the night. They set up camp on the path, with their backs to the tree and the river to their side. As Nia was quick to point out, there were less avenues of escape, but also less angles they would need to watch.

As they were setting up camp, Ainslee suddenly stopped in the middle of laying out her bedroll and surveyed the area. "Any reason we can't have a fire tonight?"

Ethan gave the dwarf a disapproving look, but she brushed him off with a wave of her hand. "Don't give me that look, wizard-boy. Look around. There's no plants on this path - they're all dead. And we can get wood from the fallen tree. Ain't no harm in that, right? I mean, it's already dead."

Looking around, Ethan saw that the dwarf was right. There was no vegetation on the path. He surveyed the surrounding area. It was barren too. Turning to Yuliana, he gave her a questioning look. "Do you think it's okay to have a fire here?"

The elven druid bit her lip and inspected the area, walking around the path and then to either side of it. When she was done, she pivoted back towards the group. "I don't see any plants that would be harmed."

"Are we even worried about the stupid tree people anymore? We ran into that vine plant that almost killed us, but we didn't see no tree people. Unless that was one of them?" Ainslee sighed and gestured to the fallen tree behind them.

Yuliana shook her head. "That was not one of the caretakers."

"Exactly. We ain't seen no tree people." The dwarf scowled, gesturing around. "So, let's have a proper fire. The moving plants people claimed to see was them viney things."

Michalus's gaze moved between Ainslee and Yuliana. The druid's brow was furrowed, and she bit her lip again. The wizard moved close to her and put his hand on her shoulder. "That is a possibility...."

"See," the dwarf interjected, pointing at the wizard.

"...but," Michalus continued, giving Ainslee a disapproving stare, "you still sense the grove or whatever you sensed earlier, correct?"

Yuliana looked over at the wizard and smiled. "I do."

The green-haired elf swiveled her head towards the dead tree, but her eyes were unfocused. It was as if she were looking through the tree to the ruined city beyond. She frowned and the lines on her forehead deepened. "The feeling is coming from the city."

"The city?" Ethan asked, confused. When he'd scouted out Camelot, there hadn't been any sort of grove or vegetation in the ruins. At least, none that he had seen from that distance. Could there really be a grove somewhere in the ruins?

"It is there." The druid nodded.

"So, there's a mess of magic down there and some sort of grove?" Ainslee grumbled. "And everyone's okay with just marching into that?"

"Well..." Ethan started but Ainslee cut him off.

"This is not normal!" the dwarf said. "People just don't rush into some place that has all kinds of crazy magic! I'm telling you, wizard-boy, this is my last adventure. You promised me an anvil so I can start the forge - and that's what I'm going to do when we get back to Hawkshead."

Not sure how to respond, Ethan just nodded. "If that's what you want to do."

"It is," the dwarf snorted, crossing her arms over her chest.

Ethan hated to lose the dwarf. Well, part of him hated to lose the dwarf. She could definitely be annoying at times. Yet, he'd gotten used to her. And he did always know where he stood with her.

She had never seemed happy about adventuring, or even being on this world. Not that any of them enjoyed being on this world. He paused. Was that really true?

Ainslee obviously didn't enjoy being here. Yuliana was always so quiet, he never knew what she was thinking. He did know she'd rather be back at her grove. That much was obvious.

Then there was Nia. Thinking about her, Ethan shot a

quick glance at the foxgirl. Given what he knew of her life before coming here, she seemed better off. He didn't know what her previous husband was like, but she seemed to like Ethan more. At least, that's what she told him. Unlike her, Ethan couldn't sniff out a lie.

Realizing the dwarf was still looking at him, Ethan nodded. "I'll keep my promise," he told the dwarf. One way or the other. I'll get you an anvil and you can start up the forge in the village."

Ainslee nodded and then snorted. "Assuming any of us fools live."

"Assuming we live," Ethan repeated.

ETHAN WAS SHAKEN AWAKE LATER that night. He felt like he had just lay down after pulling a double shift with Nia. Groggily, he sat up, blinking the sleep from his eyes. He glanced around, looking for danger but the light from the campfire blinded his still-sleepy eyes.

"What?" he half groaned, and half yawned. Beside him, Nia was sitting up too and immediately began moving her head around, sniffing the air.

"Uh, Ethan," said Par'karr. "Trees are here."

Confused, Ethan focused on the kobold. The reptilian face was hard to read, but one thing was certain. Par'karr was terrified. "What do you mean?"

"He means," Ainslee said from the other side of the fire, "we're surrounded."

The dwarf's words brought a jolt of adrenaline to Ethan, snapping him out of his grogginess. Growling, Nia rolled out of her covers and sprang to her feet, weapons in hands.

"Ainslee is right," the foxgirl said, her head darting around. "We are surrounded."

He trusted his wife's keen sense of smell and her excellent night vision. If she said there was something out there, he believed her - even if he couldn't see it himself.

Pushing himself to his feet, Ethan scanned the camp for Luna. He expected to see her up and growling. Instead, she was still lying next to Yuliana. The cat was awake and alert but appeared unconcerned. Why wasn't the big cat reacting to the intruders? Ethan squinted into the dark.

Even the horses, who seemed to whinny and want to bolt at any perceived threat, were quiet. It was very strange. Ethan looked from Par'karr to Nia, his forehead wrinkled. "Surrounded by what?"

"Trees," Par'karr repeated, gesturing frantically towards the edge of the firelight.

Ethan blinked, his eyes finally adjusting the firelight. Just out of range of the campfire's light, Ethan could make out the shapes of large tree trunks. He moved his eyes in a semi-circle around the camp. Par'karr and Nia were right. They were surrounded from the trunk of the downed redwood to the edge of the river. Surrounded by trees.

He cursed. "Wake Yuliana! Quick!"

Straining his eyes, Ethan could make out the vague outlines of about ten large tree trunks. They weren't redwoods, the trunks were much too slender. From what he could tell in the dim light, they looked more like oak trees from back on Earth.

Cursing again, he face palmed himself as he realized

these were the same type of trees that he'd seen on the hill that Camelot stood on.

"Ethan! What is it?" Nia asked, noticing his reaction.

"These are the same type of trees that surround Camelot," he retorted, looking around the semi-circle of trees. There was no way they could have grown there in a few hours. That meant, they'd moved. He shot Ainslee a look. "Or should I say... tree people."

"Loki's balls! I figured out that much myself," the dwarf growled. She glanced over to Ethan as she bent down next to Yuliana. Flashing Ethan a crooked smile, she shrugged. "Guess I was wrong. They do exist."

Even as Ainslee put her hand on the elf to shake her awake, Yuliana suddenly sat upright, eyes wide. "They are here!"

Ainslee turned to Ethan and rolled her eyes, then turned back to the elf. "Yeah, we figured that out on our own."

Michalus sat up too, awakened by the noise and movement. Blinking, he stifled a yawn. Peering into the darkness, his eyes opened wide and he struggled out of his bedrolls. "Thor's hammer. Are those... the tree-folk?"

"Not sure what else they would be," he said.

"What I would like to know is," Nia growled, eyes narrowed, "how they came to be surrounding us?"

The foxgirl glared from Par'karr to Ainslee. Par'karr withered under her stare but Ainslee just rolled her eyes. "One moment they weren't there, the next moment, they were."

"You did not hear them?" Nia demanded.

"Par'karr not hear them," the little kobold replied, his head down.

"I didn't hear them." The dwarf shrugged. "It was just the rustle of leaves and some creaking of wood. The same thing we've been hearing for days."

"But there are no trees nearby!" Nia retorted.

Ainslee seemed about to issue her own retort, but Yuliana walked in front of her. The green-haired elf had her head cocked and walked almost as if she were in a daze, or maybe a trance.

"Yuliana!" he called. "What is it?"

The elf didn't answer but kept walking away from the fire, towards the trees. Ethan was about to start after her when she stopped. She turned her head to look over her shoulder at him and smiled.

"They are the caretakers," Yuliana said softly, her voice almost like a whisper. Even in the dim light, he could see the smile on her face. "And I can hear them!"

49

Everyone's head snapped towards Yuliana. They all were wondering the same thing but Ainslee blurted it out first. "Well, what in Odin's good eye are they sayin'?!"

As the dwarf gave voice to the question, they were all wondering, Ethan took the opportunity to scan them.

```
Elder Tree Lord
    Level: 25
    Skill increase: Analyze +1%.
```

Ethan's eyes went wide, and he swallowed unconsciously. Level 25! That was the highest-level person or creature he'd seen on this world. He had never gotten to Analyze the dragon they'd encountered - it had been too far away - but as it stood, these things might be the most powerful things on this world.

He cursed silently as he slowly surveyed all of the

trees, analyzing them one by one. They were all level 25. On a plus note, he did receive an increase in Analyze for each one he checked out in his HUD and on the second to last caretaker, he received a rank increase.

You have reached Rank 4 in Analyze.
    +1 Intellect.

Unfortunately, he didn't really have time to revel in the new rank, since the group was surrounded by these tree lords with unknown intentions.

Nia slowly moved over to him, her brow furrowed. She leaned in and whispered to him. "You have analyzed them?"

"Yeah," he whispered back. He actually had no idea whether or not the tree lords, or caretakers, or whatever they were, could actually hear or how good their hearing might be if they could hear.

"They are very high level," the foxgirl told him quietly. "This means they are very powerful, yes?"

Ethan looked around and gave a slight nod of his head. "Very."

"I do not know how to defeat one of these, let alone so many," Nia admitted. "I have no tactics for trees."

Nodding, Ethan turned to her. "Me either. Let's hope they're friendly."

"They are not happy we are here," the elf replied.

Ethan and Nia exchanged glances. So much for them being friendly. Then again, if they were hostile, they probably could have killed them by now.

"That seems obvious," the dwarf muttered, gesturing around at the trees surrounding them.

He noticed that the elf was cocking her head one way and then the other, almost as if trying to listen in on a conversation. He suspected some sort of mental link. If that were the case, maybe he could use his *Mental* magic. "How are you communicating with them?"

"I hear and speak with them in my thoughts," Yuliana responded, "just as I do on my world."

"Why are they not happy we are here?" Nia asked. The foxgirl still had her scimitars in a ready position, ready to attack or defend. Ethan just didn't know what - if anything - her scimitars would do against what was effectively a tree.

Ethan watched expressions flash across the druid's face as she communicated with the caretakers. As he watched her, he tentatively reached out to the tree in front of her with a *Mental* probe. He frowned as his probe encountered nothing. It was as if the caretaker wasn't there at all.

He probed all around the tree and as high up as he could manage but there was nothing. Either they were throwing up some sort of *Mental* shield that blocked his probe or their physiology was so different that the magic simply didn't register their thoughts.

"They think we mean to help their charge," Yuliana said with a shrug, her forehead wrinkled in confusion.

"Help their charge?" Michalus asked, moving to stand by the druid. "What does that mean?"

"Their charge?" Ethan echoed. Were the caretakers

watching over someone or something? If they were, why wouldn't they want his group to help them?

Yuliana's face went through several more expressions before she turned back to them; she bit her lip for a moment before replying. "They say others have come and tried to free their charge, but they cannot allow that."

Ethan could tell she was holding something back. "What else?"

The green-haired elf bit her lip again and her face looked almost embarrassed, but there was also a hint of fear. "They would already have killed us, but they sensed me and were curious."

Nia growled and the group looked around at the large trees surrounding them. Ethan didn't think he had much of a chance against the caretakers. None of them did. Not that he knew how the creatures attacked.

"Tell them we're friendly," Ethan offered. "Tell them we just came to find the library in Camelot."

Yuliana nodded and turned to the trees. Her face contorted into several expressions, almost too quick to follow before she turned back to the group.

"They say we cannot go into Camelot," she replied. "Their charge is there, as are some who made it through."

"Some what made it through?" Ainslee scowled. "I still have no idea what they're talkin' about!"

Ethan understood the dwarf's frustration. The tree lords were talking in abstracts. Were they doing it purposefully to obscure something? Or was it somehow lost in translation? After all, to Ethan's *Mental* magic, they didn't even register as a mind.

The druid shrugged and turned back to the trees. After a few minutes she turned around and looked embarrassed. "The caretakers have forgotten what they are watching. They made a promise, long ago to a tree friend. They promised not to let it out, but not to kill it either."

"Tree friend?" Michalus asked, eyebrows raised. "What does that mean?"

"I'm not sure," she told the wizard. "It is not a term I have heard used before."

Ethan was wracking his brain for what it would be that they were guarding. Could it be Excalibur? But that didn't make sense. They said they promised not to let it out. Swords didn't just grow legs and walk out. Unless.

Was Arthur the tree friend? Were the tree lords protecting Excalibur for him? Ethan shook his head. No. He remembered what he read in the journal. Merlin had originally given Excalibur to Mordred but then later took it back and embedded it into the stone because of his grandson's lust for power.

Suddenly pieces began to fall into the place. Was Merlin the tree friend? Had he asked the tree lords to guard Excalibur to keep it out of Mordred's hands? That made sense.

"Ask them if the tree friend was named Merlin," Ethan suggested.

Yuliana nodded and turned back to the trees. When she turned around, she was smiling. "Yes! They say they remember 'The Merlin'. They say the Merlin asked them to guard it and make sure it did not leave Camelot. They have done as the tree friend, Merlin, asked."

Ethan nodded. It made sense now. Merlin didn't want

Mordred getting the sword or the Grail. He'd enchanted the Grail to make high-pitched sounds to keep his grandson from getting his hands on it. The sword, he'd embedded into stone and set guardians around to make sure Mordred couldn't reclaim it.

While he would have liked to have seen Excalibur, maybe even tried to pull the sword from the stone, it was really the Library he was interested in. Now that it was so close, he could almost taste it. He desperately wanted to get his hands on some real books about magic and this world in general.

"Ask them if we can go into the city if we do not try to remove their charge," Ethan told the elf.

The druid turned around and then seemed to begin a longer conversation. Judging by the expressions that splashed over her face, either it was an argument or a very passionate conversation. Finally, after several minutes, she sighed and turned towards them.

"They will not allow us to enter," Yuliana told him. "The only ones who enter serve their charge and try to steal it away. They cannot allow this."

Ethan cursed silently. He really needed to get into the city and find that library. Taking in all of the trees around them and remembering how many of the trees were surrounding the castle, he knew he had no hope of making it past them. Or did he?

He noticed that everyone was looking at him to make a decision. Part of Ethan's mind was already formulating a plan, but he wasn't about to tell everyone right now. At least, he wasn't going to tell them while surrounded by tree lords.

"Ask them if we can camp here tonight and leave tomorrow," Ethan said.

Yuliana nodded and had a short conversation before turning back. "They will allow us to camp here because of me, but they insist we put out the fire. They say fire burns. Destroys."

Ethan heard Ainslee grumble under her breath, but he nodded to the druid and, with a little *Water* magic, he pulled some water from the river to extinguish the fire.

"Ethan!" Nia hissed and his attention snapped back to the trees. Or rather, his attention snapped back to where the trees had been. He could just make out the retreating shapes of the large trees as they moved away.

"Not ones for long goodbyes," Ethan commented. Then he squinted and realized he couldn't see them at all. "How are they moving so fast... and so quiet?"

"See!" Par'karr squeaked. "Trees sneaky!"

Nia, who had excellent night vision, stared into the darkness. She moved her head one direction and then another. "They move on roots that resemble spider legs when they move."

"Spider legs?!" Ainslee shivered, eyes wide.

"They just resemble the movement," the foxgirl amended, seeing the wide-eyed dwarf.

"We're giving up?" Michalus asked Ethan.

Ethan looked around the area before turning to Nia. "Are they all gone?"

Nia glanced in every direction. "I can no longer see the tree people."

A grin spread across Ethan's face. "We're going into Camelot."

Yuliana's shocked expression was almost comical. "But you said..."

"I said we would leave tomorrow," Ethan reminded her. "I said nothing about going into the city before we left."

"Ethan," Nia said, her face grave. "We cannot defeat those... tree people."

"We don't have to defeat them." He grinned. "We just have to go into the city."

Par'karr and the women looked confused, but a look of understanding came over Michalus's face. He rubbed his chin. "You plan to portal to the city."

Ethan grinned and nodded. If he couldn't physically go through the tree lords, he would portal through them.

50

"You want to go into the city, surrounded by fifty-feet-tall tree people?" Ainslee scoffed. "And then expect to get out of this forest alive? You saw how quickly those things could move on their..."

"Spider legs?" Par'karr offered helpfully.

Ainslee flinched and glared at the kobold. "Roots! I was going to say roots!"

The dwarf folded her arms over her chest and turned her glare on Ethan, tapping her foot expectantly.

But Ethan had already worked out the details in his mind. Ok, maybe not ALL the details - but enough. "I think I can create a portal large enough for the horses to get through..."

"Ethan, my boy," Michalus started but Ethan stopped him with a raised palm. He already knew the wizard's concerns.

"I can do it," Ethan said, trying to sound more confident than he felt. "I got a couple more increases in intellect and have more mana now. It should be enough to open a portal large enough for the horses to get through - though we'll need to be quick. With something that large, I won't be able to hold it long."

Michalus closed his mouth and rubbed his chin. "You've already been able to open portals larger than I'm able to...but, it's risky."

"How risky?" Nia demanded, her eyes flashing from Ethan to Michalus.

The wizard scratched his head, then brought his hand down to rub his chin, a look of concentration on his face. Finally, he blew out a breath. "It's hard to say. He did open a large enough portal for us to get through from the village. I've only known one other wizard who could do that. But I've heard of plenty of wizards who have tried... tried and burned themselves out or weakened themselves considerably."

At that, Michalus's eyes darted from Ethan to Nia and back and he raised his eyebrows in a knowing look. Ethan got the hint. The wizard was reminding him of the permanent stat drain he'd received when he'd used too much *Mana* fighting the Cthulhu remnant that had been in Nia.

"What does that look mean?" Nia asked, picking up on Michalus's expression.

When Ethan didn't answer right away, Michalus opened his mouth to speak. Ethan beat him to the punch, giving the wizard a hard look. "He means I lost a permanent point of hardiness when I was battling the creature in your mind. He's saying that could happen again if I use too much mana."

Nia's expression became hard. "Then you should not

do it. There is nothing in that city that is worth you permanently hurting yourself. You must be strong!"

Ethan let out a frustrated breath. He wasn't sure that any of them would really understand why he needed to get into Camelot and find the library. Well, maybe Michalus could. The wizard knew the value of knowledge and books were knowledge. And right now, Ethan needed knowledge. He needed those books to learn everything he could about this world and about magic.

"I need to get to that library," Ethan told Nia. "I need the books in there to make me stronger."

He turned to the rest of the group. "The books in that library can help me understand more about magic and this world. It might help me understand why someone from the myths of my own world ended up in this world. I need to find that library."

It was frustrating to him that no one else understood the importance of the library. He felt himself getting angry. The others he could understand. But why was Michalus being so overly cautious. The wizard should be encouraging him to go, not trying to hold him back.

Pushing down his anger, Ethan gritted his teeth. "None of you have to go with me. I'll go myself. You can start back through the forest. With the horses, you should be able to outrun the tree lords."

"Ethan..." Michalus started but Nia interrupted.

"No!" the foxgirl cut in, she looked Ethan in the eye. "You are my alpha. If you go, I go."

"Par'karr go with Ethan!" the kobold added, crossing his slim reptilian arms over his chest in an imitation of Ainslee.

Michalus looked from Ethan to Nia and then down at Par'karr. The wizard let out a breath. "I was just trying to caution you. You seem oddly fixated on a library that may not even exist."

Ethan blinked at the wizard. What did he mean, it might not exist? Of course, it would still be there. It had to be there. Didn't it? He furrowed his brows. He felt it was there, though he couldn't explain exactly why?

The wizard must have seen Ethan's expression and pushed on. "You saw what I saw when we scouted the city. It's nothing but ruins. There's not enough stones standing to house a library."

He frowned. Michalus's words made sense but something told him it was still there. It didn't make sense, but it was as if the library was calling to him - wanting him to find it.

"I can't explain it," Ethan told the wizard, "but I know the library is still there. I just know it. I can feel it."

"And what about your quest?" Michalus asked. "Didn't you say it said there was corrupted magic? The same magic we've been sensing for days."

Ethan frowned. He and Michalus had been sensing something. But that could be whatever magic the tree lords were doing to protect Excalibur. Or it could be Excalibur itself. Plus, the quest didn't say anything about defeating some monster. It just said to find the source of the corrupted magic.

Ainslee uncrossed her arms and put her hands on her hips. "Let's say you actually make a portal to the city. Then what? You think those tree thingies are going to just stand by and allow us to wander around the city?"

Nia bit her lip and even Par'karr looked thoughtful.

"I'm not sure they can actually get into the city," Ethan replied quickly. He recalled from his scouting that the outer city wall was still intact. The walls had to be at least forty feet tall. If the tree lords could climb it, wouldn't they already be in the city?

"You willin' to bet all of our lives on it, wizard-boy?" Ainslee growled.

Ethan's first reaction was to say yes but he caught himself. That didn't sound like him. He wouldn't really put his friends in harm's way just for a bunch of books that may or may not be there. He frowned. Or would he? Wasn't that what he had just been insisting they do?

He rubbed his temples as he fought with the conflicting emotions. Part of him knew the library was there, waiting for him to find it. He knew it. He'd known it since he first learned about the library from the journal. Ethan knew it was there and he knew he had to reach it.

Biting his lip, Ethan corrected himself. No, that wasn't true. He didn't know it was there, he FELT it was there. It was an interesting difference he wasn't used to dealing with.

As a computer technician, his mind was used to using logic and deductive reasoning to figure out problems. It wasn't just at his job either. His whole life he'd always been more of a rational, logical person instead of a slave to his emotions.

When he thought about it, he really wasn't an emotional person at all. Sure, he enjoyed certain things, got mad at his work and people who cut him off in traffic, but his life had always been ruled more by rational thinking.

Now, he was suddenly trusting his feelings and that seemed strangely out of character for him. And yet, he couldn't help himself. He felt so strongly that the library was there, and he couldn't rationally explain why he felt that way.

"What is it, Ethan?" Nia asked, looking at him in concern.

"What?" he asked, her question breaking him out of his thoughts. He surveyed the group and saw that everyone was looking at him. "What?"

"You just stopped talking, wizard-boy," Ainslee said.

"Sorry," Ethan apologized. "I... I was just thinking about something."

"Thinking we should go home now and forget this daftness?" the dwarf asked hopefully.

Ethan wasn't quite sure how to answer. His mind was still at war. It was feelings versus logic. Did he go with his feelings - his gut? Or did he go with logic? Michalus's argument and logic was compelling but this feeling in his gut was strong.

"You're starting to do it again, wizard-boy!" the dwarf chuckled.

"Sorry," Ethan told them, feeling silly for having to keep apologizing. "I was trying to weigh the options."

Ethan glanced at his companions. "This may not seem like the most logical choice, but I really feel the library is there and I feel that I need to find it. I'm not sure why, it's just a gut feeling. I need to go. But as I said, the rest of you can leave."

"I don't think we can." Michalus shook his head. "The tree lords, as you called them, seem to be able to move quickly and we cannot ride on the broken road without risking the animals. Most likely, if they came after us, they would catch us."

The group was quiet as the wizard's words sank in. Michalus waited for nearly a minute before continuing. "If you go, we must all go."

"Loki's balls!" Ainslee growled and threw her hands in the air. "That's just great!"

"I guess it's up to you," Michalus said, giving Ethan a grave look. "Our fate is in your hands."

Ethan knew he should think about and weigh his options. He should look at the pros and cons and then make the most logical choice. And yet, his gut was telling him strongly that he needed to go - needed to find the library. He felt more strongly about it than nearly anything he'd felt in his life. He had to trust that feeling.

"We go," Ethan said, hoping he was making the right decision.

51

Ethan waited until morning before sending his air elemental back to Camelot to scout it out. He wanted to get a better look at the city now that they were closer. Most importantly, he needed to get a very good look at the area so he could portal inside.

So far, Ethan had only ever portaled to someplace he knew extremely well, like his house, or someplace marked with runes. This would be the first time he would try opening a portal to a location he'd never been to - or even seen with his own eyes. He prayed it would work.

He commanded his elemental to circle the city. As it did, Ethan formed a mental map of the place. He'd done the same thing with countless dungeons and cities in the MMORPGs he had played back on Earth. It was almost second nature to him at this point.

He kept his eyes open for anything that looked like a library. Unfortunately, there were so many ruined buildings, it was hard to tell if any of them were the one he sought. But it had to be there. Ethan felt it. He just needed to find it.

With a clear picture of the area in his mind, Ethan focused on a collapsed stone building. He memorized the specific pattern of the ruin. *Mentally*, he traced them in his mind until he could mentally redraw them with his eyes closed. Once he was certain he had memorized it, he returned his consciousness to his body and dismissed the elemental.

As Ethan stood up, Ainslee handed him her circlet of protection from mental attacks. They'd already agreed that since hers was the only circlet that would actually fit him, she would lend hers to him so that he could drop his *Mental* shield and allow his *Mana* to regenerate.

He slipped the circlet on his own head and dropped his shield. Ethan waited but there was no pressure in his head, and he didn't get an increase in *Mental* magic. He looked at Ainslee. "You feel anything?"

"Nothing. I feel the same." The dwarf shrugged. Then she grinned. "Maybe a little hungry."

"Just stay alert," he told the dwarf. "If you feel anything at all unusual, let me know."

"Yeah, yeah, wizard-boy," the dwarf replied, waving her hand dismissively. "I'll let you know, alright!"

His *Mana* needed some time to regenerate so he took the time to go over the plan with them and line them up in order. They had agreed Nia would go first, since she was the best and most agile warrior. Ainslee would follow her and then Michalus. Finally, Yuliana would go through, while Par'karr would bring up the rear. Once everyone else was through, Ethan would go.

By the time his companions and the horses were in line and ready to go, Ethan's *Mana* was back up to full.

Mana: 86

He put up his mental shield and removed the circlet. Ethan handed it to the dwarf, who slipped it onto her head. He looked at Ainslee. "I think I'm ready."

"Aye," Ainslee growled. "But are we?"

"I can do this. And once we're in, I can rest and then portal us all the way back to Hawkshead," he told them. He looked at the dwarf. "You'll be drinking mead before nightfall."

Ainslee perked up. "Well, why didn't you say so. Let's get moving then!"

Ethan didn't miss the looks of concern on his friends' faces and he momentarily felt guilty for dragging them into the situation. But they'd see, once he found the library. Everything would be okay. He grinned. He could even create some runes in the library and portal back whenever he needed to.

Still smiling, Ethan addressed the group. "Okay, I'm going to open up a portal. As soon as I do, go in, single file and then immediately go to one side so the next person can come through. Get in as quickly as possible and I'll come through last."

"We will," Nia assured him. He saw that the foxgirl was holding the trident he'd taken from the fish-man wizard.

He raised an eyebrow. "Found a new favorite weapon?"

"No," Nia snorted. "This is for you."

The foxgirl tossed him the trident and he caught it easily. He furrowed his brow in confusion.

"It will give you reach against any opponent," the foxgirl told him. "Use it like a spear or use it like a staff."

"It also makes you look like a proper wizard," Michalus added, gesturing at his own staff.

Ethan looked at the trident with its large Chymera crystal and shrugged. He did a few practice thrusts with it to make sure he knew the weight and balance. Finally, he nodded and smiled at his wife. "Thanks!"

Everyone grew quiet then as all eyes turned to him. He took a deep breath. This was it. He wiped his sweaty palms on his pants and prepared to conjure the portal. "It's showtime."

"Time for show?" Par'karr asked, his reptilian brows furrowed.

"Figure of speech from my world," he told the kobold and then turned to the open space in front of Nia. They had agreed she would go first, followed by Ainslee, then Michalus, followed by Yuliana and finally Par'karr would bring up the rear. Once everyone else was through, Ethan would go.

Ethan opened up his HUD and brought up his *Mana* score. It was still at max. He sighed and muttered "here goes nothing" under his breath as he prepared to will the gateway to open.

This time, rather than channeling his *Mana* through the crystals in his pouch, he channeled them through the crystal in the trident. Fixing the spot in his mind, he willed *Mana* into the trident's crystal and then pointed it at the spot in front of Nia.

The crystal on the trident flared a brilliant blue, much like Michalus's staff, and a glowing portal appeared, and he felt the strain on his *Mana*. Surprisingly, it was less than he expected. It was almost as if the larger Chymera crystal made it easier.

His HUD was up, so he was able to keep track of his stats.

Mana: 47

He felt the strain of maintaining the portal and watched his *Mana* continue to fall. With an effort, he willed it larger and larger until it was large enough to accommodate the horses.

Mana: 39

He stared into the gateway, making sure it was in fact the right place. He saw the white stones of the ruined buildings and knew he'd done it.

"Go!" he growled through gritted teeth. "Hurry!"

Nia immediately plunged through the portal, pulled his and her horses with her. As soon as the horses were through, she led them off to the side. Then it was Ainslee's turn.

The dwarf hesitated, looking into the portal first one way, then the other.

Mana: 35

"Hurry!" he repeated, and the dwarf gave him a withering look and then hurried through. Michalus followed on her heels, then Yuliana and Luna went in immediately after him.

Mana: 31

"Par'karr go through magic portal!" The kobold grinned excitedly and hurried through. As soon as Par'karr was clear of the portal, Ethan dove in and entered the Bifrost.

One moment, Ethan was next to the giant, fallen tree and the next moment he was in the rainbow tunnel of colors he'd come to call the Bifrost, after the Norse rainbow bridge that led from Earth to the realm of the gods.

Like his previous experiences, he seemed to be traveling through the bridge for much longer than the instantaneous travel would seem to allow. Was it something like Einstein's theory of relativity? Was he simply experiencing time at a different rate while in the Bifrost?

Just as he was starting to ponder the reasons, the swirling rainbow of colors disappeared and he was outside once more, next to his friends.

He glanced around, taking in the white stones, the barren earth and the tall, white walls that surrounded the area. He grinned and looked at the others. "We did it!"

But now that he was through the Bifrost, the feeling of wrongness that he'd been feeling seemed to magnify. It was so much stronger than it had been just a few miles away. It almost felt like insects crawling on his skin. Ethan looked at Michalus. "You feel it too?"

The wizard looked pale. "I've never felt anything like this in all my long years."

"What do you think it is?" Ethan asked.

"I'd say it was a demon," the wizard replied with a shiver. "But it feels fouler. Stronger."

Much stronger, boomed a voice inside their heads.

52

Ethan's head snapped around to look behind them. It hadn't been a real voice, just words in his head. Yet, he instinctively knew the mental voice had come from behind him.

Standing there, over six feet tall, was a thin, robed figure. The body was close to that of a human, but unnaturally gaunt and willowy. While Ethan couldn't see the legs beneath the robes, the arms appeared slightly too long. Glancing at the thing's hands, he saw the fingers were also long and slender and, from his vantage point, appeared to have an extra joint.

Most striking was the creature's head. It resembled a squid's head with six tentacles hanging down. There were four tentacles that were about two feet long while the remaining two were at least four feet long.

Ethan gasped as he recognized this creature as a live specimen of the desiccated creatures they'd found in Arthur's tomb. Only this one was alive. And it was dressed in faded silky robes embroidered with some sort of pattern he couldn't make out.

Oddly, this creature looked shriveled up as well, with blotches of bright grey on its hands, head and tentacles. Looking closer, Ethan saw skin flaking and peeling atop its head as well. It looked sick, or maybe just old.

Before he could ponder the creature and before any of his companions could do anything, the creature's tentacles reached out towards them and then two things happened at the same time.

First, Ethan felt a wave of "something" pass over him and a pressure in his head. At the same time, the crystal in his trident flared and several messages flashed across his HUD and his *Mana* dropped several points.

```
Skill increase: Mental Magic +1%.
  Skill increase: Mental Magic +1%.
  Mana: 29
```

Second, Luna and the horses bolted and took off down a clear section of the city opposite the squid-headed man. They tore away so quickly and so violently that none of his group had a chance to stop them.

"Luna!" Yuliana screamed after the big cat, but she didn't slow.

The squid creature's eyes opened wide for an instant before the skin over his eyes furrowed in anger. *You resist my attacks. How amusing.*

Ethan quickly Analyzed the creature in his HUD.

Mordred Pendragon

```
Greater Demon
Channeler
Level 25
```

Eyes going wide, Ethan swore loudly as he read the message in his HUD. This was Mordred Pendragon. Mordred, the son of King Arthur. Mordred, the grandson of Merlin. And Mordred, the channeler who was over a thousand years old and had completely transformed into a greater demon!

```
Quest Complete.
    Ruins of Camelot II
    Find the source of the corrupted
magic (1/1).
    Reward: 1000 experience
    You gain 1000 experience.
    You gain +5 Fame.
    You have received a new quest
"Ruins of Camelot III"
    You have discovered that Mordred
Pendragon is the source of the
disturbing magic from inside of
Camelot. Defeat Mordred Pendragon.
    Defeat Mordred Pendragon (0/1).
    Reward: 2500 experience
    Accept quest (yes or no)?
```

Ethan saw the new quest and automatically accepted it. Somehow, he didn't think he'd have a choice about defeating Mordred since the channeler had immediately attacked them with some sort of *Mental* attack.

Judging by the lack of reaction from his companions, the circlets had held against Mordred's attack. Ethan's *Mental* shield had held as well, though it had drained several points of his *Mana*.

"We don't mean you any harm," Ethan said quickly. Despite the quest, he'd prefer not to kill Mordred if he didn't have to.

That elicited a sound, which could have been laughter, that came from underneath the tentacles. Mordred. Ethan remembered from the corpses they'd found the creature did have some sort of beak-like mouth. The squid demon turned its black eyes on Ethan. *You do not mean me any harm? How amusing. Does the ant mean any harm to the boot before it is crushed?*

Mordred followed up his mental communication with another wiggle of his tentacles towards the group and Ethan felt another wave of energy pass over him and once again, he received messages in his HUD.

```
Skill increase: Mental Magic +1%.
   Skill increase: Mental Magic +1%.
Mana: 25
```

Mordred's eyes narrowed and then darted around the group before resting on the circlets everyone wore. The demon snorted. *How long do you think your primitive magic can protect them? How long do you think it can protect you?*

"Kill it!" Ethan yelled. "It's doing some sort of mental attacks on us!"

The group started to move but before any of them had so much as taken a step, a form emerged from behind a nearby piece of stonework. It was a young woman. And it was quite possibly the most beautiful woman Ethan had ever seen.

The young woman looked to be in her early twenties, clad from neck to feet in black plate mail armor. A long mess of honey-blond hair fell down her back to her waist and she had the palest blue eyes of anyone he'd met. But there was something strange about those eyes.

Unlike her smooth face, the eyes looked old, as if they belonged to a much older woman. They were also vacant, as was her expression. It was almost as if she were sleep-walking with her eyes open.

Mother, the demon said. *I'd like you to meet our guests. Remember, don't kill them. I need them alive.*

The beautiful armor-clad woman twisted her head robotically to look at Mordred and then just as stiffly nodded. Then she turned and began advancing on his companions.

Ethan blinked. Had he called the woman, Mother? Did Mordred mean that literally? Was this woman Guinevere, wife of King Arthur, mother of Mordred and Queen of Camelot? The idea was mind boggling.

He remembered reading in Merlin's journal that Arthur and Guinevere had drank from the Fountain of Youth. If that were the case, then the former queen could certainly still be alive if she were effectively immortal.

The armored woman moved closer and Ethan was able to Analyze her.

Guinevere Pendragon
   Human
   Knight
   Level 10

It was Guinevere! The Queen of Camelot was still alive after thousands of years. But why was she helping Mordred? Was it a mother's love? Or did that vacant expression mean that the demon was controlling her with *Mental* magic? Did that mean Guinevere was a victim?

"Try to subdue her!" Ethan yelled to his companions. "Mordred might be controlling her."

"Who?" Ainslee shouted back, looking between the armor-clad woman and the demon.

"Michalus and I will handle the demon," he told them. "The rest of you try to subdue Guinevere!"

Michalus cast a glance over his shoulder at Yuliana before stepping up next to Ethan. "You have a plan, my boy?"

"Keep throwing spells at him until he dies," Ethan replied with a shrug.

The wizard snorted. "Crude, but it might work..."

Michalus was finishing his sentence when Mordred made a gesture with his hand. Ethan sensed magic but it wasn't one of the elemental magics. Before he could call out a warning or try and deflect it, Michalus was yanked off his feet.

The wizard flew suddenly to the left and crashed into the large white stone Guinevere had emerged from behind. Ethan flinched as he heard a smacking sound and Ethan thought he saw Michalus's head hit the stone.

Then, the wizard dropped to the ground in a boneless heap, either dead or unconscious.

Enraged, Ethan pointed his trident at Mordred and shot a beam of white-hot fire at Mordred's chest. The demon gestured with his hand and the beam of fire curved around him and struck the stone behind him, scorching it black.

Mana: 20

Mordred chuckled. *You are a child playing with magic.*

As if to punctuate his remark, the channeler gestured again and Ethan felt magic coming at him. He was sure it was some sort of *Mental* magic attack, possibly telekinesis of some sort. Ethan tried to counter it, but he was too slow and felt himself lifted by invisible hands and raised into the air.

What a pitiful excuse for a wizard, Mordred chuckled in his mind. *After all this time, I had hoped for a bit more of a challenge.*

Ethan started to point the trident at the demon but with a gesture, Mordred yanked the trident out of his hand.

Foolish child, the demon scoffed. *Did you really think you stood a chance against me? Even my own grandfather wouldn't face me. What hope did you think you had?*

Hearing groans and shouts from behind him, he craned his neck to check on his other companions. Unfortunately, they were not doing well. As he looked, the armored woman bashed Yuliana in the head as she tried to heal Par'karr, who was down on the ground. At the same time, she sidestepped a strike from Ainslee's hammer and parried one of Nia's scimitars.

Seeing Ethan's gaze, the squid-headed demon glanced at the melee. It chuckled. *Mother has been fighting for over a thousand years. She is more than a match for your band of misfits.*

Mordred glided closer to Ethan, and he snapped his head back around at the demon. He struggled against the invisible force that held him, but physical force was useless. He needed to use magic.

Ethan reached out with his *Mental* awareness and felt the tendrils of magic, *Mental* magic. Channeling his power through the crystals in his pouch, he grabbed hold of the tendrils with his will and pulled them apart, dropping him to the ground.

Mordred staggered a step and bent over making a strange sound. Was that coughing? Ethan tried to take advantage of the demon's distraction and was about to conjure a firebolt at his head, but he was suddenly tossed sideways and slammed into one of the large stones.

Mordred Pendragon crushes YOU for 11 damage.

Head ringing, Ethan couldn't react quick enough to prevent Mordred from pulling back and slamming him into the stone again.

Mordred Pendragon crushes YOU for 13 damage.
    YOU are stunned.

Mordred released Ethan then. Head and ears ringing, vision blurred and bleeding from a gash on his head, he dropped heavily to the ground. Part of him realized he probably had a concussion, but he couldn't remember what he should do for it.

You surprised me just now, Mordred told him. *Something no one has done in hundreds of years. For that, you will be the first one I impregnate and transform.*

"What?" Ethan moaned, holding his hand to his head. Did Mordred just say he was going to impregnate him?

Unfortunately, for you, the process is quite painful, came the demon's gleeful voice in his head. *But in the end, you will shed your human form and take on my magnificent form. You will become a demon as well - under my control, of course.*

53

The squid-headed demon looked past Ethan and with a wave of both hands, sent Nia and Ainslee soaring through the air to slam into pieces of the stone ruins. Blinking, he watched them get slammed over and over until the two collapsed onto the ground.

Anger and hatred welled up in him and he tried to strike out at Mordred with a fist of *Air* but the channeler countered it with his telekinesis. Then, an invisible force struck him across the face rocking his head to the side and he saw stars.

Mordred Pendragon bashes YOU for 3 damage.

Mordred snorted, or at least, it sounded like what passed for a snort from a squid's beaked mouth. *You have fight in you. That is good. Soon, you will fight for me and help me break free of this tree lord prison my grandfather created for me.*

Ethan shook his head to clear it but that just caused pain to shoot from the front of his forehead to the base of his neck. He guessed he must have a concussion, possibly a fractured skull.

The demon loomed over him and looked down with black eyes. He clicked his beak in laughter, apparently thinking that Ethan's headshake was an act of defiance. *You may think you are strong, but you are weak.*

Trying to ignore the pain in his head, Ethan looked around for a weapon or anything he could use to strike out at Mordred but nothing was nearby. His trident was lying several yards away, as was the magical shotgun. He hadn't heard the kobold fire it - probably because he'd told them to take Guinevere alive. He cursed himself for being a fool.

You think you can defy me, but you have been my puppet since the first time I touched your mind in my father's tomb, Mordred said in his mind as he stared down at him with disdain. The demon made a dismissive gesture with his hand. *You have been doing my bidding ever since.*

"What?" Ethan muttered, brows furrowed. There was pain behind his eyes, and it made it hard to focus but he tried to comprehend what the demon was talking about. How could Mordred have touched his mind back in the tomb? That made no sense.... Unless.

Ethan's eyes went wide. "The amulet?"

Maybe you are not as stupid as I thought, Mordred said. *Yes, from the moment you touched the amulet, I was able to reach out to your mind. I have been manipulating you ever since.*

He shook his head and this time he wasn't trying to clear it. "No... not possible... I..."

No? You think it was your idea to come find Camelot? You think you actually read about a library in my grandfather's journal? The demon chuckled, clicking his beak together under the tentacles. *So easy to manipulate. Just offer you the chance for knowledge and power and you came running.*

Ethan's head was starting to clear slightly but he couldn't believe what Mordred was saying. Had the demon really been implanting thoughts in his head this entire time? Had he really been manipulated the entire time?

His eyes darted to one of the pouches on his belt. Suddenly he remembered the amulet was still there. It had been there the whole time and yet, he couldn't remember thinking about it since putting it in the pouch.

Grinding his teeth, he realized it was true. Mordred must have been playing with his thoughts the entire time. Keeping the amulet on him. Not remembering the amulet. Thinking he read about the library in the journal.

Even now, he couldn't deny that he was still feeling desperate to find the library and gain the knowledge it held. Had he really not even read about a library in the journal? Or was Mordred manipulating him now? Making him doubt himself.

He looked over to his companions. Guinevere was lining up their bodies in a row - getting them ready for impregnation by Mordred. Impregnation and then transformation into the same creatures they'd found in the tomb. Manipulated or not, it would be Ethan's fault.

Mordred saw what he was looking at and looked down at him in amusement. *Yes, you convinced your friends to come with you. You sealed their fate. And I didn't even have to manipulate you to do that.*

Seething with rage, Ethan wanted to reach out and strangle Mordred with his bare hands, but he knew he had no chance against the demon. Then again, wouldn't he rather die than become one of the creatures they'd found in the tomb.

"Why?" he asked, looking up at Mordred defiantly. "Why did you send the others to the tomb?"

The demon's squid-like features turned into an expression that Ethan thought might be frustration and anger. *Nearly a thousand years I've been seeking the cup my grandfather stole from me! My birthright! With it, I would have ruled this planet!*

It took me hundreds of years to find my father's tomb, the demon's voice said in his mind. A faraway look came to the black eyes. *It was a painfully slow process to reach out to travelers and entice them in. Few made it here but those that did, I turned and sent to the tomb.*

Mordred turned his gaze back to Ethan. *I sent dozens of minions over the span of four hundred years, and finally... FINALLY... it was within my grasp. I saw it through the medallion. It was right in front of them.*

"The spiders," Ethan muttered.

Yes, the spiders, Mordred spat. *Once more, I was robbed of my prize. Of my birthright! Of immortality!*

Mordred's eyes flicked to Guinevere and a low growl

came from under the tentacles. *My mother has not aged a day since I've been alive and yet I grow old and wither. This once-human body cannot take the strain of all of my power.*

Ethan looked at the blotchy and flaking skin and realized the truth. Mordred was dying. The demon transformation didn't grant him immortality. It just prolonged his life. "You're dying."

The tentacles quivered and a look of rage passed over the demon's face but quickly disappeared. *I was dying. Demons are immortal, they do not age. But my flawed human body has its limits, despite embracing the transformation. I need the cup to restore my vigor and grant me immortality like my mother.*

Mordred's eyes brightened as he looked down at Ethan. *But you have killed the spider queen and her brood. Once you are transformed, you will retrieve the Grail for me, and I will unlock its secrets and finally have immortality! Then, I will finish what I started over a thousand years ago and rule this pitiful world.*

Remembering their fight against the spiders and his near-death experience, Ethan was reminded of the reason they'd ventured into the tomb at all. Merlin had taken the Grail from his grandson and hidden it in his father's tomb.

The legendary wizard had also placed an enchantment on the chalice to prevent Mordred from ever getting it. The enchantment on the cup caused it to emit a high-pitched sound whenever it was removed from Arthur's sarcophagus. Ethan's eyes flicked to his portal pouch and he made a quick grab for it.

Unfortunately, Mordred caught the movement and suddenly invisible tendrils of force grabbed him by the wrists and ankles and lifted into the air so he was eye to eye with the demon. *No more tricks. No more games. I have waited long enough. You will join me as my servant now.*

The demon's tentacles reached out for Ethan's head and he tried to twist away. "I'll never do your bidding!"

The tentacles stopped as Mordred laughed. *You think you are so noble. So good. And that I am evil to be vanquished. Such a child, like my mother. She thought she could reach me with love. Instead, I twisted her mind and made her my servant.*

Mordred looked Ethan in the eyes. *Just as I will now do to you.*

"Wait!" Ethan blurted. "If you let us go, I'll give you the Grail."

Oh, you are a child. You expect me to believe you? Mordred's mental tone tripped with sarcasm. *I should just let you go, and you'll go running back to the tomb and bring me the Grail?*

"No," Ethan replied, calmer now. "Let me go and I'll give it to you right now."

The demon's eyes narrowed. *You do not have the Grail on you. I would sense it if you did.*

"You're right," he replied. "I don't have it on me. I created a portal pouch to it. That way it's safe until we need it."

The demon's eyes went wide, and Ethan felt the invisible grip on him loosen slightly. Unfortunately, he was still held too tightly to break loose. Mordred's eyes dropped to Ethan's pouches and then darted back up.

Mordred's eyes narrowed again. *How do I know it's not some trap? Lower your shield and let me in your mind.*

Ethan shook his head. Despite his repeated pummeling, he'd managed to keep his *Mental* shield up. Once he'd seen what the demon had done to his own mother, he wasn't about to drop the shield. "No way. I won't let you turn me into a zombie like your mother."

The demon's eyes flicked to Guinevere and he chuckled. *Mother does make an excellent servant.*

That gave Ethan an idea. If Mordred wouldn't let Ethan reach into the pouch and he wouldn't reach into it himself for fear of a trap, maybe dear old Mom could help. "If you don't trust me, have Guinevere reach in and pull it out. Just let me and my friends go."

An interesting proposition, Mordred replied, tentacles wiggling. *I think I will have my mother retrieve it. Which pouch is it in?*

"The big one on the right side of my belt," he replied. "Take it and let us go."

Oh, I will take it, gullible child, Mordred replied. *And then I will transform you and your friends into my minions.*

Ethan had been expecting it, but he had to sell it. He screwed up his face in mock outrage. "But we agreed!"

Mordred chuckled as his mother walked over as if in a trance. The demon took several steps back and then, without him telling her to, Guinevere pulled open the flap of the pouch.

We will see if you are telling the truth, Mordred told him.

Guinevere reached her arm into the portal pouch and Mordred's eyes went wide, then darted to Ethan. *It is the Grail. You did not lie!*

"I didn't lie. I'm good, not evil like you," Ethan snapped. Though he knew that was actually a lie.

A moment later, Guinevere pulled the Grail from out of the portal pouch and for a moment, Mordred's face held a look of triumph. And then he screamed.

Mordred's hands went to the sides of his head and he let loose an inhuman, high-pitched scream while his tentacles flailed in all directions. The invisible bonds that had been holding Ethan dissolved as both the demon and his mother fell to their knees holding their heads.

Ethan landed unsteadily on his feet and didn't hesitate. Reaching out his hands, he grabbed the trident with *Air* and sent it flying into Mordred's back with as much power as he could muster. The demon arched his back as the trident buried itself into him.

You pierce Mordred Pendragon for 23 damage.

At the same time, with another tendril of *Air*, his magic shotgun flew into his hand. He remembered a line from one of his favorite movies and pointed the gun at Mordred's head. "Good. Bad. I'm the guy with the shotgun."

Then, Ethan pulled both triggers and sent a double volley of stone slugs into the demon's skull.

You critically pierce Mordred Pendragon for 31 damage.
You critically pierce Mordred Pendragon for 27 damage.
Mordred Pendragon dies.

```
You       gain       250       experience.
Experience to next level 2,135.
```

Mordred's lifeless body crumpled to the ground and at the same time, Guinevere fell motionless to the ground as well, the Grail slipping from her fingers.

```
Quest Complete.
    Ruins of Camelot II
    Defeat Mordred Pendragon (1/1).
    Reward: 2500 experience
    You gain 2500 experience.
    You gain +5 Fame.
    Congratulations!
    You have reached level 7.
    +1 Attribute Point.
    New ability: Energy Affinity III.
```

He'd achieved level 7 but all he could think about right now was his friends. Reaching down, he scooped up the Grail and hurried over to his unconscious companions.

54

Ethan scrambled over to his friends with the Grail. Since his water bottle was on his horse and he had no idea where it was at the moment, he used *Water* magic to pull liquid from the surrounding area.

One by one, he poured some of the water into their mouths, reviving them. Once they were all revived, they sat up and looked around.

"Where's the octopus guy?" Ainslee demanded, searching the area for her hammer.

"Dead," Ethan said, glancing back at Mordred's body.

The dwarf swiveled her head, looking from Mordred to Guinevere. "And that blonde-haired banshee?! She dead too?"

He looked back at the unconscious form of Guinevere near her dead son. Even from her, he could see the rise and fall of her chest and knew she was still alive. "I don't think so. I think she's unconscious."

"We should tie her," Nia said. The foxgirl had retrieved her scimitars and was removing her sword belt. "I will use my belt to bind her hands."

"Tie legs too," Par'karr said, rubbing the side of his head. "She kick Par'karr in head."

"That's probably a good precaution. At least until we can question her," Ethan agreed and took a sip from the Holy Grail. Instantly, the bruises and scrapes he'd taken from Mordred's pummeling disappeared. He checked his stats:

Health: 30
  Mana: 97
  Stamina: 60

Not only were all of his stats back to full, his head felt clear as well. That's when he noticed the lack of something he'd been feeling for days. "Michalus, do you feel that? Or should I say... NOT feel it?"

Michalus cocked his head and then nodded. "The corruption is gone."

"Yes," Ethan confirmed and looked around the ruined city. "But I still sense magic. Strong magic. Is that from the walls? Or could Mordred still have a spell active?"

"I'm not..." The wizard started but Yuliana interrupted him.

"The caretakers," she said suddenly, eyes wide. "They are talking with me again."

"I'll bet they're not happy," Ainslee said out of the side of her mouth. "You'd better be able to get us out of here, wizard-boy."

He gave the dwarf a stern look and then turned his gaze on the druid. "What are they saying?"

Yuliana tilted her head one way and then the other. "They are upset..."

"Told ya," Ainslee said and Ethan shushed her. She rolled her eyes. "Well, I did."

"They are upset," Yuliana continued. "But also happy. Their charge is finished."

Ethan remembered Mordred's comment about the tree lords. "They were charged with keeping him contained."

After a moment, Yuliana nodded. "They were charged by the Merlin to keep the demon from leaving the city and they have kept that charge for over a thousand years."

"Long time," Par'karr whistled.

"Why didn't they just kill him?" Ainslee asked.

Yuliana posed the question to the tree lords but Ethan already knew the answer. "Because Mordred might have transformed into a demon, but he was still Merlin's grandson. Merlin asked them not to kill him."

"They don't know," Yuliana told them. "They were asked only to keep him here but not to harm him."

"A life sentence, but where life is over a thousand years." Michalus shook his head. "The creature must have been a little mad after all that time alone."

Nia stepped next to Ethan. "He was not alone. He had the woman with him."

"His mother," Ethan clarified. "That's his mother and who knows how long he's been controlling her mind."

"You're assuming she wasn't helping him of her own free will." Ainslee frowned.

"I am," Ethan said. "But I think it's a fair assumption. They both collapsed at the same time and even the high-pitch sound seemed to affect her at the same time, even though she's human. I think he was mentally controlling her - making her his puppet."

Suddenly the feeling of strong magic began to fade. Within only a matter of seconds, it was gone completely. Ethan looked at the wizard. "Did you just feel that too?"

"I did," Michalus replied. "Whatever magic was over the area, it is now gone."

"Mordred magic?" Par'karr asked.

"The caretakers have removed their magic from around the city," Yuliana told them.

"Ah." Michalus nodded. "It seems the magic we felt was some sort of shield or barrier to keep the demon contained."

"Makes sense," Ethan said. "But I thought it would be some sort of wizard magic since we could feel it. I mean, I can't sense Yuliana at all when she's healing. Why could we sense the tree lords?"

"For all we know," Michalus said with a raised eyebrow. "The tree lords ARE wizards."

"An interesting thought," Ethan said. "What did the barrier do?"

Yuliana was quiet for a moment then looked up at them. "It prevented the demon from leaving the city."

Ethan thought back to the two squid-headed bodies they'd found. Obviously, some of his minions had made it through the barrier. "Why could those he'd turned get through the barrier?"

"They say," she told the group, "that the lesser demons

left before their transformation was complete, so the barrier did not stop them."

"He was clever, you have to give him that," Michalus said, with a glance at the dead body.

"The caretakers say they will stay and heal this area before returning to their home," Yuliana told them.

"Their home?" Ainslee asked. "They're...uh... trees. Don't they... live in the forest?"

"They live in the forest," Yuliana said. "But not here. They live to the east and the north."

"How long will it take them to heal the area?" Ethan asked.

Yuliana cocked her head, then nodded. "One hundred years or so. Time passes differently for the caretakers but I think what they told me equates to around one hundred years."

"A hundred years," Ethan whistled. "That's a long time."

The druid bit her lip and was quiet for a moment before speaking again. "I... I will stay with them."

"Stay here?" Ainslee said, wide-eyed. "There's nothing to eat!"

"The forest will provide," Yuliana countered. She looked around the group. "I will tend their grove, nurse it back to health and help the caretakers. That's all I ever wanted."

Ethan let out a breath and nodded. Since they met the tree lords, Ethan had been wondering if the elf might want to stay with them. He wasn't really surprised.

"I will stay with you," Michalus said, looking at Yuliana. "I mean, if that's okay with you."

Ethan blinked. He hadn't been expecting that, though he guessed he should have. He looked to Yuliana.

The elf smiled and nodded. "I would enjoy the company."

"Excellent," the wizard said with a schoolboy grin.

He opened his mouth to speak but couldn't think of the right thing to say. He closed his mouth, then opened it, then closed it again. Finally, he nodded. "I'll be sorry to see both of you leave, but I understand."

"You'll know where to find us," Michalus said with a grin. "And now that you know this location..."

"I can open a portal to it." Ethan nodded. He walked over to a piece of broken white stone and picked it up. Using *Earth* magic, he shaped the stone into a thin rectangle with three runes he carved. He handed it to Michalus. "Just keep this some place open... and not your pocket."

"Most definitely," the wizard smiled.

"So, we can go back to Hawkshead now?" Ainslee asked.

"Not quite yet," Ethan said. He turned and looked at the still-unconscious form of Guinevere. "We still need to interrogate her."

"Why?" Ainslee asked. "What do you think she'll tell us?"

Ethan stared at the armor-clad woman. "For one, we can find out if she was a partner or willing participant with Mordred or whether or not he was controlling her mind."

"Like she's going to tell us the truth." Ainslee frowned.

Ethan put his arm around Nia. "Lucky, we have someone who can smell the truth."

55

———

A buzzing sound filled the air and they all looked around.

"Do you hear that, my dear?" Michalus asked Yuliana. "Is that the tree lords?"

The green-haired elf cocked her head to the side. "They say..."

"Ethan!" Nia screamed and he felt himself tackled to the ground as a large shape flashed overhead, barely missing him.

As the two of them tumbled to the ground, he heard the buzzing of large insect wings. Were they being attacked by giant bees?

Ethan heard a scream as he rolled to his feet. Looking around, he saw that two giant insects were on the ground. Both had bodies that resembled a giant praying mantis, though hundreds or thousands of times larger.

The insects were six feet tall, with long bodies, triangular heads that had bulbous eyes and long antennae.

Four feet supported their lower bodies while a thinner "torso" part of their body spouted two arms tipped with scythe-like endings.

```
Queen's Collector
   Doemenagg
   Assassin
   Level 5
```

Ethan did a double take at the race of the creature. This was one of the Doemenagg. It was one of the creatures who had killed Arthur, over a thousand years ago. And now, here it was, suddenly attacking them out of nowhere.

The nearest creature spun, its eyes rotating to lock onto Ethan. The other insect creature had hit Michalus. It was now on top of him with one of its sharp forearms impaling his shoulder.

"Help Michalus!" he ordered Nia.

The foxgirl glared at him. "My place is by your side."

Before he had time to argue, a roar echoed through the ruins as Ainslee charged the Doemenagg. The dwarf barreled into the insect, knocking it off the wizard.

The Doemenagg facing Ethan and Nia rubbed its antennae together and Ethan felt magic. He felt Air magic being channeled against Nia and he channeled his own Air magic to counter it.

"They can do magic!" he yelled.

His Doemenagg clicked in annoyance and then charged Nia with surprising speed. There were several clangs as bony forearms struck scimitar blades. The foxgirl was able to deflect the blades, but they seemed nearly matched in speed.

Ethan shaped four spikes from a nearby piece of white stone and sent them soaring at the creature's back. One of the bulbous eyes rotated - apparently the Doemenagg could see behind itself. The antennae rubbed together, and the spikes hit a shield of <u>Air</u> a foot from the assassin's back.

But the distraction had cost the insect. It might be able to move its eyes independently and see Ethan and Nia, but it still had to split its concentration. The momentary lapse allowed Nia to score a hit along its torso area, drawing a thin green ichor.

If the creature noticed the strike, it didn't react. Instead, it moved its antennae again and this time Ethan felt the hairs on his head standing up. He'd spent enough time around electricity as a computer tech to know about a static charge. Cursing, he dove to the side just as a small bolt of lightning flashed in the place he'd just been.

He scrambled to his feet and saw the Doemenagg's thorax vibrating. He had no idea what that meant but he'd played enough MMORPGs to think that was some sort of special attack. "Jump back! Now!"

Nia didn't hesitate. She leapt back with uncanny dexterity a second before the insect released a spray of green mist. Ethan had no idea what effect the mist might have, but he was positive it was nothing good. The foxgirl backed further away, making sure not to let the mist come near her.

Ethan tried a blast of fire at the creature's head but

once again, the insect countered his spell. This time, it conjured a blast of water, causing the fire to fizzle.

Nia had circled around the insect, bypassing the lingering green cloud of mist. She rushed in and attacked with both scimitars, forcing the creature to defend itself.

Taking the moment's reprieve, Ethan glanced over and saw Ainslee and a wounded Michalus battling the other Doemenagg. The dwarf was in front of the wizard, catching the insect's strikes on her shield as she occasionally swatted back with her hammer. Behind Michalus, Yuliana was resting her glowing green hands on Michalus, pouring healing magic into him.

Ethan gritted his teeth in frustration. The Doemenagg were not only excellent melee combatants, but apparently wizards as well. Or rather, they were able to use wizard magic to both attack and defend. He needed to find a weakness in its defenses so he could get an attack through.

Forming another stone spike, he sent it flying at the creature's body. At the same time, he sent a stream of fire at the creature. He hoped to overwhelm the creature by using multiple attacks of different elements. Unfortunately, the creature countered both.

Nia moved in to attack as the creature was distracted. This time, the Doemenagg jumped up and over her, using its wings to augment its jump. As it passed over the foxgirl, the assassin kicked out with two of its legs. The blows hit Nia in the head, and she collapsed.

"Nia!" Ethan screamed as he saw Nia go down. He wasn't sure if she was unconscious or dead. Just the possibility that she was dead filled him with white-hot rage.

Ethan threw spell after spell at it. He hurled rocks, sent fire bolts, even managed to duplicate the creature's lightning bolt spell. But other than keeping the creature at bay and draining his *Mana*, the attacks did no damage. The Doemenagg countered every one.

He checked his stats:

Mana: 31

Two-thirds of his *Mana* was gone, and he hadn't even made a dent in the creature. He needed to think of something! And he needed to do it quickly!

His attacks had dropped off as he checked his HUD and the creature seized the opportunity to spring forward. Before Ethan could evade, he felt the icy pain of its blade-like forearms drive into his shoulders and he screamed.

The creature began to slowly raise him, causing the forearms to dig and slice deeper into him. He gritted his teeth against the pain and saw something was emerging from between its mandibles. A sharp, cylinder-like appendage. He cursed and panicked at the same time.

He'd watched enough horror movies to know this wasn't a good thing. Either this thing was about to implant some alien embryo in him, or it was about to suck his brain out. Neither option was particularly appealing to him.

Ethan pushed down his panic and tried to think what else he could do. He was getting close to the creature's head and the pointed appendage, so he had to think fast. Was there anything he knew that couldn't be countered?

Could the mana blade be countered? What about

portals? Could he create a portal underneath it? Ethan was almost eye level to the Doemenagg. He needed something now.

He remembered his mental battle with the Cthulhu. Could he use *Mental* magic as a weapon? Ethan had never tried using it that way before, but he was out of time. He only had time for one attempt.

Trying to ignore the pain in his shoulders, he gathered his will and thrust it into the creature's mind like a knife. This time, the creature didn't - or couldn't - counter the *Mental* magic. He felt the creature shudder and jerk to a halt but then things shifted.

Skill increase: Mental Magic +1%.

Ethan felt the creature's will as an almost living thing, much like the bit of Cthulhu he'd fought against in Nia's mind. He wrapped his will around it and squeezed as hard as he could.

Skill increase: Mental Magic +1%.

The thing that was the creature's will twisted and squirmed as it tried to escape his vice-like grip. He picked up strange sensations and images from the creature's will but it was impossible to make sense of them.

Skill increase: Mental Magic +1%.

He maintained his grip and continued pressing. More images and sensations - almost like feelings - leaked from the creature's mind to his own. He saw bits and pieces of the insect's memories. A scene. A feeling. It was all very strange, seen through multifaceted eyes.

Skill increase: Mental Magic +1%.

Ethan felt the creature jerking, causing spikes of pain in his shoulders. The creature's will began to shrink beneath his onslaught and he pressed his advantage.

Skill increase: Mental Magic +1%.

The insect's forearms went slack and he slid off and fell onto the ground. Grunting as he hit the ground, he maintained his lock on the creature's mind. It shrank in on itself and Ethan felt something new.

Skill increase: Mental Magic +1%.

It was a different will. A will that was not the creature's. It was another will the assassin was linked to, something far away but connected to him. He was curious what this other will was and whether or not he needed to destroy it as well.

Maintaining the attack, Ethan probed towards the other will. He sent a tendril of his own mind down the path that he sensed. It seemed to Ethan that he was going south, far south but it was just a feeling and he wasn't sure if he could trust it.

One moment he was speeding along and the next he was confronted by a much larger will than the one he was attacking. It was another creature. A powerful creature. Ethan probed gently and flashes of images assaulted him in rapid succession.

There were images of a jungle world with a red sun, huge swarms of the mantis warriors, and a gateway opening and sucking one of them through. Then he saw images of this world, the twin suns and the black hole. Other images came too, taking people, injecting something into them and then new mantis creatures exploding from their bodies.

He shuddered at the images but then went cold as he sensed the other will take notice of him. It was more curious than alarmed, though his impression of it was that it was powerful. Much more powerful than the creature he was currently fighting.

The new will reached out its own probing tendrils. Ethan instantly put up his mental defenses but not before he felt something wiggling in his mind. He shuddered again and slammed his mental fortress shut, locking out the probes. He began to feel the strain on his mind, as it became difficult maintaining an attack and an active defense. He knew he couldn't do both and hope to succeed.

The tendrils began trying to wrap themselves around his own fragment of will and he knew it was about to either attack or at the very least hold his will in place. Panicking, he slipped away and raced back down the connection to the mantis warrior whose mind he'd invaded.

Ethan's panic level increased exponentially as he sensed the other mind, he'd contacted begin to come along the same link he was traveling. He cursed mentally, several times. Whatever this other will was, it was following him!

Suddenly he was back inside the Doemenagg's mind, still surrounding and crushing the creature's will. He sensed the other will was right behind him and with a Herculean effort, he crushed the last of the creature's will, killing it and severing the link. With nothing to latch onto, Ethan was thrown back to his own body.

He looked at the praying mantis creature in front of him. The assassin Doemenagg shuddered, went limp and collapsed into a heap.

Quickly probing the area with *Mental* magic, he sensed no trace of the other creature's will - the one that had followed him.

He was relieved but didn't have any time to rest. He staggered to his feet, his shoulders bleeding. He reached up and pressed his hand against the wound to stop the bleeding. Looking around, he spotted Nia on the ground. He wanted to go to the foxgirl but the other Deomenagg was still alive.

Looking over at his other companions, he saw the Doemenagg collapsing to the ground without a head. He blinked, unsure who had killed the creature.

"You all okay?" he called out.

Michalus smiled weakly. "We are. Thanks to our new friend."

"New friend?" Ethan asked, looking around.

From behind a piece of rock near the dead body, an armor-clad woman stepped out with a grim expression. Her armor, shield, face and blond hair were smeared with green ichor. But even covered in insect blood, the woman had a regal bearing to her that he hadn't seen before. It was the bearing of a queen. The bearing of Guinevere Pendragon, wife of King Arthur and Queen of Camelot.

"Oh boy," he muttered.

56

———

Ethan nodded his acknowledgement to Guinevere and, keeping an eye on the blond woman, rushed over to Nia. Her chest was still moving, but she had a nasty-looking lump on her head. He cursed and reached for the pouch with the Grail before realizing he'd already used it on her once today.

According to the description, the Grail only worked on a person once a day. He remembered he'd tested it once, back in Hawkshead and, true to the description, it hadn't healed him a second time in the same day.

"Yuliana!" he called out. "Nia needs healing!"

The green-haired elf rushed over, and Ethan pointed at the lump. "See if you can focus your healing there!"

"I will do what I can," she responded and green energy enveloped her hands as she placed them on the foxgirl's head.

Ethan waited nervously as the green healing magic surrounded Nia's head. Yuliana continued to pour healing magic into the foxgirl for over a minute until Nia's eyes fluttered open. She looked around and started to rise but Ethan put a hand on her chest.

"Just lie still for a moment," he said. "You took a nasty blow to the head."

Nia stopped trying to sit up and moved her hand to the lump on her head. "My head is spinning, even though I am not moving."

Ethan cursed under his breath. He was pretty sure that meant a concussion. Unfortunately, he had no idea how to treat a concussion. It wasn't something he'd ever had to know back on Earth.

He looked down at the lump that was still on his wife's head. Some of the damage might be healed but the druid's magic couldn't fix everything. The lump was still there and whatever was causing her vertigo. He took the foxgirl's hand and gave it a squeeze.

"You have a head injury," he told her. "We've already used the Grail on you once today, so you'll have to wait until tomorrow."

"I can get up," Nia insisted but Ethan put his hand on her chest again.

"You fought well," he told her. "Now rest. That's an order from your Alpha."

Surprisingly, the foxgirl gave a slight nod of her head and settled back down. He gave her hand another squeeze, then released it and stood up.

"Keep an eye on her," Ethan told Yuliana and the elf nodded.

Ethan turned to face Guinevere and the rest of his companions.

"You are the leader?" Guinevere asked as their eyes met.

He nodded. "I am."

"And a wizard," the woman said. It was a statement, not a question but he answered anyway.

"I am," he replied.

"I am..." the woman started.

"Guinevere Pendragon, daughter of Merlin, wife of Arthur and mother to Mordred," he finished.

A look of annoyance passed over the blond woman's beautiful face but then her face relaxed and she let out a small chuckle. "I had forgotten how annoying wizards can be, always seeming to know everything."

"Sorry, your majesty," Ethan said. He hadn't been trying to be annoying, but as she just pointed out, maybe that was a failing of many wizards - and computer geeks.

The woman snorted. "I am Her Majesty no longer. My husband has been dead for over a thousand years and Camelot fell shortly thereafter. I am queen of nothing."

Ethan didn't know how to respond to that, so he nodded. "What shall we call you, then?"

She smiled. "Just... Guinevere."

"Nice to meet you, Guinevere, I am Ethan." Ethan returned the smile and began gesturing to his companions. "This is Michalus, Ainslee, Par'karr, Yuliana and Nia, my wife."

Surprise flashed across Guinevere's features when he introduced Nia but then she resumed a more neutral expression. "Well met, all of you."

The former queen looked down at Mordred's body, her face betraying the sadness she felt, and it struck

Ethan that they'd killed her son. Actually, HE'D killed her son.

"I'm sorry about your son," Ethan blurted out. "I had no choice..."

"I know you had no choice." Guinevere sighed and looked away from her son's corpse. She looked back at Ethan, seeming to take stock of him. "And I know my son had fallen to the path of evil and depravity - oh, I know it better than anyone. And yet, it makes it no easier to know that he is dead."

The blond woman fell silent for a long while and Ethan didn't interrupt her silent reverie. He waited patiently until she spoke again.

A tear rolled down Guinevere's cheek. "I came here, against my father's wishes. I thought I could redeem him - talk sense into him. But my father was right. The demon had wrested control of his mind. I guess you could say, my son died a long time ago."

"He gave himself over to the demon he was channeling," Ethan said, remembering Merlin's journal.

The former queen raised an eyebrow. "You are remarkably well informed."

"I have one of your father's journals," he replied sheepishly. "Possibly the last one he ever wrote."

Guinevere bit her lip. "I see. I had hoped that... perhaps you had spoken with my father. That he was still alive."

"He drank from the fountain too, right?" Ethan asked, confused. "He should still be alive, just as you are."

The blond woman looked shocked for a second before

nodding. "You read about the fountain in the journal, I take it."

"Actually," Ethan grinned, "we found it - the fountain of youth. Your father entombed your husband there, along with the Grail. We've all drank from the fountain."

"You've been to my husband's tomb?" she asked, her brow wrinkling in pain.

Ethan nodded.

She chuckled mirthlessly. "I was never able to get to it. I tried but my father never told me the secret to the traps there."

"It wasn't easy," he told her.

"But you found the tomb and the fountain of youth?" she asked.

"We did," he replied.

Guinevere shook her head. "Then, I pity you."

Ethan gave her a confused look and furrowed his brow. "Why?"

She chuckled mirthlessly. "At first it feels like a gift. The gift of eternal youth. Who would not want that? But then, as the years come and go and those around you - those you loved - grow old and die, you are left alone. Utterly alone. And then you realize that it is not a gift... it is a curse."

He hadn't really considered the long-term ramifications of immortality and wasn't even sure he would get to a point where he regretted it. He could still die of something other than old age and considering the recent combats, death seemed always just around the corner.

Both of them were quiet for a long time before Ainslee

finally broke the silence. "Not that this conversation isn't exciting, but I'm going to go find the horses."

"Par'karr go with you!" the kobold said and scrambled after the dwarf.

"You are leaving?" Guinevere asked.

Ethan looked around the ruins. "It depends. Your son said he was manipulating my mind, making me believe there was a library here. Is that true? Is there no library?"

"There was a library, but it was destroyed when the city was razed." The blond knight gestured around to the destruction. "The nobles sacked the city and anything of value was taken, even Excalibur."

"Wait! What?" Ethan said in shock and confusion. "Someone drew Excalibur?"

"Those pig herders? Ha!" The woman smirked. "Not one of them was worthy. No, from the reports of some of the survivors I questioned, several of Lord Bryan's wizards cut the stone and the earth underneath it and took the whole thing."

"Ha!" Ainslee yelled from a few dozen yards. "I heard that! That's what a dwarf would do!"

Ignoring the dwarf, Ethan pressed on. "I take it that Merlin enchanted the stone as well?"

She nodded. "I was still here when he did that. The stone was enchanted to repel magic and mundane tools. Only someone worthy and pure of heart can draw it. But they cut the area around the stone he'd enchanted."

"What does worthy and pure of heart mean?" Ethan asked.

Guinevere shrugged. "You'd have to ask my father. He never told me." She looked sheepish for a moment. "I have to admit, I did try drawing it myself. Unfortunately, my father's own enchantment didn't find me worthy."

"That's strange," Ethan replied. "His own daughter isn't worthy?"

"I thought so," the woman agreed with a crooked smile. "But that was my father."

"And you said the sword was taken?" he asked.

"Yes, a thousand years ago," she confirmed.

"Do you have any idea where it is now?" Ethan asked. He was more curious than anything else. He suspected that if Guinevere wasn't worthy, he certainly wouldn't be considered worthy.

The warrior shook her head and glanced at Mordred's body. "I've been here, under my son's control, for centuries. I lost track of it when I came here one last time to try to redeem my son."

Ethan nodded and gave her an apologetic look. "I'm sorry again for your son."

Guinevere waved his apology away, taking a deep breath. "I came here to redeem him or kill him, and I failed at both. He made me his slave and sent me out to bring back people for him to... change. I saw it all like it was a dream, but I had no control of myself. It was maddening."

The woman looked away from her son and back to Ethan. "It is better this way. Perhaps he is finally at peace."

They were quiet for a long moment before Ethan broke the silence. "What will you do now?"

The woman shrugged. "I haven't thought about it."

"You can come with us for now," he said, "if you want. We're based in a village not far from your husband's tomb and I can portal you there once I have time to rest."

Guinevere considered his suggestion, emotions playing over her face before finally nodding. "I will join you, for now. Everything I knew is gone."

"Good." Ethan smiled at her. "We can talk more about it later. For the moment, what can you tell me about these Doemenagg?"

57

Michalus, who had been staring down at the Doemenagg the entire time, looked up at Ethan. "I'm not sure what she knows, but I can tell you this: A creature like this is what attacked me just before the village."

Shocked, Ethan raised an eyebrow. "You remember now?"

The wizard nodded. "I think I do. Seeing it again jarred something in my memory. I'm certain it was one of them."

Ethan whistled. "And you fought it off all by yourself."

Michalus snorted. "Well, I am a wizard, my boy."

"Yeah," Ethan replied, walking over to the creature's head and nudging the antennae with his foot. "But I'm pretty sure they are too. Or, at least, they can obviously do different types of magic."

"I did notice that as well," he replied.

"Yes," Guinevere agreed, stepping over to them. "These

are assassins. They drink the brains of people and feed them to their queen. Somehow, she is able to gain their memories."

Guinevere cursed as she stared down at the insect corpse. "My father said that Arthur had killed the queen. He'd sacrificed his life to end her. It seems like he was wrong. My husband's sacrifice was for nothing."

Both Ethan and Michalus exchanged looks. It was obvious they were thinking the same thing. All the killings of wizards and the sucking out of their brains, it had been the Doemenagg.

Ethan turned to Michalus. "You're luckier than you knew. You're the only wizard to survive these things."

"Now, you too," the wizard pointed out. "And I almost didn't survive the first time, but you used the Grail on me."

"But why does the queen Doemenagg want wizard brains?" Ethan asked.

"When we fought them," Guinevere said. "They couldn't do magic. These two could. I think the queen learned a new trick."

"Are you suggesting that they are learning magic by consuming the brains of wizards?" Michalus gasped.

Guinevere nodded grimly. "From what my father told me, the Queen learns and then decides what information gets passed to her brood. If she knows magic, then all of them may know magic. That's an army that would be difficult to face."

"An army of insect wizards?" Ethan said, rubbing his temples. "Are you serious?"

"Insect wizards?!" Ainslee said from behind him. "I told you, wizard-boy, this is it. First spiders, then fish people and walking trees... now an octopus demon and insect wizards. That's it! No more adventures. Just get me back to Hawkshead and let me work the forge."

Ethan turned and nodded to the dwarf. She was tying off one of the horses to a rock outcropping and then put her hands on her hips.

"If that's what you want, then I'll figure out a way to get you an anvil," Ethan assured her.

"You'd better," the dwarf huffed. "You gave me your word."

"I will," Ethan promised her. "We have the money from the river. Hopefully that will be enough."

Ainslee huffed and walked off, presumably to help find the other horses. He heard her mumble as she walked away. "Insect wizards!"

"If gold will help you," Guinevere offered, "you can follow me back to our dwelling. My... son... had been taking all of the gold from those he turned over the years. It's not a fortune, but it might help you."

"You're his next of kin," Ethan countered. "You should get it."

"I want nothing that my son's corruption tainted," the woman spat. Her expression turned sad. "I will remember him as he was once."

Ethan flashed her a smile. "Thank you. I appreciated that."

He gestured to the insect corpse. "So back to the Doemenagg. You really think they might be forming a magic army of insects by eating wizards' brains?"

"What else would they be doing?" Guinevere asked.

"They failed the first time, learned from their enemies and will try taking over the world again."

Michalus and Ethan exchanged looks. They both scratched their chins at the same time. Then a thought occurred to Ethan. "How did they find us? And how did they find Michalus before?"

The blonde woman shrugged. "I do not know. Last time, they didn't come after wizards."

Guinevere paused and looked thoughtful. "Actually, that might not be true. They did start coming after wizards at the end, but we thought they simply wanted to eliminate them. We had no idea that they could actually learn magic from eating their brains."

"So, Arthur killed the queen," he said, "but not before she ate some wizard brains and learned magic. If that's the case, why hasn't she attacked sooner? I mean, it's been like... what... a thousand years. Why are they attacking now?"

"Wizards have been dying for several years now," Michalus corrected him.

"True," Ethan admitted. "But still, that's a long time for them to not be seen."

"Perhaps the queen has been building her army," Guinevere suggested. "Those are sound tactics. Amass your army in secret, then launch a surprise attack and overwhelm your enemy before they even know what hit them."

"But a thousand years?" Ethan asked aloud.

"We don't know their lifespans," Guinevere said. "Perhaps a thousand years is nothing to them, like it is for you or I now."

Ethan couldn't help but notice the bitterness in her voice when she spoke of living a thousand years. He wondered if there would come a time when he was like that as well - old and bitter. He hoped not.

"If these creatures are somehow able to track magic," Michalus said grimly, "then wherever we go, we and the people around us will be in danger."

Blinking, Ethan remembered Odelina, the butcher and hunter in Hawkshead, saying something similar. Her father had been there when her mother was attacked and had been left little more than an invalid. As they would say back on Earth, collateral damage.

"You're right," Ethan said, thinking of Nia. He looked over and saw that she was still lying down where he'd left her. "We are a danger to the people around us."

"You fought well against these," the former queen said, gesturing to the two bodies.

"Because of you," Ethan pointed out.

"No." Guinevere shook her head. "You defeated yours alone and had I not intervened, you would likely have killed the other one, once it was two against one."

"Speaking of which," Michalus said, turning to Ethan. "How did you kill that one?"

Ethan grinned and made a squishing motion with his fingers. "I squished its brain. Or rather, I crushed its... mind with *Mental* magic. Similar to the Cthulhu fragment that was in Nia."

He remembered the other presence, the other will, he'd encountered. The queen. It had to be the queen. Whatever it was, it had been connected to the creature he'd fought. "I think... I think the queen's mind was connected to the ones we fought."

Both Michalus and Guinevere looked alarmed. The blonde warrior looked at him with concern. "How do you know this?"

"I... felt her," he replied. "I mean, I felt something but now I'm convinced it's her."

"Then she knows of this battle and that her assassins failed," Guinevere said. "Most likely she will send more. And this time, they will know your tactics."

"How do you know?" Michalus asked.

"During the first war," she explained, "we would win a skirmish with the Doemenagg when we tried a new tactic. Whenever we tried the same tactic, it almost always failed. They remembered - even if none lived. My father thought they might be linked back to the queen but could never prove it."

"Well, that stinks," Ethan said. "And chances are, if she sent one for you before and sent two this time, next time she'll send at least three."

"That would be logical," the wizard admitted. Michalus looked across the ruins in the direction Yuliana had run off. His forehead wrinkled and when he turned around, his face was stern. "I can't stay with her. I would put her in danger."

"Yeah, but..." Ethan started but the wizard stopped him with a raised hand. "I was her target and now the queen knows about you as well, so you'll be a target too."

Ethan nodded. That meant his friends were in danger now. And if they went back to Hawkshead, they'd be putting the entire village in danger. He cursed. They needed to find this queen and kill her.

"How did Arthur kill the queen last time?" Ethan asked Guinevere.

The woman shook her head, her eyes certain. "I don't know for certain. No one who was there in the final battle lived and my father would never speak of it. He loved Arthur like a son. All I know for certain was that Excalibur was critical."

"But that's lost now," Ethan said.

"Yes and no," the former queen admitted. "Lord Bryan took it south to Avalon. From what I remember, it was displayed in his throne room until he died, then it disappeared."

Ethan raised an eyebrow. "Buried with him?"

"That was my thought," the woman said with a shrug. "But since I knew I couldn't draw it, I never bothered investigating."

"Maybe we should investigate it while we're down south," Ethan suggested.

"Avalon was overrun years ago," Michalus told him. "It's a city of orcs now."

"Still, we're down this far," Ethan suggested, "we should at least check it out. If Excalibur killed the queen last time, then we might need it as a weapon."

"Assuming one of us can draw it," Michalus retorted. "And that's a rather large assumption."

"Even if we can't draw it," Ethan countered. "It might give us a psychological advantage if she knows we have it. Plus, if we study it, maybe between the two of us, we can figure out how to make a copy or a similar sword."

The wizard looked skeptical but after a moment, he shrugged. "Do you think you can convince the others?"

Ethan shrugged. "Maybe. Some of them. Not Ainslee."

"And not Yuliana," Michalus said. "She won't give up her chance to be with the caretakers."

"How about you, Guinevere?" Ethan looked at the blond warrior. "Would you like to join us in finding Excalibur?"

"A quest?" the woman said with a grin. "It's been a long time since I was on a quest. Count me in."

58

While they waited for the rest of the group to return with their mounts, Guinevere wanted to bury her son. Ethan wasn't about to deny a mother's request to put her son to rest, so he helped by using *Earth* to dig a grave for the creature. Even so, he kept a wary eye out for any more Doemenaggs. They still had no idea whether more were coming.

When he went to help her move the body to the grave, he saw a silver medallion necklace around Mordred's neck. It looked like an almost exact match for the amulet he'd found on the squid-headed demon in the tomb.

"A Scrying amulet," the former queen told him as she saw what he was looking at. "My father made them for my son and I... when he was a child. I never took mine off..."

"He took it off you, didn't he?" Ethan asked, already knowing the answer. The Scrying amulet he'd found in the tomb had to be Guinevere's. It was how Mordred had touched his mind and manipulated him into coming here.

Guinevere nodded, her face unreadable. "After he... took control of me, he took the necklace off. He said he didn't need it any longer and neither did I. He gave it to one of the people he'd converted before sending them out."

"I found the person, demon actually," Ethan explained, "and the necklace in your husband's tomb. Mordred somehow made me forget I even had it."

He reached into his pouch and gingerly pulled out the amulet he'd found in the tomb. This time, there was no sudden headache and no intrusion into his mind. It seemed like a plain, silver amulet.

The blonde warrior stared down at the amulet and nodded. "He was a master manipulator and he could twist and control even the strongest mind."

Ethan offered the amulet to the former queen. "This belongs to you then."

Guinevere shook her head. "No. I have no use for it now. Keep it."

He looked from the amulet in his hand to the amulet around Mordred's neck. Guinevere seemed to read his mind and shrugged. "Take it. I want neither of them. I now realize my son used the amulet to feed thoughts into my head. I would prefer not to be reminded of that painful episode."

"Thank you," Ethan told the warrior and slipped them into his pouch. This time, he'd remember them, and he'd experiment with them to see what abilities they had.

Ethan levitated Mordred's body into the grave and then filled in the grave with dirt. As the last of the dirt went on top, he caught tears streaming down Guinevere's cheeks. He was trying to think of something to say when the others returned with the horses.

"We get them all!" Par'karr said, leading two of the mounts.

"Should we set up camp here?" Ainslee asked.

"No," Guinevere said. "There is a better place. Follow me."

After a last, lingering look at her son's grave, Guinevere led them to Mordred's lair. The rest of his companions led the horses and Ethan floated Nia along on a stretcher made of stone. Of course, she'd objected at first, but had eventually relented once she realized she couldn't stand without vertigo.

He worried about Nia. He didn't know much about serious concussions, but given how long the vertigo had lasted, he was concerned. And yet, there was nothing he could do for now. According to the foxgirl, her HUD said she was at full health. That meant it was some sort of "condition" and not an injury. Unfortunately, all he could do was to wait until the next morning when she could use the Grail.

Guinevere led them further into the city and then stopped in front of one of the few buildings he'd seen that were still intact. The blond warrior turned to them. "This has been our - my - home for a long time."

Ethan looked over the building. The structure was flush against the outer wall. It was a two-story stone home or store, though stones of other buildings rested against both sides. It wasn't a particularly large structure, maybe fifteen or twenty feet wide and thirty or thirty-five feet long.

Given the tons of rock that was leaning on either side of the place, Ethan wondered how stable this structure really was. He raised an eyebrow. "Is it safe?"

"As I said," she answered, gesturing around at the stone structure. "This has been my home for a long time. In all that time, it has remained."

He looked at Ainslee. "What do you think?"

The dwarf blinked and looked up at him in surprise. "What?"

"What do you think, Ainslee?" he asked. "Is it safe to stay in?"

The dwarf turned and glanced around the exterior of the building. Walking over, she looked at one wall, then the other. Finally, Ainslee announced, "Looks structurally intact."

Guinevere rolled her eyes and gave Ethan a "I told you so" look. He shrugged and then followed the woman inside the building. She led Ethan to an area in the back of the first floor and showed him a small chest.

"This is the treasure he's collected from his victims over the last thousand years," she said bitterly. "They are dead - or worse - so take it and use it to fulfill your promise."

Walking over to the chest, he opened it up. Belatedly, he thought about traps but luckily, nothing happened, and he sighed in relief.

Inside the chest were a collection of coins of all types, along with gold, silver and even some copper jewelry. Some of the jewelry was encrusted with gems of various colors, and there were some loose gems as well.

Ainslee whistled from behind him. "Not bad. Not bad at all!"

"I think there's enough here to get you an anvil," Ethan muttered, closing the lid.

He turned around. "This seems like a good place. Ainslee, can you go upstairs and check out the defensive situation. I want to seal this place up so there's no more surprises from our giant insect friends."

"I won't argue with that," the dwarf said and went upstairs. "Par'karr, can you set your rabbits on watch duty outside?"

Par'karr nodded enthusiastically and ran out the door.

"Someone keep an eye on Nia while I see what all I can secure with some extra stone," he told them.

The group spent the rest of the day securing the place, but no more Doemenaggs appeared. When night fell, Ethan and Michalus sealed them in so it would be more difficult for the insect wizards to get in. Then they set double watches.

THE NEXT MORNING, Ethan gave Nia a sip from the Grail and she was instantly better. Once more the magical cup had proved its use and, seeing the foxgirl better, he was glad they'd found it.

Ethan and his companions ate breakfast and then decided their next steps. There wasn't much discussion. In the end, it was as he expected.

Ainslee insisted on going back to Hawkshead. With the money they had recovered, she wanted to order an anvil from Castlehaven and get her smithy up and running.

Despite the danger, Yuliana insisted on staying with the tree lords. Because of the tree lords' constant draw on the land to keep a shield around the city, the nearby grove was in shambles and she told the group she was desperately needed. Plus, it was what she'd always wanted.

Michalus had told everyone that he would come with them to find Excalibur. Ethan knew the wizard wanted to stay with Yuliana, but they both knew it put the druid in danger. There weren't any reports of random people getting their brains sucked out - just wizards. Anyone around them became a target. And the wizard wasn't about to risk Yuliana.

Guinevere, Par'karr and Nia all decided to come along, and Ethan was glad. The blonde warrior had already proven that she was a capable fighter and had been able to kill one of the Doemenagg. Par'karr and Nia had already proven themselves as well. With their help, he was confident they could find Excalibur.

The group said their goodbyes and then Ethan opened a portal to his house in Hawkshead. Ainslee stopped at the entrance and looked back. He thought she looked a little watery eyed, but maybe it was a trick of the morning sun. She smiled. "I'll have the forge up before you lot get back!"

"Sounds good!" Ethan said and called out right as she turned to walk through the portal. "One favor!"

"What?" the dwarf eyed him suspiciously.

"Can you wash out my chest," he asked with a grin. "It stinks like fish!"

The dwarf rolled her eyes. "Sure thing, wizard-boy."

Ainslee turned and stepped through the portal without another word and Ethan let it dissolve behind her.

He looked over at Yuliana and Michalus just as they broke their hug. "You sure you don't want to come with us?"

The druid's eye flicked to Michalus but she shook her head. "No, my place is here, with the caretakers."

Ethan handed her a foot-long piece of stone he'd made with three runes. "For when we come back. Just keep it some place in the open."

The elf took the stone and slipped it into her pack. She gave the group a smile and then walked back towards the entrance of the city. Michalus watched her until she disappeared behind some of the ruins.

"We go on adventure now?" Par'karr asked brightly.

Ethan looked at his companions and walked over to his horse. "Yes, Par'karr... we go on an adventure now."

EPILOGUE

The Queen chittered in anger, causing nearby drones to flee her chamber. One of the drones was a little too close and she stabbed it through the thorax with one of her long, sharp forearms. The thing squirmed as she lifted it to her mouth and bit its head off.

Spitting out the head, the Queen dropped the lifeless corpse to the ground. She glared at the drones around her.

Despite their fear, the drones instantly obeyed. They skittered over and dragged the body and head away, mostly likely grateful to be out of the Queen's presence. Not that she cared. They were drones. Workers. Slaves. Their only purpose was to serve her.

She was angry that she hadn't been able to fully touch the wizard's mind. She had only managed to catch glimpses of him. Yet, even that brief contact had shown her some of his memories, and that excited her.

Like some of the other wizards, this one could open a

portal. Unlike the other ones, this one had opened a portal to another world! She had seen it in his mind! He had actually visited the other world.

It had been brief, but she'd seen a world with a large red sun and another world with a smaller yellow sun. Neither was this forsaken planet.

Her mandibles moved happily as she thought about this new wizard. Yes. This new wizard held the key. The key to leaving this strange world and returning to her own world.

Her world. Yes, she needed to get back there. She'd been away for over a thousand years. In her absence, one of her drones would have laid another queen egg. That meant she'd have to fight the new Queen for the right to rule her world. That was fine. She was confident she would defeat her and take her brood back. After all, there could be only one queen.

She needed the wizard's brain. But she couldn't send a collector to get it. No. The Queen needed to drink it personally from his primitive skull to absorb all the memories possible. She could not afford to miss out on any important memories.

Yes, when the drones retrieved a brain from one of the primitive species on this planet, she did get some memories. After all, that was how she had learned about magic and how she had altered her collectors to be able to perform magic as well.

It had been a good system and safe for her. She sent the collectors out to find brains and then bring them back to her. She would drink the brains and absorb some of their memories. That was how her species learned, after all.

Then she'd gotten the brain of a wizard and it had opened her eyes to a world of magic. Magic that her species had never encountered before. It was something that could make her the greatest of her kind. She clicked happily at the idea.

And yet, she was still hesitant to leave her lair. Her kind rarely left their lairs, except to battle other Queens. She'd left her lair on this world only once - the time she had been killed by the Arthur and the Merlin using that accursed sword.

The Queen seethed at the thought, despite the fact that she had killed the Arthur. She had still died. Died to that awful blade. So much of her brood had been killed that day as well, though they were replaceable.

It had taken her hundreds of years to build up her nest again, once she was reborn. And once her nest was rebuilt, it had taken her hundreds more years to breed just the right sort of collector that could work the newly discovered magic.

She had done it slowly, so slowly, to avoid the notice of the Merlin. Despite the Arthur being the one to actually kill her, it had been the Merlin who had destroyed most of her brood. Destroyed them with magic. Had the Arthur not killed her, she knew the Merlin would have.

But now she had the magic as well. Had learned how to use it from the minds of many wizards. And yet, her own power still seemed to be lacking, compared to what she had seen the Merlin do. She still didn't dare face the Merlin. Not yet.

The Queen clicked her mandibles together in annoyance. She had learned her lesson. She would not venture from the nest. Not this time. She would have her collectors bring her the wizard - intact. Then she could drink his brain, personally.

Skittering out of her chamber and into the birthing chamber, she looked down at the six collector eggs. Within a day they would hatch. Then, she would use her nectar to accelerate their growth.

In a week, perhaps a bit longer, she would send all six of them after the wizard. Then, finally, she would have the knowledge she needed to return to her world. Return and conquer. It was a pleasant thought. A very pleasant thought.

JOIN THE ADVENTURE

Thank you for reading this book! If you enjoyed it, please consider leaving a review on Amazon or tagging me on social media.
Tag me @authorjohncress on Twitter and @authorjohncressman on Facebook and Instagram!
Reviews help readers like you find this book. More readers means more sales, and more sales help independent authors like me to be able to write more books!
To learn more about the author and his other books and projects, visit the author's website at:
https://www.johnecressman.com
Or visit him on Facebook
https://www.facebook.com/authorjohncressman/

LITRPG

To learn more about LitRPG, talk to authors including myself, and just have an awesome time, please join the <u>LitRPG Group</u>.

MORE LITRPG

For more information on this book and other exciting LitRPG/GameLit books, please visit the following Facebook groups:
LitRPG Books
https://www.facebook.com/groups/LitRPG.books/

and

GameLit Society
https://www.facebook.com/groups/LitRPGsociety/

ACKNOWLEDGMENTS

I'd like to acknowledge all the members of the LitRPG Authors' Guild who helped me in so many ways! Without your help, I could never have gotten this far!

Also, a big thank you for everyone who had bought one of my books. Your support really means a lot to me.